*W*hat the critics are saying...

෪

"Tides of Time is an uplifting, inspirational, and heartwarming read for people of all ages." ~ *Steve Azar, Mercury Records Nashville*

"A novel that makes you laugh, makes you cry, and makes you sing." ~ *Kathryn Falk, CEO/founder of RT BOOKreviews Magazine*

"Her hero and heroine ... face and triumph over many obstacles in this classic love story set against the backdrop of the country music industry." ~ *Tara Gelsomino, RT BOOKreviews Magazine*

# SONYA KATE CHILDERS

# TIDES OF TIME

CERRIDWEN PRESS

A Cerridwen Press Publication

www.cerridwenpress.com

Tides of Time

ISBN 1419955659,9781419955655
ALL RIGHTS RESERVED.
Tides of Time Copyright © 2006 Sonya Kate Childers
Edited by Mary Altman
Cover art by Julie Barnes & Kenneth Barnes

Electronic book Publication September 2006
Trade paperback Publication December 2006

Cerridwen Press is an imprint of Ellora's Cave Publishing, Inc.®

# About the Author

~

Sonya Kate Childers is a wife and mother. Missouri natives, the Childers family recently relocated to the gentile state of Louisiana. In her new environment, the author enjoys lazy summer days writing from the comfort of her poolside veranda overlooking the many whispering Live Oaks adorning the property. During her free time, Sonya can be found touring haunted plantations, strolling the French Quarter in New Orleans or salt water fishing in the Gulf.

This author blends a bold and exciting style of writing derived from critical life experiences. With a unique marketing campaign, Sonya has combined her passion of writing with her love of country music and its artists. While these characters may unfold from real-life experiences, her story lines develop through dreams. The computer keys are ablaze long before the first cup of morning coffee is poured as Sonya types what she dreamt the night before.

Charities are dear to Sonya Kate's heart. Due to her own struggles with Lupus, the family is involved with charities including St. Jude's Children's Hospital, SOS America, Inc. and Lupus Awareness. Her husband and children have remained constant and positive influences and sources of strength and guidance in the author's day to day struggles.

Sonya welcomes comments from readers. You can find her website and email address on her author bio page at www.cerridwenpress.com. You can write to her at Uptown Marketing & Promotions, Attn: Sonya Kate, P.O. Box 870, Springfield, Louisiana 70462.

# Dedication

&

First and foremost, this book is dedicated to my husband, Bert, my daughter, Melissa, and my son, Josh, for always being there and for giving up so much to get me to this point. It's been a hard year for our family, but with the Childers resolve there are no obstacles too big for us to overcome as a family.

Kathryn Falk, Kenneth Rubin, Carole Stacey, Nancy, Giselle, Jo Carol and RT BookReviews Magazine — thanks for all your wisdom, guidance and always challenging me to be a winner. This book is a testament to the philosophy "We can sleep when we're dead".

Tina, Patty, Jeania, Raelene, Mary and Cerridwen Publishing — thanks for believing in this book and project of merging publishing with country music as much as I did. You girls have always "thought outside the box" in trying new and exciting marketing techniques. I'm lucky to have found partners with so much in common.

Penny Hussey, Audrey Jones, Fran Garfunkle, Karla Hallowell, Misty Easterling, Sid & Terry Baumgartener, Carol Hoerl, John Ratcliff, Lauren Katz, Nina, Cheyenne, Charles & Tara McPhail, Helen Doyle, Ray, Becky, Brenda, Lil Froggie, Jackie Profitt, Friends of Darryl Worley's Fan Club, Friends of Steve Azar's Landing, Tom Lord of Mercury Nashville, Mike Kennedy of KBEQ, all of the members of Sonya Kate Childers MySpace site and finally, all country music performers and fans — thanks for all your prayers, support and promotion.

A special dedication to my adopted Papi, Rudy. Thank God you came into my life…your inspiration keeps me going.

# Special Dedication

෨

By the grace of God, I was blessed to meet Virgie, a charming woman from the heart of the Mississippi Delta. Everyone needs a special friend, somebody outside their family, during the low points in life. There's never a day I can't call on this lady for kind words of encouragement.

I suffer from a variety of debilitating illnesses, including Lupus and Anti-Phospholipids Disorder. Four years ago, I suffered a stroke. When I awoke to the frantic screams of my children, paralysis claimed my right side. Apparently I'd been ill since childhood — remission had already come and gone. The doctors told me I had seven "good years" left. Some days the pain slices through my bones and organs like a knife, so excruciating it is unbearable and my limbs are useless. Although we've never met in person, whenever those bad days come, Virgie has been there, lifting my tired spirit through e-mails, phone calls and prayers.

Virgie's husband, children and grandbabies are her constant, and she lovingly instills in them her belief that dreams really can come true. Of course it takes hard work, determination and a whole lot of heart — and unconditional love from one's parents doesn't hurt, either. Not surprisingly, then, Virgie is the mother of one of the most fantastic singer-songwriters to emerge from the Mississippi Delta. Country superstar Steve Azar, like his remarkable mother, has also become my friend. There's a lot of Virgie's strength and character in Steve's songs.

Steve, we both grew up in sleepy towns that adorn the Mississippi. Although we've never forgotten our roots, we look toward the future with great anticipation. Sharing the same goals, ethics and love of telling stories, we entertain — you, through song and me, through books. You and your mother have been a huge inspiration to me in the writing of this book.

You've kept me going when I felt like giving up. Whether it's through your songs or videos, the love and strength of that incredible family of yours shines through.

Joe Sr., Virgie, Steve, Joe Jr., and Katie, I can never thank your family enough for all your encouragement and support of *Tides of Time* and, more importantly, of the work done at St. Jude Children's Hospital. It seems a crime of nature for children to suffer from horrible diseases, to miss out on simple pleasures healthy children take for granted. That's why our work and dedication to St. Jude is so very important. Thank you for being the first to rise to the challenge, taking on this project with me. The world is a better place because of all of you, and I count myself lucky to have crossed paths with your family! Therefore, *Tides of Time* is dedicated to you. God bless your entire family, and may serious childhood illnesses one day become a thing of the past.

# A Personal Note

&

I would like to take this opportunity to thank the city of Galveston, Texas, and the wonderful folks living there. My love for your island, people, and the great state of Texas inspired the setting for this novel. Stewart Beach in Galveston was the first place I experienced the ocean. The Gulf has been my one true passion ever since, and my seaside trips create peace and tranquility in my life.

*See end of book for Bonus Gift offer of free*
*Steve Azar song.*

# *Trademarks Acknowledgement*

The author acknowledges the trademarked status and trademark owners of the following wordmarks mentioned in this work of fiction:

AA/Alcoholics Anonymous: Alcoholic Anonymous World Services Inc.

Big & Rich: Alphin, Kenneth Individual USA and Rich, John Individual USA

Borders: Borders Properties, Inc.

Bose: Bose Corporation

Bud Light: Anheuser-Busch, Incorporated

Burberry: Burberry Limited Corporation

Capital: Capital Records

Chance: Chanel, Inc.

Chanel: Chanel, Inc.

Chevy Trucks: General Motors Corp.

Chippendales: Chippendales USA, Inc.

CNN: Cable News Network LP.

Chevrolet Corvette: General Motors Corp.

Diet Pepsi: PepsiCo, Inc.

Dolly Parton: Parton, Dolly, Individual USA

Dom Perignon: Chandon Champagne Corp.

Exxon Corporation: Exxon Corp.

Fender: CBS Inc.

Ford: Ford Motor Company

Fox Cable News: Twentieth Century Fox Film Corp.

George Strait: George Strait Productions, Inc.

Gibson: Gibson Guitar Corp.

Grand Ole Opry: Gaylord Entertainment Co.

Jacuzzi: Jacuzzi Inc. Corporation

Jeep: DaimlerChrysler

KBEQ Young Country Q104: CBS Radio Holdings, Inc.

Landrey's Restaurant: J.R. Landrey and Sons Inc.

Lifetime Networks: Lifetime Entertainment Services Cable LT Holdings, Inc.

Lions Club International: International Association of Lions Clubs

MacGyver: Paramount Pictures Inc.

Mercury Records: Universal International Music Group

Moody Gardens, Galveston, TX: Moody Gardens, Inc.

Oreos: Nabisco Inc.

Playskool: Playskool, Inc.

Publisher's Clearing House: Publisher's Clearing House LLC Ltd.

Pyramids of Moody Gardens: Moody Gardens, Inc.

RCA: General Electric Co. Corp.

Red Bull: Red Bull GMBH Ltd.

St. Jude Children's Research Hospital: St. Jude Children's Research Hospital Inc.

Shania Twain: Lange, Eileen, aka Twain, Shania Individual Canada

Shiner: Gambrinus Importing Co., Inc. Corp.

Sony: Sony Corp.

SOS America, Inc.: Support Our Soldiers America, Inc. Corp.

Southern Comfort: Southern Comfort Properties, Inc

Southern Living: Southern Living, Inc., Corp.

Stetson: John B. Stetson Company

Support Our Soldiers: Support Our Soldiers America, Inc. Corp.

The American Legion: The American Legion

Top Ramen: Nissin Foods, Co., Inc.

USA Today: Society for the Advancement of Education, Inc.

Waldenbooks: Waldenbooks Properties, Inc.

Walker Texas Ranger: CBS Worldwide Inc.

Wal-Mart: Wal-Mart Stores, Inc. Corp.

Wranglers: Wrangler Apparel Corp.

# TIDES OF TIME

ဆာ

# Chapter One

## ഇ

Rebecca Roberts unlocked the squeaky front door of the boarding house and wearily faced the narrow staircase leading up to the third floor. The grocery bags in her arms suddenly seemed heavier than they had at Wal-Mart, which offered the distinct advantage of air-conditioning. That she could take a sauna in the oppressing heat of the stairwell crossed her mind as she mopped her brow with her handkerchief.

"This is not another day in paradise—it's just a dog day afternoon in small-town Galveston," she muttered, adjusting the weight of the bags and feeling the wetness of melting ice cream on her palms. "Damn," she swore.

She'd check her mailbox later. Nothing good was ever in it. The rusty, old box was probably stuffed full of junk mail she wouldn't read anyhow. It was highly unlikely that she'd win millions in the Publisher's Clearing House drawing this week. Or receive a letter from Jason Engles, Mr. Country Superstar.

Long ago, she'd given up on both and shortly after that she'd stopped believing in Santa Claus. The next to go—the Easter Bunny, she joked to herself for the thousandth time. Groaning, she began making the treacherous ascent of all forty-four stairs. Counting each one distracted her from the discomfort.

Putting down the bags after the final step, she took a breather. She brushed back the wisps of blonde hair falling into her eyes before making her way through the shadows of the hall.

The doorknob, when she and the groceries with the melting ice cream finally reached it, turned, but it wouldn't budge. Hot and exasperated, Rebecca kicked open the black door in frustration instead and stifled a curse when she banged her toe.

Shutting the door in a terrible hurry, she locked it and muttered some frightful words as she sped to the kitchen with the dripping bags. The freezer felt good, like a cold wind, when she tossed in the containers of ice cream. She couldn't wait to pour herself a tall glass of raspberry lemon iced tea and collapse.

But first she hit the switch for the air conditioner and turned on some vintage George Strait tunes. It was a happy moment. She swayed to the up-tempo beat of "Fool Hearted Memory" as she methodically put away the rest of the groceries in her spotless mulberry potpourri-scented kitchen. At least the air works, she thought gratefully as she walked over to the window and patted the misting cooler. She was thankful for small favors. It had taken her quite awhile to save up enough money to buy that little beauty. When finished with her chores, she plopped down on the recliner, kicked off her sandals and stretched out her long shapely legs, ready to relax and sip good old Texas tea.

Looking around, she was content that all was well in her shabby little world. Seeing everything in its place gave Rebecca great satisfaction—even as she realized that she was really trying to make up for her mother's slovenly house. Dirt was not in Rebecca's vocabulary, although heartbreak, poverty and an alcoholic parent certainly were.

Her mother's violent tantrums and alcoholic rages had haunted her until she'd fled from the house at twenty and found her own place. *"You won't amount to a hill of beans, Rebecca, wait and see. You'll be back."* JoAnne's words were embedded in her consciousness. This is why Rebecca consistently challenged herself to succeed, no matter how small the milestone or the apartment. Her failure wasn't a victory she'd give her mother willingly. Intent on never moving back in, she still visited daily to help take care of her ailing uncle and avoided seeing her mother whenever possible.

Maybe she wouldn't make it as a songwriter—the secret goal her mother didn't know about. But she could make her way and pay her rent on her own.

In her heart she held on to the words of a talented boy named Jason, who told her when she was sixteen that he loved her, that she was beautiful and artistic. "Every girl should hear that at least once in her life," sighed Rebecca, putting the chilled glass of tea up to her cheek as she remembered the magnificent summer they'd written songs together.

She was so afraid to speak up. As a result, any kind of public speaking at school had caused Rebecca's voice to shake and she'd pinch the top of her hands to distract herself from being frightened. Only her late-night, closet writing enabled Rebecca to articulate words and create an outlet for thoughts.

But reality was closing in. A number of years had passed since Jason's departure. She had graduated high school and was still working a dead-end job. In her spare time, she'd been trying to make a living by selling her lyrics with minimal success. She'd confided her hopelessness only to her uncle and her best friend, Whitney.

"Hit songs that touch the emotions of millions are not so much about expression as they are about communication." When the topic of songwriting came up, big, burly Uncle Burt liked to lecture like a scholar rather than simply talk to her as they sat together late at night when JoAnne was either out of the house or out like a light and they could enjoy a peaceful moment. "While expression is simply letting thought and feelings flow freely, communication is the transmission of information, thought or feeling so that it is satisfactorily received to be understood by the listeners. There is a vast difference between the two. I'm going to give you a helpful analogy."

Like a favorite bedtime story, he would tell her the familiar tale of Noah's Ark. "You remember how it goes," he'd chuckle, drawing her close. "After forty days of floating around on the endless ocean, Noah sends out a dove to see if there is any sign of vegetation. The first time he sends the dove out, it has to return because there is no place for the bird to put its foot on anything but water. A few days later Noah sends it out again. This time it returns with an olive branch in its mouth indicating that the water is receding. Finally, when Noah lets the dove out for the third time, it doesn't return at all. It is then that Noah knows the flood is almost over.

"The listener's mind is much like Noah's dove. It is flying around over a flood of thoughts — family concerns, problems at work, preoccupation with traffic, etc. When your song begins to play, the listener subconsciously searches for a place to mentally connect with you in the experience of the song — a place to 'put their foot down' and ride to the end. You as the songwriter must offer solid ground for the mind to get attached and stay interested all the way through."

"How do I do that?" Rebecca would ask. "If I can learn to master it, will I truly be on the way to a place in the Songwriter's Hall of Fame? Like Jason, or like you might have before Vietnam?"

Instead of an answer, he'd give her some "life instructions", as he called them. "The key to writing any kind of 'hit' is to make sure that your audience understands what you are trying to communicate and that they identify with that message. Accomplishing this goal involves developing a tightrope walker's sense of balance. Musically, the melody and harmonies must be familiar enough so that the expected musical payoffs occur and enable the listener to hum or whistle the melody after the song is over.

"But, on the other hand, the music must also be fresh enough to surprise and delight the ear. Similarly, the lyrics must be conversational and understandable but, at the same time, stated in a slightly unique and original way to bring home the point of the song. Mega-hits usually flow from the pens of artists who write like song craftsmen, but who listen and think like ordinary people.

"Great songwriters know what listeners expect to hear and then they craft songs that will meet and exceed those expectations. But not only do great songwriters know their listeners, they also respect them. An audience can tell by the way you write whether you have taken the time to really craft a song they can understand or whether you are simply giving vent to your own personal emotions.

"They can also tell if you are writing songs in order to sell them a slick and clever product or whether you really have something heartfelt, true and well-crafted to communicate. If you sincerely respect your audience, you will take the time to make sure they 'hear your heart' in both your words and music by carefully and meticulously shaping every note and word so that your listeners can receive what you are trying to express. They need to know that you are speaking their language, getting on their wavelength and that you consider yourself one of them."

Rebecca never forgot those lessons. She'd often stop and think for a moment about how Uncle Burt, and for several years, Jason, had made the deepest impressions on her life. They were not people who'd talk down to you, or over your head, or preach at you in a condescending manner, like her mother.

"Almost always," Uncle Burt would remind her, as if he was trying to offset the negative influence of his sister, "the greatest impact comes from people who genuinely and honestly share with you until you are able to connect with them and with what they are trying to say. The effective songwriter must approach the task of writing with that same honest and humble spirit."

As Rebecca's imagination reworked lyrics even when asleep, her uncle's soft, Southern voice often floated to her ear. "The responsibility lies with the communicator—not the receiver—as to whether or not the material is assimilated!"

She was twenty-three. She'd been writing songs since she was a teenager. And she knew the mantra. *The responsibility for ensuring that listeners stay attentive does not lie with the listeners, but with the songwriter. Create lyrics that 'make the light go on' in the eyes of your audience and perhaps even produce a few tears.*

But could she?

Rebecca gazed out of the window then turned, reaching for a notebook and pen from a nearby table. Noisy sea gulls fluttered past her windows and toward the beach until she couldn't hear the squawks anymore. Lines from an old folk song flashed unbidden in her mind, "Are birds really angel spirits carried home by gentle, heavenly winds?" She had an irresistible urge to compose a new song. Her method of writing lyrics was to scribble bits and pieces of ideas that had a central theme related to the song idea.

But something else was going on—she felt it. For some reason she was feeling uneasy about her uncle. A little voice in the back of her head kept repeating that he would be okay alone in the house, but Jo Anne was so unpredictable. Rebecca's apartment was too small for two adults and had too many flights for her uncle to climb with his cane, but she couldn't afford anything larger. Besides, since he'd come out of the VA Hospital after Vietnam, he'd committed himself to looking after his widowed older sister as best he could.

*"He knows something I don't know,"* Rebecca would sigh. Her relationship with JoAnne was more than strained and dysfunctional—it was nonexistent. It was as if she'd regretted the day Rebecca was born and would easily have traded her for her husband who was killed in a car wreck the same week.

Rebecca had few answers but she had her humble home, as she called the crooked floors and cracked window sashes. This was her space, but if need be, one could eat off her floor—or at least that's what Uncle Burt bragged to his friends. With the help of some of his friends from the VFW hall, they'd carry him up the stairs for occasional visits.

Rebecca leaned forward in front of a window, massaging her throbbing feet. Concentrating on her aching arches, she watched a pair of seagulls squalling on a metal light post. If only she was as carefree as a bird. Some days she felt like water in a hot skillet—going in different directions.

"God, Whitney'd better make the supervisor's position with Exxon Corporation happen. If I work for that ambulance chaser much longer, I'll need a good criminal lawyer for what I'd like to do with him," she grimaced.

The clock chimed three o'clock.

Coming home this early was unusual. Normally Rebecca would've stopped by her mother's place to see Uncle Burt. But today he was working at the VFW hall helping fellow Army buddies prepare testimony for the House Veterans' Affairs Committee.

This change of routine worked better anyhow. She could relax and spend some time on new song lyrics, or maybe take a nap until she met up with her uncle.

After eight-thirty she'd miss seeing her mother, which was an added bonus. It was Bingo and Dollar Margarita Night at the Blue Moon Bar & Grill and her mother would never miss that. It was Galveston's social event for cheap drunks.

With luck, Uncle Burt wouldn't be too tired to look at her latest efforts. They needed polishing and his fine ear, attuned to years of listening to the Grand Ole Opry.

Lynne Robin Green, head of Back Roads Music Company, was Rebecca's mentor and stepping stone in the industry. The last thing Rebecca wanted to do was disappoint her. So far five songs had passed the test and were recorded by Back Road's up-and-coming artists. It wasn't much, but it was a start.

When Lynne first told her that she liked the lyrics because the verses came from the heart, Rebecca had walked on air for a week. She couldn't imagine feeling any higher—except so long ago, when she was a carefree sixteen-year-old on Galveston Bay. It was when she'd written a song for Jason, her high school sweetheart. When he told her she had the heart of a poet and could be a great songwriter, Rebecca "saw the light" as her uncle called it, and she knew what her true calling would be.

Reading favorable mention of her pseudonym, J.R. Neels and good reviews in Country Today and On The Edge! Country Music was encouraging, but that didn't pay the bills. Writing for smaller, independent labels was a start, but a slow one.

For the moment she just wanted to quit her job and find a better paying one. Her friend, Whitney, had submitted her name to the personnel department at Exxon and for the past month kept telling her the position would happen, it was just a matter of time.

"Great title for a song, Whit," Rebecca would say to her, in a sulk. "If only Randy Travis hasn't jumped on it first."

Rebecca wanted the new job so badly she could taste it. Not only would she escape her lecherous employer's advances, she'd make more money and not have to work Saturdays. Weekends could be totally devoted to her writing, Uncle Burt or a refreshing swim in the Gulf.

Maybe it was a pipe dream, but Rebecca prayed she could someday afford to head for the bright lights of Nashville, taking her uncle with her. She felt it might be within her grasp after Cheyenne Knolls, country's hottest female newcomer, called to congratulate her on "Tell Them I Won't Be Long".

A lengthy buzz from the doorbell jolted her out of her reverie, half dozing and half thinking. No way was she going to answer it, she thought. She'd had more than enough dealing with people for one day, but the ringing persisted. Rousing herself to stand up, she walked to the front window overlooking the porch and flung open the shutters.

"Who is it?" she shouted.

Hearing the clicking of high heels against the wooden planks and seeing the flash of curly reddish hair, she knew her quiet time was over. "What is it, Whitney? You're interrupting my catnap."

"Buzz me in or you'll rue the day," she shouted, her eyes as wide as her smile.

Rebecca wasn't up for whatever her friend had planned. Judging by her killer outfit and three-inch heels, which could have doubled as deadly weapons, she was prepared for a wild night out on the town. Or as wild as Galveston could get on a muggy night.

"So are you going to let me in, or what?" demanded Whitney as she irritatingly hit the buzzer a couple more times.

Rebecca let out a deep sigh and buzzed her in. Knowing Whitney, she'd run up the stairs in those heels and the heat. With any luck the humidity would frizz her hair—maybe then she'd change her mind and not want to go out looking like Yuck-Yuck the Clown.

Wrong.

"Oh, girlfriend, you're going to perk right up when you hear what I have to tell you." Whitney tugged on the knob, kicking the door open as Rebecca had done.

"This had better be one spectacular piece of news." Rebecca hoped it was an interview.

"Oh," Whitney's green eyes were twinkling, "you don't know the half of it."

Rebecca curled back in the recliner while Whitney pulled up a chair. As usual, Whitney wore her favorite perfume, "Chance". The expensive Chanel scent was sweet and comforting.

"Becca, my friend—my poor, tired, dateless, no-life-whatsoever friend—no time for vegging tonight. You get your dancing shoes on, because we're going out!" Whitney looked about ready to jump out of her skin with excitement.

"Oh no. Nope. No way I'm going anywhere tonight." Rebecca shook her head. "I have a date with a carton of Double Fudge Royale and an Orlando Bloom pirate DVD—no way." Rebecca made a shooing gesture with both hands.

"This is important. Really important."

"I'm not in the mood to waste time on losers in some bar. Let's just do this some other t—" Suddenly, she shot forward in her chair. "Or did I get the job?" Rebecca's heart began to race.

"I don't know anything about that yet. Sorry. What I have to tell you is far more earth-shattering." Whitney bent down and shook Rebecca lightly. "This could be the rest of your life I'm talking about, not some modern-day pirate movie fantasy."

"Work is the rest of my life, Orlando is my secret pleasure and the answer is still no. I'm pooped and staying home. After ice cream and a movie, I'm planning on spending time with my uncle. We're working on…on a family project."

Whitney shook her head as if to say "you're impossible". "Your family project will be there tomorrow. Tonight, you're coming with me." Whitney grabbed Rebecca's hand and pulled. "Come on, let's check out your closet."

Rebecca did her best to wiggle out of Whitney's grasp. When her fiery friend got into nagging mode, there was just no shutting her off.

She compulsively visited every dance club within 100 miles looking for Mr. Right, downing margaritas while she danced herself into oblivion. Too often she dragged a reluctant Rebecca along, insisting that she needed to get out — have fun. Going out on the town like this wasn't exactly her idea of a perfect evening, although, to be fair, Rebecca had liked a few of the guys she met. And they liked her. But her relationships hardly lasted more than a couple of months. Jason Engles still haunted her thoughts. Dating other men seemed as if she were being unfaithful to him. Not that he likely gave a damn.

He'd walked out of her life seven years ago and never looked back. Spending time with guys after being with Jason was like comparing a cheap Chevy to a red Corvette convertible.

She tugged her hand out of Whitney's grip. "Read my lips. I don't feel like going out. I don't feel like drinking. I don't feel like dancing. I'm just not in a very good mood."

"Well, you'd better get into a good mood. I'm talking an once-in-a-lifetime, life-altering experience for you."

"Come on, Whit, stop being a drama queen. What's on your agenda this time?" Rebecca said to humor her friend. "A shipment of designer shoes at Sole's Discount Shack? A two-for-one coupon at some new restaurant? Oh, I know — a lingerie clearance at Love or Lust."

"I am being totally serious with you — tonight you are Cinderella, and me? I'm your fairy godmother!"

"Fairy godmother, huh?" Rebecca looked her friend up and down. "Well, at five feet on a good day and armed with the ability to nag someone to death, I guess you could pass for a fairy. But a fairy godmother in those heels? Not impressive enough. Sorry," she winced.

"What do you mean, 'not impressive enough'?" Whitney leaned down and poked her with a perfectly manicured finger. "We can't all be gorgeous, have waist-long blonde hair and legs that go on forever like 'thou'. But I'll have you know there's a lot of magic in this red head of mine, as well as my ample cleavage. So you just listen up."

"Go ahead." Rebecca smiled at her vivacious, full-of-life friend in spite of herself. "I'm too tired to argue."

Whitney dug into her purse and fished out a small, yellow envelope. Teasing Rebecca, she waved it in front of her face. "Do you know what I'm holding in my magical hands?"

"An envelope?"

"No need to get smart," Whitney replied in a singsong voice. "Good thing you're sitting down. This little envelope, my dear, contains two front-row-center tickets for tonight's America Supports You concert in Houston."

"Why don't you invite someone else, Whit? I'd rather spend an intimate evening with that ice cream I was talking about than with a zillion country fans yelling and pushing. In this heat, I appreciate the thought, but I'm just not interested."

Whitney giggled, twirling around. "You have no idea who's performing tonight, do you?"

Rebecca hesitated. It couldn't be. "No, and I don't much care either," she replied, but her heart begin to pound.

"What planet have you been living on for the past few weeks, my grumpy friend? Sometimes I think you're an old lady trapped in a young woman's body." She put her hand against her forehead in a melodramatic gesture. "I can't believe you don't know who is going to be singing his heart out just forty-five minutes up the road."

Rebecca's heart was really pulsing now, as if she'd been running a marathon. "Who?" she managed to ask.

"Jason Engles—your Jason Engles—and his band, The Fighting Eagles." Whitney laughed triumphantly. "He's performing at the benefit to help the military families. Apparently, he's been doing these benefits all over the country, but this time it's in our backyard."

Feeling overwhelmed, Rebecca tried to catch her breath as she gripped the arms of the recliner. She hadn't felt this way since—well, never. God, this couldn't be happening. Or could it? Finding it increasingly harder to breathe, Rebecca stood and walked into her small kitchen. Propping herself up against the counter, she tried to think, but her thoughts were a wild scramble.

"I knew you'd flip. I told you so." Whitney followed her into the kitchen. "Guess you're speechless, huh?"

Rebecca gulped in some air and then nodded her head. There were so many images whirling through her mind. Finally she managed to get out a intelligible sentence. "How in the world did you get seats?"

"I won them! Front row seats too," Whitney crowed with an exuberant gesture. She'd been rooting for a Jason-Rebecca reunion long after Rebecca herself had lost hope. *"In love, anything can happen"*, was Whitney's motto, and she'd always stuck to it.

"I just won them over the radio. I even got to talk to that hunky DJ, Mike Kennedy. Isn't that fabulous?" Whitney was bubbling over with excitement. "Once I heard that KBEQ was giving them out as a promotional concert, I've been trying for the past three days. I just knew you had to be there, Becca." She reached over and gave Rebecca a quick hug. "Now do you believe me? That I'm a fairy godmother and I come bearing gifts?"

Rebecca was stunned and she found it increasingly harder to think straight. Her body began trembling. She was feeling so many emotions right now that it made her lightheaded. Could all this really be true? What would she say to Jason, if she were lucky enough to talk to him?

Rebecca looked around the room. Not knowing what to say first, she felt tongue-tied as usual, but managed to force words from her lips, "That's quite a gift, Whit. I...I don't know what to say."

"How about yes?" Whitney laughed. "Come on, smile. This is great news."

Rebecca began to pace the kitchen, touching the edge of the counter occasionally for balance. "Don't get me wrong. The concert sounds exciting. But..."

"But what?" Whitney interrupted her. "You know you still love the guy. And this is your chance to see him up close and personal. Well, as personal as you can get among a million other fans."

"Whit, he walked away from me. He left and never looked back." She could feel her face tightened with anger.

"Becca, he didn't just walk away from you," Whitney said gently. "He explained his reasons. You were still in school, just a kid and he was looking out for you in his own way." She put an arm around Rebecca to stop her from pacing. "He was pursuing his lifelong goal. He's doing what his father never did and that's a lot on a boy's shoulders. He had to try to get that hardheaded man's approval. Besides," she said, smoothing Rebecca's hair in a motherly way, "he needed to grow up."

Whitney shifted so that they were face-to-face. "But you're not sixteen and he's still single. Call me a cockeyed optimist, but I think there's a message there."

Uneasy, Rebecca said nothing. She was too afraid. For years she'd been resentful and emotionally wounded by Jason leaving. She felt herself pinching her hand red to push down the fear of speaking up and saying how hurt she felt.

"Listen to me, Becca." Whitney jostled her to listen. "I saw a show last week about a couple whose parents split them apart when they were teens. After more than thirty years, they got back together and picked up where they'd left off. There's no reason you can't too. Go for it, Becca. Do it for all us hopeless romantics who have daydreams like this."

Fairy tales. Fantasies. Rebecca sighed deeply. She knew that life wasn't a fairy tale and that storybook endings were few and far between. "Life isn't that simple, Whit," she said. "Jason and I said our goodbyes. We can't all have a happily-ever-after."

Rebecca couldn't afford to let Whitney's boundless optimism fill her head with impossible dreams that she couldn't handle emotionally. The disappointments had piled up, from JoAnne to her miserable job.

The old desires were still there. Her throat caught as she let a few memories of his face and smile float to the surface. She couldn't deny that she desperately wanted to see Jason again, even if it was just up on the stage. Who knew, maybe he'd changed. Maybe she'd realize that she didn't care about him anymore.

"Whit, just because we're sitting in the front row doesn't mean we'll actually get to talk to Jason. Besides, what if he has a girlfriend? What if he doesn't want to see me again?" She linked her hands together so tightly that her knuckles popped. "Can you imagine how painful that would be for me? It would be like losing him all over again."

Whitney sighed and rolled her eyes. "Becca, the gossip magazines say he's single. That's all you have to know."

"What makes you think he'd want to see me now anyway?" she demanded. "In all these years, he hasn't contacted me. Not once. He certainly didn't send me an invite, now did he?"

"Use your head, silly girl. He told you seven years ago that he was making a clean break so that you could get on with your life. So quit throwing a pity party for yourself, and get on with that life — tonight!"

"Whitney..."

"Don't you 'Whitney' me. You are no wet blanket, Rebecca. If that were true, you would have given up years ago, but you didn't. You've hung in there and moved away from your mother's wrath, concentrated on your music. Did it never occur to you that maybe he's been as chicken as you're being right now? The male ego is a fragile thing, you know," she chuckled. Then her voice softened and became more serious. "It's about time you knocked down that fortress around your heart, Becca, and open up to the world."

Rebecca pondered the thought. Had she barricaded her wounded heart behind a barrier for the last seven years? Crippled by her past, she found it hard to trust or think highly of herself. Was it this wall that had held her back from pursuing her dreams of becoming a well-paid songwriter?

She'd been telling herself that it was her mother and staying in Galveston out of concern for her uncle, but maybe she had just shut down.

Maybe she should take a chance and bulldoze down those bricks. After all, she didn't feel like a coward. And Jason had often told her how brave she was. Maybe this was the step she needed to take to set herself free. And she'd never know if she stayed home with that carton of ice cream.

Rebecca stretched the kinks out of her body as she wished she could stretch them out of her blasted ego. Running her hands through her limp hair made her connect with how she looked. As beat as she felt?

But hey, that wasn't anything a hot shower, a curling iron, and some artful makeup couldn't fix. If she had the tiniest chance of seeing Jason again, she was going to look her best.

"Becca? Hello?" Whitney laughed. "Earth calling Becca?"

Whitney's voice broke into her thoughts.

"So, what's it going to be? Ice cream and a movie all by your lonesome?"

"If you put it that way, you've got me."

"I do, don't I?" her friend said with deep satisfaction.

Rebecca couldn't help but join her in a hug. Leave it to Whitney to find some way to make her smile even at the scariest of times. When she was in the hospital, Whitney had arrived with a roomful of balloons. Whitney always knew how to exaggerate her generosity to try to make up for JoAnne's insensitivity.

"No matter what happens, it'll be worth it to learn how it feels to see him again." She reached up and gave Rebecca a gentle punch on the chin. "You snooze, you lose. Besides, Bec, I'll be there with you."

"Okay, you win. Call me crazy, but I'll go."

"Great! Now you go get a shower and do your hair. I'm going through your closet. Before I'm finished with you, you're going to be the ultimate femme fatale." Whitney rubbed her hands together. "This is going to be fun."

"If you say so. Make sure I'm home by midnight and your car doesn't turn into a pumpkin."

"Don't be a smartass. Get going, girl. Time's a-wasting."

Thoughts of Jason, lazy summer days and young love filled her head minutes later as Rebecca stood humming softly in the shower, letting the strong pressure of the hot water stimulate her skin. She picked up the citrus-scented soap resting in the carved dish and started scrubbing herself. First her hands and arms. She rinsed the suds off her wrists and continued up over her forearms to her shoulders, which lacked the tan she'd always had when she was a teenager. Another rinse, then she scrubbed her torso, glancing down between her breasts to rub the thick lather over a belly she'd taken pains to keep flat. She slid the soap down over her thighs, which were lean but muscular. If she'd been shorter, they'd have seemed ungainly. She softly scrubbed them with a sense of wry affection.

At that point, Rebecca rested her head against the cool shower tile and began to question her earlier decision to go. "What on Earth are you getting yourself into?"

It hadn't been hard to keep tabs on Jason all these years. Rebecca had learned from his mother when he'd landed a gig in Nashville as the opening act for Dream On.

But the real shocker came a year later when Mrs. Engles, who was leaving town and getting a divorce, told her that Jason had given up singing to join the Marines. That felt like a real betrayal for Rebecca. He'd left her for a singing career and now he'd chucked it, too!

When Jason resumed his singing career and made it really big, she had secretly hoped he would contact her. But after months with no word, she resigned herself to the fact that he simply didn't love her. She told herself again and again to move forward and quit finding things wrong with every man she met, but somehow she never could.

As the water sluiced down her body for a final rinse, Rebecca remembered the night of the big confrontation—the crying, anger and the blood. Knowing Jason was leaving Galveston for Nashville, she'd poured her heart and soul out to him in a lengthy letter and poem.

Tears flowed uncontrollably that evening. Rebecca slipped out of the house and walked over a mile to deliver the note, but it was too late. Jason was gone. His mother took the envelope and promised she'd get it to her son.

Weeks later Jason sent back a heartbreaking note, explaining that he missed her so much but keeping in touch would just make it harder for him to live without her. He urged her to forget him.

After that she never mailed another letter, but continued to write poems, pouring out her heart through thick black ink quills written on countless reams of paper. Uncle Burt finally persuaded her to turn those love letters into song lyrics. That was the "family project" they would work on together. Uncle Burt enjoyed the sessions and called it their "Music of the Night".

He had a way with words, something he proudly told Rebecca she'd inherited from him, and he had passed on his passion for country-western music. Also, almost losing his legs in a helicopter crash kept him in constant pain and on opiate drugs.

Rebecca was so grateful for his attention, and writing song lyrics was excellent therapy. It was her channel for articulating her hypersensitive feelings after Jason left her. She clearly recalled when the big decision was made for her.

Rebecca had brought Uncle Burt dinner that night—fried chicken, mashed potatoes, coleslaw and biscuits from Chicken Champ.

"What's all this, honey? Looks like you got all my favorites," he had said with a delighted grin.

She patted his hand. "You bet I did. I know how much you like your fried chicken, and I figured my mother doesn't make it for you very often."

"Are you kidding? She don't cook for me at all, Becca. If it weren't for you bringing groceries into this house and the lunches down at the VFW, I'd never get a decent meal."

"So where is she tonight?" Rebecca knew the answer even before she asked the question.

"I'll give you three guesses. Heck, I hardly ever see her unless it's the first of the month—then I see too much of her." The pair laughed, and Rebecca got up to give her uncle a big hug.

"You fix your plate, Uncle Burt, and I'll make you some iced tea. Do you need apple butter for your biscuits?"

"You shouldn't fuss over me so, Rebecca." The old man dug into the hot food. "You'll spoil me and yes, I'd love some apple butter."

"I love spoiling you." She looked at him over her shoulder. "Besides, it isn't like I have anyone else in my life to spoil now, do I?"

"I worry about you, sweetheart." Uncle Burt's smile faded. "You're happy on the outside, always cracking jokes, but on the inside…" He shook his head. "I can tell your heart is breaking and I know why."

Tears burned behind her eyelids and she busied herself with Burt's tea. "You want to share your observations?" she said once she had herself under control.

"You still miss that boy."

"What's done is done. He made his decision a long time ago." Rebecca moved her shoulders in what she hoped was a casual shrug. "And I've gotten on with my life."

"No, you haven't." Uncle Burt's fork clattered on the table. "You're going through the motions of life, but you're not living. You've never gotten over Jason."

"Well, what if I haven't?" She couldn't keep the annoyance out of her voice.

"One thing the war taught me was that you can't erase the past, but you have to move on. You should go to Nashville and find that young man—make your dreams come true."

"No. As much as I love and miss him, there is no way I'm going after him." Rebecca sat down next to her uncle.

"Every day is a gift, Becca." He put his hand on Rebecca's. "Don't let it go to waste."

"If life is such a gift, why do I have a mother who hates me? A father who abandoned me? Why did the man I love leave me without any warning?" She looked straight into her uncle's eyes. Rebecca knew these were hard questions, but she wanted to see if her uncle had any answers.

"Your pride is telling you not to go to Nashville—that's fine. I understand that. But, Rebecca, you're a talented young woman. It's time you explored what's deep inside you and used that to make things better for yourself."

"What's inside of me is just one sad country song after another," Rebecca replied sharply.

"That's exactly what I'm talking about, darlin'. You need to write this stuff down. How long has it been since you put words to paper and written a song? You used to show me such beautiful poetry."

"It's been a while, hasn't it?" Rebecca admitted.

"It's about time you started writing again." Uncle Burt reached over and took her hand. "Put that brain of yours to work for yourself instead of that ambulance and skirt chaser you work for. Make a name for yourself. If you don't do it, no one else will."

Rebecca's eyes welled up with tears. "Uncle Burt, I don't know if—"

"You can do it and you will become a success if that's what you're afraid of. I can feel it in my heart."

Rebecca threw her arms around her uncle's shoulders and gave him a squeeze.

"Look, your mother is out for the evening. Go grab some paper and a pencil and get to work."

Rebecca found a notebook and a pencil, cleaned up the remains of their dinner and helped Uncle Burt settle into his favorite chair. He was right about her life, she thought. It was boring and she'd kept her emotions hidden for too long.

"What should I write?" she asked as she sat down on the carpet at her uncle's feet.

"You write what's in your heart. Write about your life, lost love and new adventures. A song has to come from deep within your soul. It's a small novel just waiting to tell someone a story. Tell your story, Becca, and let the world know what's in your heart." He smiled, patted her shoulder and settled back.

Rebecca felt content as the words began to flow from her soul onto the paper. From time to time, Uncle Burt would look down at her or stroke her hair. After she read what she had written aloud to him, he made some suggestions for improvement.

"We make quite a team, Uncle Burt," she told him as she helped him up the stairs to his room. When he sat down on his bed, she bent down and gave him a kiss on the temple. "I love you, Uncle Burt."

"I love you, too, Rebecca. I'm so proud of you. You took a big step tonight."

She smiled. "I did, didn't I?"

"I'd love to read what you've written again. Can I keep your songs? I'll put them in my metal strongbox for safekeeping."

"Sure, Uncle Burt. We'll work on them again the next time I visit."

Writing those songs had become a mainstay in her life. And, in an odd way, Jason had remained her inspiration.

"Hey, Becca." Whitney's voice interrupted her memories. "Get out of that shower before you turn into a prune. We all know what prunes are good for. Do I have a dress for you!"

"Give me a couple minutes." Rebecca turned off the water and hurriedly toweled off. She vigorously rubbed rose-scented lotion all over her body to smooth and perfume her skin. After all these years of never getting him out of her mind, in a few short hours she'd be seeing him again. It was a terrifying thought, yet exhilarating. Soon she'd know for sure why he was the one love of her life.

# Chapter Two

ഌ

Rebecca and Whitney pressed their way through hordes of enthusiastic country music fans looking for their row and seats. Recorded music from one of the groups' albums on sale at kiosks filled the air, as did the chattering voices of overzealous and over-endowed Texas girls selling Jason Engles' Fighting Eagles T-shirts. Adding to the loud, noisy crowd were the voices of burly vendors, carrying heavy containers and shouting out "Red Bull, Bud Light, Shiner," the beers befitting the Texas palate.

Rebecca and Whitney were indeed front row center. They scooted in and found their seats. Roadies were busy scurrying across the darkened stage and up onto ladders finalizing the stage lighting. Video film crews repositioned their cameras for the main event. It was all overwhelming for Rebecca — to see how a concert worked and just how far Jason had come. Frenzied fans were filling up the enormous Houston Stadium. The smell of beer and cigarettes filled the air.

Looking around, it wasn't hard to see which charities Jason and the Eagles were supporting. A glittery white banner stretched across the proscenium arch. "America Supports You Concert for Support Our Soldiers America" was lettered in red and blue metallic. Hanging from the side walls were thirty-foot posters of America Supports You and SOS America, Inc.

The audience oohed and aahed and applauded when a back curtain was slowly raised to reveal two Apache helicopters at the rear of the stage.

As Rebecca and Whitney intently watched ticket holders parade around in the latest western fashions — the year's newest cowboy hats, tank tops, boots and larger than life shiny belt buckles. The crowd was growing increasingly impatient and demanding Jason and his band in a deafening cacophony. Rebecca had to yell into Whitney's ear if she wanted to talk. Her arms were covered with goose bumps—not from the air-conditioning but from nerves and all the second-guessing in her mind as they were driving to the stadium.

Rebecca squirmed, not entirely comfortable with the revealing outfit Whitney had forced on her. There was entirely too much skin showing—her midriff was exposed between the spangled red baby doll top and the above-the-knee ruffled white skirt. She'd bought the outfit months ago on a dare from Whitney but never had the courage to wear it until now. And her feet felt unaccustomed to the strappy high-heeled sandals Whitney had insisted she wear. "They show off those long legs, Becca," she'd said. Being barefoot would have been oh so much better.

Looking for a mirror, Rebecca frantically searched through her purse. Taking it out, she checked her lipstick for the tenth time and flipped her long hair off her shoulder to reveal the red crystal shoulder-duster earrings loaned by Whitney. God, how she hoped Jason might recognize her and if so, like what he saw. It was hard for her to believe a big star would still be interested in a simple girl like her.

"Don't worry, Becca, you look fantastic!" Whitney told her emphatically and placed her hands around her mouth, shouting to her. "I wonder how Jason will look."

"Well, in his last video he had a mustache, long hair and defined pecs," Rebecca yelled back.

"Yeah, well, they can do wonderful things in the editing room these days," her friend teased.

Rebecca forced a smile but that didn't do anything for her nerves, which were stretched as tightly as a guitar string. Her hands were twisting in her lap like she had done the St. Vitas dance.

How much *had* Jason changed in the past seven years? Not just physically, but deep inside? Did he even remember how they'd made music on the beach? How they'd made love? Or had his ambition and his father's dream made that long-ago summer simply an episode he'd long since forgotten?

She blinked, adjusting her eyes as the house lights suddenly dimmed. The clamor from the fans dropped low enough for her to hear Whitney's voice in a normal tone. "Here we go, Bec!" She gave her arm a squeeze while darkness began to grow.

Rebecca tried not to be swept away by the thrill of the moment, but nothing could stop the butterflies dancing inside her stomach. She felt the excitement mounting even as she told herself she was crazy.

From the back of the stage, pulsating red, white and blue lights swirled through wisps of fog and mist. Rebecca could feel her nerves tense as music started up that matched the rhythmic gyrations of the laser show. The chords of Jason's latest chart-topping hit, "Courage Under Fire," began to throb over the speakers. Her body began to buzz with a rush of adrenaline so powerful that suddenly anything seemed possible.

Through the colored haze, tall silhouettes began to emerge and the crowd went wild with roars of enthusiasm. The shadowy figures one by one solidified into band members. Rebecca strained to find Jason. Still, she couldn't stop herself from standing and clapping to the rhythm of the haunting ballad. She couldn't see him, but she could feel his presence. Her pulse quickened in anticipation, her excitement growing even more because she now had no idea what to expect.

From the stadium's catwalk, a huge American flag topped by a bald eagle unfurled toward the stage, signaling to Jason's fans that he was about to appear. An explosive cheer from the delighted, impatient crowd vibrated through Rebecca's body as the roar of countless feet stomped and hands clapped. Voices chanted his name, and tears of pride filled Rebecca's eyes. He'd made it big-time, as he always said he would.

The stadium rocked to the sounds of Jason's music as the band played in front of over ten thousand fans. The entire audience behind her stood and surged forward. Rebecca looked around at the seemingly endless sea of people packed into the stadium who were clapping approvingly at the fabulous visual effects. The sweeping lights were like another musical instrument, pulsating and slamming against the walls and ceilings with the force of an electric storm.

"Get ready!" Whitney shouted. "Any second now your sexy beast of a man is going to walk out onto that stage." She pointed to the bright spotlight illuminating center stage, just within her reach. "Maybe he'll pick you up and carry you outta here, like in the movies."

"Fat chance," Rebecca yelled back.

The music surged, getting louder and stronger with every electrified beat. Rebecca couldn't take her eyes off the stage. Somewhere up there her fate was about to appear. She didn't want to blink and miss a second. Her thoughts drifted off toward their reunion and how he would put his arm around her, scoop her up and carry her away from all this.

In a few minutes, seconds, she would see Jason again. She almost felt sick with the waiting, as if her entire life came down to this one moment. Nothing existed but this instant, this stadium, this seat, this tiny space of floor upon which she weakly stood.

Finally, she heard a bold, rugged voice—his voice—as it slipped through the lights and the mist. The crowd clapped and screamed with exhilaration, but Rebecca heard only the sexy baritone that stole her breath and made her heart yearn.

Fans pushed forward in a wave, trying to reach the stage and touch or get pictures of their favorite singer. Girls climbed up onto their boyfriends' shoulders to get a better view. Some fans had smuggled in camcorders, digital cameras and contraband booze. Whitney pointed and squealed with excitement. Rebecca was no exception. Although she didn't shout like the others, she was truly captivated, awestruck by her surroundings.

It was hard to imagine that all this hoopla was born out of one songwriter's heartfelt words. A group of carefully mastered sentences and phrases made for all this grandeur. Without the songwriting, Rebecca's true passion, there'd be no concerts or country superstars. Her desire for a career in this business now raged into full-blown determination to make her life a success. To top it off, the object of her teenage passion would be singing merely a few feet away.

Within seconds, a smaller spotlight pooled on the stage, illuminating a lone guitar player dressed in black, complete with a coal-black Stetson. Jason Engles strummed his signature Gibson acoustic. The spotlight caught a scar along his temple and cheek, and Rebecca's heart skipped a beat. Besides Whitney, she was the only one in the stadium who knew where that had come from.

"Oh, God, Whitney, look at his scar," she shouted, not taking her eyes off the stage. "I hope he doesn't hate me because of it."

"Come on, quit blaming yourself for that. Besides, it adds character. He's about the sexiest thing I've seen in a long time." She leaned over toward Rebecca and laughed. "How come I let you have him in high school? I should have made my move on him that day at the beach when I had the chance."

Rebecca didn't reply but kept her eyes on Jason, her heart pounding so hard that it felt as if it would burst—or at the very least jump out of her chest. She supposed his scar did add character, but to her, it was a haunting reminder of their painful farewell. She kept studying his body as the spotlight's radiance danced across him and his guitar, seeming to cast an illuminating halo all around him.

Standing before her was the embodiment of all her dreams. The moment seemed so unreal that she was tempted to think Jason was just another of her fantastic imaginings, but Whitney's hand squeezing her arm went a long way toward reassuring Rebecca that this was reality.

He was born to be up there. This had been Jason's birthright all along. It was tough to admit it, but he'd made the right decision in leaving Galveston behind. Even harder to admit was the fact that his father had been right about the career choice. Being up there on the stage in front of a crowd of people was his destiny.

Years ago, she'd dreamed of success for him, for them. Except now someone else wrote the lyrics to his songs.

The ballad started soft and slow, but it built, becoming more powerful, more compelling. Jason's stage presence was electrifying as he strode across the stage in time to the beat, his tight black Wrangler jeans looking as if they had been painted on his body. Rebecca felt a thrill as his muscles rippled through the dark, thick material. Jason looked more like a "bad outlaw" than a singer.

"He's still definitely eye candy!" Whitney shouted to Rebecca, but she barely heard her friend.

His white and black long-sleeved shirt was unbuttoned from his throat to the middle of his chest, showing off his muscled upper body and corded neck. Rebecca remembered the texture of his skin so precisely that her hands flexed as if she were back in time, touching him all over again. More wiry hair covered his chest than she remembered and her fingers tingled as she thought of how his chiseled flesh would feel now.

"He looks even better than I remembered, Bec. I'm definitely turned on." She grinned. "Not that I'm trying to poach on your man or anything."

"Whitney, any man who breathes turns you on. You could be on life support, but put a man within a mile of you and you'd turn over and shave your legs," Rebecca shouted back, all the while never taking her eyes off Jason.

When the song ended, the audience clapped and cheered and called for more.

"Thank you all kindly." Jason waved to the crowd. "It's a great night for a concert, isn't it, Houston?"

The crowd went wild with excitement. Women of all ages whooped and hollered as if they hadn't seen a man for years. And Whitney was no exception. If she weren't her best friend, Rebecca might have been upset by Whitney's flirty shouts, but she knew that it was just her coquettish style. Rebecca watched Jason grin like a delighted little boy and make a formal bow to his fans. Then, straightening, he lofted his Stetson high into the air above the crowd.

Rebecca watched, stunned that women were going crazy screaming and climbing over one another trying to grab for it. The whole event was like watching a feeding frenzy of starving sharks, or worse, a dozen bridesmaids tackling one another to catch a lone bridal bouquet. "I bet that smaller lady in the middle gets it. She looks like a scrapper," Whitney giggled.

Several minutes later, after a fierce fight, Whitney's predictions came true. Her lady emerged the winner, clutching the hat tightly to her chest. Rebecca smiled, remembering that Jason had always hated hats and, if forced to wear one, always managed to get rid of it as soon as possible. "If only that woman knew how little that Stetson meant to him, perhaps she wouldn't have gone through so much agony," Rebecca muttered.

A high-pitched noise came from the sound system. Everyone's attention once again turned toward the stage. "It's great to be back in the Lone Star State and the glorious Bayou City of Houston," Jason shouted.

At the mention of their city, the locals whistled and whooped. Jason waited for the crowd to quiet down before continuing. "I'd like to thank all of you for coming and contributing to SOS America. Support Our Soldiers is such a worthy cause and one very close to my heart, as it is with many citizens across our great country. This concert will be broadcasted to our troops overseas, so let's give a big round of applause for the men and women fighting in Afghanistan and

Iraq and let their families know just how much we care about them."

Jason started to clap, and the crowd let their patriotic spirit take over as they responded with thunderous applause.

"You know," Jason, continued, "I've got a good friend, Charlie Wallace, over in Iraq right now. Charlie's a character, as I'm sure his buddies in his company, the Pit Bulls, would tell you, but he's one of the bravest men I know. His wife, Tara, and their children are somewhere in the crowd tonight." He shaded his eyes and peered out into the audience. "Let's give her and the kids a big hand and let them know we're here for them."

A spotlight searched the audience for the Marine's wife. She was crying, overwhelmed and reluctant to acknowledge the crowd's reaction, but the audience gave her a standing ovation. That was just like him, Rebecca thought, and she felt her heart expand with love. He might be famous now, but he hadn't lost his caring, generous nature.

"Some of you may know that I was born and raised not too far from here," he continued in a chatty tone, as if he were just shooting the breeze with a bunch of old high school friends. "In a little town called Galveston. Anyone heard of it?"

Again the fans broke into a deafening din. Whitney poked Rebecca in the side with her elbow while clapping with the rest of the audience.

"Yep," he continued. "Some of the best times of my life were spent in Galveston, swimming at Lake Travis, fishing the outlying bayous, and let's not forget those late- night parties on the jetties." He chuckled and the crowd roared and whistled their approval at the local reference. "Yeah, y'all know what I'm talking about."

Jason adjusted a string on his guitar as he walked toward the stage apron right in front of Rebecca and Whitney. He strolled past them, tuning the guitar, never looking in their direction. Rebecca didn't know whether to be disappointed or relieved. All she knew was that every nerve in her body felt as tight as the twangy string Jason was adjusting.

"I'll bet most of you have memories of hot summer weekends swimming with friends, drinking beer on deserted country roads where the law couldn't find you and lazy, hot nights with the girl—or boy—of your dreams. In my case, girl," he laughed.

The strum of the E string flooded Rebecca with memories. If Jason had a guitar in his hands and was the least bit nervous, he always played with that damned E string. It was such a little thing, but it made her feel special to know that she was probably the only one in the entire crowd who knew that.

He finally got the string tuned to his satisfaction, then headed back over to the band. He whispered something to the drummer and then turned to face the audience again.

"This next song is one of the first I ever wrote the music to. Being home in Texas brought it to mind, I guess, and I'd like to sing it for you." He smiled a sexy little smile. "It's about those lazy summer days at the shore and the long-legged girl with golden hair who shared 'em with me."

He turned to the band and counted off the beat. "One...two... a one, two, three, four!"

Suddenly, the words Rebecca had written so many years ago pulsed through the amplifiers and into her heart. Immediately, the images of those sultry summer evenings when she and Jason had sat under the shade of an old willow tree, dangling their feet in the cool lake while he struggled to put music to the words she had written the night before was so clear in her memory. All the sensations, all the salty, piney scents of that night came flooding back to her.

"Gentle Winds, Tender Heart" had been their first collaboration, and it had been good enough for Jason to win a local talent contest sponsored by the American Legion. He had played an old six-string Gibson that had once belonged to his grandfather—his most prized possession.

"Nothing makes music like a Gibson," Jason had often told her. Now, of course, he was playing a state-of-the-art Gibson acoustic, but his old scratched-up guitar had made such beautiful music.

Now, after all those years, as she listened to the song, tears filled her eyes. Damn it! She tried to blink back the tears. It was hard enough just looking at Jason without having to hear their love song and listen to him reminisce about their time together which had just become a line in his act about the good old days.

*Gentle winds and tender heart forever in my soul.*

*As years fly by, and life leads me afar,*

*It's the gentle winds and your tender heart that call me home…*

*To you.*

Rebecca knew every word, every note, as if they had been burned into her memory for eternity. The images washed over her. They would sneak off to the lake to be together when Jason got off work at the docks. Jason and Rebecca had felt so much joy being together and escaping from their everyday world—Rebecca from her mother and Jason from his own version of hell. For a moment, she found herself wondering what it would be like to be with Jason in that special way again, but she immediately reined herself in, reminding herself that fairy tales didn't happen in real life.

"I love this song," Whitney sighed, not noticing her friend's tears.

"Yeah…it's a wonderful song," Rebecca replied with a crackle in her voice.

What would Whitney say if she told her Jason hadn't written this famous song alone? That she had, in fact, composed the words and Jason had translated the poem to music? It was Jason's first big win. Uncle Burt was the only other one who knew she'd helped him win that first contest, and if her uncle hadn't talked when the Viet Cong had him, he wouldn't talk now.

"He did mention a long-legged Texas girl with golden hair," Whitney pointed out when the song ended. "See, Becca? He was talking about you!"

Rebecca just shook her head, unwilling to believe it.

"Well, who else? He said that being back in Texas brought back those 'steamy' memories." The twinkle in Whitney's eyes made Rebecca blush. "Obviously he *has* been thinking about you."

"Well, fairy godmother, are you going to sprinkle some of your magic dust and make it be true?" Rebecca asked.

But what if it was true? What if those words weren't just part of his act? What if he thought about her when he sang that song? Or those long, late nights when he couldn't sleep? Her stomach twisted in knots at the mere idea.

"My magic dust dispenser is in the shop," Whitney said.

"What good is a fairy godmother without magic dust?" Rebecca demanded.

"So why don't you make it happen yourself?" joked Whitney. "You've been working out. Do a little chin-up and just hoist yourself up on the stage."

"Sure, make a fool of myself, why don't I?" Rebecca shrugged. "Either way, since he never got in touch with me, it's not too likely that Jason would want to see me again now."

"Don't be too sure about that. My money is on the two of you getting back together and living happily ever after." Whitney tapped her on the shoulder. "There just *has* to be at least one couple in this crazy world who can live happily ever after. Or else what's the purpose of love, anyway?"

"You mean besides the perpetuation of the species?" It felt good to relieve her stress by joking with her friend.

"Yeah," Whitney giggled. "Besides that. If love doesn't last, then why did God invent it in the first place?"

"Who said God invented it? Probably men invented the concept—to keep the women barefoot and pregnant while they went off and did whatever they wanted."

"Too bad." Whitney shook her head and gave a mock frown. "I was really counting on a happily ever after. It's a damn shame. Besides, if my species looked that good, I'd be pregnant all the time cause I'd never leave the bedroom."

"You just can't help yourself, can you Whit?"

The banter with Whitney helped Rebecca relax. During their chatter the band moved on to another tune that had the audience singing along and dancing in the aisles. With her mind back on the music, Rebecca couldn't resist picking up the beat, as well. She and Whitney clapped along with the crowd and watched Jason as his hips gyrated in time with the music.

He put his Gibson aside and clapped to the music's beat as he sang to his fans. Dancing a two-step across the stage's apron, he slapped the hands held out to him. God, Becca thought. He was born to do this. He looked so perfect up there, with the music pulsing through his blood. It made sacrificing him all those years ago almost worth it.

"He's coming this way, Becca. Oh, God, he's coming this way." Whitney grabbed her arm and shook her. "Get ready! Do something! He needs to see you."

Whitney pushed Rebecca closer to the stage. She wanted so badly to raise her hands out to the magnificent performer up there on the stage, but her fear was greater. If she touched him, even the tips of his fingers, she knew a jolt of attraction would slam through her—it always had. And who knew how she would embarrass herself then?

"Come on, Becca!" Whitney tried to push her still closer to the stage. "Let him spot you so he'll know you cared enough to come tonight."

"I can't, Whit…I just can't." She pulled back. "Trust me, it's for the best."

Rebecca remained standing next to her friend while Jason returned to the band. The women and younger girls in the audience screamed like maniacs, happily making fools of themselves. She admired their ability to let loose and have a good time even though she cringed at how ridiculous they looked doing it.

Whitney sat back down and gave Rebecca a serious look. "You aren't getting into the spirit of this thing," she reproached her. "Here's your chance to hook up with the love of your life and you're hanging back. What gives?"

"How do I know he'd even want to see me? He might want to toss me out on my butt after what my mother did to him." She twirled a lock of hair tightly around her thin finger. "Don't you see? That would be the worst thing of all."

"You have to take the chance, Becca. Otherwise you're still letting your mother come between you—she wins. You don't want that now. C'mon, what do you have to lose? If he doesn't want to see you, you'll be no worse off than you are now." Whitney sighed impatiently. "And at least you'll know where you stand, and maybe then you can get on with your life. You have to go for it!"

"Let's just drop the whole subject and enjoy the rest of the show," Rebecca said, starting to get annoyed. "Okay?"

"Fine! But you'll thank me if you take the gamble and win and you'll hate yourself if you let your chance go. Got that?"

"Yeah, I got that." She forced herself to smile. "Now be a dear and shut up so I can hear the music."

When Jason and the band began the opening bars of "Texas Cattlemen's Club," one of Rebecca's favorite songs, all her annoyance with Whitney's pushing faded from her mind. The song was fast and wicked with a wild, driving beat that rocked her to her feet. Thoroughly caught up in the music, she danced and sang along.

Being in the front row allowed her a wonderful view of Jason and the band. She saw how artfully the men interacted, joking and talking between tunes. Their chemistry reverberated throughout the audience. The band worked together like a well-oiled machine. And Rebecca couldn't take her eyes off Jason. He'd always been a gorgeous specimen of masculinity, but now he was stunning. Jason had obviously done some serious working out and the charming laugh lines around his bedroom eyes could melt the clothes off a girl. Even the scar enhanced his sexy, rugged good looks. His hair was still the color of cornstalks drying in the fields, but it was cut short now, reminiscent of a military style.

Really, she mused as the music continued to thrum through her veins, there wasn't a single thing about Jason's appearance she would change. Would he think the same if he saw her, she wondered?

The arena went pitch-black again, and from deep downstage a solitary drum tapped out a beat. After two measures the bass joined in, and then a slide guitar began its eerie wail. The crowd recognized the tune and whistled and shouted its approval.

"Looking for a Way Out" had been Jason's first hit to go platinum. The entire audience leapt to its feet, stamping to the rhythm and chanting the opening line. The atmosphere became so intense that Rebecca felt herself being carried by the energy of those around her. Her heart raced as she swayed to the rhythm. All thoughts and worries melted away and she threw herself blissfully into the music. This was where Jason belonged, performing onstage. And this was where she needed to be.

The intensity built and Jason sang the words as if they were being torn from his soul. Of course, she knew what the lyrics meant to him. At the time that song was written, he was looking for some way to break loose from his father—to prove himself as a man. He moved across the stage like a flame, flaring out to his fans, pouring out his power as if he wanted and needed to share it with the audience. To give it away until there was nothing left of him. The performance consumed him and the audience couldn't get enough.

His glistening body dripped sweat until he looked as if he had just stepped out from behind a waterfall. How could he do this night after night, Rebecca wondered. His strength and stamina must be amazing. He was like a red-hot meteor blazing across the sky and she just watched in awe.

Jason moved down to the front of the stage and before she knew it, he was standing right in front of her, singing his soul out to the crowd. His eyes sparkled with excitement and his voice washed over her like a forceful ocean wave.

Then, inevitably, their eyes met and held and she saw the moment of his awareness of her as his chocolate-brown eyes widened with shock. His voice caught on a phrase, but he didn't lose a beat. His gaze frozen on her face, he finished the song with a flourish but then stood stock-still in front of Rebecca as cheers and applause washed over him.

Rebecca, too, stood still. Everything around them disappeared as if they were in their very own universe. Part of her wanted to reach out to him, touch him, but she couldn't move. And then there was that flicker of pride that wanted him to take the first step toward her. Her eyes on his, she willed him to reach down toward her. Reach down and make her heart come alive again.

# Chapter Three

**ഌ**

Rebecca felt like a deer caught in the blinding headlights of an approaching car. She couldn't move, couldn't speak, her mouth was as dry as a West Texas desert in late August and she could barely breathe. All she could do was stand perfectly still, look into Jason's eyes and pray that he would reach for her.

She could see the turmoil in his eyes and knew that he was wrestling with his own tangle of emotions. Was he remembering a simpler place and time where only two young lovers and their music, the tides of the Gulf and warm, gentle breezes existed? Was he as flooded with emotion as she was, oblivious to the rowdy crowd?

As she watched the shock in Jason's face recede, her heart pounded so loudly that it was like a drumbeat echoing in her ears. His eyes came alive with an internal fire and she would have shaken her head in disbelief if she'd had the strength to do so. Was it possible that he hadn't forgotten? That he burned as brightly for her as she still did for him?

"Becca, say something!" Whitney shouted at her, but she heard her voice as if it were hundreds of miles away. "Reach for him. Let yourself go! It's time to take a chance."

Whitney shook her arm, breaking the spell, and Rebecca dragged in a gulp of air, realizing that she had almost forgotten to breathe. The world snapped into focus, and once again she found herself in the raucous stadium with thousands of fans chanting Jason's name.

Jason, too, seemed to emerge from a similar spell, and he blinked hard as if trying to concentrate.

"Becca?" he asked in disbelief, his words coming through the speakers as clear and sharp as glass. "Is that you?" He began to reach down toward her.

Rebecca could feel the stares of thousands of onlookers. Hearing the sound of her name was frightening. She could feel the goose bumps once again rise on her arms. More than anything, she felt the need to reach out to him, to take his hand, but pride and uncertainty held her back. Her flesh burned for the heat of his touch. Rebecca slowly leaned toward the stage. In an instant, she could feel her mouth begin to form the beginning sounds of his name.

Before she could totally respond, Jason's bass guitarist grabbed his arm and hauled him back toward the band. A techie dashed offstage and the microphones suddenly fell silent. All she could hear was the thunderous roar of the crowd, but it was clearly visible that the band members were having a heated discussion.

"Well, well," Whitney said with a smug smile, "I guess that answers the question about whether he remembers you." She briskly fanned herself with her program. "Now, I wonder what's next."

Rebecca was feeling dizzy and nauseous again. "Oh no, Whitney, the last thing I wanted to do was cause any trouble and it looks like I've caused plenty!" Rebecca started to panic and began searching the ground for her purse. "Quick. Let's get outta here."

"Not a chance, girlfriend. I want to see what happens." Whitney laughed. "We're going to get our money's worth, come hell or high water."

Rebecca turned to look at Whitney's delighted face. "You're having a pretty good time at my expense. I can't believe it. You didn't even pay for the tickets," she pointed out.

"Yeah, but I still deserve to watch the rest of this show and the fireworks that are sure to follow." Whitney winked and turned her attention toward what was happening onstage.

Led by the drummer, the band quickly exploded into another number, loud and hard. Rebecca didn't recognize the tune—not that it mattered. Jason knew she was here now.

She looked back up at the stage. Jason played his guitar and belted out the song as if nothing unusual had just happened. He was back in his star persona, putting on an electrifying show for all the people who had paid good money to hear him sing. Well, what was he supposed to do, she thought. Although part of her did wish that he hadn't slipped back into his supremely confident persona quite so easily.

The band put on a phenomenal performance, with back-to-back upbeat numbers. Toward the end, the bass player and Jason began dueling guitars and the crowd loved it. Jason ran up a ramp stage left and out amongst the crowd while the other guitarist climbed atop a huge amplifier. Aiming their instruments like guns, they "shot" at each other with every note they played. The drums played along while the steel guitars screamed out the emotion of the patriotic song.

As the music built to a climactic crescendo, the other guitarist pretended to be mortally hit. He dropped from the amp and rolled across the stage, tucking his guitar tightly to his body without missing a single note. He bounced up to his knees and shot another volley of notes at Jason, who had also climbed atop a huge sound system.

With the crowd screaming encouragement, Jason finished his adversary off, plucking out the exciting finish to the instrumental battle. With a flourish and a jaunty grin, he jumped down from the platform and landed center stage, arms outstretched to receive the exuberant applause.

He was a consummate professional, Rebecca thought. He'd really made a name for himself in the past two years, after having been voted country music's "Most Promising Newcomer" and winning a country music award for his first album. To earn honors like that, he had to know how to put on a show and work a crowd.

Rebecca looked at her watch, increasingly edgy. Maybe thirty minutes remained of the show, and she tried to figure out how she could find a way out of there before then. All she wanted to do was disappear. She looked back up at the stage and saw that Jason, his guitar hanging off his back, a microphone in his hand, was looking toward her again.

"Hey, Houston," he called out, his breath still ragged after that spectacular performance. "I told you this was a homecoming for me."

Rebecca's stomach twisted into knots as she wondered what he was going to say.

"There are some good friends I haven't seen in years out there in the audience. I'd like to give those people a big hello and a huge thank you for coming tonight and for their support over the years." His smile was brilliant as he waved. "You know who you are and I never would have made it this far if it wasn't for you."

Well, that said it all, Rebecca thought. She'd known fairy tales didn't happen in real life. And so much for the fairy godmother sitting next to her. Not very impressive, indeed.

Bending down, she continued frantically searching the ground for her purse while the crowd clapped and whistled, welcoming Jason's friends. She grabbed it and straightened, pulling down her skirt. But at his next words, she froze.

"You know that long-legged girl with the golden hair I told you about earlier?" He aimed the full wattage of his smile straight at her. "Well, this girl with her bright eyes and a smile that could melt any heart, she's out there tonight, too."

More whistles and a few catcalls erupted from the audience and Rebecca wanted to disappear into the floor. As a poor second choice, she sat back down in her seat.

With a large smile on her face and a glint in her eye, Whitney leaned close and said, "That's you he's talking about, Becca."

"This next song is dedicated to you, my long-legged golden girl."

Rebecca gasped, her hand fluttering up to her throat. He was dedicating a song to her? It was every little girl's dream come true. An entertainer of his magnitude acknowledging her — it was almost too amazing for words. Still gazing directly at her, Jason dipped his head in a slight nod of acknowledgment and her heart soared, her eyes filling with tears.

"This is our new single, 'Lay Your Heart Next to Mine'. A very talented lady I once knew wrote the words for me years ago." He dipped his head closer to the microphone and his voice lowered. "I hope you like it."

Rebecca was stunned. It was the poem she had composed the night Jason had left and she'd put it in with the long letter she'd written him so many years ago. In trying to make sense of his leaving and the emptiness she felt, she had likened her life to the ocean tides that brought new treasures onto the shore while taking old ones back out to sea. She'd poured her heart and soul into the words, wondering if her life could be like that, its empty spaces filled by the tides of time. She still thought it was the best poem she'd ever written. Jason had coupled those words with a gorgeous melody that was sure to be his next hit. She tried to listen to it objectively, from a fan's perspective. Tonight's crowd certainly seemed mesmerized by the song. She hugged herself and smiled.

Jason didn't take his eyes off her as he sang the chorus, and the emotion was audible. Was he just being a fabulous entertainer or was he trying to convey a special message to her, she wondered. Her breath caught on a sigh. She wanted to believe that more than anything.

"My God," Whitney whispered in her ear. "Look at the way he's singing to you, Becca. He looks about ready to pick you up and carry you offstage." She grinned mischievously. "Or maybe like he could strip you naked and have his way with you right here."

"Sounds like you've been reading those steamy romance novels again." She shook her head. "They should ban you from Waldenbooks and Borders—or have they already?"

"Don't you see that he's telling you he still loves you? Who says there are no fairy tales or romance in real life?"

Was Whitney right, Rebecca wondered. The thought thrilled and scared her all at the same time.

Still holding her gaze, Jason sauntered across the stage, a sexy swing to his hips, and stopped right in front of her seat. The band kept playing as he unstrapped his guitar and placed it on the floor beside him. Then he sat on the apron of the stage, his legs dangling, his knees only inches away. If she wanted, Rebecca could have easily reached out and touched him. And the entire time he sang her words directly to her, sending goose bumps racing all over her body.

This is a dream. It can't be real, she thought. Jason couldn't be singing a love song to her in front of the crowd. It was better than anything she could have imagined or dreamed. She wondered if he would disappear if she touched him. Maybe it was all an illusion. Whatever it was, she stood and gradually inched her way closer to the stage. So close, she could feel the coolness of marble against her bare stomach.

As if reading her mind, Jason reached out and caressed her cheek. Her skin tingled at the warmth of his touch and she shivered as if chilled. He drew one finger down along her jaw, holding her gaze all the while. It was as if he was searching for something in her eyes. When his finger drifted across her lips, she thought she would melt into a puddle at his feet.

He tipped her chin up, giving her a devastating smile, and she felt her blood burst into flame. She burned for him and she could see that he knew it. An answering flame lit his eyes just before he rose and extended his hands toward her. The song came to a gentle, romantic end.

"Come on, Slim," Jason said, his voice as smooth as honey. "Looks like we've got some catching up to do."

The crowd gasped in surprise.

"Oh, Lord, Becca, he's...he's asking you up onstage. Go!"

"No. I...I can't... I don't...my skirt...underwear..." Rebecca was so rattled that she couldn't put a sentence together to save her life.

By now, the audience was standing and going wild with excitement.

Dazed, Rebecca reached for Jason's hands. He grinned and tugged her closer. Then he bent down and, circling her waist with his hands, he lifted her up. Before she knew what hit her, she was onstage with the man she adored. Talk about fairy tales, she thought, her head spinning.

Rebecca looked out into the crowd. If Jason hadn't been holding onto her, she would probably have fled. She spotted her "fairy godmother's" joyous face and sent her a tremulous smile.

Stunned, Rebecca felt herself being spun around. She was now face-to-face—and body-to-body—with Jason, only his microphone between them.

A hush descended over the crowd.

"It's been too long, Becca." Jason leaned close to Rebecca and looked deeply into her eyes. "I've missed you."

Rebecca wanted to say something, to tell him what was in her heart, but she couldn't speak. She could only stand there trembling with emotion as tears of happiness stung her eyes. He was the only man who could make her heart beat slower and faster, all at the same time. She felt as if she could just float away.

"Folks." Jason turned toward the audience. "I hadn't planned to play this song tonight, but it's just too perfect a time not to. The song is brand-new and the band and I have only practiced it a few times, so I hope you get your money's worth. The song is called 'A Girl Like You' and this beautiful lady was my inspiration." He reached out and put his arm around her shoulders.

At his beckoning gesture, an assistant brought a long-legged stool down to the front of the stage and Jason lifted her up on it. Rebecca was so stunned that she almost forgot that she was onstage in front of a huge crowd wearing a skimpy outfit.

The crowd let out a deafening cheer but quieted down as soon as the music began. The words tugged at the heartstrings and Jason's beautiful voice was so full of emotion as he sang that there wasn't a dry eye in the place.

Rebecca resolutely blinked back her own tears. She felt as if she were dreaming. Only the hot lights shining on the stage and the man singing to her as if they were the only two people in the world reminded her that this was real.

At the close of the performance, Jason gave Rebecca a sweet kiss on the cheek, then turned back to the audience and waved. "Thank you, Houston! It's been great!"

He flipped his guitar around to his back and bowed deeply, grabbing for Rebecca's hand. "How about this little lady...isn't she something?"

The crowd cheered, and hearing the deafening applause from the stage, looking out at the sea of enthusiastic faces, she understood why people got addicted to success. It must be a heated rush, she thought, to have thousands of people applauding you like that.

"I know you'll never forget our fighting soldiers or the sacrifices their families are making for us, Houston. Please remember to keep them in your thoughts and prayers. They need our full support. God bless you all for your generous donations and God bless America! Good night!"

# Chapter Four

### ❧

The massive stage was plunged into darkness and the crowd immediately started chanting, "Jason! Jason! Jason!" The audience clapped and stomped their feet in unison, attempting to lure their favorite country crooner back onto the stage for an encore.

Jason squeezed Rebecca's hand tightly as he led her across the stage, down a set of steep, narrow metal stairs and a long hallway. When she stumbled in her high-heeled red shoes, Jason swiftly put his arm around her waist. "It's okay, sweetheart," he said with a quick grin. "I'm not going to let you fall.

"Go to the dressing rooms up ahead and wait for me," he added, pointing down the hall. "We're gonna have to do an encore, but promise me that whatever you do, you won't leave." He cupped her face so that they were eye-to-eye. "Just don't leave, okay?"

Rebecca looked at Jason, his shirt and hair wet from his athletic exertions during the performance. In her heart, she knew she wasn't going anywhere. She didn't want to be anywhere in the world but here. "Okay," was all she could get out.

He gave her a warm smile of approval, hugged her and jogged back the way they had come. She watched his trim backside as he moved down the hallway and was thrilled when he turned back to look at her.

Once he disappeared, Rebecca found what appeared to be the dressing room. She looked around in horror.

"Oh, my God, would you look at this place? I've never seen so much shit in one room in my entire life, not even at your mom's."

Rebecca jumped at the unexpected voice. "Whitney! How did you manage to get back here?"

"Oh, I've got my wicked ways." Whitney grinned and wiggled her strawberry blonde eyebrows.

"Just what did you promise Security to get through the guarded doors?"

"Not much. Don't worry. A fairy godmother has to have a few secrets up her sleeve," Whitney said breezily. She stepped farther into the room and gingerly walked to a folding table covered with clutter.

"This is the dressing room of a superstar? I was expecting elegant furnishings, a table loaded with lobster and caviar and flutes of iced champagne. This is a dump!" The look of mock horror on Whitney's face was comical as she picked her way through the stadium's crowded locker room.

Rebecca followed her friend, stepping over an open box of cold pizza and empty beer cans that littered the table and floor. The smell of stale cigarette smoke permeated the room. "This place needs a can of air freshener," she observed, surprised that she could make an everyday comment when mere moments before she'd been speechless with emotion.

"Air freshener? Are you joking?" Whitney kicked another box of trash out of her way. "This place needs a friggin' bulldozer."

The bright yellow walls boasted what looked like fifty years' worth of graffiti. The table was covered with newspapers, fast food wrappers, overflowing ashtrays and sheets of music. Rebecca picked up one of the music sheets and tried to decipher the pencil scratchings, but it was too much of a jumble for her to read.

"So much for hanging out with the rich and famous. Just where are we supposed to sit?" Whitney asked. "There's no way I'm putting this designer-clad butt on that filthy couch."

"I think I'll stand, too," said Rebecca, not wanting her white skirt anywhere near the couch either. "Besides, the concert is almost over."

"Let's hope they don't do more than one encore," Whitney said, looking around at the litter and filth surrounding her. A roach crawling out from between the pages of a gossip magazine put her over the edge. "This place is creeping me out."

Rebecca wandered around the messy room trying to calm her racing heart and scale back all those hopes that had sprung back to life when Jason had lifted her onto the stage. The craziness he exhibited in front of hundreds of fans indicated that Jason still felt something for her, but she still didn't want to expect too much from him.

Maybe it was all a performance. Perhaps this was just her night, as she happened to be someone he recognized sitting in the front row. A hometown girl's picture, not to mention their past history together, would no doubt make for a good newspaper story.

The thought burst the little bubble of excitement and hope that had been building inside her.

"Whit, do you think Jason sings like that to some girl at every concert?"

Her best friend stared at her for a long moment before she shook her head. "Becca, sometimes I swear you must come from a different planet. If I hadn't been your best friend since fifth grade, I'd pack you up and send you to NASA for experimentation." She gripped Rebecca's arms and gave her a light shake. "Jason recognized you and poured out his feelings for you right there for the world to see. Where do you come up with these dumb ideas?" Whitney broke her grasp and walked toward a table, halfheartedly thumbing through the pages of an old USA Today.

Rebecca wanted to be an optimist, but she'd grown up hearing from her mother how everything always went wrong.

And she'd certainly been told how worthless she was often enough.

"Well, think about it. He's such a pro. Jason could single out a girl at every concert—like a publicity stunt, you know? How many times have the tabloids reported incidents like this?"

"Listen to me. Will you stop worrying?" Whitney tossed aside the newspaper and turned back toward Rebecca, accidentally stepping on the pizza box so that her spiked heel got stuck in a slice. "Oh, crap. I was going to take these damn things back tomorrow." She began balancing on one foot as she tried to pick the goop off her shoe with a napkin. "You're driving me nuts, Becca. In a couple of minutes you can ask Jason yourself." Losing her balance, she grabbed Rebecca's arm to steady herself. "Then you can put all of us out of our misery." She laughed. "Maybe I'll have to put this poor shoe out of its misery, too."

"Thanks for the reality check, Whit." Her best friend could always make her smile, she thought. Boy was she glad to have her here now. Whitney always knew what to say to make her feel better. "You're right. I'll stop obsessing and just wait for Jason."

"Hell, Becca, thank *you*. Now I can recoup my investment," she wiggled her glittery blue and gold clad hips, "and impress one of those sexy band members."

Rebecca laughed, but the laughter froze in her throat when she heard the door open. She turned to see Jason standing there, looking as excited as a little boy with a new toy on Christmas morning.

Inside, Rebecca's heart was turning to mush. She wanted more than anything to run across the room, throw her arms around him and cry, but she refrained from doing so. She'd let him come to her. It was a wiser choice to let him make the first move. After all, he'd been the one to leave her.

Jason stopped and ran his fingers through his damp hair. Rebecca remembered he'd always done that whenever he was nervous or unsure of himself. It was a good sign, him being nervous. That meant he still cared for her. Regaining his composure, he smiled, held out his arms and continued walking toward her. "Becca, I can't believe it's you. Look at you. All grown up and more beautiful now than ever."

She stood frozen. God, she wanted to say something, anything, but fear and emotion blocked her words and her eyes filled with tears and spilled over.

In two heartbeats he crossed the room and gently put his hands on her shoulders. "Please tell me those tears are a good sign."

She still couldn't say anything, but she nodded and smiled.

He immediately gathered her into his arms. "Becca, Becca, it's so good to see you, sweetheart," he whispered. "It's been so damn long."

"Jason…"

It was a dream, an illusion—she felt it—but even in cautioning herself, Rebecca knew that she was going to enjoy this moment as long as it lasted. She hugged his waist and buried her face in the side of his neck. He wore expensive musk-scented cologne, but she'd recognize his personal scent anywhere and he smelled delicious. Jason held her tightly and for the first time in what seemed like forever, Rebecca felt whole.

"And what am I? Chopped liver?"

Whitney's voice broke through Rebecca's dreamy state and she pulled herself together and stepped away from Jason.

"You remember Whitney—Whitney Harmon—don't you, Jason?"

Jason extended his right hand to Whitney. "Sure I do," he said with an easy smile. "How are you doing, Whit? Good to see you. How's that big brother of yours…Donny? Is he still hell-bent on racing those formula cars?"

Rebecca moved aside as Whitney came forward to shake Jason's hand.

"Yep, Donny's been trying to qualify for a couple of years now. I don't know if he ever will, but it keeps him happy."

"That's great. I hope he makes it. Dreams come true, you know." He looked toward Rebecca and snagged her hand, pulling her back toward him.

"Well, Mr. Country Music Star," Whitney said with exaggerated awe, "it sure looks like you've made the big-time. I'll bet it takes at least a dozen platinum albums to rate a dressing room as great as this, huh?"

"Whit!" Rebecca wailed, wanting to sink through the floor. Whitney was a great friend, but a diplomat she wasn't.

"Actually, this isn't my dressing room," Jason said. "I'm down the hall. I guess Rebecca found the wrong door."

Rebecca had so many questions to ask, but she held back, unsure of how to handle the situation.

"Hey, listen." Jason broke the tension. "This isn't any place to renew old friendships. Why don't you two wait for me in my bus? I have to do some meet-and-greets with a few honchos and with the fans who won backstage tickets. It won't take me more than half an hour, tops. Is that okay?"

"Sure. That would be great, Jason." Whitney's face lit up. "But can we just get on the bus? Won't security stop us?"

"I'll have Rick take you. He's my drummer, best friend and a really cool guy. You'll like him. Come on." He motioned for them to follow him. "Let's see if we can dig him up somewhere."

Backstage was buzzing with people packing up instruments, lights and amplifiers, all of them talking and laughing and, it seemed, smoking cigarettes.

Jason led them through the smoky haze and maze of boxes and wires toward a group of young women talking to a couple of band members.

"Hey, Rick, can you pry yourself away from the ladies and come over here for a minute?"

At Jason's call, a tall, handsome man disengaged himself from the fawning females.

Rebecca heard Whitney's sharp intake of breath and turned to look at her friend. She was smiling like a cat who had just spotted the canary, and that prompted Rebecca to look at Rick again.

The man's white band T-shirt did nothing to hide his muscular frame. A pair of tight black leather pants showed off long, firm legs. His clean-shaven face was bronze-colored with high cheekbones and deep brown eyes that had a slight, exotic tilt to them. His full, well-shaped lips were curved into a slight smile. But it was the man's hair that was truly remarkable.

A straight, shiny river of silky black hair fell past his shoulders and ended in the middle of his back. His face had been hard to see behind the drums, but now up close, he was sure easy on the eyes.

"Oh, God," Whitney whispered to Rebecca. "Look at him! I bet he's Native American. I wonder if he tastes as good as he looks."

"Be quiet, Whit. He's coming this way," whispered Rebecca.

"What's up, boss?"

Rick stood about three inches taller than Jason. That would make him about six foot four, Rebecca calculated—a whole foot taller than Whitney.

"Rick, these pretty ladies are old friends of mine. This is Rebecca Roberts and this is Whitney Harmon. Ladies, this is Rick Youngblood, our drummer."

"Hi," Rick said as he shook their hands. "You must be the newest gals in our little henhouse, huh? A man can never have too many, you know."

"Cretan," Rebecca whispered under her breath so only Whitney could hear her.

Whitney grinned back at her friend. "I think he's wonderful."

Rick smiled at both of them, but his eyes lingered on Whitney with a good deal of warmth.

"I have to do some meet-and-greets backstage. Could you take Becca and Whitney to the bus and keep them company for about thirty minutes or so?"

"It would be my pleasure," Rick said with a gleam in his eyes.

"I'll be there as soon as possible. The radio station only sent about ten people this trip. The fan club line is a little longer, but I shouldn't be too long."

Rick wrapped an arm around each of their shoulders. "I'll keep them entertained until you get back."

"Not too entertained, Rick. Behave yourself." Jason narrowed his eyes with a hint of concern.

"Don't worry. Ladies?" he said, looking at each in turn. "You look like you could both use a drink." He turned them toward the bay door, which stood open to the back parking lot.

"Hey, Rick!"

Rick stopped and looked back at Jason.

"Behave yourself. I mean it. These two are special."

"I can see that. And I'm always good." Rebecca felt the man's body shake with a soft chuckle. "Come on, ladies."

"Yeah, right." Jason laughed and shook his head. "Good is what I'm worried about."

The bus was parked across the lot, away from the cars and trucks of the stadium's employees. The walk gave Rebecca an opportunity to get a good look at the oversized vehicle, which was dramatically painted in black and gold with Jason's name on the sides. The windows were tinted dark so there was no hint as to what the inside looked like.

What must it be like to tour to different towns and states and live a life without anything to tie you down? She had such a humdrum life that being free and seeing new places and meeting fabulous new people everyday sounded like the most wonderful thing in the world. It was an experience so alien to hers that it was hard for her to even imagine a life like that.

The inside of the vehicle was even more dramatic than the outside. Behind the driver's compartment, the front section of the bus had been turned into a posh living area complete with light beige leather recliners that matched a long, comfortable-looking couch, a huge flat-screen TV and a stereo system with more flashing lights and dials than an airplane cockpit. Nearby was a mahogany dining table with four swivel chairs upholstered in a knobby brick red fabric. Further back it looked like sleeping compartments.

Rick removed a couple of beers from the refrigerator. "Glasses, ladies?"

"No, thanks," Whitney answered for them both. "The faster we get some of that cold beer down our throats, the better it's going to be."

Rick grinned. "A lady after my own heart."

While Whitney and Rick got to know each other, talking about country music and traveling, Rebecca halfheartedly followed the conversation, zoning in and out, only really paying attention when she heard Jason's name as Rick described playing for the troops at Camp LeJeune and Camp Pendleton. At their Fourth of July concert, even Vice President Cheney had been in the audience.

She felt as if she were in a daze. The last time she'd felt like this had been when she was in the hospital, pumped full of painkillers after her mother had kicked her down the stairs in a drunken rage. The memory made her shiver, and she tried to shake off the brain fog and participate in the conversation.

Only three minutes past the time he'd promised— according to her watch, which she'd looked at every two minutes—Jason entered the bus. "I'm glad you're still here," he said to Rebecca and Whitney. "I hope you weren't too bored." He winked in Rick's direction.

"Are you kidding?" Whitney smiled at the drummer and touched his arm lightly. "He made us comfortable, got us drinks and entertained us with some great stories about life on the road."

"I can always count on Rick to entertain the ladies," Jason said wryly. Then he turned to Rebecca, sat down at the table with her and immediately began firing off questions. "So, how have you been? Are you still living at home with JoAnne? Or are you married?"

Rebecca smiled and felt herself relax. This was still her Jason, always questioning things, even if he was a big country star.

"No and no. I have my own little apartment and I'm not married."

His shoulders relaxed and he sighed. Was he relieved, she wondered, or was she just imagining things again?

"Are you writing? Going to school?"

"I work for a lawyer now, but I've interviewed for a position with a good old Texas company, the Exxon Corporation, where Whit is an executive assistant." She twirled a strand of hair around her finger. "I'm hoping that a job in their advertising division will come through soon."

"Well, that sounds interesting. What else have you been doing?" Jason urged her to continue with a subtle gesture of his hand.

"Not much," Whitney spoke up. "She could use a change in her life." She grinned. "For that matter, I could use a change of pace myself. Got anything in mind, boys?" At this last question, she sent Rick a flirty glance.

"I'm sure I could think of something," he replied with a grin. Then he leaned over and whispered into her ear and Whitney giggled like the high school homecoming queen she had once been.

"Hey, Rick, ol' buddy." Jason dug into his jeans pocket and pulled out a set of keys and some crumpled bills. "Why don't you and Whit take the car and bring back some pizza? You still like pineapple?" he asked Rebecca. At her surprised nod, he continued to Rick, "Get a large Hawaiian with extra pineapple and a large of whatever you and Whitney want." He tossed the keys and money to his friend.

"What an excellent idea," Whitney purred, and she sent Rebecca a wink. "I'm sure Jason and Rebecca have a lot of catching up to do." As Rick pulled her to her feet, she looked up at him with a seductive smile and linked her arm with his.

"My pleasure." Rick caught the keys and pocketed the money. "Come on, gorgeous lady," he said. "Let's leave these two alone and go get the food. It should only take us a couple of hours or so," he joked.

Rebecca watched the two exit the bus. "They seem to be getting along well," she said after a brief moment of silence.

"Yeah. All the ladies love Rick." He rubbed his hand over his stubbled cheek. "It must be that Native American mystique."

"Oh?"

"Yeah, Rick's full-blooded Apache. The ladies love that dangerous warrior aura." He shook his head with a grin. "It never fails."

The air around them subtly changed. Rebecca looked straight at Jason, suddenly utterly aware of how beautiful his mouth was, how deeply she could look into his expressive dark brown eyes.

"What about you?" she asked, her voice just above a whisper, her breathing unsteady. "What about your mystique? Do the ladies love it too?"

"There's nothing mysterious about me, Becca."

"Really? That's not what the fan magazines say. They say Jason Engles is all mystery and magic and that all the women chase after him wherever he goes."

He gave her a sheepish grin and went back to drawing little circles in the condensation her drink had left on the table.

"Well, do they?"

"I guess they do." He shrugged. "What else do the magazines say?" He had captured her fingers with his and was now making those little circles on the back of her hand.

"They say you leave all of them craving more."

Rebecca knew she was babbling, but she just had to keep talking if she had any chance of withstanding the spell Jason was casting on her with his eyes and his intoxicating touch.

"Really?" He turned her hand over gently, rubbing her palm, his eyes still on hers.

Despite the air-conditioning in the bus, Rebecca suddenly felt a wave of heat. "I do wonder sometimes how they know, though."

"Know what?" Jason asked.

"That the women crave more." She heard her voice slowing down as Jason continued that featherlight touch. "Do they ask them?"

She was melting. How could a simple touch get her to melt like a pat of butter on a summer day? Come to think of it, Jason didn't look particularly cool himself.

"Ask who?"

"The ladies." At this moment, she would sell her best friend for a fan.

"What ladies?"

"The ladies who crave more of you."

She was getting all mixed up and couldn't even remember how the conversation got started. Rebecca wished he'd just lean across the table and kiss her. Did he still kiss like an angel, she wondered as her gaze slipped down to his mouth.

"Do you crave more?"

She blinked. What was he asking? "Crave what?"

Jason laughed as his fingers moved up to her wrist and traced those maddening circles across her pounding pulse.

"Me." He swiped his tongue across his bottom lip. "Do you still crave more of me, Becca?"

A fire burst into flame in the very center of her. Her breath started hitching as if she'd been running. She didn't know what to do. What was the right answer, she thought, panicking.

Jason took her hands into his. Rebecca could feel the roughness of his palms against her skin. The serious expression intensified. It was easy to feel the sexual tension burning deep within both of them. "Because I still crave you, Becca."

She shook her head, not sure if she'd heard right. Then she watched Jason's eyes dip down to her mouth. His gaze was so intense that she was sure that if she licked her lips, she would taste him. She felt another wave of heat that made her thighs tingle with delight and she wished someone would turn down the air conditioner.

He leaned toward her slowly, as if giving her the time to pull away if she wanted. "It's been so damn long, Becca," he murmured, his mouth just a whisper away from hers, soft lips almost touching softer flesh. "Will you let me kiss you?"

# Chapter Five

&

As Jason's firm mouth softly touched hers, Rebecca closed her eyes in frenzied anticipation. This one moment was what she'd been craving for so long. Casting inhibitions aside, she leaned into his kiss and parted her lips. His coarse stubble tickled her skin but she didn't care. Turned on by the wonderful sensation, she flung her arms around his waist and drew nearer to him. She had no idea which one of them gasped in pleasure first, but the sounds excited her.

The feel of Jason's chiseled body combined with his warm and inviting pine-scented musk cologne led Rebecca to lose control. Feeling more relaxed, her hands glided up toward Jason's wide, muscular shoulders. The energy of the moment led their lips to tighten as they explored every inch of one another's mouths. Breaking the kiss, Rebecca tilted her head slightly backward, hoping to feel Jason's lips upon her neck. Instead, one rough hand began to caress the hollow of her throat while the other moved smoothly down her back, pulling their bodies closer.

A more confident Rebecca kissed his neck, then slipped her hands from around his shoulders toward the contours of his face, brushing her lips over his. In a sense, it was the first time she'd kissed him like this — well, the first time since the incident. Rebecca accidentally caressed the jagged line of skin. Her thoughts immediately traveled back to her youth. She'd wanted so badly to go to him that night, to stoop down beside him and tell him things would be all right and that she'd miss him terribly, but her mother kept her away.

Between the guilt over the scar and the edge of the heavy mahogany table cutting into her thighs, Rebecca broke away from the kiss. As if Jason read her mind, he muttered, "Damn table," as he, too, broke his contact to move to the chair beside her. The interruption distracted her just enough for questions, reason, guilt and sanity to return.

"Jason, please wait."

"What's wrong?" he asked, frowning.

Rebecca placed her hands on his chest, preventing him from closing the small space between them. For a moment, the disappointment, the need on his face almost weakened her resolve. But she maintained the gap separating them even though she was on fire for him. The muscles tightly rippling under her fingers didn't make stopping him any easier.

"Jason, we need to talk. Please." She pushed against his chest. "Can we just talk for a little bit?"

The passion slowly subsided from his eyes. "Oh damn, Becca." He sat back and ran a hand through his hair. "I'm so sorry. I didn't mean to rush you, sweetheart." He touched her cheek lightly. "Guess I just lost my head for a second." He stood up and paced the room, his back to her.

"It's okay. You didn't do anything wrong. I got a little scared for a moment," Rebecca said, sensing his frustration. "Sit down so we can talk. Please?"

Jason scratched his head. "What's the matter Becca? You look so serious," he said, continuing to stand.

Rebecca briefly looked down at the table and back up at Jason. He was towering over her. Here was her chance to say all the things she had been denied seven long years ago. "I'm so sorry about your face. If I could go back in time, relive those moments and take it back, I would."

Jason delicately put his hand on her shoulder. His touch warmed her skin. Any contact with him made her feel secure and loved. "Rebecca, my face is not your fault. I don't hold you responsible for the actions of a crazy old woman—never did."

"But I thought—"

Jason tilted her face upward and once again placed his mouth over hers. She cupped her hand around his chin and lightly began stroking his stubble with her fingertips. Then, in another bold move, she threw her arms around his neck and kissed him like never before. Almost as if they'd not been apart, Jason cradled Rebecca's body. His eager movements gently brushed her against the cabinet.

This wasn't going quite the way Rebecca had ever imagined. In her wildest dreams she hadn't thought they would be in each other's arms within minutes of seeing one another again. Rebecca couldn't begin to guess exactly what that meant. There were so many questions once again racing through her mind that it was hard to focus. She needed answers to long-burning questions and she needed them now. Abruptly breaking free of the kiss, she leaned back in her seat and stared out the window.

"I think you need to give me a few minutes, Jason," Rebecca managed to utter before resting her head against the window.

"Tell you what," he said in a slightly puzzled voice. "I'm going to take a shower. I'm all sweaty and grungy from the concert. I relax better after a shower anyway. If you could fix us a pot of coffee, I'll be back in fifteen minutes and we can talk then. Deal?"

She lifted her head and returned his tentative smile. "Deal."

"Promise me one thing?"

"What?"

"That you won't disappear as soon as I get into the bathroom. I'm so sorry I practically jumped you just now. I don't know what came over me. Guess I never could keep my hands off you," he said a bit ruefully. "But I promise to behave myself if you'll just stay and talk."

"Okay," she nodded. "I'll stay." Jason turned and began walking toward the back of the bus. "You're right, you know?"

Jason stopped in mid-stride, turning toward Rebecca with a half-puzzled look on his face. "Right about what?"

"You never really could keep your hands off me." She grinned, bit her lip and pushed a strand of hair behind her ear.

Jason threw her a cunning smile and started for the bathroom quickly. He turned and retraced his steps back to her. The desire in his eyes triggered a response throughout her body, and her knees turned so weak that she grabbed the edge of the sturdy table to brace herself and keep herself from following him to the shower.

"Do you have any idea just how much I've missed you?" His deep voice caressed her senses like warm honey dripping from the comb. He pushed a curl back from her face, and then let his fingers drift gently down her cheek. "I didn't think it was possible, but you're even more beautiful than I remembered."

His words touched her heart, warmed her soul and stole her breath. Rebecca wanted nothing more than to slip back into his arms, recapture their steamy embrace, and to hell with talking. He truly sounded regretful for upsetting her. Only he hadn't upset her, she thought. She had loved every second of his passionate kisses. But she wasn't here to become Jason's latest one-night stand.

"Where's the coffee?" she asked, damning the quaver in her voice.

Jason led her to the next room, which was a glistening, top-of-the-line modern kitchen complete with dishwasher, espresso machine and wine cooler.

"I'll be right back," he said after taking the coffee out of a cabinet. He bent down and gave her a quick kiss on the temple. "I'd better get out of here before I forget my manners again." He sent her a quick, wicked grin and jogged toward the bathroom.

Needing to keep her hands busy, Rebecca quickly started the coffee and then rummaged in the refrigerator and cabinets for something to nibble while she waited. Her last meal had been lunch, almost twelve hours before. When Whitney and Rick got back, she'd probably jump them for the pizza.

She found grapes and cheese and crackers and placed them on a plate, all the while listening to the hiss of water coming from the bathroom. She half expected him to start singing and was a little disappointed when he didn't, but then, he had just done plenty of that. She sat down, but within a minute she was up and pacing. Listening to Jason in the shower was not a very relaxing activity.

How would he look with the hot spray hitting his hard, tanned body, soapsuds trailing down his glistening skin? Rebecca kept imagining that warm stream of water cascading down his back, gliding over his buttocks and sliding down his long legs, caressing each firm muscle like a lover. Oh, how she wished she was that bar of soap.

What would happen if she walked into the bathroom and pushed back the shower door? She could almost see herself standing in the shower with him, lathering his shoulders, his hips, his buttocks. She could almost feel the silky wetness of his skin under her hands, the way his muscles would bunch and swell beneath her fingers. She could almost taste his skin, she thought as her eyes closed.

Her entire body grew warm and languid. If he walked out of the shower this minute and tried to kiss her, Rebecca knew she would welcome him with her whole body. Just thinking about him made her weak with wanting and suddenly she imagined waiting for Jason to emerge from his shower every day for the rest of her life.

Her eyes flew open at the sound of a door closing just in time to see the object of her dreams step out of the bathroom with only a towel wrapped around his waist. Oh, what she wouldn't give to see that towel slide ever so slowly down his naked body. Then she caught Jason's gaze and felt a hot blush flood her cheeks.

"Coffee smells great. I'll be right there," he said, politely ignoring her indiscreet look, although a corner of his mouth did quirk up in a little grin. Then he walked down the hall to a door at the back of the bus.

Foolish, foolish girl, she chided herself. How could she have let him catch her staring at him like some star-struck groupie? She'd better get her head out of the clouds before she started making plans for the rest of her life.

Needing something to do to cover her embarrassment, she busied herself by bringing the cups and snacks over to the table. She poured the dark brew into both mugs and then sat down to wait. Somehow she had to get her shaky nerves under control, she thought, linking her hands together tightly.

Jason stepped into the kitchen, rubbing his hair with a thick terry towel which he then draped around his neck. He was barefoot and bare-chested. He shook his head and a few droplets slid down his tanned shoulders. Another pair of skintight jeans hugged his long, lean frame, riding low on his hips. She found her mind wandering—boxers or briefs? Her eyes fixated on the trail of soft body hair from his chest to his belly. Those images alone made her swallow hard before dumping half the sugar bowl into her mug. Okay, she thought, now it was official—she looked like a star-struck dork.

"Um…here's your coffee." She slid his mug across the table, indicating where he should sit.

He looked at the mug and then at her but took a seat without protest. "You're right, Rebecca. We do need to talk." Concern shadowing his eyes, Jason met her gaze full-on. "So, how come you didn't bring your boyfriend to the concert tonight?"

Rebecca wasn't sure what she had expected him to say to her, but it certainly wasn't a question about her boyfriend. Or her lack of one.

"Whitney invited me," she hedged. She fiddled with her spoon, stirring her coffee to keep her hands busy. "She won the tickets from a radio station. Backstage passes, too." She glanced up at him. "But I guess we didn't need those."

Oh Lord, she cringed inwardly, why had she just said that? How lame could she get?

"No, you didn't need those. You never would have needed one to see me." His voice sounded solemn. "I guess that explains why you came with Whit instead of the boyfriend?"

"I don't have a boyfriend. Why would you even ask something like that?" She surprised herself with her annoyed tone, wondering why his questions made her angry.

"Call me curious. What's wrong with the guys in Galveston that someone as beautiful inside and out as you doesn't have a boyfriend?"

His face was serious, his eyes dark and focused. Rebecca had never seen him like this, and she wasn't sure how to respond. Just what was he getting at?

"Well, apparently I'm not as beautiful inside and out as you think, then." Her snippy tone dismayed her and she took a deep breath before continuing. "Okay, turnabout is fair play. Where's your girlfriend?"

A slow grin spread across his face, lightening his countenance and clearing the shadows from his eyes. The laugh lines deepened around his mouth, giving him a devil-may-care look.

"Sweetie, like you, I'm unattached." He reached across the table and took her hand. "Funny how that worked out, huh?"

She smiled back at him. It was a relief to know that a girlfriend wasn't going to be popping out of a closet somewhere. But there were so many other things she had to know.

"Yeah. Funny, and odd. What's wrong with the girls in America that a big country music star as handsome and talented as you doesn't have a girlfriend?"

"I guess that's a fair question." He rubbed his thumb gently over the back of her hand. This unsettled her, and his smug grin told her that he had seen it. She gave her hand a little tug and he released it.

"You know how it is." He took a sip of his coffee and leaned back in the chair. "My music keeps me pretty busy."

"What about all those groupies I saw hanging around out there?" she blurted. The minute the words were out of her mouth, she wanted to kick herself for sounding so childish, so jealous.

Hearkening back to a conversation they'd had seven long years ago about life on the road, Rebecca knew the last thing she wanted was to sound desperate. She realized she'd have to change the condescending undertone and fast.

"Aw, hell, Becca." He took another long, slow sip of the coffee and then used his towel to wipe away a few drops that had dribbled past the rim of the cup.

For the first time, Rebecca realized that Jason might be nervous about this meeting too. He always fiddled with things when he was nervous. Maybe they should just ease into things by talking about something that wasn't quite so personal.

"So," she asked, her voice as neutral as she could make it, "how did you get involved with SOS America, anyway?"

He drained the coffee from his mug and poured himself another cup before he answered.

"I guess you know I joined the Marines a little over a year after I left Galveston. Mama was so proud—I think she told everyone."

"Yes, I heard," she said quietly. "It was quite a surprise."

He rubbed his face with his hands as if he were rubbing away thoughts or memories or maybe even regrets.

"I never told anyone the real reason I joined up, not even Mom," he said. With a deep sigh, he leaned back against the chair and closed his eyes. "It seems I've been waiting forever to tell someone." He sat forward again. "To tell you."

Rebecca reached across the table, caressing his forearm with her fingers. She didn't know exactly what he needed, but she could see that he needed something. Encouragement? Strength? Support? Whatever it was, maybe she could give it to him.

"I'd been making the rounds night after night, playing two-bit dives and occasionally opening for some decent bands. I was getting exposure and picking up a lot of stage savvy." His eyes grew shadowed again. "The guy who originally got me to go to Nashville all but promised me a contract with a big studio — RCA, Sony, Capital or even Mercury. He said anything was possible and, hell, what did I know? I was so starry-eyed that I believed him.

"Back then, I was young and full of dreams and way too naïve. You always hear those stories of how a singer is discovered and makes it big almost overnight. The guy kept me going by telling me the next gig would be my big break. The next song would hit the charts." He rubbed the back of his neck. "It was always the next, then the next. Nothing ever happened when it was supposed to. The waiting game took all the enjoyment away from my music.

"After a year of broken promises, the gigs got worse and worse and I had nothing to eat but bologna sandwiches. Finally, I paid off my contract with the guy and decided to go it alone. I thought not having a manager would give me more operating money and I could upgrade my diet to peanut butter and jelly," Jason said with a half-grin.

"Was it any better?"

"I walked the streets, pounded on doors, stapled flyers on every telephone pole in the city and took any gig to come my way. Hell, at this point, bread for my sandwiches was a luxury. Pretty soon I came to realize one big truth — I wasn't gonna make it." He shook his head. "Next to leaving you back in Galveston, that was the hardest thing to bear."

Rebecca opened her mouth to say something comforting, but she was so stunned at his revelation that not a word came out. When she attempted to speak, he pulled his hand away and touched her lips to hush her. She understood that he had to exorcise his demons, and she had to be there for him while he did.

"One night I was playing in a hole-in-the-wall biker bar. I did my first set and the crowd wasn't into the music much. During my break I sat at the bar with a beer. I was entitled to two free beers each night—the management was generous.

"I was right in the middle of a pity party for myself when this dude sits down next to me and we get to talking. He's in the Marines and he makes it sound like heaven on Earth with a bunch of wonderful opportunities. Plus, I'd get three squares and a roof over my head. I wasn't really into his pitch, but I stuck his card in my pocket." He got up and started to pace around the room.

"Then when I almost got heckled out of the place during my next set, I decided that I sucked big time. No matter what I did, how hard I practiced, I was always going to suck, so what was the point? There was always something missing when I played, you know?" He looked over at Rebecca, his eyes sad. "Never quite put my finger on what it was."

He returned to the table, sat down, took another gulp of his coffee and stared into space for a few moments. He looked lost and alone, Rebecca thought as she waited in silence. Again she reached out and took his hand.

"Anyway," he finally said, waving her hand away as if he didn't want pity. "The next day I was looking for a guitar pick in my pocket and I found the guy's card. I took a walk to the address printed there. Sure enough, it was a recruiting station. I talked with the same guy again and within thirty minutes, I was Uncle Sam's newest recruit.

"It was probably the best thing that could have happened, really. I did a lot of growing up in the military. It taught me how to fight for what I wanted in life, and once I got out, I went after my singing career with a tenacity and single-mindedness I didn't know I had." He smiled. "And here I am today."

Resting his hands behind his head, he once again sat back. "Nope. You won't find any bologna in that refrigerator, but don't get me wrong, I still respect what it's like to earn money. Terri Clark taught me that. She says 'a country singer is only as good as his or her last hit record' — so she reuses her tinfoil and buys clothes at Wally's. She shared that story with me after her performance at the Opry last year."

Rebecca looked into his eyes and felt her heart swell with love and pride. She had to face it — she would never get this man out of her system, no matter what happened. Even if he told her he never wanted to see her again. He was her soul mate and nothing would ever change that.

"And here you are," she repeated with pride.

Jason removed his hands from behind his head and reached over, took her other hand in his and brought it to his lips. "Now, why don't you tell me why you're here?"

# Chapter Six

**෨**

Once again turning toward the window, Rebecca stared out into the darkness of the parking lot. Searching for the right words to say, she couldn't help but compare that big, empty parking area to her own life. She had felt so alone without this man. Rebecca hated to feel so pitiful, but it was true. Jason had exorcised his demons—now it was her turn to step up to the microphone and sing. The time was now and the words began to pour out her mouth as naturally as if she'd written them on paper.

"I'm here to find out what happened to you, to us. Do you have any idea how difficult it was for me to come here tonight after seven years of silence from you?" Drawing on a source of strength hidden deep inside her, a source of strength she hadn't even known she had, she answered frankly without softening her words. "I have to know, once and for all, if I need to finally put you out of my mind and get on with my life."

Now that she had finally gotten over the hurdle of speaking openly, she couldn't seem to stop. "I've never felt whole since you left. Not ever." She pulled her hands out of Jason's grip and linked them tightly. "I had to see you once more to figure out how I could put myself back together again."

Baring her heart in such a way was not something Rebecca did often. Her emotions were a private place, reserved only for her writing—strangers weren't allowed in. Despite the fact that they had been lovers, the man in front of her was now a virtual stranger. But there had been a time when he had known her heart and soul, sometimes better than she'd known them herself. Rebecca desperately needed to know if he was the same man whom she had loved so deeply, so completely, or if his stardom had changed him. Now that she was here, she couldn't wait any longer and had said far more than she wanted. But at least it would be over now, she thought. Right here, right now she would finally learn the truth.

She watched his face intently for any hint of rejection, of distance. When she saw none, she felt a spark of elation and tried to ignore it. But then she saw his eyes warm with deep tenderness. He reached over and caressed her shoulder gently, patiently. The movement almost made Rebecca slide off the slick leather chair. Then, still touching her, he stood and urged her up until they stood face-to-face.

"I was a naïve, ambitious boy who took a long time to grow up. Back then, I thought I knew everything. I thought I had all the answers, but I didn't."

"And do you have the answers now?" Rebecca asked quietly.

"Some of them. Now I know exactly what I want out of life." He pulled her tightly into his arms and she went without a murmur. "If you put me out of your mind, Becca, I'll lose mine, because I couldn't bear to let you leave." His fingers drifted through her hair as he kissed her temple, her earlobe. "Stay with me, Becca," he whispered. She could feel the warmth of his breath against her skin. "Now that you're finally here, stay with me."

Was she dreaming? Was she really hearing what she thought she was hearing? All her hopes and dreams seemed to be coming true. Or were they? She uttered the only words that came to mind. "What…What do you mean, Jason? Are you saying that you want me to…to stay the night with you?"

Oh God, she thought, her heart pounding so loudly she was sure he could hear it. She didn't think she could take it if all he wanted from her was one night. As much as she loved him and wanted to make love with him, there was no way she would be willing to ruin her wondrous memories with a sordid one-night stand.

"Tonight and every night. I want to sleep with you forever. I want to know what it feels like to wake up with you in my arms." He smiled and kissed her lightly on the mouth. "I can't lose you again, Becca. I was a stupid kid back then. My only excuse is—well, there is no excuse." He gathered her tightly in his arms.

"We had something so special. I should have waited for you, but I was too impatient, too hungry and much too busy putting old ghosts to rest. But now that you're here with me, I can't let you go—not for a second time."

Rebecca didn't say a word. She couldn't. She just stood there wrapped in his arms and breathed his wonderful, familiar scent. It was like coming home after a long, hard, cold journey.

"Aren't you going to say anything, sweetheart?" Jason pulled back a bit and looked at her. "I thought you were telling me that you still love me—or at least are fond of me. Please let me know that it's true. Tell me I wasn't dreaming."

He drew her closer, his lips barely touching hers as if to tease her. As the coolness of his wet flesh met and meshed with hers, his kiss was even sweeter and more passionate than before. Her arms slipped around his neck and her hands moved through his hair. It was damp and silky and she could have gone on touching him for hours, but there were more questions that needed answers.

"I—I can't believe this is happening," she said breathlessly. "I never stopped loving you, Jason. Never. But I thought you stopped loving me."

"Never, Becca. I was an idiot to believe I could make it without you." He punctuated his words with kisses. "You were what was missing when I played. I was such a fool when I told you to get on with your life without me. What I didn't know was that I couldn't get on with my life without you."

"Why didn't you come back? Call me? Write? Sometimes I thought you blamed me for what happened to your face."

With a look of longing, Jason drew Rebecca closer and hugged her tightly. "I'm sorry. There's no good excuse. I should've called. But we're together now and it's gonna be all right," he whispered.

"No Jase. It's not all right. Don't you see? I tried conning you into staying that night. I thought if we slept together that one last time, you'd stay. It was a stupid, desperate idea. Then my mom attacked you with that ashtray. If JoAnne hadn't caught us making love, if you hadn't stayed and had left when you wanted, you never would have been injured."

Rebecca took a deep breath, trying desperately to control the never-ending trail of tears running down her cheeks. "I poured my heart and soul out to you that night in a letter. It was weeks before I heard from you again. Then you sent this most awful note back to me. I thought you'd blame me forever." Rebecca sat back down on the bench and put her head in her hands, weeping.

Jason quickly knelt beside her. "Sweet Becca," he said in the most soothing of voices. "You've got to put that whole incident out of your mind. The scar is in no way your fault. I wanted to stay. The memory of us making love that last night got me through some tight spots. My face was a small price to pay for that memory."

Slowly Rebecca straightened up, grabbing for Jason and eventually resting her head on his shoulder. The butterflies in her stomach began to calm.

"Do you know how hard it is for a man to admit he's been a fool?" He softly chuckled as if to calm his nerves. "Sometimes it's easier to just go on hurting. I hadn't realized I'd hurt you in the process."

"I don't want you to hurt, Jason." Overcome with tenderness and love, Rebecca stroked his stubbled face. "I don't want either of us to hurt. We've had far too much of that in our lives."

"It crossed my mind every day that maybe you'd moved on with your life. Every time I'd think about that possibility, I'd put it out of my head. One thing's for sure though—I've always loved you, Becca, and I always will. Promise me you won't leave me. Stay with me?"

His words were murmured between kisses, as if he couldn't get enough of her. Together they tumbled onto the long leather couch, hungry for each other's touch like when they were two teenagers experiencing passion for the first time.

Rebecca's head tipped back against the soft leather as Jason's touch nearly sent her spiraling into ecstasy. She wanted to stay like this for the rest of her life, to give herself to him completely, but she knew it was too soon. They couldn't allow themselves to get carried away like this. Reluctantly she pressed her hands against his chest and he sighed.

He sat up and pulled her up beside him, brushing the hair out of her face. "You're right, we need to talk and cuddling on the couch isn't the way to get it done," he admitted. "Besides, Whit and Rick should be knocking on the door any minute now. But I'm not letting you go." He tilted her face up to his. "And that brings me to another important question."

"What question?"

"This was my last gig for a couple of months. My manager's letting me get some rest, so I was planning to hole up in a special place I know. How long will it take you to pack? You don't need a lot of stuff." His voice was quick and eager. "Anything you don't have, we'll buy."

"Wait a minute." Shifting out of his embrace, she held up a hand and jumped up from the couch. "Let me understand this. You've been out of my life for seven years and you want me to go with you on a two month vacation just like that?" She snapped her fingers.

"Sweetheart, I don't think you're quite getting this." Jason remained seated on the couch. "I want you with me always. As in forever. But I don't want to rush you." He sat forward and linked his hands loosely between his knees. "I want to give us a chance to catch up—so I'm thinking a vacation by the ocean for a few weeks could kind of ease you into forever and always." He sent her one of his heartbreaking little boy grins.

"For real?" She looked down at him, her arms tightly crossed over her chest. "You expect me to just pack my things and take off? What about my life? What about work? Who's going to take care of Uncle Burt?"

So many thoughts were rushing through her head that she had trouble concentrating. She couldn't just walk away from her job without notice. Jason's proposal was oh, so tempting, but it wasn't practical. Could she really take this risk, this gamble? If she gambled wrong, her life would be a shambles.

And then there was Uncle Burt. She couldn't leave him alone and at the mercy of her mother. Her uncle was the main reason she was still in Galveston at all. She was terrified that JoAnne might take out her fury on Uncle Burt.

"To hell with work," Jason told her. "You said you were looking for a new job, anyway. So take some time off before getting another one. Or don't work at all, if that's what you want. I have enough money for both of us."

"I can't just live off of you," she protested, resenting his high-handed assumption that she would just drop everything to go with him. "It wouldn't be right. Not for me."

"Calm down, honey." He stood up and put his hands lightly on her shoulders. "When I said forever, that means for the rest of our lives. And if living off of me, as you put it, bothers you, I'd be willing to bet that you'll be making big bucks with your songwriting in no time." He grinned. "I might have a couple of connections, you know. Then we can work as a team, just like the way we once dreamed."

"But what about my uncle? I can't just leave him with my mother. She'd destroy him."

"Not to worry, sweetheart. We can take care of your uncle."

"How?"

"I could hire a full-time nurse to stay at the house."

"That would cost you a pile of money. Besides, JoAnne would never allow a stranger to live in the house. No," she said, shaking her head. "That wouldn't work. You know how Mother can be."

"Okay...what if we put him up someplace where he'd get lots of care? Someplace where he could still see his friends? Have transportation whenever he needed to go somewhere?"

"You mean a nursing home?" She'd never put Uncle Burt into a nursing home. She once promised him that would never happen so long as she was overseeing his affairs. Once people went into a nursing home, they just gave up on their lives and died.

"No, not a nursing home. I'm thinking more along the lines of a hotel or resort where they have hot tubs in the rooms and masseurs and specialty chefs. Then I could hire a nurse and put him or her up at the place, too." He smiled. "That way he'd be having a good time and still getting whatever care he needed. It would be like a vacation for him too, Becca. He'd be away from your mother and having a little fun."

"You'd do that for him?" she asked, incredibly touched by his generosity.

"For Burt." He tucked his hand under her chin and stroked her lower lip with his thumb. "And for us."

She threw her arms around his neck and kissed him as if her life depended upon it.

Jason broke away from Rebecca and moved back into the cushions of the couch. A sheepish grin adorned his face as he looked at Rebecca with great amusement. "Hey, if I'd have known I'd get that kind of response, I would have mentioned helping your uncle sooner."

She laughed but then grew serious. "I can't let you do all that, Jason." She shook her head. "It'd be way too expensive."

"I'm made of money these days, sugar," he said with a grin. "I can do anything I want. Besides, I like Burt. Always have. If I can give him some happy memories, relieve his pain and give you some stress-free time off, it's worth any price to me."

"Are you sure? Are you really sure?"

"As sure as Texas is God's country."

She smiled as he used his mother's favorite phrase. "Whit always says I need to take more chances. Maybe she's right. One thing I do know is that I can't walk away from you. The thought of never seeing you again…" She took a deep breath. "When were you thinking of leaving?"

Jason wrapped her in his arms and swung her around the room, whooping.

"Put me down, you crazy man!" She was breathless from the decision she had just made, from laughing, from everything. "Behave yourself or I might just change my mind."

"Behave myself?" He bent down, slipping an arm behind her knees and lifting her as if she were a baby. "Behave myself, woman? I'll show you what behaving is." Jason twirled around toward the couch, then tossed her onto the soft leather and followed her down, tickling her stomach mercilessly with the coarse stubble on his face. "How's this for behaving myself?"

She laughed with delight. Now that she had taken that big first step, she felt so lighthearted she could sing.

"Uh…did someone here order pizza?"

They both froze as Whitney's voice sliced through their laughter. As one they turned their heads to see Whitney and Rick standing in the doorway, each holding a pizza box.

"Ever hear of knocking?" Jason growled.

"For your information, Mr. Big Star, I did knock," Rick drawled. "But then I heard Rebecca here screaming for help, so naturally I came in to investigate."

"Naturally," Jason said as he stood and helped Rebecca to her feet.

"Sorry, boss," Rick said as he walked to the table and put the food and drink down. "Didn't mean to cramp your style there."

"What the hell is going on in here, Becca?" Whitney put in playfully. "I leave you alone with this guy and come back to him crawling all over you. Have you gone through a personality change? For a moment I thought you were acting like me." She broke into a grin. "Looks like your fairy godmother came through for you, and it's not even midnight yet!"

"Never mind what we were doing. Where on Earth have you two been?" Rebecca sat down at the table. "I'm starved. Let's eat."

Rick opened one of the boxes, releasing the mouthwatering aroma of warm pineapples, ham and spices.

"Help yourself, missy," Rick told her as he slid the box in front of her. "Jason, grab some napkins."

"All right, Cinderella," Whitney stage-whispered. "We'll eat first, then you can tell me what was going on. I want the juicy details — all of them."

"Sure," Becca said between bites. "As soon as you tell me why going for pizza took that long." She looked from Whitney to Rick and back. They had apparently hit it off well. Rebecca's eyes moved to the two undone buttons on Whitney's blouse. However, her mind didn't remain on Whitney for very long.

Thoughts flashed back to the beautiful, gentle words he had said to her. And his passionate kisses. She'd never been on a real vacation in her life, she thought, and here she was going on a two-month vacation with the man she loved more than life itself. Maybe fairy tales did come true. But right now, she was starving and reached for another piece of pizza.

# Chapter Seven

ହ

It took a lot of reasoning, but Rebecca finally convinced Jason that she had to do more than pack a toothbrush before she could just up and leave on vacation with him. Jason had to understand that there were just too many loose ends to tie up, including Uncle Burt, her job and apartment.

"Take Whitney with you when you go to see Uncle Burt," he insisted. "If JoAnne finds out that you're going away with me, she'll come down on you harder than a drill sergeant on a raw recruit the second day of boot camp."

Rebecca laughed to cover up her nervousness because she knew he was right. "It sounds like you're speaking from experience."

"You better believe it." He put his hands on Rebecca's shoulders and ducked his head a little so he could look directly into her eyes. "I'm serious though. The less JoAnne knows, the better it'll be."

"I could make all the arrangements with Burt," Whitney volunteered. "That way you wouldn't have to go to the house at all. It'll be like *Romeo and Juliet*." She winked at Rebecca. "I'm game to play the Nurse and pass along messages."

"Don't mean to burst your bubble or anything, but *Romeo and Juliet* ended badly, my dear," Rick said, chucking Whitney playfully under the chin.

"Yeah, but they sure had a whole lotta fun while it lasted. Besides, what the heck do you know about it?" Whitney demanded. "I bet you skipped English class the week you had to read it."

"I'll have you know I aced English lit. Yeah, the long-haired Fabio in the back of the band has a mind." Rick sent Whitney a killer grin. "Who'd have thought it?"

"He's our resident intellectual," Jason pointed out. "Rick was the valedictorian of his graduating class and the real boss of this outfit."

"That's pretty impressive," Rebecca said.

"A brainiac, huh? My, my, how looks can be deceiving." Whitney boldly looked Rick up and down.

They laughed and settled down to work out the final details of Operation "Romeo and Juliet Go on Vacation."

The foursome spent most of Saturday together playing tourists in Galveston. Jason hadn't been back for a lengthy visit in years. Rebecca could tell by the glint in his eyes he enjoyed being home. They went to the Aquarium and the Rainforest Pyramids at Moody Gardens, then rummaged through the shops in the Strand's Historical District and laughed their way through a carriage ride along the beach. Topping off the afternoon, Jason treated everyone to margaritas and fried calamari at Landrey's oceanfront veranda.

Whitney was especially enjoying herself. She had apparently struck relationship pay dirt with Rick, and Rebecca found herself envying the easy camaraderie between her and Rick as they bantered and argued. There was still a subtle tension between her and Jason. With so much unsaid between them, they were still tiptoeing around each other.

But Whitney and Rick never stopped talking and the tension between Rebecca and Jason seemed to ease when they were all together. That night, Jason took them all out to a steak dinner at the The Lone Star Roadhouse and then they saw an action movie.

Rebecca paid more attention to Jason holding her hand than the movie. Afterwards they went to The Cream Factory for homemade butter pecan cones. It was another wonderful evening.

"I don't suppose you're going to invite me upstairs," Jason asked later when they stood on Rebecca's porch saying their long goodbye.

She thought he was cute, much like a puppy begging for table scraps. "You supposed right," Rebecca said, softening her words with a kiss.

"So can I see you tomorrow?" He let his fingers drift through her hair. "Or do you have plans?"

"I did have a date with Johnny Depp, but I might be persuaded if you made me an offer I can't refuse." She flipped her head and smiled teasingly.

"Well." He maneuvered her toward the wicker love seat that stood in the shadows. "What do you say we spend the day at the lake?" He squeezed her waist. "I have some very fond memories there."

Rebecca rested her head on his shoulder, thrilled that he remembered. His Uncle Luke's private lake held so many of her most cherished moments and she couldn't think of a more romantic spot to spend the day. She'd written great poetry and lyrics during her times there. Perhaps she would again.

Underneath the glow of the moon, they continued to sit outside, enjoying one another's company. Rebecca kept fidgeting. The old wicker bench was uncomfortable and dug into her backside something awful, but she'd endure the discomfort. She was having fun talking with Jason about their reunion and the touching wasn't half bad either. After a bit, the evening air became too cool, and fearing Rebecca might be cold, Jason decided to call it a night. As they walked arm in arm toward the porch, she liked the feeling of the love of her life by her side.

Rebecca and Jason spent the afternoon swimming and talking about old times. He acted like a teenaged boy — one minute playing pranks, like scaring her by placing a small tree frog on her leg and then the other kissing her madly. Little by little, they got reacquainted and caught up on their activities over the past seven years, but as if by tacit agreement, they avoided discussing anything too emotionally charged. When they touched, Rebecca felt a flare of desire, and the look in Jason's eyes told her that he was feeling the same way. She made sure they didn't touch too much. It would have been too easy to let go and throw caution to the wind. They both wanted to. It was better to be careful. They'd have plenty of time together once they left Galveston.

Leaving the lake, Rebecca was delighted to be sitting close to Jason. Her hand rested gently upon his thigh. Every so often she'd stroke his leg or touch his cheek. Jason threw his arm around her and flipped the radio on. They both laughed as the local station played one of his first hits. Rebecca liked the feeling of the wind whipping through her hair as they drove. Jason spotted a local Lions Club carnival just as the fiery Texas sun was about to set.

"Hey, look at the lights. Do you know how long it's been since I've been to a fair where I didn't have to perform?" He patted Rebecca's shoulder. "Do you still like the rides?"

"I don't know. I haven't been to one since high school. There was this boy who used to win me stuffed animals." She smiled up at him. "I still have every single one." They were all lined up in her bedroom and sometimes she touched them because that made her feel closer to Jason and good times past.

Rebecca squeezed his biceps. "Think you can win me a prize?"

He scored her a pink armadillo first time out, and then they gorged themselves with cotton candy, funnel cakes, caramel apples, hot dogs and blue raspberry slushies. They had ice cream in twist waffle cones on the Ferris wheel and watched the city laid out below them like tiny jewels scattered on black velvet. As if he were a love-struck teenaged boy, Jason kept trying to steal kisses from his girl.

It was nearing the end of a magical day, but Jason was too quiet during the ride home. Rebecca sensed something was on his mind.

"I'm worried about you, Becca. Promise me you'll take Whitney with you, when you go see your uncle tomorrow," he said as they sat in his rented SUV in front of Rebecca's house. "And I'll pick both you and Burt up in the afternoon."

"I can take care of myself, Jason. You've forgotten that I've been doing that for a long time."

Jason was silent and stared out into the night. "I know I let you down, Becca."

Oh, no. She hadn't meant for that last sentence to come out the way that it did. "You did what you needed to do." She curled her hand over his.

"Don't make excuses for me, Bec." He lifted her hand to his lips. "I screwed up."

"Thank God for second chances."

His arms went around her. "How did I get this lucky?" he asked. "I'll make it up to you every day of my life, Becca." He kissed her passionately. "I mean it."

Rebecca hugged him tightly, thinking she was the lucky one.

When Monday morning arrived, Rebecca wished she really did have a fairy godmother that could wave a magic wand so that it would be afternoon. Then everything would be behind her. There were a lot of things on her "to do" list today. If she didn't get going, they'd never get done.

Taking a deep breath, she walked into her boss's office and pretended there weren't any butterflies waltzing in her stomach.

"Mr. Peddleston—"

"Well, Becky, you look all rested up from your weekend." His leer made his jowls wobble like gelatin. "You sit right down and we'll do a little multitasking for the week."

Rebecca just wanted to yell "I quit," but she wanted the back pay he owed her, so she bit down her words.

"I'm sorry, Mr. Peddleston, but I'm giving notice. My uncle isn't well and I have to take care of him. He's being moved this afternoon."

"You can't do that," he roared, fist falling on top of the desk. "You can't quit. You won't get any unemployment and I can take action against you."

"Not when it's a legitimate family emergency." She looked him straight in the eye and quoted the relevant federal laws that covered The Family Leave Act. "Like I said, my uncle is being moved today."

"How about you stay this week, Becky, until I get a replacement?" He stood up and went around the desk, but Rebecca skillfully moved out of his reach. "I'll give you a bonus."

"It's Rebecca and I'm sorry. But I'd like my pay for last week and the back vacation pay you owe me."

Grumbling about how hard it was to find good help, he sat back down at his desk with such force his chair cracked and popped. "You're a pretty cool customer, but don't think you'll be getting this job back." He took out his checkbook, wrote the check and flipped it across the desk and onto the floor, making her pick it up.

"Thank you." Rebecca glanced down at the amount and wished she could do a happy dance right then and there. The old creep may have made her bend down to retrieve her check for one more glimpse of her bum, but he'd actually given her all the money he owed her.

On her way out of his office, she passed the storage area and grabbed an empty recycling box. Quickly she packed a few things from her desk and scooted out of there.

Okay, she thought, heaving a huge sigh of relief as she walked down the stairs. One down, one more obstacle to go.

There was no way she could avoid seeing JoAnne, not this morning. The bars didn't open this early.

Rebecca let herself into the house and quietly went up the staircase, avoiding all the places where she knew the steps squeaked. She had long since memorized all of them.

Uncle Burt was sitting at the window of his room with a cup of coffee in his hand. He always said how he liked having the morning sun on his face.

"Uncle Burt," Rebecca knelt next to his chair. "I have a surprise."

Quickly, she explained the plan and the accommodations Jason had reserved for him. He was a proud man and at first was hesitant about leaving his familiar surroundings and letting someone else pay his way.

"But, Uncle Burt, Jason wants to do this," Rebecca assured him. "He's even hiring a nurse who'll be staying at the hotel with you. Plus you'll have a full-time driver and car, so you can still attend all your veterans' affairs meetings and see your buddies."

"I don't know about accepting so much from a virtual stranger."

"You should know better than anyone, Uncle Burt, that Jason's no stranger. I didn't ask him to do this. He offered." She touched his arm. "And if you don't want to do it for yourself, do it for me. I'll feel so much better if you're somewhere else while I'm out of town."

"You sure make it hard for a guy to say 'no'." Uncle Burt smiled and patted her on the cheek. "I can't wait to see what this nurse looks like."

Rebecca started to tell her uncle that his nurse was a male but couldn't quite make the words come out of her mouth. She'd won one battle, she thought. Why push things? She'd tell him later.

Suddenly the door flew open and Rebecca looked up to see JoAnne standing there. She was barefoot and wore a tattered housecoat over her nightgown.

"I thought I heard voices. What the hell are you doing here at this hour?" she demanded. "Why aren't you at work?"

"Nice to see you too," Rebecca whispered, rolled her eyes and turned to face her mother. "If you must know, I quit my job this morning."

"You did what?" She swiped her tangled hair out of her face. "Well, don't come around here expecting a handout, missy. This bank's gone dry and we don't feed strays here."

"Don't worry. I haven't ever asked you for a handout, and I don't expect to start now," Rebecca said calmly.

"What's the big dream this time? Go off to Vegas and become a showgirl?" She took a drag from her cigarette. "I sure hope not. Your boobs aren't big enough and you ain't got the guts."

Rebecca said nothing and grabbed for her Uncle's hand.

"And how are you planning to make a living?" she demanded when Rebecca didn't answer. "On your back?"

Rebecca whirled around to face the older woman. "I'm not going to dignify that with an answer. Besides, I don't think that's any of your business."

"It's not, is it? Then why don't you just get the hell out of this house?"

Rebecca bent down and whispered in Uncle Burt's ear, "Jason and I will be back this afternoon to pick you up. We'll help you pack your stuff then. Don't say anything."

Warily, Rebecca walked past her mother, ready to defend herself with the moves she'd learned in her self-defense class if JoAnne tried to hit her.

She turned around one more time at the door. "I'll see you later, Uncle Burt."

"I don't want you hanging around here." JoAnne's voice rose. "Now that you don't have a job, you'll probably steal from me."

Rebecca bit her lip to keep back the words on her tongue. It was better not to antagonize JoAnne until they got her uncle out of there. She just kept going and ran down the stairs.

She'd been hoping that her mother would be out when they came to pick up Uncle Burt, but no such luck. JoAnne probably sensed something was up and stayed home to spite her. Hand in hand, Rebecca and Jason walked into the house.

The TV was blasting away and JoAnne was sitting on the filthy couch in a cloud of cigarette smoke watching a rerun of Walker, Texas Ranger. She'd always envisioned herself with Chuck Norris — like she ever had a chance.

"What are you doing here?" she shouted over the gunshots on the TV. "I thought I told you to stay away from here."

"We're here to pick up Burt," Jason said, his voice quiet and polite. "We'll be gone in a few minutes."

"Whaddya mean you're pickin' my brother up?"

Rebecca started to speak, but Jason squeezed her hand, signaling her to let him do the talking.

"Burt's going on a little vacation while Becca and I are out of town, Mrs. Roberts."

"Going out of town, are you?" She got up and walked toward them. "Didn't I say this morning that you'll be earning your living on your back, you slut?"

Jason shifted to stand between her and Rebecca. "You've got no call to be insulting Becca. If you'll just step aside, ma'am, we'll get Burt and be on our way."

"Who do you think you are?" JoAnne yelled.

"I'm the two-bit singer that finally got his priorities in order," Jason answered, maneuvering Rebecca up the stairs.

Within half an hour, Uncle Burt was seated in Jason's car as they loaded the rest of his things.

"Once that playboy is through with you, Rebecca Lynn Roberts, you'll be back," JoAnne yelled at them from the stoop. "All he wants is a piece of ass, just like before. He'll leave you again. I promise you that!"

They ignored her and that seemed to make her even angrier. "Don't you ever come back here, Rebecca," she screamed.

Rebecca tried not to let JoAnne's cruel words get to her, but by the time they finished loading the car, her eyes were filled with tears.

"Whatever you do, don't cry. You are too good a person to be upset by someone so emotionally troubled. We'll be gone in just a minute," Jason whispered and touched her hand.

"I'm changing the locks, girl," her mother bellowed, a cigarette dangling from her lips. "So don't you even think about ever coming back here!"

"Don't worry," Rebecca assured her. "I won't."

"He won't stay with you, girly. His kind never does."

Jason took Rebecca's arm and helped her into the car.

"Burt!" JoAnne yelled. "You better come back soon, you hear me?"

"I hear you, woman." Burt stuck his head out the car window. "Now shut your damn mouth and get back into the house before someone calls the cops on you for disturbing the peace." He leaned forward and tapped Jason's seat. "Get the hell outta here, boy. I need some fresh air."

By six that evening, Burt was comfortably settled in his hotel suite and Steve Ryan, his male nurse, had scheduled the daily regimen of therapeutic massages and special meals. Rebecca's uncle seemed a little overwhelmed at first and uneasy about a male nurse, but as Steve got him acquainted with the space, showing him the way to the phone, the big screen television, Bose radio and the hot tub, he began to get used to the idea.

"It's so nice of you to do this for Uncle Burt," Rebecca whispered as Steve was showing her uncle around. "I don't know how to thank you."

"You don't have to thank me, sweetheart. It's my pleasure."

"It's a relief knowing I won't have to worry about him while we're away."

"My thinking exactly." Jason grinned. "I wouldn't want you being anxious and worrying while I'm wining, dining and courting you." He put his arm around her and pulled her toward him "Besides, it's the least I can do. I know how much you love the guy."

Rebecca stretched upward and kissed him on his stubbled chin. "You're a sweet man, Jason Engles."

Jason smiled. "We aim to please."


Rebecca relaxed against the plush beige leather seat of the convertible. Jason had taken the SUV back and rented the sporty red Corvette just for her, remembering it had always been her dream car. As they flew down the interstate with the wind whipping through her hair and the radio blaring her favorite country tunes, Rebecca sang along with the radio and Jason. She could hardly remember the last time she had felt so young and free. Had she ever? Years of worry and sadness faded away, and she basked in this moment of perfect happiness.

Jason had only told her they were going to a special place on the ocean but hadn't revealed any more than that. She'd find out soon enough and anywhere he took her was bound to be wonderful. Just being with him like this, with the wind in her hair, the smell of the ocean and the sound of music was like being in heaven.

They left the car at Hobbie Airport, where Jason had chartered a private jet to Destin, Florida. Destin, she thought. As in destiny? It had to be destiny that they were together again.

Jason didn't volunteer any further information. He just held her hand and smiled like the proverbial cat that had swallowed the canary during the boarding process and throughout the flight.

A white limousine waited for them at the airport and drove them to a hotel that was like something out of the Disney movies she enjoyed as a child. Rebecca felt like Cinderella, one of her favorite fairy tale characters.

Since Jason was being so mysterious, Rebecca decided to keep her questions to herself. She figured two could play that game. Besides, she couldn't possibly express how wonderful it was to be able to trust someone to take care of her needs and put aside her worries and anxieties. She tapped her foot and grabbed for Jason's arm. She couldn't wait to see where they'd end up.

A bellman opened the door to their suite and Rebecca stepped into the most sumptuous room she had ever seen.

The focal point of the black marble-tiled foyer was a fountain carved in the shape of dolphins, water spouting merrily from their mouths. A maid came out of a side room and hurried to open the plush drapes that ran the length of the room. The sapphire blue silk revealed a majestic view of the Gulf of Mexico, its expanse of turquoise dotted with green barrier islands.

Rebecca took the two steps down into the living area to get a better look out the window, and the lush carpeting all but swallowed her feet to the ankles. She stared outside in amazement. Not only was there a spectacular view of the Gulf, but also a private balcony complete with a small lap pool and bar area.

She marveled at the delights outside their window and then turned back toward the room that would have done justice to a spread in *Southern Living* magazine. A cabinet of rich, reddish teak held the TV and the stereo system, and the furniture was upholstered with raw silk and damask in watery blues and lush greens, held together with creamy beige and bright sapphire accents.

When the door closed behind the bellman and maid, she turned to Jason with excitement. "This place is gorgeous." She laughed and twirled around. "I feel like a movie star."

He joined her in the living room. "I'm glad you like it, darlin'. But this isn't the special place I'm taking you."

"It's not?" She wandered around the room, running her fingers over everything like a child in a toy store. "This looks pretty darn special to me."

"We'll spend the night here, but tomorrow we'll take a boat to our final destination. I think you'll like it." He followed her as she moved around and took her hand. "At least I hope you'll like it."

Rebecca was stunned by the questioning tone in his voice. How could anyone not like all this? "As long as you're with me, I'd love any place on Earth."

"How about this?" He tugged gently on her hand and led her through a set of double doors into another room.

The tropical theme continued in one of the luxuriously appointed bedrooms. The walls were covered in shimmering silk of the palest green, but the focal point was a large raised bed beneath a canopy of multiple layers of sheer green, blue, and silver silk.

"Oh, Jase. It's the most beautiful bedroom I've ever seen! I feel like a queen." She threw her arms around his neck and hugged him. "Where are you going to sleep?"

She laughed when he raised his eyebrows.

"Right here with you, precious—if you'll have me." The tone of his voice told her he had a secret.

She felt herself blush but said boldly, "I wouldn't dream of letting you sleep anywhere else. We belong here together."

Jason's eyes grew dark with passion and Rebecca's body responded immediately. Lord, she thought, he barely had to touch her to make her want him to carry her to the bed and make love to her right then and there. She wanted to feel his skin against her own.

Jason enclosed her in his arms and gave her a deep, sensual kiss as he ran his fingers through her hair. She moaned and pressed herself against him, but he broke the embrace. "Not so fast, little lady. Let's make this night last a long, long time." He took her hand again and tugged her across the room. "This suite is gigantic and that's not the only bedroom. C'mon, I have a little surprise for you."

Rebecca followed Jason into the bathroom and stopped. The room was enormous. It was almost as large as the bedroom and decorated in sandstone tiles with touches of terra cotta, echoing the beach below their window. Vanilla-scented candles glimmered around the room, reflecting off the many mirrors and sparkling fixtures.

"It's lovely," she murmured as she stepped in farther, bending down to touch a washcloth that had been twisted into the shape of a seashell.

Hidden by a half wall of glass and tiles, she found a huge, raised black marble hot tub with shiny golden fixtures. Two marble steps led to the tub, which was surrounded by more candles. Crystal vases filled with white gardenias scented the area with their own heavenly fragrance. Soft music filled the air and a bottle of champagne was chilling in a golden bucket.

"What do you think?" Jason asked eagerly. "Are you surprised?"

Rebecca turned and gave him a huge smile. "It's the most beautiful place I've ever seen." She had the sudden urge to write and put all these wonderful, warm feelings into a song. Too bad there was no pen or paper handy—but for now she was deeply anticipating his touch.

He put his hands on her shoulders, sending thrilling little chills down her spine. The day had been hot, and she had chosen a blue and white sundress to wear for the trip. His hands drifted over her bare shoulders, his fingers slipping under the tiny straps to caress her sun-kissed skin.

"This is all for you, Rebecca." He bent down and brushed his lips over her shoulder. "I'm glad you like it."

"I love it, but you didn't have to go to such trouble for me, you know. I would have been happy in a tent as long as you were with me."

"Well, I guess you could call that teepee over the bed in there a tent." His mouth quirked into a sexy grin. "But I don't think that's exactly what you meant."

"No, it wasn't. But I guess it'll have to do," she said, happily throwing her arms around his neck.

She lifted her hands and stroked his face, feeling as if her heart could burst right out of her chest. Could he see the love in her eyes, she wondered? Did he know it almost hurt to love him so much?

As if he could read her mind, he began running his fingers through her hair, around the outline of her ear and then finally down around her mouth. Forcing her lips apart, he gently caressed the inside of her bottom lip, teasing her tongue. Rebecca felt like she'd go mad—the tingling between her thighs was uncontrollable and she needed Jason to make love to her soon. His roaming fingers found a firm breast. She was now putty in his hands. Ever so slightly he drew himself nearer and began fondling both of them.

A chime sounded and they jumped apart like kids caught with their hands in a cookie jar. Rebecca could tell by Jason's eyes that something special was about to happen. She followed him into the living area and watched as he opened the door.

"Oh, I'd almost forgotten that I'd been expecting you guys." Jason looked back at Rebecca with a devilish smirk.

"Sir, your dinner is here," said the waiter—a dapper man in his late forties who wore his spotless uniform with style and pride.

Rebecca turned her eyes from the elaborate table and looked at Jason. He was staring at her as if he were seeking some kind of approval. With a smile, she nodded. "Ah yes. That would be fine, thank you."

The room service staff entered and proceeded to set the table with creamy linens and sparkling crystal and china. The silver serving plates gave off the most heavenly aromas, and Rebecca couldn't wait to taste what delicacies were hidden underneath the silvery domes.

Jason walked to the bar, which she hadn't noticed before, and stepped behind it. "Would you like something to drink?"

Rebecca wasn't a big drinker—she had her mother's example to demonstrate to her that alcohol consumed in large quantities was never a good choice. But she did enjoy a glass of wine or a cold beer on occasion. This seemed to be a very big occasion, so she hesitated only a moment. "I'd love a glass of white wine."

"Coming right up."

As Jason uncorked the bottle of wine, Rebecca perched on a stool and watched the preparations for their dinner. She had spent most of the last few days with Jason, but she still felt as if all this wasn't quite real. To have her wildest dreams and hopes fulfilled so suddenly just seemed too good to be true. It was hard for her to take it in. It frightened her to think how close she had come to not going to the concert. She owed Whitney big-time for making her go and for pushing her to attract Jason's attention. It had indeed been as much of a life-changing night as her friend had predicted.

And tonight, she knew, would be another.

She couldn't deny that she was nervous. Even though Jason had said again and again that he loved her, she was worried she wouldn't measure up to his expectations after all this time. The last time they'd been together, they had both been inexperienced kids. How would she, with her limited sexual experience, compare to the women he'd surely been with over the years?

Tonight would be magical for her, but she wanted it to be as wonderful for him. She wanted to prove to him—and herself—that they belonged together. Yes, she thought. No matter how it turned out, tonight would be life-changing.

Jason handed her a glass of wine, then reached for her hand and led her from the bar area to near the dinner table. "Make yourself comfortable and relax." He rubbed the tense muscles at the base of her neck.

Rebecca guessed that Jason was saving his "real" moves until after dinner, but what he didn't realize was that every little touch sent sparks throughout her body. She was on fire for him, so it was a safe bet to stay away from alcohol and just sip iced tea. Maybe the tea would cool her blood. She'd heard wine had more of a warming affect. But all the cold drinks in the world couldn't chill what was burning inside her most delicate areas. Jason's scent and touch lit a fire inside her and her entire body ignited and tingled with need.

The waiter prepared to leave. "Everything is as you requested, sir," he said with a dip of his head. "Enjoy your evening."

The door closed with a soft click and they were gone.

# Chapter Eight

## ഔ

Jason removed the crystal wineglass from her hand and placed it on a glass and cherry wood end table. Maintaining eye contact, he gently tucked a strand of silky hair behind her ear and cupped her cheek with one palm. Rebecca breathed in the sweet smell of his thick Burberry cologne and closed her eyes in anticipation, turning her face into the warmth of his fingers.

"Becca, I've imagined this night a thousand times."

The deep timbre of his voice sent shivers racing through her. She wanted him. No, she ached for him. When he caught her lips in a gentle kiss, the need inside escalated, almost stealing her breath. She slipped her arms around his neck, drawing him closer and deepening the kiss so she could savor the taste of him.

"What did you imagine?" she asked, breathlessly breaking away from the sensual embrace. "Tell me. What were your wildest dreams?"

He ran his fingers down her neck, exploring the swell of her breasts. "I imagined us holding one another like this. We'd have some wine while we got reacquainted with each other's touch and feel—ever so slowly, so we could savor the experience. And then…" He slid his finger under the fabric of her dress between her breasts.

She gasped with the pleasure of it and ran her own inquisitive hands across his powerful chest, broad shoulders and up into his smooth hair. Pulling his head softly onto her chest, she buried her face in his hair. Traces of the expensive citrus shampoo he'd used that morning still lingered, enticing her.

Jason rose and she rediscovered all the planes and angles of his face, his sexy stubble tickling her fingertips. When she reached his mouth, her fingers caressed his full lips with a featherlike touch. She arched back and sighed when Jason sucked the tip of her finger into his mouth and playfully stroked it with his tongue.

"Like this?" Rebecca breathed the question against his corded neck, her mouth open so she could taste his skin.

Jason moaned appreciatively as he turned his head, allowing his tongue to tantalize her lips. At the same time, he trailed his hands down her sides, exploring her in return. "Yes, exactly like that."

He kissed her again, using his tongue to tease her lips apart and explore her mouth. His touch made her feel soft, alive, hot all over and she loved it—needed it.

Rebecca explored his hips and the area of skin just along the waistband of his jeans, playfully forcing an exploring finger into the material's depths. She could feel his hard arousal pushing against the denim and she knew he was as turned on as she was. Teasing them both, she played with the zipper of his jeans. Fumbling with the metal button, she was startled at her own boldness. She moved her hands up instead, as if to tease him, and started to undo his shirt, running her fingers through his wiry chest hair. She could feel him relax.

He moaned again, nuzzling her cheek and neck. "If we don't stop now, all that food is going to go to waste. Our dinner is getting cold."

She sighed. "Do we care?"

"Sweetheart, we need to eat to build up our strength for the night ahead," he said with a throaty chuckle. "At least, that's how I imagined it."

Reluctantly, she pulled back from him and lightly giggled. He must be some super lover to already anticipate an entire night of passion. There was little doubt in her mind that just being near this man made her reckless and bold. And all he had to do was put his hands on her to bring her to a state of careless, screaming abandon. Hopefully, dinner wouldn't take too long.

Having been without Jason for seven years, she didn't want to wait another minute.

"Okay. Let's eat. I know you're on a tight budget," she said playfully. "I'd hate to see all that extravagant food go to waste."

He tugged her up gently from the couch and led her to the table. Chivalrously, he pulled out a chair, and as she sat down, he bent toward her and kissed the spot where her neck and shoulder met. She was racked by emotions, but one thing was for sure—she felt like a queen, or perhaps a real English lady. There was no fantasy she'd ever had that could have compared to the love and security she felt at this moment.

Seated in the ornate dining area, Rebecca could fully appreciate what a stunning view of the ocean this room would have in the daylight. Now, the fading glow of the brilliant sunset cast its light into the dusk. The balcony door stood ajar, allowing a cool ocean breeze and the sweet scent of roses and island flowers into the room. The sound of waves crashing onto the sand was a majestic counterpoint to the water rippling in the fountain in the foyer.

Red and white roses filled a lead crystal vase set in the middle of the table, adding their fragrance to the breeze from outside. The sterling silver place settings and white china with a fine gold rim gleamed in the candlelight. Rebecca felt overwhelmed at her surroundings. She looked at all the forks and wondered which one to use first. She'd never had a dinner that was as elaborate as this.

"Everything looks so beautiful," she said in amazement.

"Not as stunning as you, Becca girl," Jason replied as he poured them each a flute of sparkling champagne.

"You make me feel like a princess with all this attention."

"You deserve it. And more." Jason picked up his glass and held it out toward her "To the most exquisitely genuine, good-hearted woman in the world."

"You make me feel so beautiful, Jason," she said quietly, realizing that it was true.

The bubbles tickled her nose as she sipped the champagne. Jason gave her a devastating smile over the rim of his glass and her heart lurched. She felt as if she should pinch herself so that she would know she wasn't dreaming.

Now that she was surrounded by all the delicious smells of spicy seafood, rich cream sauces, herbs and fresh fruits, she realized how hungry she was. It had been hours since she had eaten.

"I hope you like everything I picked out for our dinner," Jason said. "Try the French onion soup."

"This is delicious," she exclaimed as she tried the unfamiliar soup with a piece of bread and cheese crust. Taking another spoonful, she concentrated on finishing everything in the bowl.

Each time she looked up from the table, Jason's eyes were upon her, shining with what looked like love and contentment while his fingers eagerly thrummed the champagne flute. His gaze warmed her in ways she couldn't begin to describe. She would have loved him no matter what, but she was so proud of him — that he'd finally achieved what he'd wanted so much.

Rebecca was amazed to find that she was still hungry even after she'd finished the soup and a salad of baby greens garnished with toasted pecans, tomatoes, goat cheese and honey vinaigrette.

"What else are you going to feed me?" she asked, as she put their salad plates aside.

He winked and slanted his face with a subtle smile. "We'll save that question for later."

"Jason, you beast." Rebecca placed her hands over her face to hide the blushing.

Quickly changing the subject, he said, "Do you still love crab and shrimp as much as you used to?"

"They're my favorites."

"Well, I'm in luck then." Jason took the covers off the other platters that contained shrimp and crab and sides of seafood-stuffed mushrooms, oyster etouffée, twice-baked potatoes with cheese and sour cream and asparagus tips topped with a rich buttery sauce. This wasn't just a dinner—it was a banquet fit for royalty.

"There's more food on this table than I could ever eat. This all looks so good, I believe I'll sample some of everything." His thoughtfulness overwhelmed her. "You didn't have to do all this for me, Jase."

Rebecca felt delighted by the look of adoration on Jason's face. Anyone, including her, could tell he was in love. He continued gazing at her as if something were on his mind. Perhaps he did want to make amends for all his earlier mistakes and indiscretions. "You deserve so much. I wanted to give you this, my sweet Becca. And much more…"

Tears welled in Rebecca's eyes. She'd waited her entire life to hear those words, to feel this way—secure, in love and oh, so content. Her mother had been wrong about her and Jason. This was the beginning of an exciting new chapter in both their lives and she couldn't wait to get started.

Sampling all the delicacies, she felt like a glutton, but the food was so fabulous that she devoured it, savoring every morsel. Rebecca hadn't eaten so well in her whole life. This food was so much better than Top Ramen or those cheap microwave dinners she'd usually buy.

"That was truly amazing." Rebecca folded her napkin and sat back in her chair, patting her tummy contentedly.

"I'm glad you liked it," he said. "A woman like you should be wined and dined on a regular basis. I've decided that it'll be my life's work to make you happy and keep you well-fed."

Although he spoke jokingly, she saw the emotion in his eyes as he laid his napkin across his plate. Rising from his seat and sauntering around the table, he gently tugged her out of her chair and into his arms. "Dance with me, Becca."

Rebecca was shocked. In all the time she'd known him, he'd never asked her to dance. She rested her head on his shoulder and closed her eyes. With every movement, every heartbeat and touch, Rebecca felt as if they had been partners all their lives. Her heart filled and overflowed with love and she prayed these magical moments would never end.

The delicious food, soft music and sensual atmosphere put her at ease and, at the same time, aroused another hunger deep within her. She appreciated the fact that Jason wasn't rushing her into anything, and the dancing was lovely, but at the same time her body felt impatient, humming with expectation and need.

She opened her eyes and looked up at him. His eyes were closed and a content look shone upon his face. Rebecca smiled and began to wonder what he was thinking. Feeling.

"Will you kiss me, Jason?"

At the sound of her voice, his eyes opened. "With the greatest of pleasure," he murmured just before capturing her lips in a deep, searing kiss that rocked her inner core.

They stopped dancing and stood, Rebecca on her tiptoes as their bodies pressed tightly. The kiss went on and on until it seemed they were drinking from each other's souls. But it wasn't enough. She needed more of him. Making an impatient sound, she pressed even more firmly against him, her breasts aching with that wonderful pressure.

Jason bent down, "You mean the world to me, Becca." He lifted the tips of his fingers to her cheek and glided them across her face. His hand slowly meandered its way down her neck and she noticed that his eyes were fixated on her bosom. Intercepting his hand before it reached the object of his fascination, she moved his fingers toward her lips, lightly sucking them. Each touch seemed to burn its way through her entire body. Then, in one surprising motion, he scooped her up into his arms.

Jason carried Rebecca down a small, dimly lit hallway, gently setting her down next to a closed door made of Brazilian hardwood. Rebecca was puzzled—this was a room she hadn't yet seen. "This is what I definitely imagined," Jason whispered as he looked at her. Ever so slowly he turned the knob and opened the door. There awaited the most romantic setting she'd ever seen. It was much more stunning than the earlier room Jason had showed her. Placing her hands over her mouth in amazement, she walked to the door and stopped.

A full moon and ocean mist scented candles illuminated their way, casting the bedroom in a magical glow. The thick aroma of the islands filled the air from hundreds of mixed flower petals, which were strewn on the blue satin quilt of the canopied bed and about the floor. Large tropical citrus and vanilla scented pillar candles adorned the fireplace mantel, casting an even more intoxicating fragrance. These subtleties all added an aura of romance that touched her deeply. The soft, sexy music from the other room followed them, wrapping them in a cocoon of sensuality.

Jason once again took his place next to Rebecca, gently lifting her into the air. As if she were made of glass, he delicately placed her on the edge of the bed. He looked into her eyes as if to sear the moment into his memory. "This is a miracle, Becca. I thought I had lost you forever."

"You never lost me, Jase." She reached out to touch his shoulder. "I've been here for you all along and I'm here now."

He knelt on the bed and gathered her into his arms. She felt his heart beating against hers, strong and steady like the tides. Then, in unison, their heartbeats sped up as the anticipation of the magical night sure to come intensified.

"I want tonight to be special," he whispered, brushing her hair away from her face, letting each strand cascade through his fingers.

In disbelief, Rebecca let out a deep sigh and murmured, "It already is." She reached up to run her fingers along the line of his jaw.

"You and I were always meant to be together. Can you forgive me for not recognizing that way back when?"

"Does it look like I've forgiven you?" She smiled.

"I want to be with you. I want to make you mine." He stroked her hair, her face. "Tell me you want it, too."

"You know I do, Jason." She held out her arms to him. "Make me yours tonight. Make me yours now."

Hungrily complying, Jason breathed her name into her skin as he rose, straddling her. His knees digging deeply into the mattress, he drew himself nearer until his lips touched hers. She could feel the heat from his body as he began teasing her with his tongue. They both became breathless as he slid his mouth down the nape of her neck, stopping where the neckline of her dress began. As his tongue slipped slightly under the delicate fabric, she moaned and lifted her hands to the button closure of her dress.

He stopped her hands. "Please, Rebecca. Let me undress you." His fingers eagerly played with the top button. "I've been waiting for this moment for so long. Will you let me?"

His words sent electric shivers dancing across her nerves, making it impossible for her to move or breathe. She couldn't speak. All she could do was nod.

Jason's hands touched her as lightly as butterflies as he undid the long row of buttons one by one and then eased the thin garment from her body. Jason stood, extending a hand toward Rebecca. She began to shiver as she slipped off the bed, standing before him with nothing on but a strapless white lace bra and delicate pink silk panties. A bit uncomfortable and not able to read his reaction, Rebecca rubbed the back of her calf with her foot.

For long moments, Jason didn't touch her. Instead he walked circles around her, every so often teasing her with a gentle glide of his fingers across her back, stomach and neck. She watched as his eyes feasted on her while flooding with desire and turning dark and heated. Her own body was moist and ready. She'd gone without him for years and she didn't want to wait another minute to feel him inside her.

She was trembling with need and lifted her arms in invitation. "Do you like what you see, Jase?" she pleaded softly. "If so, come here and be with me."

"Not so fast." He smiled, but his breathing was accelerating. "We're going to make this last, remember?"

"I want to feel your body against mine," she whispered in his ear, hoping Jason would give in to her needs.

"Soon, baby doll. I want to see all of you. My eyes need to take in every square inch of your lovely form." A few moments passed as he continued to tantalize her body with every teasing touch. She thought she'd lose her mind if he didn't hurry.

Once again, he eased her back, taking a strand of hair and pushing it aside. "Rebecca, your hair smells like the islands. You always smell so good." She smiled up at him, wishing he would make his move. Rising to his knees, he lifted her to allow access to the clasp of her bra. He tossed the lacy garment aside and gently laid her back on the bed.

She felt a wave of heated embarrassment as he studied her. For a moment, she wanted to reach for the satin quilt and cover herself. But only for just a moment. His loving expressions calmed her insecurities. Now, more than anything, she was ready to give everything to Jason.

Moonlight cascaded over the bed, illuminating the creases of Jason's ever-widening smile. "Oh, sweet Lord, Becca." Jason positioned his body on the bed next to her. She could feel the fine hairs on his torso tickling her side. Slowly reaching a shaky finger up to one of her puckered nipples, Jason then gently cupped both her breasts, kneading them between his fingers. Lowering his head, he placed his mouth between her breasts, gliding his lips and tongue from one to the other. Resting his chin upon her chest, he gazed up toward her. "In all my born days, I've never seen anything as beautiful as you nor experienced anything as sweet."

His continued fondling sent a bolt of lightning rocketing through her. She couldn't hold back the soft whimper as he held her full breasts in his hands, massaging them. When he bent his head to kiss each nipple, she thought she would go mad with wanting him.

Begging for more, Rebecca cradled his head against her breasts, sifting his hair through her fingers. Her eyes closed as tears of happiness streamed down her face. She was aroused and overflowing with need and desire, but her heart was so filled with tenderness and love that she couldn't hold back.

He rained kisses on her—from her neck down over her breasts and back again. She moaned as he took an aching nipple into his mouth. As he drew on her breast, the sensation stoked the flames in her blood to an even higher pitch. Was it possible to want someone the way she craved this man? For years, she had hungered for his touch, his kisses, never quite believing she would experience them again. Now, like a miracle, he was here, his lips and hands on her skin. Her heart was so full of emotion, and the overwhelming sensations that his skillful caresses created were so wonderful that she sighed.

As his hands scraped lightly over her panties, heat washed through her. The ache of wanting built and built until it became a hard knot of passion in her belly. His fingers slipped under the elastic and slid between her legs. Without conscious thought, she opened for him, welcoming every single sensation he evoked in her.

"Ah, sweetheart, you're so ready for me."

Rebecca wanted to respond, to tell him that she'd been ready for him forever, but he stole her breath with a long, hard embrace. She eagerly leaned forward and gave him the response his tongue demanded. His mouth and hands never stopped touching her, branding her as his.

Writhing under his caresses, Rebecca moaned and rubbed her slender body against his. She thought she would die if he didn't make love to her soon, and the words somehow found their way to her lips.

"Soon, sweetheart, soon," he whispered and continued to touch her.

After a lifetime, an hour, a moment, Jason released her lips and straightened. Still kneeling beside her, he gently ran his hands down her body. "Will you let me see the rest of you, Becca?" he asked softly.

She couldn't speak, but she shifted wordlessly toward him. Gently, he hooked his fingers into the elastic and slowly, slowly pulled down the last bit of fabric that covered her. Full of impatience and need, she whimpered as she lifted her hips to allow him to pull the panties down. But then self-consciousness took over and she started to shift onto her side.

"Shh, don't." He stopped her movement with a hand flat against her belly. "You have a beautiful body. Don't be embarrassed to let me see," he murmured.

Trembling, she tried to lie quietly beneath his heated gaze. Silently, she watched him devour her with his eyes as the breeze from the open window caressed her.

But her embarrassment was soon forgotten. The flames of desire had burned away everything but the need to unite her body with Jason's. Every part of her tingled with wanting him. She thought she would go insane if he didn't touch her soon. "Jase…"

"I still can't believe you're really here. That this is really happening."

"Jason."

"What?" He looked into her eyes, his own heavy-lidded and sexy.

"You know."

"Tell me." He slipped his fingers slowly into the nest of curls between her thighs, and she gasped at the bold touch. "Let me hear you say it."

"I need you." Her breath was unsteady. He was teasing her. Jason knew exactly what she wanted, but he was going to make her say it. His fingers withdrew from her heat and she moaned, signaling her distress at losing his touch.

"Say it," he urged. "Tell me that you want me."

"I want you…madly, desperately, you know I do." Her hips writhed. "I need you—now!"

His fingers dipped into her curls again and explored. "So wet and hot and slick," he whispered, his voice hoarse with passion. "Are you ready for me?"

"Yes." She moved her hips to meet his fingers.

He again captured a nipple in his mouth and tongued it tenderly while using his fingers to drive her wild. She was panting as though she had run a marathon, and the need was like a flame in her blood. Rebecca moved desperately against his hand while he maintained his languid pace. She cried out with frustrated desire.

"Do you know what you're doing to me?" she asked, almost sobbing with need.

"Oh, sweet Becca," he said, looking at her face while he worked his wicked way with his fingers. "I do know." He smiled. "And if I didn't, your body is telling me."

"I don't want to wait anymore."

"Shh, not yet. We have the whole night ahead of us," he said and continued to touch her.

Just as she thought she would slide off the edge of the world into ecstasy, he withdrew his hand from her. She forced her mind back from the brink. He kissed her lightly once more and stood. As he unbuttoned his shirt, the moonlight poured its silver light over his smooth, firm skin, his broad shoulders and well-defined muscles. He held her gaze as he slowly unbuckled his belt. With the flick of a finger, he undid the silver button at the waist of his jeans, and his fingers slowly worked the zipper down.

Rebecca's mouth went dry as he opened his pants. He snagged a foil packet out of his pocket and eased the tight jeans down those firm thighs. He stepped out of the denim and stood before her in nothing but a pair of blue boxers. She lay without moving, waiting for that last piece of clothing to hit the floor. Her body was tingling with eagerness.

Finally, deliberately, Jason hooked his thumbs in the waistband and slid the boxers down his legs and over his feet. Silently he straightened and stood still, giving her the chance to study him. He looked even better than when they were teens. He stood proud and firm, a powerful testament to the fact that he burned as hotly for her as she did for him.

"You're beautiful, Jason." She lifted herself up, supporting herself on a bent elbow. "And we don't need that," she said, tipping her head toward the condom packet he held in his hand. "I won't get pregnant." She pushed away the flash of regret, refusing to let it spoil the moment. "But if you don't come to me now, I'll—"

"You'll what?" He gave her a hungry grin.

"I'll come after you and have my way with you."

He slipped into bed. "We wouldn't want that now, would we?" He pulled her on top of him and her hair fell forward, cascading around them like a curtain.

"Jason," she whispered, "I love you so much."

"And I love you. We're together now, and that's all that matters. You're mine and I'm yours." He moved beneath her so that she felt the hardness of him rubbing against her feminine core.

He captured her mouth in a kiss that touched her very soul, then rolled over and tucked her underneath him. All her insecurities, her anxieties forgotten, she opened for him, welcoming him home.

Jason shifted his body to find that special place. There was none of that adolescent awkwardness that had marked their lovemaking so long ago. That uneasiness had bloomed into secret adult indulgences. They moved together in a dance as old as that of Earth's first lovers. Flesh lovingly rubbing against flesh, the momentum built, churning with heated sensuality and hidden desires. Between sighs and moans, kisses and caresses, they came together in an explosion of passion that rocked Rebecca's very soul.

After their lovemaking had come to a climactic end, they lay together, their bodies pressed close. Jason's eyes were shut, so Rebecca moved slowly, careful not to disturb him. Only a sheet covered his lower half. She caressed his stomach with her fingers, gradually moving them up to his chest. A tear came to her eye as new emotions began to stir within her once again. She moved her arm to wipe the tear away when Jason opened his eyes. "Thank you for trusting me, Becca."

She smiled against his shoulder. "How could I not?"

He ran his fingers through her hair. "We'll make so many wonderful memories together, and I will earn that trust. You'll see," he said as she snuggled against him.

Rebecca was floating in the circle of her lover's embrace. After years of hurt and unfulfilled dreams, she had found her fairy-tale prince again. They'd be together forever, she thought, the moment filled with love and unclouded by doubt. With a contented sigh, she drifted off to sleep.

# Chapter Nine

ɞ

Rebecca watched the morning sun touch Jason's face as he slept. The golden light seemed to tip the sandy stubble along his jaw with tiny diamonds, giving the impression that he glowed with some inner light. His long lashes lay against his tan cheeks like sable, and she had an urge to stroke them with a gentle finger.

As he lay there quietly, she couldn't help but compare the man to the boy she'd known years ago. His face had been smoother then, without the touch of life's thumbprint. Now lines around his eyes and mouth told her he had lived hard during the years away from her. His face was more mature now, more interesting. How much of the boy she had fallen in love with all those years ago was still a part of him?

The stubble around his lips accented their sensual shape. She tingled all over when she remembered what those clever lips had done to her last night. Every moment of their adolescent lovemaking had been beautiful, but it was nothing like the mind-blowing pleasure he had given her last night. It might be petty, yet she couldn't help but think about all the women he had been with in the past seven years. And judging from his skill last night, it must have been quite a few.

How could one man give a woman so much pleasure? She gave her head a tiny shake, telling herself that it didn't matter where or when he'd learned how to do all those things. The only thing that mattered, as he'd said, was now. She decided that she would simply think of those other women as mere practice for the real thing — her. His lifelong soul mate.

The way he was laying, she couldn't see the scar her mother had given him. Oh, how she wished she could touch his face and just magically remove it and the awful memories. But it was an indelible part of him now, as were his memories, good and bad.

Suddenly all the anxieties that need and desire had washed away the night before came rushing back. Right now, she felt safe, even protected, with Jason but she couldn't help remembering how he'd left her before. She'd had no warning about his plans. He'd hidden them from her well, and she had been devastated.

Now he had achieved his goal, but that very success made them hugely unequal. He had all the power. Calling all the shots about their future. What if life threw him another reason to leave her behind? Would he go, as JoAnne predicted, without even seeking her say-so?

"Good morning, sweetheart."

Jason had opened his eyes, and his sleepy smile and greeting awoke tenderness inside her. It was wonderful waking up next to someone, enjoying that space together night after night. She could definitely get used to this kind of life. Rebecca's heart overflowed with love. More than anything, she longed to spend eternity with this man. What wouldn't she give to be the mother of his children?

They would have made such beautiful children together—a little boy as adorable as Jason, with sandy hair and dark eyes and little girls with golden curls and long legs, like their mama. That would have been so perfect. If only… No, she thought, resolutely pushing the regrets away. Now was not the time for dark thoughts.

"Good morning, Jase." Pushing her hair back, she leaned over to give him a sweet kiss. "Did I wake you?"

"Uh uh." He stretched like a large cat. "I've been awake for awhile." Reaching out, he brushed a finger down her arm. "It felt so good to know that you were here beside me."

Rebecca smiled. She was just thinking the same thing. "Did you sleep well?"

"Best sleep I've gotten in a very long time." He gave her a meaningful smile and reached up to tuck a strand of hair back behind her ear. "Best sleep I've ever had, in fact."

She smiled. "I slept pretty well myself." Feeling a bit shy with him in the light of day, she hitched the quilt up against her breasts.

"Are you trying to tell me something?" he asked playfully and hooked a long finger into the quilt.

"I'm sure I don't know what you mean." She answered his grin, getting into the spirit of the little game.

He gave the quilt a tug, but she was holding on to it tightly. He tugged again, harder this time, so that she slipped off her elbow and fell onto the pillow next to him.

His mouth was level with the edge of the quilt, and he pulled it down a little further, following the path with his mouth. His breath was hot against her skin and, forgetting her earlier discomfort, Rebecca shifted back against the pillows to give him better access.

Jason rolled up onto his knees and straddled her. Capturing her hands in his, he stretched them over her head and looked.

"You're even more beautiful in the sunlight than you were in the moonlight," he whispered. She could feel his hardness through the quilt and took delight in knowing that she excited him.

"Are you ready for breakfast?" he asked, his voice soft, barely audible.

The look in his eyes told her what he really wanted, and it wasn't pancakes.

"I wouldn't mind some breakfast," she said, deciding that two could play at this game. "I bet they do real fine here." She grinned up at him.

"Real fine," he agreed, and shifting back, he gave the quilt such a hard tug that it slipped off the bed. Bending down, he kissed the soft skin between her breasts. Then his mouth traveled downward. When he dipped his tongue into her navel, she sucked in her breath and clenched the sheets with her hands. It tickled her, but the feeling of his tongue against her skin sent an arrow of heat between her thighs.

Jason shifted over her and twined his legs with hers. "I can't get enough of you. I've never felt this way." He rubbed his body against hers. "What have you done to me?"

He released her hands and she immediately trailed them down his back and over his buttocks, pressing him closer. Without any urging, she opened to him and he fit himself inside her as if they were two parts of one perfect whole.

She welcomed him with a moan of pleasure, lifting her legs to hug his waist as he moved against her in a way that soon had her spiraling out of control. Their lovemaking was fast and hard, their bodies straining before they let go and fell into the vortex. Jason lay on her, panting uncontrollably.

"I always liked the thought of more than one course for breakfast." He gave her that wicked grin of his.

"Maybe we can have bacon and eggs now," she said with a little twist of her hips, telling him that bacon and eggs were the furthest things from her mind.

"Oh, I like your thinking." Just as he ducked his head to take her mouth again, the phone on the nightstand began to ring.

Rebecca threw herself back against the pillow in disgust. This was her time—no time for phone calls.

Apparently Jason was thinking the same thing. "Damn it." Jason rolled away to grab the phone, nearly knocking over a lamp. "Hello?"

Rebecca laid on her back, looking up at the canopy overhead, the blue silk like a pale summer sky. Her body still thrumming from his touch, she listened to Jason's end of the conversation, savoring the certainty that she'd made Jason feel just as good as he had made her feel. Content and smiling, she ran her fingers down the length of her torso, hoping his hands would soon follow.

"All right. We'll be there. Thanks for the info." He hung up the phone and then quickly turned back to her. He gathered her up into his arms, stroking her hair.

"Who was that?" she asked, not really caring about anything but being in Jason's arms.

"A guy I know." He kissed her, then patted her on the rear. "Time to get up, sweetheart. We have a boat to catch in an hour."

"A boat?" Rebecca was puzzled. What the heck was he thinking?

Jason stood and stretched as she watched him walk, naked and nonchalant, toward the bathroom. She loved the look of him from any direction, but his butt was to die for.

"I told you last night that this wasn't our final destination. We make the rest of the trip by boat, but there's a storm coming. We've got to hurry." He turned around at the bathroom door. "Get a move on, woman, time's a-wasting."

"Time may be a-wasting, but I'm not getting out of this bed," she said, feeling content and not ready to get up just yet. She wanted to finish making love. Besides, the bed felt heavenly. Running her hands over the plush mattress, she gave herself a lazy, long stretch, pulling a pillow under her head.

A moment later, Jason came back, giving Rebecca an ornery grin. As if he were a tiger flying through the air pouncing on prey, he jumped, straddling her. Knees digging hard into the bed, he began tickling her sides, occasionally running razor stubble over her belly. Rebecca's stomach muscles started to ache from laughter. "Stop, I give! Uncle! Uncle!"

"Will you get up if I promise that we'll finish where we left off later?" he said, holding her arms above her head.

"Promise! I was hoping you'd say that." Rebecca rolled over and laughed.

He rustled his hand through her hair, messing it up even more. "I've got wonderful things to show you today, Rebecca Lynn Roberts. I'm almost tempted to tell you about where we are going...almost," he teased. "Now let's get showered and dressed. We have places to be."

Their trip to the small Gulf island was a choppy one. Rebecca was uneasy in the small boat surrounded by the angry swells, but Jason kept his arm around her the entire time. Dark, menacing clouds had started to spit misty rain when the dock at Cinnamon Bay came into sight. The wind was gusting with the approaching storm, and lightning and claps of thunder split the air in the distance. They needed to find shelter quickly.

Upon their approach, Rebecca saw that the island's residents were also heeding the storm warnings. Fishermen secured their boats to the docks and stowed their equipment while homeowners rushed to bring in lawn furniture and laundry.

Through the mist Rebecca also spotted a few commercial buildings on the bay. A small grocery store, a pharmacy, a gas station and a boat repair shop huddled under the questionable protection of a stand of trees—just enough businesses to sustain daily life on the island. Cinnamon Bay appeared to be a very private place.

Although Rebecca didn't much care for the white caps, strong winds and lightning, she loved the refreshing rain smell. Back home she could tell when it was about to storm—there was always a distinct, clean scent in the air. The island was no exception, except that it had more tantalizing floral fragrances mixed into the rain's freshness. This was an aspect she could definitely get used to—well, as soon as she was safely on shore.

The mist and waves were intensifying. Finally getting her sea legs, Rebecca looked around the boat for a raincoat. No luck. In a storage box next to the life vests she found someone's old baseball cap. It wasn't much, but it was better than nothing. Her eyes were stinging from the saltwater and wet hair beating against her face. Pulling her damp hair back into a ponytail, she placed the hat on her head and hoped for the best.

"Ugh—I must be a mess. A drowned rat probably would look better right now," she mumbled while images of that nice, warm hotel room ran through her mind. Jason still looked unscathed. No amount of wind or water would mess his hair up. He was just one of those people who could towel dry his hair and make it look good.

Engrossed with thoughts of Jason naked in the shower, Rebecca was oblivious to him coming toward her. The tug nearly startled her out of the boat.

"Hey, Becca, if you look over there to the right, you can see a blue rooftop."

"Where?"

Jason pulled her closer and pointed with his free hand. "If you look right over there, past that row of palms, you'll see it."

Rebecca spotted a little white Spanish-style cottage. This wasn't her surprise, was it?

Later, as Jason pulled into the driveway and parked, Rebecca got a clearer picture of the small homestead. Large palm trees around the house, a screened porch, a veranda, and even a little gable-roofed well out front gave the place a lot of charm. Rebecca thought it would look even prettier with some bright flowers and shrubs planted all around it. A hammock for those sultry summer afternoons would be a nice touch too.

The house's stucco front glowed white with dark blue shutters and a gray door. Blue Spanish tiles adorned the roof while thick patches of bright green ivy grew up the east side. Several large, ceramic flowerpots contained plants that had dried up, and the shrubs needed a major manicure.

"The grounds go way back around the place," Jason said as they scurried hand in hand up a pathway that was laid out with fieldstone. "There's even a little orange grove." He gave her an anxious look. "Do you like it?"

The cottage and expansive grounds had great potential, but they cried out for care and love and a family to make the whole place complete.

"Well, it needs some work, but it's got loads of charm. Whose house is it?"

"Yours."

"Mine?" Why would this be her house?

He seemed to be fumbling for the right words and after a few tries, Jason managed to get out a complete sentence. "Well, ours," he corrected himself. "It's our house, Becca."

Rebecca felt her heart thumping in her chest. Was this another part of the fairy tale? Or was this real life? Her head began to whirl. Things were moving way too fast. She loved him, yes—but for him just to assume they were going to live together, here… What if she didn't like being stranded out in the middle of nowhere? Was this his way of keeping her out of the public eye? Did he really plan on marrying at some point?

"Why didn't you get a house closer to Nashville?" she asked.

"I wanted a home far away from the city lights and prying eyes, and this is it. Like you said, it needs attention, but we have time to do that now." He squeezed her shoulder and pressed a kiss to her temple. "I was going to hire an interior decorator, but now that I've found you, I want you to make this our home—if you want to, that is."

Overwhelmed by what Jason was saying, Rebecca was silent.

"If you want a designer, or if you just plain hate it, we'll unload the place," Jason said just as the wind kicked up and rain started falling. "Looks like we'd better head inside before things get bad."

They grabbed their luggage and ran up the stairs to the screened porch just as it started to pour.

After Jason stopped and set down the luggage, he took Rebecca's bag and put it down as well. He unlocked the door, scooped her up in his arms and carried her inside the house.

Bowled over by his actions, Rebecca broke out in laughter. "I'm surprised after that dinner you fed me last night that you were able to pick me up so easily."

Jason grinned. "Nope. You're still light as a feather. Besides we got plenty of exercise to burn off that meal—or are you saying *I* got all the exercise?"

Rebecca threw him a playful grin, then raised her eyebrows. "Jason, you're awful. Now put me down," she said, playfully slapping his arm. He cringed like she'd really hurt him. Rolling her eyes, she turned away.

"Bec. You've got to come here." She eagerly complied and followed him deep into the sun porch, which looked into the main part of the house.

Rebecca was stunned. She couldn't believe how beautiful the view of the bay was and how well she could see the now raging storm. Turning toward the kitchen, tears welled in her eyes.

"Hey, darling, are you crying?" Jason asked, putting his hands on her shoulders, ducking a little so that he could see her face. "I'm sorry. You don't like the cottage?"

"No. No, that's not it at all." She swiped at her tears with the backs of her hands. "I love it. It's just that—"

"Tell me why you're crying and I'll make it right. Or try to, at least."

Rebecca drew a deep breath. "You have to understand that my life has changed so much within the past few days—so many wonderful things have happened. I'm just overwhelmed." She took his hand. "I'd love to make this house our home, but I'm worried that we're moving too fast. We've only been back together for such a short time. What if I give up everything to come here permanently and it doesn't work out?"

Jason was visibly upset. "Rebecca, I love you. When I said that I wanted us to be together, I meant forever. Look, if you don't like the house it's fine. I only bought it as a place to escape to whenever I needed some privacy. We both love the beach and each other, or so I thought… Maybe I read too much into the last few days."

"I do love you, but I don't want us making a mistake. Things have changed — we've changed. You might not like living with me or I you."

"Like what? What could I possibly not like about you?"

"That's what I'm talking about Jase. This isn't puppy love anymore. It's for keeps. I clip my toenails on the sofa as I'm watching Lifetime movies for God's sake. When I'm depressed I eat ice cream right out of the carton and drink milk out of the jug. I leave my underwear on the bathroom floor 'cause I'm too lazy to walk to the hamper."

"I leave my underwear on the floor too. What's your point, Becca?" Jason said with a sharp tone. "Look I hope you're not having second thoughts about us. I know that I made some big mistakes. We've covered that. But make no mistake about this — I love you and intend on making a life for us whether you clip your toenails in the living room or not."

Rebecca turned toward him with a haphazard grin, removing the ball cap and releasing her hair from the confines of the ponytail band. Perhaps she was just being silly and nervous.

He pulled her into his arms. "What do you say? Will you take a chance and spend the rest of your life with me?"

Rebecca's heart filled with love and joy. Answering him between hiccups and tears, she said, "Yes Jason, I'll take that chance. I've never wanted anyone more in my life — I want you now."

"You have me," he whispered as he gently put her down.

The storm was now in full rage, completely engulfing the island in its wrath. Rain was blowing in through the screened windows.

Jason delicately cupped Rebecca's face with his hand as tiny rain droplets slowly slid down her cheeks. He bent down to taste the salt of her tears as his free hand sifted through her damp hair, released from the cap and ponytail earlier. His touch ignited a raging inferno within her as the pounding in her heart became harder, more intense. She was ready to give in to him again.

After breaking their embrace, Rebecca ran her hands over his chest and began to unbutton his shirt. Feeling incredibly brave and bold, she pulled the shirt out of his jeans and glided the sleeves down his arms. She glanced up at him, suddenly unsure, but he smiled to encourage her.

Jason stood motionless and looked down at her as she opened the button of his jeans and slid down the zipper. Running one hand a little farther south, she felt the hardness of him. She wrapped her fingers around him and gently squeezed. Jason moaned with pleasure and pushed his hips forward, inviting her touch. It thrilled her that he let her take charge.

Pressing up against him, she stretched for a kiss as her hands felt their way toward his buttocks and began pulling his jeans down.

"Becca," he breathed against her mouth. "You make me crazy. Crazy for you."

Like a pirate grabbing treasure, he whisked her up into his arms. She closed her eyes, dizzy with excitement, as the storm crashed around them. He lowered her into the chaise and stood looking down at her hungrily.

She felt wanton as the wind and rain tore through the screens, and she pulled him down to her and rolled atop him. Taking the lead again, she yanked at his jeans as he pushed up her sundress, and they came together in a frenzy of tangled clothing and clutching hands.

The storm outside paled in comparison to the fiery energy Rebecca felt coursing through her as she straddled Jason. She moved her hands up and down his chest, reveling in the feel of his damp, wiry chest hair and the rippling muscles underneath. His hardness gently brushed against Rebecca's most tender of treasures. This sensual sensation was overwhelming and she began pressing her delicate area even firmer against his. When the wanting became intolerable, she maneuvered upward, placing him deep inside her.

He slightly arched back and trailed his hands over her breasts, her stomach. Then his hands slipped down to feverishly caress her where they were joined. Rebecca moaned in ecstasy as she sped up her gliding movements in time with the storm raging around them. The wailing wind blew silken droplets of rain through the screen to cool their heated flesh. She didn't care about getting wet. All that mattered in the world was being in Jason's arms and slaking the storm of passion that had brewed within her since they'd met again.

Desperate with need, Rebecca quivered, throwing her head back in ecstasy, her wet hair streaming down her back. She could feel the pressure of Jason's hands around her waist. On a burst of thunder, she cried out. His hips arched upward and he joined her as their lovemaking came to a climactic end.

Rebecca gazed down at Jason, her ragged hair pushed to one side. She moved forward, kissing Jason's lips lightly as her hands cupped the side of his jaw. "I think I'll be happy here. We can make our own memories—and storms."

Jason stretched his arm outward, fumbling to pick up his shirt with one finger. "Here you go, babe. Put this on before you get too cold." Rebecca took the shirt, slipped it onto her body and took her place beside him.

In the aftermath of their passion, Rebecca lay against Jason's chest and listened to the distant rumble of thunder as the storm moved off. Her heart rate began to slow and her breathing returned to normal. With Jason she felt invincible, as if no harm could ever come to her again. To her, their lovemaking against the storm was a symbol, proof that together they could withstand any tempest that life brought them. They were meant to be together. Always had been. Always would be.

They lay there for a long time, savoring their fulfilled passion.

"Becca?"

"Mmm?"

"I've been doing a lot of thinking since Friday night. And I'm sure that you have, too."

Rebecca tensed, wondering what he was going to say, and rose so that she could look into his face.

"I may be jumping the gun here, but I have to ask you something."

"Jason—"

"Hush, let me get this out." He lifted his arms, took her face in his hands and kissed her with a tenderness that nearly broke her heart.

"I'm so grateful that God brought you back to me. And I can't let you go, Becca. I just can't do it again. And this is not just a living arrangement for me either."

Throwing her arms around his neck, she buried her face in his shoulder. He stroked her hair and rubbed her back. "Becca, I've never done this before, so I know I'm making a mess of it... Well, hell. Sweetheart, will you marry me?"

Rebecca began to smile. "Yes, Jason. I will marry you—on one condition."

"What's that?"

"That I can continue with my music?"

Jason grinned. "With me, we'll make music everyday." Even he couldn't keep a straight face after that line. "Corny, huh?"

Slapping his arm once again she said, "Be serious. This is almost all too perfect. There's no doubt I love you, but you've picked out the house, made all the decisions so far. I want to write more than anything. I want my own music career."

"The apple doesn't fall too far from the tree in this family, does it? I guess you and I will become a regular Porter Wagoner and Dolly Parton."

"Uh, they were never married, dear. Perhaps this country idol needs to study up on his country music trivia," Rebecca scoffed.

Jason grinned. "I bet Porter wanted to marry Dolly."

Rebecca was feeling testy. "Will you support me in a music career or what?"

With a quick move, Jason rolled Rebecca over, pressing her back into the cushion. "Well, what do you think?"

# Chapter Ten

## ∽

After Rebecca had time to process Jason's stunning proposal of marriage, the next couple of weeks fell into a deceptively comfortable routine and Rebecca found herself happier than she had ever imagined being.

Spending time with Jason was always wonderful, but mornings were the best, she thought as she awoke from a sound and peaceful sleep with Jason's arms lovingly wrapped around her.

Sometimes they'd cuddle under the covers and talk. They'd talk about everything from wedding plans to remodeling the old beach house. Jason would share stories about his life on the road and how he performed at concerts and charitable events in fascinating cities all over the map. He promised her that soon she'd be living those stories rather than just hearing about them. Soft talking often turned into sweet lovemaking before they got up to begin their day.

It was paradise, she thought as she stretched, loving the feeling of his skin against hers. The sound of the waves gently lapping onto the shore outside their bedroom windows made it even more romantic. For the first time in her entire life, Rebecca felt truly safe and content. Just doing everyday things with Jason gave her a sense of security and normalcy she'd never known.

"I think someone's awake," Jason murmured against her hair.

Rebecca could smell the rich aroma of freshly brewed French vanilla coffee. The smell tantalized her, making her crave a cup of the thick brew. Jason must have set the timer before bed last night.

He nuzzled his face deeper into her hair and whispered in her ear, "Can I interest you in a cup?"

"I'll get us a cup. We can pretend it's cappuccino."

"No." Jason sat up in bed. "I'll get it." He grinned down at her. "I actually remembered to set the timer last night."

Rebecca whispered, "It's like I'm psychic."

"Did you say something, Becca?"

"No, just mumbling to myself."

After a bit, he returned with two steaming cups of fresh coffee. A hint of cinnamon spread throughout the room. Jason had granted her wish. He'd topped off two cups of coffee with whipped cream, sprinkled with cinnamon and sugar.

"We can pretend it's that fancy coffee you like from the restaurant back in Galveston." Rebecca sensed from his actions that he was happy to please her.

He did please her. In fact, she felt like a queen being waited on hand and foot. She turned away from him for a moment. God I hope this fairy tale bubble I'm living in doesn't burst, she thought.

He slipped back under the covers and offered her a bite of one of the chocolate chip cookies she'd baked last night.

"That's not exactly my idea of a nutritious breakfast."

"Well, I could offer you something more substantial." He wiggled his eyebrows in a mock leer. "If I had some incentive."

"I'm sure you could." She laughed lightheartedly. "But I said 'nutritious' not 'substantial'."

"How about substantial first and nutritious later?"

Rebecca set her coffee cup aside and opened her arms.


They took turns making breakfast, and to Rebecca's surprise, Jason had turned out to be a decent cook. She recalled that when he'd been a teenager, he considered boiling water a challenge. Rebecca, of course, had been cooking since she was in elementary school, but preparing Jason's favorites—bacon, scrambled eggs and hash browns—was somehow much more fun and rewarding as she basked in his appreciation and love.

One morning, Jason surprised her with the news that his mother was coming to visit. "You don't mind, do you, Bec?"

"Mind? Don't be silly. How could I mind that?"

"Well, not every woman might appreciate it when her future mother-in-law comes for a visit."

"I guess I'm not every woman."

"No." Jason wrapped his arms around her tightly. "No, there's only one of you in the entire world and you belong to me."

"Did your mom ever tell you that I went to see her after you left?" Rebecca asked as she went back to making breakfast.

Jason shook his head.

"The morning after JoAnne found us together." She paused, remembering. "I don't think I ever walked a mile that felt that long—or that hot." She dished up some sliced fruit and brought the bowls to the table.

"Do you want to tell me?" Jason asked. "But I'll understand if you don't want to talk about it."

"No, it's okay." Rebecca smiled and touched his hand. "Now that we're here together, it doesn't hurt as much to remember. I wanted to make sure you were okay after my mother flung that ashtray at your head." Rebecca wiped fruit juice from her hand and began to chop vegetables for the omelets. "And to apologize."

Jason looked worried as Rebecca began removing the cheese from the wrapper and placing the rest of the ingredients into the skillet. "I guess I was hoping that I'd be able to persuade you to stay in Galveston—at least part-time." She laughed a sad little laugh as the intoxicating aroma of a hearty country breakfast filled the kitchen.

"I was geared up to give this whole silly speech." Rebecca continued preparing the omelets, flipping them occasionally in between pouring orange juice and making toast. "I was going to tell you about how I didn't want you to put your ambitions on hold or postpone your dreams. How I understood that this was a great offer that could go on to bigger and better opportunities. About how I'd quit school the minute I was seventeen and come and join you."

With her ramblings she'd forgotten about the toast. Thick, gray smoke poured from the toaster, but Rebecca didn't miss a beat. Removing the burnt toast and tossing it into the sink, she automatically began to prepare fresh pieces. "I knew I couldn't go with you no matter how much I wanted to get away from my mother. She would have called the police and reported you as a kidnapper or a rapist if I'd gone. I couldn't let that happen to you."

Rebecca began to fight back the tears. Her mother had done so much damage to her life, but one day she'd have to come to terms with that. By now the breakfast was sitting on plates in front of them, but they were too engrossed in thoughts and conversation to notice that it was getting cold.

"Once I got to your house, I think it took me half an hour to work up the courage to just climb the porch steps and knock," Rebecca said. Jason put his arms around her for comfort. "I can still hear your mother's words. She told me that I was a sweet girl, that you cared for me and that we'd see each other when you came home, but you never did—you never came home."

Jason said nothing and ducked his head. Rebecca could feel his fingers caressing her shoulder as if to console her.

"Sarah said you'd come back to me. She said she was as sure as 'Texas is God's country'. You know, I use that phrase all the time now."

"I'm so sorry, sweetheart. No words I can possibly say right now can make up for my mistakes." Jason squeezed her tightly as if he didn't ever want to let her go.

"We're here together now. That's what matters."

Mrs. Engles was overjoyed that her son had finally proposed to his teenaged sweetheart. Rebecca felt both honored and humbled to be so welcomed into this loving family.

Rebecca gave her a hug. "Oh Mrs. Engles, I've waited for a long time for this day. It's such an honor to be part of your family. There is a saying, 'you can't pick your family, but you can pick your friends'. Well, in this case I did pick my family. I couldn't have asked for a better mother than you."

"Call me Sarah from now on, Becca," his mother told her. "You and I are going to be good friends. I always thought you were a wonderful girl—and so good for my son. Besides that, we have our love for this boy here to keep us close." She gave Rebecca a warm hug. "I'm proud to welcome you into our family."

"Rebecca can you get Mama a glass of iced tea?"

"Sure. Sarah, want some lemon?"

"Whatever's easiest, dear." She smiled, placing her purse on the table.

"Did you bring it Mom?" Rebecca overheard Jason whisper with worry.

Mrs. Engles patted her son's hand. "Yes. Calm down. It's right here. I took it out of my bag a few minutes ago."

As Rebecca retuned to the table with iced tea for everyone, Jason stood and dropped to one knee. She could feel her cheeks warm and hands shake, almost to the point of dumping her own glass onto the floor.

"This is my grandmother's engagement ring, Becca. It was brought over from Europe—Bohemia, to be exact, when my grandfather came to this country. His dream was to place it on the finger of a beautiful woman with enough grit to handle ranching in the rugged Red River Valley. After a month of looking he found her teaching school. Grandpa figured if she was tough enough to handle all those kids, she surely could manage him and a ranch. Grandma passed the ring on to Mom to hold, until I—I know it's a little old-fashioned, but we can fly to New York and buy you the biggest Harry Winston diamond you want."

Rebecca was stunned. With their quick reunion and Jason's whirlwind proposal, she'd totally forgotten about a ring. Her heart raced and she began to cry. Between the tears, she managed to get out a few intelligible sentences. "Oh, no!" she protested. "I love you for you, not for what you can buy me. This ring is perfect, and as it did for your grandparents, it symbolizes our relationship. We have 'enough grit' to handle whatever comes our way." She looked at it sparkle on her finger and smiled. "I don't want a big diamond. This ring represents family and that's more than a new piece of jewelry could ever do. I'll cherish this for the rest of my life."

She turned toward her soon-to-be mother-in-law. "Sarah, please know that I will take good care of this ring. It means more to me than anything I've ever gotten. I meant what I said. I'll cherish it always."

Sarah smiled at Rebecca. She too was teary-eyed when she emerged from the table for another hug.

Jason smiled his approval and put his arms around both women. "You're right Rebecca. This ring does symbolize family and now it's my turn to start a new branch of the Engles tree. It starts right here, right now with the two women I care about most."

Uncle Burt, too, voiced his approval of the match in a lengthy phone call that Rebecca had with him later that night.

"I'm really happy for you," he said. "I always liked Jason, and I hated seeing you cry your eyes out after that boy left Galveston."

"Well, I'm just glad I had your shoulder to cry on, Uncle Burt." Rebecca gripped the phone, wishing her uncle was there so she could share the good news in person and give him a big bear hug.

Uncle Burt sounded overjoyed. "I know that I've been encouraging you for years to find a good man and get married, but I guess it's a good thing you didn't take my advice."

"I knew you meant well, Uncle Burt, but my memories of how special everything had been with Jason... I just couldn't imagine committing to anyone else," she said, looking out the window into the bay.

Uncle Burt chuckled. "Well, like I said, it's a good thing. By the way, have you told him that you've sold songs under the name J.R. Neels?"

"No. I don't want Jason to think that I'm using him in order to hit it big myself. It's important that I do this on my own. He knows I want a career songwriting, but he doesn't know I've already started. I'll tell him about J.R. Neels in good time. " She tried keeping her voice down so that Jason couldn't hear.

"That boy has got more sense than that. You should tell him, Becca," her uncle urged. "You didn't much like it that Jason kept secrets from you. What makes you think he'll like it any better if you keep secrets from him?"

"This is different," she protested. "The house concerns us both. It's something we can build on together. Songwriting is *my* legacy as a person. His legacy is already written. He knows the road to success. If Jason paves the way for me, it takes away from the accomplishment. I'll never know if it was *my* talent or his connections. When Jason left me, he made a name for himself on his own. It is important for me to do the same—earn my own independence."

"If you're getting married, then everything either of you does concerns the other person. I believe it is always better to be open. Please think about it long and hard, Becca."

"Okay, I'll think about it," she promised only to humor him. She'd know when the time was right to surprise Jason.

When Whitney heard the news, she was so elated that Rebecca could hear her jumping up and down. "Didn't I tell you your fairy godmother would take care of you, Ms. Doubting

Thomas? You need to start listening to me. Not to toot my own horn or anything."

Rebecca and Jason decided to talk to Whitney on the speakerphone. It would be easier to share her noisy antics that way.

"So, when's the big day? I need to clear my calendar. I am going to be your maid of honor, right?"

"We haven't set a date yet," Rebecca told her. "We're going to wait a little while. And, yes, you will be my maid of honor and Rick will be Jason's best man."

"Hey, Jason," Whitney said. "You got the engagement ring, but you'd better get a wedding ring on that girl's finger, you hear me? But not before we have a huge bachelorette party. I'll plan it. We can all go out for Mexican and margaritas. Then we'll go to that bar—I think it's called Bottoms Up. I'm thinking they have an all-male dance revue with men hunkier than Fabio or those Chippendales dancers. I'll start looking into that right away. Oh, and I've got to get some of those gag novelties like penis key chains and stuff. This is going to be research I like." She giggled.

"Whit, I don't think I want one of those wild things. Let's just have a low-key get-together with Jason and me, you and Rick, Mrs. Engles and Uncle Burt."

"Now what kind of bachelorette party would that be? That's going to be one boring event. C'mon now."

Rebecca held her ground. "I don't think so. And anyway, I don't have eyes for any other guys anymore—just my Jason here."

"You're no fun whatsoever. Can you tell I'm pouting right now guys?"

"Tell me that *you* have eyes for other men these days, Whit." Grinning with satisfaction, Rebecca knew she was pressing her friend's buttons for a change.

"Have you never heard of 'look but don't touch'?" Whitney laughed.

"Come to think of it, where is that tall drink of water of yours?" Jason asked.

Whitney was silent for a long moment and Rebecca almost started to ask the question again. Finally, Whitney said, "Rick went home to Arizona for a few days. I guess he's going to break it to his folks that he's hanging out with an Anglo gal."

"So he's thinking about taking you to Arizona to introduce you to his family? That's great."

"We'll see how his folks take the news that he's dating someone without a drop of Native American blood in her veins. I guess his dad is a real stickler for Native American traditions."

"So are you guys just…dating, or is it more serious than that?" Rebecca asked.

Whitney's voice became serious. "Let's put it this way. When Rick isn't around, my dancing shoes don't get much of a workout."

Rebecca laughed. "Knowing you, that sounds pretty serious to me."

Whitney sighed. "I'm not really sure how Rick feels. We have a great time and all, but he doesn't talk about emotions much. We'll figure it out somehow."

"I know you will. Rick may not know it yet, but you two are perfect for each other."


When Rick and Whitney finally came to visit, the two couples went to the mainland for a special dinner with other members of the band and their dates. They had a great time talking and laughing and catching up. Until dessert, that is. By then the local paparazzi had gotten wind that Jason's band was in town and photographers converged on the restaurant seemingly from out of nowhere.

One of the newsmen got aggressive and approached them with personal questions. The man asked Jason if he had any comment on the rumors that had been flying around ever since the Houston concert. Was he planning to marry the girl he had brought up onto the stage to sing to? Jason just grumbled that he had no comment and signaled the manager of the restaurant, who had the reporter escorted out.

As they left the restaurant, the friends tried to ignore the photographers and reporters and the flashbulbs popping in their faces. Rick and Whitney and the other members of the band ran across the street to the parking lot and dove for their vehicles. Jason grabbed Rebecca's hand and ducked between two buildings when attention was briefly diverted away from them by the sirens of a passing ambulance.

"They'll just get in their cars and follow us if they think we're with the rest of the group. Let's stay here for a bit and let them follow the others. Then you won't have to deal with them."

After a little while, he cautiously led her down a narrow alley.

Rebecca was appreciative that Jason was going to all this trouble to take good care of her. She was glad that he was with her during her first paparazzi encounter. Apparently, he knew all the tricks.

"I think we lost them," he whispered. "Come with me." He looked both ways before stepping out into the street. In a hushed voice, he said, "C'mon."

"Where are we going, Jase?" Rebecca clutched his arm tightly. She was still worried after almost being attacked by the reporters.

"I hate to see our special evening end so miserably. Somebody must have called the newspaper, so I'm taking you someplace safe until things quiet down. When I take off running, run as fast as you can, okay?"

"Whatever you say, Jase." She was still worried. It was pitch-black outside and the area had no lights coming from inside any of the buildings. Apparently the stores closed early in this part of town.

"There's a little place down on Harbor Shores Road. This older couple owns it, Gladys and Opie Worley. They were friends of my father and they retired here. That's how I got to know this area and realized how great it was before I bought the beach house."

Rebecca continued to tag along, thinking that it was a good sign that he trusted her enough to mention his father. He almost never spoke about him, and she knew he was ashamed of him and his alcoholism, even though his father's drinking was much milder than her mother's. She knew that Jason had been so driven by his career because he'd always had a fear of becoming like his dad.

"Here it is. Let's get inside."

"This place?" she questioned. It looked more like a mirage. How could someone locate a restaurant in a quiet neighborhood like this and be successful? But there it was. Gulf Bar & Grill flashed in neon above the door. The place looked respectable and he held the door for her as they entered.

As Rebecca had suspected, the bar was nice with large booths and tables, a small dance floor and area for a band. Beer signs and strands of white Christmas lights lit up the inside. It was a likeable place other than the thick cloud of cigarette smoke that hung heavily in the air. Apparently the ventilation system didn't work too well.

"Jason!" A little round, red-faced woman with long, dark hair streaked with white and tied back in a ponytail squealed his name and raced across the room, dodging tables and chairs to throw herself into his arms. Rebecca judged her to be in her mid-sixties, although she certainly moved like a much younger person.

"Gladys, it's really great to see you. It's been too long." Jason picked the woman up and gave her a bear hug. "Where's Opie? Don't tell me he's heading up another protest somewhere."

"No. Op's protesting days are over with. That last right-to-life demonstration for that brain-damaged girl in Milwaukee took the wind right out of his sails. He's in the back. He'll be out in a minute." She ushered them into the room and put them at a table close to the bar. "Have a seat."

She wagged her finger at Jason. "And shame on you for not stopping by sooner. I heard you bought over on the island, but I refused to believe it until I heard it from you personally. Thought you would have been by before now to tell us. You better have a good excuse why you haven't."

Jason held out the chair for Rebecca and sat down next to her.

"The reason I've not been here sooner is this little lady." Jason boasted putting his arm around her waist and nudging her forward. "See, I bought the property, then left to do a concert in Houston and, well, I got reunited with my high school sweetheart, Rebecca Roberts."

"Really!" chimed the little round lady. "That's wonderful. Our little boy is all grown up and starting a family of his own now. How exciting!"

"Be kind to her, Gladys. Her intelligence is suspect, because she's agreed to marry me." Rebecca caught him throwing her a teasing glance and laughed.

The little woman stopped bustling around and stared at them. "When's the wedding?"

"Who's marrying whom?" A burly man with long auburn hair cut in a mullet walked through a side door and stood beside Gladys.

"Opie, it's great to see you." Jason jumped up to greet the newcomer. The two men grinned and pumped hands like competitors trying to best the other in arm wrestling.

"Break it up, you two," Gladys told them in a stern voice. "Andrew, this here is Rebecca Roberts, and she's agreed to marry our crazy country crooner." She turned to Rebecca. "This old man who thinks he can still out-wrestle any young buck coming through the door is my husband, Andy."

"Old woman, how many times have I told you not to call me that? Ms. Roberts, my name is Opie."

"Oh, shut up, you overgrown baby." Gladys teasingly tried hitting her husband with a rolled-up menu.

Rebecca could tell that Gladys didn't take any flak from her husband. "It's wonderful to meet you both." Rebecca shook Opie's hand and waved shyly at Gladys.

"She's a looker. Makes me wish I was twenty years younger, boy," Opie told Jason. "Did you come all the way from Nashville to tell us old folks about the wedding or were you just in the area and decided to grace us with your presence?"

Like a little kid, Jason began to explain what he'd been up to. He seemed so happy he was back among old friends—his roots. "We've been staying at the house I bought in Cinnamon Bay."

"And you haven't been by to tell us, boy?" Opie grinned. "Well, I guess you've had something better to do than hang out with a couple of old fogies."

Jason laughed. "Stop fishing for compliments, Opie."

"So what brings you by tonight?" Opie asked.

"We were being chased by some paparazzi. Rebecca and I lost the photographers and headed here." Jason put an arm around Rebecca. "I thought you wouldn't mind putting us up for an hour or two until the coast is clear."

"Gladys, do you think we can hide these two kids for awhile?" Opie seemed happy to help and seemed to be trying to act like a father figure. His round face and bright red hair probably made him intimidating to people who didn't know him, but Rebecca could tell he was nothing but a big teddy bear.

Gladys struck a thoughtful pose, as if considering her answer carefully. "Depends on how much money they have," she said with a chuckle. "Or maybe they'd like to work off whatever tab they run up."

"Just what I was thinking myself, my dear." The two of them grinned in unison like a couple of Cheshire cats.

"Wait a minute." Jason put his hands up as if to ward off an attack. "If my manager finds out, he'll take his percentage out of my hide."

Rebecca watched the interaction among the three friends. Opie and Gladys slowly advanced on Jason while he backed up. All three of them were laughing.

"Gladys, go get the Gibson. We're going to have us some entertainment. That's how you can repay us for our services."

As understanding began to dawn on Rebecca, she added her encouragement. "Oh, yes Jase, you gotta play for us. I've not heard you sing since Houston. Please do it for me?"

Soon the few patrons at the bar realized Jason Engles was in their midst and they began to clap and cheer. Laughing at his friends' antics, Jason agreed to the arrangement with good humor.

"Bar the door, Opie, my dear," Gladys told her husband as she went in search of the guitar. "We're going to have us some fun and we don't want those camera people horning in!"

Rebecca sat by Jason's side as he accompanied himself on the guitar and sang well into the night. He performed many of his early songs from his Nashville days, and when he played his hits, the bar patrons sang along. What better way, she thought, to celebrate their engagement than to be with him while he did what he loved best.

During the course of the evening, Gladys came to sit by Rebecca. "He gets his voice from his daddy. He was a damn good singer thirty-some-odd years ago."

"You knew Jason's dad?"

"Sure. Me 'n Opie were part of Eddy Engles' band when he'd been trying to make it as a country singer. But it just wasn't in the cards."

"What happened?"

"Sarah got pregnant and there were a lot of medical bills, so Eddy had to get work on the docks. He hated that and it started him drinking." She shrugged. "And I guess you know the rest.

Hard to go touring when you've got a wife and a baby. Even harder to get good gigs when you're on the sauce."

So that was it, Rebecca thought. Jason had been afraid she'd get pregnant and then his hopes for a career would go downhill just like his father's. That was the big secret he never would talk about? Rebecca was puzzled as to why that was so shameful. But it did shed light on a few things. All that time apart for nothing. If Jason was keeping something like this a secret, what else was he hiding?

Gladys leaned over to her. "That old Gibson that Jason is playing right now belonged to Eddy. One day he just quit playing and gave the guitar to Opie. Doesn't surprise me that he took to drink after completely giving up his music like that. It does my heart good to see that old guitar come to life in the boy's hands. He sure can play."

"Yes," Rebecca agreed, her eyes on Jason. "He had the ability to reduce me to tears with his voice when we were kids and it hasn't stopped. I melt every time I hear him."

Somewhere around 2:00 a.m. they decided to call it a night. Opie and Gladys drove them to the marina and made Rebecca promise to call if she needed anything and Jason wasn't around. The two women hugged.

"Don't be a stranger. Come and visit us," Gladys said.

Jason woke the owner of the marina to find someone to ferry them to Cinnamon Bay.

"We'll get a boat of our own so we won't have to go through this every time we want to cross." He was agitated that they had to wait. "When I get bac—I mean later on, we'll buy one of those cabin cruisers. It will be small enough to dock over here or take it on down the coast."

"I don't mind using the ferry." She put her head on his shoulder and yawned sleepily. "You were wonderful tonight. Gladys said that guitar was your dad's." Rebecca hoped he would open up and tell her more about his family.

"Yeah, well..." Jason began wringing his hands and turned away from her.

When he didn't volunteer any further information, she tried a more direct route. "Gladys told me that she and Opie were in your father's band. She said she was sure he was going places when the bottom fell out. What happened?"

"Gladys has a big mouth." The dark expression on Jason's face was almost scary. She'd never seen him look so angry before.

Trying to calm him down, Rebecca placed her hand over his. She thought he wasn't going to answer her question, but finally he spoke so quietly that she almost missed it. "My sister and I happened."

"Are you telling me you still believe that your dad quit music simply because he and your mom had kids?"

"Yep. He said he had to get a real job to support the family. He told me plenty of times that if he hadn't married Mom and had us kids, he'd have been a star. Dad always said it was Mom's idea to have children. He really didn't want any."

"What a cruel thing to say," she exclaimed, hugging his arm while burying her head into his shoulder. "You poor thing. Didn't he take any responsibility? What about the fact that he liked his booze a little too much and simply gave up?" She was so upset her stomach ached. "What if your mom hadn't gotten pregnant and he'd failed anyway? He held you and your sister solely responsible? That's crazy."

"Hell, Becca, it isn't half as bad as what you went through at home. Besides, my mom was always great. I got over it." Jason stood up, running his fingers through his hair, turning back to Rebecca. "I feel bad even complaining to you."

Rebecca wondered if that was true—not being as bad as what she went through. She'd assumed that his having two parents somehow made his life more normal and less traumatic than hers. Looking down at her lap, she suddenly felt ashamed. Perhaps he shouldn't have been pushed for an explanation. Her heart ached for the pain he'd been through. She'd been there many times herself.

It was clear as day now that Jason had refused to take her with him to Nashville because his father's experience had convinced him he could never be successful with a wife or girlfriend tagging along. Especially if there was a chance she might become pregnant. His father's view of life had affected Jason — and her — deeply, whether Jase acknowledged it or not.

"We both have a ton of baggage from our youth. But we're together now, despite it all, and we can finally move on. Right?"

He studied her for a moment before bending to touch his lips to hers. She poured as much love into her response as she could, wanting him to know just how much she treasured him. After awhile he broke the kiss and looked into her eyes. "I love you, Becca. You're so good for me. Never leave me, promise?"

Rebecca abruptly stood up as if she'd been shot out of a cannon. "I love you, too, Jason. I'll always be here for you." She flung her arms around his waist, clinging to him.

That night, instead of making love, they simply fell asleep holding each other, giving and receiving love, comfort and strength. Neither one of them, Rebecca thought as she drifted off, would ever have to bear life's burdens alone again.

# Chapter Eleven

## ဆ

Rebecca woke to the sound of linen curtains flapping in the crisp morning breeze. Slightly rising from the pillow, she inhaled the salty scent of fresh sea air that flooded into the room. She liked sleeping with the windows open. At night she'd drift off to the sounds of waves lapping onto the shore, wind softly whistling through the palm trees and the mournful, eerie sound of loons off in the distance.

Of course, having the man of her dreams lying beside her was the major source of Rebecca's contentment. Goose bumps covered her skin every time she looked at him while her stomach did fluttery flips during those long moonlit walks.

In order to keep their private moments private, it was an understood rule by all that lived on the island that no one bothered Jason and Rebecca for autographs or pictures. If even the most persistent tabloid reporter showed up, poking around, the townspeople were unwelcoming and made sure to run him off. The tightly-knit community went out of its way to protect their local celebrities. Living on Cinnamon Bay with Jason was nothing short of paradise.

Oh, it felt good to stretch out on the cool cotton sheets. Jason claimed the fabric was an expensive kind of Egyptian cotton. Being a girl from her side of the tracks, she'd never heard of it, but whatever the brand, the material felt fabulous to the touch. Raising her arms above her head, Rebecca extended one leg, then the other, before turning over to find Jason gone. The kitchen was quiet and the aroma of fresh-brewing coffee—hazelnut by the smell of it—filtered into the room. Rebecca sat up, noticing that Jason's jogging shoes and cell phone were missing. He was probably out for his morning run and had started the coffee before leaving.

It was her turn to fix breakfast. She hated to get out of bed and give up all this comfort, but for Jason she would. The hardwood floor was freezing and her feet felt heavy and cold as ice cubes. She hustled around the room trying to find socks. Rummaging through Jason's dresser, she found what she needed including his Army sweatshirt and a pair of shorts. Rebecca quickly got dressed and headed out to start preparing food.

Waltzing around the kitchen, Rebecca fixed herself a cup of Joe and then took out bacon, sausage, eggs and an array of fresh vegetables from the refrigerator. Jason had been to the store the night before and restocked the fridge and cupboards. He loved breakfast food, especially her omelets, hash browns and biscuits with honey. It was so nice preparing meals for someone who appreciated them.

Her coffee was still too hot to drink, even after adding creamer and a piece of ice. Thinking it wise to let Jason's cup cool, she poured milk into a pitcher, removed another mug from the cabinet and carefully filled it. She then grabbed the newspaper and placed everything neatly on the table. Noticing that something was missing, Rebecca found her slip-ons and headed outside to the modest garden to gather flowers for a centerpiece, the crisp morning air once again causing her legs to chill.

*Oh do I have plans for this garden,* she thought, pausing on the path to pick up a pair of shears she'd forgotten to put away. *I'm going to put lilies by the porch, miniature Yucatan palms up the sidewalk and rows upon rows of vegetables toward the south end of the house.*

Rebecca had always dreamed of having a garden. There was something exciting about nurturing plants and watching them grow. Her mother never had time to fool with one, nor was there room at her tiny apartment. Now that she had all this land, maybe she'd learn to can vegetables and fruit jellies.

The distant ring tone of Revelry interrupted her daydreams. Looking around, she saw Jason down by the beach, cell phone in hand. Deep in conversation, he turned toward the house. Noticing her standing there, he waved, finished the call and trotted to her side.

"Good morning, Sunshine." He put his arms around her, dripping with sweat and breathing heavily. "Whatcha doing?"

"Morning, Sexy." With shears in one hand and flowers in the other, she rested her forearms on his hips. "I'm cutting flowers for our breakfast table."

Jason backed away. "You think of everything, don't you?" He took off his shirt and started drying off with it. "How did I ever manage without you?" he said, grinning.

"Beats me," she responded easily, especially after just witnessing him using his T-shirt as a sponge. "I've already fixed your coffee and now I'm making grand plans for this neglected patch of ground we loosely call our garden." She pointed out at the acreage.

"Aha. The woman's a wizard with plans." He walked over to the water spigot, cupping his hands for a cool drink. "Which is a good thing. You'll get to knock yourself out once the house remodeling gets going. In fact, Joe, one of my Marine buddies, has a contracting business now and he'll be coming over later with the plans." Jason wrung the water from his hands. "I guess he's been working on them for the last couple of weeks." He walked back to where Rebecca was standing, removing the shears from her grasp and placing them on a cast-iron garden bench.

His fingers were frigid from the ice-cold well water and Rebecca cringed at his touch. "Well Jason, looks like our home is in good hands with your friend, then." Rebecca sat down, placing her hands between her thighs for warmth.

"Yeah, we were together the entire four years, starting in boot camp. But he signed up for another tour when I got out." Jason looked away. "He was deployed to Iraq and wounded during the first days of the war. When Joe came back home, he started his own building business down here."

Rebecca was surprised and anxious. Anytime she met someone with a war injury, it took her back to what her uncle had been through. "Was he hurt badly?"

Jason began pacing the sidewalk, taking his time in answering. "Joe's missing an arm, Becca. An RPG hit his tent. Lots of guys died in the blast. He was one of the luckier ones."

She could see the anguish in his eyes and sensed there was more to the story. "If you say so," she said grimly.

Reaching up, he grabbed for a loose branch, yanking it from the tree. "He's bringing the prints for us to look over and you'll get to see what your new home's gonna look like."

"I can't wait." This was exciting. A real home of her own. She couldn't help but ask, "Were you on the phone with Joe just now?"

Jason paused for a moment, looking as if he'd just seen a ghost. "The phone, uh, no..." He looked concerned, disturbed.

"What's wrong?" Rebecca stood, feeling compelled to rush to his side.

Jason walked away from her to the edge of the yard, tree branch in one hand, resting his other on a corner of the house. "My mom's been looking after my apartment in Nashville and picking up my mail."

Rebecca was puzzled. "Well, what's wrong with that? Don't you want her there?"

He hit the side of the house with his open palm. "It's not my mother. A letter came today..." He turned toward her. "I was going to wait and tell you tonight."

"Tell me what?" A familiar, sickening feeling pierced her insides.

"I'm getting called up again." He stared out into the ocean. "I had Mama open the letter and read it to me this morning."

Rebecca felt a swell of emotion deep inside her. "What do you mean 'called up'? I thought you were done with all that." Rebecca threw the flowers she'd cut to the ground, waiting for some type of explanation. "Looks like the fairy-tale bubble I've been living in just burst. I knew this was too good to last."

A look of helplessness spread across his face. "I'm on inactive duty for four years. That means I can get called up whenever they need me." Jason threw his arms up in the air. "And it's my duty to go when my country calls."

All the patriotism in the world couldn't hide the anguish on his face. "I understand that, but..." She closed her eyes. God, how could this be happening? Rebecca clenched her fists in anger. Just when they had found each other again, he was leaving.

"But, what?" Jason said.

Rebecca wrapped her arms around her stomach and hugged herself tightly. "Where... Where are they sending you?"

"These days, it's going to most likely be Iraq. I'll find out pretty soon."

"Pretty soon?" Rebecca placed her hands to her face and began trembling. "Oh God." She fell to her knees. "When do you have to leave?" Tears were flowing down her face as the grass cut into the skin of her knees. "How long will we have together?"

Jason knelt down, lightly touching her shoulders while facing her. "Within about thirty days. Could be before, though." He squeezed Rebecca tightly, trying to comfort her. "And about how long we have together—how about the rest of our lives?"

Rebecca remained stunned, speechless and on the ground.

He tipped her chin so she'd look at him. "Please don't be upset. This is hard on the both of us, believe me, but I'll be back before you know it. And with the house remodel and all, you won't get bored." Jason stood, pulling Rebecca to her feet.

She wiggled her way out of his grasp, shouting, "I'm not a child who needs a toy so that she won't get bored!" She defiantly pointed a finger at him. "This will be the second time you've left me. Do you have any idea how awful I feel?"

Jason again reached for her. "I'm sorry Becca. I just thought if you had something to occupy your time, you wouldn't…"

"How dare you patronize me? I don't need a hobby—I need you." She felt a rush of heated anger—anger she couldn't control. Balling up her fists, she began pounding his chest.

Jason grabbed her wrists. "Rebecca! Stop this!" He threw her hands away from him and ran his fingers over his stinging chest.

"Stop? This is your life we're talking about. I watch the news. Don't you think I know how dangerous it is?" Rebecca walked away, unable to look at him.

Jason hesitated and then ran across the yard after her. "I'm going to have plenty of Marines around me to keep me safe. And just the thought that you're waiting for me to come home, all our thoughts and plans…well, that'll be enough to get me through anything."

Rebecca stopped walking. Her back toward him, she could feel the slight touch of his body and his moist breath against her neck. He turned her toward him, cupping her cheek. "I want to remember you happy and full of life, not mad and upset. Now, how about a smile for your soldier?"

Telling herself she had to be brave, that he didn't need to be worrying about her too, she slowly slipped her arms around his body, hugging him tight. "There's no way I can give you a smile right now, but I'll be fine. I just need a little time for all this to sink in."

He gave her a tight squeeze. "Let's look on the bright side."

Rebecca looked up at him. How could there be a bright side? "What's that?"

Jason ran his fingers through her hair. "You've got me for awhile longer. So, we need to make the most of the time we have. Let's get started on those wedding plans. Besides, there's a lot we can do here between now and then."

He tried everything to make her smile, but she didn't quite return his enthusiasm.

"Just wait until you see the architect's plans, Becca. There'll be a whole new wing just for your uncle, designed specifically to accommodate his special needs. And we'll have guide rails throughout the house so he can get around easily."

"There aren't too many men who would be willing to take a disabled person into their home. You are so very special." She hugged him closely. "I don't ever want to lose you—not to another career move, and especially not to Iraq."

Jason put his arms around her waist and gave her a teeny shake. "Now stop it. Let's agree not to spend this time worrying about what we can't change." His hands remained around her waist. "Where's that breakfast you've been promising? I want to eat as much of your home cooking as I can before I leave, 'cause soon I'll have a steady diet of MREs."

Rebecca shrugged her shoulders. "MREs?"

"That means meals ready to eat. If you can call them meals," he said with a smile.

Later that morning, the backfire of an engine startled them. Jason walked over to the window and pulled the curtain aside. "Hey, Becca, Joe's here." The screen door creaked as Jason walked out onto the porch.

Rebecca had just finished straightening up the kitchen. Tossing a dirty dishrag on the counter, she went to join him. "Wow, that was fast."

Placing his arm around her waist he said, "Yeah, he was just on the other side of the island, bidding on some condos." He removed his hands from Rebecca just as his friend was getting out of his vintage 1979 Ford.

It dawned on Rebecca that perhaps Joe might be hungry since he'd apparently been working all morning. "Jase, I'm gonna see what we have to snack on, and perhaps warm up some leftover biscuits and gravy. Joe might like something to eat."

"Thanks, darling. Just don't fix fruit. If memory serves me, he doesn't like it." Jason patted Rebecca on the bottom and eagerly opened the door for his friend. "Joe! Come on in."

Joe removed some papers from his vehicle, shutting the door and happily returning his friend's wave. "Hey, Jason! Great to see you after all these months."

Jason went to shake Joe's good hand, pulling him forward for a quick slap on the back. "It's good seeing you too. I know things were hard on you there for a while." He patted his friend once more.

He grasped Jason's hand tightly with his good one. "Well, I heard this morning you were going."

Jason looked stunned. "How?"

"Your mama called me last night. She heard from you that I was gonna be out this way today and well—she couldn't get a hold of you last night." Joe removed his hand from Jason's.

Jason took the materials his friend had neatly tucked under his arm. "Let's talk about something else. Glad to hear that business is good."

Joe removed his ball cap, wiping his brow with a blue and white handkerchief. "It may be cool this morning, but I've been running my tail off—can't complain though."

"Hey, it's what you wanted," Jason said as he rubbed his fingers together in a gesture meaning "money". "Now maybe you can get a new vehicle—one that doesn't backfire, making your customers think old man Johnson is shooting rabbits again."

The two men started laughing as they made their way into the kitchen. Joe began spreading out house plans and an old, tattered notepad on the table as they talked.

"Well, getting a lot of referrals from Mr. Country Music Star didn't hurt. Thanks, Jason." Joe gave his buddy a friendly grin. "Oh, and I don't care how many greenbacks I'm knocking down—I'd part with my wife before I'd give up that old truck."

Noticing the arch of Rebecca's eyebrow as she placed a basket of biscuits and muffins on the table, Jason hurried with the introductions. "Hey, I'd like you to meet the future Missus." Jason put an arm around Rebecca. "Joe McCoy, this is Rebecca Roberts."

"It's very nice to meet you, Joe. Jason's told me a lot about you," she said, extending her hand.

"All good, I hope?"

Rebecca grinned. "Yes, Joe. Don't worry. It was all good, I assure you."

Jason pulled out a chair for Rebecca as his friend took a seat across from the both of them. "You're a lucky man, Jason."

"Yeah, Rebecca's a sweetheart. I don't know what I'd do without her." He playfully tapped her knee.

Joe reached into the basket and removed a banana nut muffin. "What does she think about you going back to kick some butt?"

Jason tensed, quickly changing the subject. "Joe, we don't need to bore Rebecca with all that military stuff."

Rebecca snapped, "Don't talk about me like I'm not here. I can speak for myself." Jason ducked his head as if to hold his tongue. "To answer your question—I'm not thrilled with any of this. In fact, I hate the whole idea of him going over to that hellhole. If you'll excuse me." She quickly stood and walked into the other room, busying herself with housework.

Rebecca could hear the men whispering. She could only assume it was about his deployment and her hysterical reaction.

After regaining her composure a few minutes later, she returned. "I'm sorry about awhile ago guys." Sensing the awkwardness of the moment, she quickly changed the subject. "Let's look at those blueprints." It took all the effort she could manage to sound upbeat and happy. "Joe, can I get you something to drink?"

"I'm fine, but thanks anyway." Joe winked. "So you want to keep parts of the old house intact, is that right?"

"Yeah. I figured that the original structure could become a huge kitchen with a big hearth and family room. The remainder of the place will spread out from there. I wanted the kitchen to be roomy and cozy for family dinners with a bunch of rowdy kids running around the table, harassing Grandma."

At the mention of family, Rebecca felt nauseous. What if Jason didn't come back? Continuing to look at Joe made her worry about Jason in combat. Then there were thoughts of her own physical ailment. She could never have children. How could she tell him now? With him leaving, it wasn't the best time to discuss old problems.

She would have wanted more than anything to have Jason's children — to hear them running through the house laughing and playing. It would be her family to love and nurture. But she knew that wasn't possible. Her womb was too scarred to conceive a baby.

Rebecca continued listening to the men talk as Joe kept taking notes. It should have been a happy day, but instead the entire morning made her uncomfortable with Jason leaving, war talk, children and now all the decisions regarding the house being made for her. It was as if she had no say in her own life. Perhaps this was more than she'd bargained for.

She knew Jason was doing what he thought best, and even though everything she'd seen so far was wonderful, part of her still wished he had asked her opinion on things. But even though it was rough, she reminded herself to focus on the positive.

"What about company?" Rebecca smiled.

"We'll build a small guest house out back. It will be a nice getaway for the band and I have a feeling Rick and Whit will end up crashing here quite often. A guest house will ensure their privacy." He took her hand.

"Oh, I love that idea." The thought of her friend being able to stay whenever she wanted thrilled her.

The group sat discussing house plans most of the morning. Joe made lists of all the things Jason wanted—from the finest fixtures to skylights, walk-in closets with timer lights, pillar columns around the master bathroom Jacuzzi tub and an indoor swimming pool complete with imported blue Spanish clay tiles that were equipped with heat strips.

Joe removed his hat, scratching his head. "This will take at least nine, ten months to complete, if not a year."

"That's fine. You know the budget, so whatever needs to be done," Jason voiced his approval.

"I know something I'd like added." Rebecca got up from her chair and leaned over the designs.

She had been so quiet, the men seemed surprised by the sound of her voice. "What's that darling? Just say it and Joe will build it."

"I'd love a writing studio. It would be nice to have a comfortable room that had a view of the ocean." She lightly squeezed Jason's arm and smiled.

Joe cleared his throat and reshuffled the pages on his notepad. "Any other specifics you'd like in this room, Ms. Rebecca?"

Her face lit up with excitement. "I'd like to have one wall full of bookshelves and a place for a sound system. I love listening to music while writing."

"You know Becca, it would be nice if you also had some type of bench or seat next to the windows—a place where you could stretch out and totally relax while you're composing."

Rebecca leaned over, throwing her arms around Jason. "That's a wonderful idea. Your mom had something similar in her house in front of the bay windows."

"That's one of the few things dad ever did for her. She loved to sit next to that window and work on her cross-stitch." Jason seemed a little sentimental. "I'm just glad I can do things like this for you. A few years ago, I could barely put food on the table. Now I can give you elegant dinners, trips and whatever else your little heart desires."

In the long, sultry weeks that followed, the couple took full advantage of the beach, going for refreshing afternoon swims and romantic evening dips. Jason would spend his mornings working out and jogging, readying himself for duty. Rebecca rarely joined him, unable to keep up with his stringent pace. Running in sand was especially hard for her. She didn't know how Jason could do it several times a day. But there were plenty of other things to occupy her besides joining in on Jason's workout sessions.

During her alone time, she concentrated on cleaning their home, rearranging furniture as different parts of the house were completed and gardening. Some days she'd head inland to do the shopping until hooking up with Jason later in the afternoon. Their evenings were just as exciting as that first night together — passion-filled. Rebecca smiled as she looked around the rooms of their home. She and Jason had christened nearly every room. She took special enjoyment from their steamy interlude in the laundry room. Jason gave a whole other dimension to the words "spin cycle". Whether it was the bedroom or the laundry, Rebecca found it hard to sleep afterward and would quietly slip from between the covers and write. It was all so perfect.

Sitting on the screened porch, Rebecca pored over the gardening books and manuals she'd acquired on her last trip to the mainland. The thought of actually seeing plants and flowers grow from seeds was very exciting. She'd never tell Jason, but she was almost more excited about being able to have a garden than about the fabulous house.

Thinking about their home always made her feel a little sad. It reminded her of all the rooms Jason planned to fill with kids. The secret was killing her. Perhaps she would tell him before he left for the Gulf. Maybe she'd make a special meal and then they'd talk afterward. It took years for her to come to terms with her infertility, and not knowing how Jason would react was tearing her heart out. She knew he wanted a boy to carry on his name more than anything. But she'd just have to think about all that later.

Voices and laughter caught her attention. Rebecca put her books on the floor. Walking outside, she blocked the sun with her hand. At first, all she could see was an empty, wide stretch of beach. Continuing to follow the noise, she found Jason throwing a football to the neighbor boys from down the road. Not knowing what to expect from the big Country Star, the boys had been shy at first. Once they realized he was willing to play ball or simply shoot the breeze with them, they just "happened" by almost every day.

Today, these scenes were bothering her. Rebecca turned from the beach toward the house. It made her heart ache watching him down there, playing enthusiastically. He would have made such a great father. The voices came closer and she hurriedly walked into the house. She knew they could use something cool to drink.

"Hey, Becca," Jason called out. "Look, I've brought company."

She popped open the screen door just in time to see Jason take the stairs two at a time, followed by a couple of freckle-faced boys.

Jason patted Rebecca on the shoulder and headed for the utility room, probably to put the ball away. "Football is thirsty work, woman."

She forced a smile. "I'm one step ahead of you. Ice is already in the glasses and there's plenty of juice and soda in the fridge." It was hard for Rebecca to tell whether Jason had heard her or not—she hadn't gotten a response from him. "I'll be there in a bit. Okay?"

When she didn't receive an answer, Rebecca headed for the porch. Sitting in her favorite wicker chair, she picked up her books and tried to read, but she couldn't concentrate. The men were making too much noise rummaging around the kitchen, talking and laughing. She kept to the porch, knowing that there was no way she'd be able to put on a happy face.

As the back door slammed shut, the two boys ran through the yard toward the beach. Rebecca tensed as a warm hand rested upon her shoulder. "What's wrong, Becca?" Jason massaged her shoulder with his fingers. "How come you didn't stay in the kitchen with us? I hate seeing you out here all alone."

"Wrong?" She linked her fingers, clasping her hands together.

"I don't want to say that I can read you like a book because I can't, but I sure can tell that something's wrong." He leaned around her, kissing her cheek. "When I came in with those kids, you looked like you were upset. Do those boys bother you? Is it that I'll be leaving soon?"

"No," she shook her head. "I was watching you down at the beach, and…"

She stood, walked to the end of the porch and leaned against a wooden post. This was it. She had to tell him. The idea of Jason planning this wonderful house for a family and keeping this kind of secret from him was too much to bear.

Rebecca began wringing her hands. The worried look on her face was bound to prompt a lot of questions, but she needed to get this out in her own time. "You remember how that first night at the hotel I said I wouldn't get pregnant?"

"There's nothing I don't remember about that first night, sweetheart." He hugged her waist as he drew her near.

Rebecca covered her face, his gentleness making it even harder to tell him.

"Well, I didn't mean I couldn't get pregnant that night." She paused and took a deep breath. "I meant I couldn't get pregnant — ever."

She heard Jason's quick intake of breath and waited for him to say something, but he remained silent. Rebecca gazed at him, but his head was down and his eyes hidden by his hair.

"When you were talking to Joe about rooms for the kids, I wanted to cry. And when I watched you today with those boys, I thought you would make such a great dad." She took a deep, shivering breath. "Jason, it makes me so sad to know that I can't ever give you children."

Since he didn't take his hands off her waist to hug her, she wondered if he was angry or just stunned. She was scared and didn't want to look too deeply into his eyes. More than anything, Rebecca needed him to give her a hug, something— anything. When he didn't, her body trembled with panic.

She stared away and out at the beach, hoping he'd make more physical contact with her soon. "I'm sorry that I didn't tell you before, Jason. But I was so afraid of spoiling…"

"Look at me, Rebecca," he said quietly. She turned as her gaze met his.

"Did you think I would love you any less because you can't have children?" He gestured for her hand. "What kind of man would I be if that were true?"

Rebecca gave a little, timid shrug. How did you tell someone that your own mother had scarred your body in such a way that she'd ruined you for life?

Jason put his arms around Rebecca, pressing her against his body. "I love you for you. Nothing will ever change that. As long as we have each other, we can figure out anything else."

His embrace made her feel whole, loved and secure. It was so comforting to have his understanding. Leaning into his shoulder, tears burned the back of her eyes and she started to cry.

He maneuvered her over to the wicker loveseat and settled her in his lap. Words remained unspoken. For comfort, Jason stroked her hair from time to time. After her tears subsided to an occasional hiccup, he kissed the top of her head. "How did you find out?"

"I was… I had an accident." She looked down at her hands. "I—I fell down the stairs, and…"

He tilted her face up to his. "Did JoAnne do this to you?"

She nodded. "It was a couple of months after I graduated from high school. We were arguing over money and she kicked me. I lost my balance and fell. My body hit all thirteen steps on the way down." Her eyes filled with tears again as she remembered. "The fall knocked me out, but she must have gone on kicking me after I fell unconscious. I don't know what would have happened if Uncle Burt hadn't come along when he did, and as usual, good ol' Whit was there in the hospital with me."

Looking up at him, she saw his jaw tighten with anger. "It's a good thing that woman isn't here right now," he said in a crumbling voice, "because I don't know if I'd be able to control myself."

Rebecca hugged his neck but couldn't speak.

His eyes remained dark and desperate. "It's my fault. If I hadn't been so selfish…if I hadn't left…"

Rebecca touched his lips to silence him. "You couldn't have known."

Jason pounded his fist against the chair. "I should have known. I knew she hit you—the cuts—the bruises. There's no reason why you couldn't have come to Nashville with me. I'm such an ass."

"I understand why you left. We both have carried deep-seated guilt around—me for the scar on your face and you for leaving me. But all that's in the past now, Jase." She stroked her hand down his cheek. "I'm just glad you're not angry that I didn't tell you before. I want more than anything to give you a child. It's like I've been living a lie."

Jason grabbed her face. "You look at me." His fingers caressed her cheek. "I love you, Becca. There's nothing that we can't face together. Besides, we can always adopt. I wouldn't love those children any differently because they weren't my blood." He kissed her again. "And you're perfect just the way you are."

"You are the gentlest, kindest man I've ever met. I love you more right now than I have in my whole lifetime." She curled further into his lap and buried her head securely against his chest.

That night Rebecca relaxed in a hot bath scented with lavender oil and thick, silky bubbles. Winding her hair up in a terry towel, she sank deeper into a lathery abyss as the warm water caressed her skin. The bubbles and flowery aroma allowed her total relaxation. Thoughts of their lovemaking to come later that night flooded her with inner warmth. She was hoping to smell like a temptress and look like a sex machine. After what that wonderful man said to her earlier, he deserved a night of unbridled passion.

Letting out a deep sigh, she moved her arms freely in the water. Things would certainly be interesting. Would Jason look at her differently because of what she'd told him? Would the day come when he would regret his decision to stay? She closed her eyes. These questions would end up driving her crazy if she kept asking herself them. All she could do was take things as they came. Right now, the most important thing was for Jason to come home alive and healthy.

Wrapping herself in a plush bathrobe of black cashmere that Jason had bought, she slowly opened the bathroom door and peered into the bedroom. Jason was leaning back against the pillows, legs stretched out, barefoot and hands resting atop his stomach. He was lightly breathing and his eyes were closed.

Rebecca knelt down on top of the quilt facing him. "Penny for your thoughts."

He opened his eyes and smiled at her. "They should be worth at least a nickel these days." He stretched out a hand toward her. "You're awfully far away."

Rebecca took his hand, holding it in both of hers, but stayed where she was.

"If you're holding out for a report on my thoughts, I was just daydreaming, I guess." He must have seen the question in her eyes because he added, "Mostly about you."

What could he be thinking? She wished he'd share his thoughts.

"C'mon over here, sweetheart." He gave her hands a tug. "I need to hold you."

Unable to resist an invitation like that, she snuggled up to him and rested her head on his shoulder.

He lightly rubbed the side of her head, twirling her hair around his fingers. "Becca, I know you wanted a nice church wedding with a beautiful gown and all the trimmings, but we won't have time for that before I have to leave."

"It'll keep until you get back. Our wedding can be your welcome home celebration." She looked up at him and nuzzled his chin. "We can have the ceremony right here. I've always wanted a beach wedding. My gown will be formal, but not elaborate and you'll wear tuxedo pants and a crisp white shirt. The bridesmaids can wear simple spaghetti strap sundresses with orchids in their hair. We can say our vows as the water rises over our toes. How does all of that sound?"

Jason stopped winding her hair around his fingers. "It sounds wonderful, but we really ought to tie the knot before I leave."

"Why?" Needing to look at his face, she sat up. She could see that his eyes were worried.

"If we're married, you'll be entitled to benefits if anything happens…"

"No!" She put her fingers against his lips to silence him. "You're not going to say that. You're not even going to think it." Hearing him talk like this broke her heart.

"Becca, listen to me." He pulled her over to him again and cradled her like a baby. "I know what I'm doing. My buddies over there know what they're doing. And coming back home to you is the biggest incentive a guy could have. But things happen. We have to think about that. Man, I could just kick myself for not taking that spot with the military band. I could be entertaining the troops instead of seeing combat. I had to be a hardhead."

"No." She shook her head. "If we get married right now just because you're leaving, I'll feel like I'm expecting something bad to happen." Reaching up, she put her arms around his neck. "You'll come back to me safe and sound. I just know it." She prayed that her words were true. "Make love with me, Jason." Rebecca kissed him urgently. "Make love with me now."

Two weeks went by, and then another. Some days, Rebecca could almost convince herself that things were normal and that Jason would be staying home, yet she couldn't help but jolt every time the phone rang or cringe whenever she saw Jason's packed duffel bag that sat in a corner of their bedroom. That awful thing was a constant reminder of his impending deployment.

Everything about their life had an urgency to it. When Jason wasn't exercising or getting business affairs in order, he worked hard alongside Joe and his crew. Even their lovemaking had a desperate feeling to it because they never knew if this would be the last time.

One night, she emerged from her bath to see him waiting for her in bed. As she unsnapped her hair tie, she noticed a single candle burning on the nightstand, which made his tanned skin gleam like bronze. The heavily scented candle filled the room with vanilla, tantalizing her senses.

"Are you waiting for someone, fella?" she teased, walking toward him with a swing to her hips while whipping her hair around and playing with the drawstring to her robe.

His face sported a blank stare. It wasn't quite the reaction she was going for. "Becca, I got a call earlier today…"

Warning bells rang in her head. This was it. This was the moment she'd been dreading. "I don't think I want to hear what you're about to tell me."

"Probably not." He ran a hand through his hair. "It's time. I've been called up. I have to leave first thing in the morning."

"Oh my God. Jason," she said, placing a hand over her mouth. Her legs felt weak, as if they were going to buckle under her. Slowly, she made her way to the bed where she sat down. She felt betrayed, not by her beloved, but by time. It was always a time issue with their relationship—it was a culprit that would never truly go away. He'd probably known all day, waiting until the last minute to tell her. He always did that, trying to protect her in some way. Struggling for words, Rebecca said, "You said you had thirty more days. That means another week." Getting more emotional by the moment, she reached for a pillow. All she wanted to do was bury her head in it and scream.

Jason grabbed the pillow. "Yeah, Rebecca, but it's like I told you—the order comes with a disclaimer to pack your bags and be ready at a moment's notice."

"We've had so little time together. I can't believe this is happening." She pulled away from him as he went to touch her.

"Honey, I'm sorry, but there's nothing I can do." He reached for her again, pulling her next to him.

She sat still, showing little emotion at his touch. "I feel like I'm losing you all over again."

"It's only temporary, sweetheart." He tried hugging her for comfort. "And with any kind of luck, my job won't be dangerous. My CO told me I'd be working primarily out of one of the makeshift bases in Baghdad."

"Baghdad?" She pulled away from his grasp, staring at him in horror. "That's the most dangerous place in the world right now. Why you?"

"It's all right, Becca. Just calm down." He stroked her back, trying to soothe her. "Please don't cry, and don't worry so much. I can't bear your being this upset. Besides, remember what you said about my coming back safe and sound? You just hold that thought."

"I feel sick." She once again squirmed out of his embrace.

Jason stood up, reaching for her. "Becca..."

"No, Jase, I feel...sick." She covered her mouth with one hand and ran into the bathroom, dropping to her knees in front of the toilet. Feeling dizzy, she threw up while Jason came to her aid, pinning her hair back with his hand. He knelt beside her, holding a cool cloth to her forehead until she felt better. Then he gently carried her back to bed. Jason hurried to the kitchen, retrieving a bottle of water to help break the acidic taste in her mouth.

Jason placed his hand underneath Rebecca's head, propping her up so she could take a sip of water. "I can't bear to see you this upset, Becca. When I see you cry or get sick, it just tears me up inside."

She finished taking a drink, wiping a tear from her eye. "I know I'm supposed to be strong. I guess I wasn't as prepared for your leaving as I thought."

"Becca, you do need to be strong—for me. I can't do my job and stay alive over there if I'm worrying about you being sick back here." He removed the bottle of water from her hand and caressed her forehead.

"I know. I'm sorry." She tried again for a smile. "But I'm going to miss and worry about you so much."

"I'm going to miss you, too and probably think about you every second—especially what's underneath that robe." He tugged her closer, grinning.

Rebecca halfheartedly smiled back. "If you think you're getting under this robe after that remark Jason Engles, you are sorely mistaken." She nuzzled her face close to his, taking a finger and tracing the outline of his lips. God how she wished she could etch this moment into her memory forever.

"I'll make some calls tomorrow morning and arrange for your uncle to come stay here with you while I'm gone. And

Steve can help you with Burt while you're working on the house. You might even be able to crank out some songs." He squeezed her tightly. "And I won't be out of touch completely. The military will let me call occasionally, and then there's e-mail."

"You don't have the greatest record of keeping in touch," she said miserably.

"Come on, baby. Don't hold the past against me, okay? Even if I do deserve it." He sat up. "I'm not as poor as I was that first time. I've got a credit card with a hefty limit, so those expensive per minute Internet fees aren't going to stop me from e-mailing you."

Rebecca tried her best to smile. She rubbed her hand over his chest and hoped that everything would be okay.

"Hey, Rick and Whit can come and visit. The band won't be doing much with me gone. And Whitney probably won't object to spending plenty of weekends here with Rick. I can have a plane shuttle them back and forth. Time will fly by. You'll see."

Jason was right. She did have to be strong for his sake. She didn't want him worrying about her when he should be paying attention to keeping himself safe. Tamping down her runaway emotions, she hugged him tightly. "I'll be fine, Jason. I'll hold down the fort while you're away. I promise."

"That's my girl." He gave her an encouraging smile. "By the time I get back, the house will be all done and we can think about adopting. I'd love to hear tiny voices filling the hallways with songs when I come home."

Rebecca nodded again, her heart overflowing with love. "What time do you have to leave?"

"Five o'clock." He reached for the belt of her bathrobe. "Now, how about you remind me what's under this robe one more time before I go?"

Rebecca awoke not to the feeling of a sea breeze blowing across her face, but to Jason's lips brushing her forehead.

"Jason…" She struggled to sit up.

"Shh, sweetheart." He perched on the edge of the bed. "I didn't get you up on purpose. In fact, I almost wanted to leave while you were still sleeping. You looked so peaceful." Leaning forward, he gave her a soft kiss. "I wanted to carry that picture of you with me over there to that sand pit."

Rebecca shook her head in disbelief. "Didn't you think I'd want to say goodbye? To see you off properly?" She couldn't keep the annoyance out of her voice. "I would have been pretty mad if you'd snuck off without waking me." She forcefully pulled him toward her.

"I knew you were up most of the night. Besides, I thought I'd spare us both a sad goodbye. And I wanted to take my memory of you lying in our bed, in my T-shirt, with those beautiful long legs of yours tangled in the covers." He urged her back down. "Stay in bed, Becca. Go back to sleep and have sweet dreams of me."

"When does your flight leave?" She flung her legs over the side of the bed, once again trying to get up.

"I've got to be at the airstrip by six-thirty. From there it's off to Camp LeJeune. I'll get my orders on to Iraq from there."

Rebecca tried to hold back the tears. While missing him was something she was all too familiar with, this goodbye seemed harder to get through. She thrust her arms around his chest and kissed him, wanting, needing to put all her love into that embrace so that their bond would never break.

Suddenly she felt dizzy and sick to her stomach, but she tried to ignore it, not wanting to let Jason see how upset she was at his leaving.

"What's the matter?" he asked worriedly.

She could barely even look at him. "Nothing. I'm just going to miss you."

"I've got to catch the ferry. The next one leaves in fifteen minutes." He kissed her one more time. "Please, don't get up, Becca. I want to remember you just like this."

As the front door shut, Rebecca jumped out of bed. Running to the living room, she flung open the shades just in time to see Jason getting into a waiting car. He paused for a moment to take another look at the house.

Apparently Joe was taking him to the ferry. But Rebecca wasn't about to miss sending him off.

She ran back to the bedroom, throwing on a pair of jeans, flip-flops and sweatshirt. There was no time for a shower or makeup. Not this morning. She ran back to the phone and dialed it quickly.

"Don, this is Rebecca Roberts. I need you to get your boat ready. I've got to get to the mainland." Rebecca paced back and forth between the kitchen table and fireplace. "No, you don't understand. I need to beat the ferry there. Well, actually I have to get to the airport right away." Rebecca continued her frenzied conversation as she ran around the house looking for her purse and phone. "Okay, I can do that." She said slipping her flip-flops on. "Great. I'll be at the boat ramp in five minutes. Oh, and Don, don't tell anyone you're taking me, including Jason, if you happen to see him."

After finding her keys Rebecca ran from the house into the morning fog. Jumping into Jason's old Jeep, she headed for the charter boats. It was a relief to see Don already waiting. Clutching her purse, she opened the door and jumped out. Sensing a movement behind her, she turned around in time to see the vehicle starting to roll. Rebecca quickly reached inside, bumping her knees against the sharp metal, putting the Jeep into park. Lord, she thought, she'd been so intent on getting to the airport that she hadn't even done that. Good thing she wasn't driving. She slammed the door and ran to the waiting boat.

"Don, I'm glad you're here. Jason leaves for Iraq this morning. He didn't want me to see him off—thought I'd be too teary. But I don't want to miss him." She reached for his arm. "I can't miss him. Please hurry."

Motioning her to quickly get situated, Don revved the motor. "Don't you worry. I'll get you there." He gave her a huge, toothless grin. Don seemed happy someone needed him. "Hold onto your hat. I'll open this thing up as fast as she'll go. You won't miss Jason. Promise."

"How do I get to the airport from the docks?"

"Don't worry about that. My brother will take you." Don began concentrating on the sea ahead. "The ferry didn't leave too long ago. We should get you to the mainland just after it."

Rebecca pulled the hood of her sweatshirt up so her hair wouldn't beat her to death. "Good, Don. Thank you."

Don took his eyes off the sea for a moment. "How come we didn't read anything about Jason leaving in the newspaper?" He looked puzzled. "I thought those gossipers over at the paper knew everything. Hell, Jason's the biggest news story we've ever had."

"He didn't want anyone knowing. The government is usually pretty tight-lipped about deployments anyway." Rebecca clutched her purse, shivering. The morning air was cooler than she'd expected.

The twenty-minute boat ride seemed like hours. The waves were choppy, and Rebecca's stomach heaved, but she wasn't going to let a little seasickness stop her from seeing her future husband off. God, she hoped she got there in time. It was a small, private airport with a locked security gate. There was no way to page or call him, unless he was outside with his cell on waiting to board.

As Don's brother and Rebecca approached the airport, there was no sign of a plane. Her stomach sank. That's it, she thought. Everything was quiet. She must have missed him. Then the loud twang of airplane engines could be heard off in the distance. Frantically searching for a takeoff, she heard some sputtering noises and then saw the propellers of a twin-engine plane revving up behind a nearby hangar.

Oh, God, where was the cell phone, in case Jason made one last call to her? Rebecca desperately searched for it, finally finding it at the bottom of her purse. She held the phone tightly in her hand, her finger on the button. Now if he called her, she'd be ready.

Rebecca watched the plane pull onto the runway, getting prepped for takeoff. Her fingers grasped the chain link fence separating her from the airstrip. He wasn't going to call, she thought. Oh, please, she prayed, I want to hear his voice one more time.

The second the phone in her hand vibrated, she had it at her ear. "Yes?" She was breathless as if she'd been with Jason during one of his jogging rituals.

"Becca! I just wanted to tell you one more time that I love you. I'll miss you, sweetheart. I wish you were here."

"Jase, look out the window." She was crying and laughing at the same time. "I am here!" And she waved her arms with all her might.

The boat ride back to the island was a somber one. She barely noticed the sun starting to break through the fog or the birds fishing for their breakfasts. Her sides ached from stomach cramps. The water was tranquil now and a slight, salty breeze caressed her face, but all she could think about was Jason and the all too brief time they'd spent together in their new home. Images of his smiling face, his sensual body and the way he'd made love to her so tenderly flashed through her mind. Oh, to have him touch her, hug her just one more time—she'd give anything.

She fought back tears and clutched the cell phone tightly to her chest. For months it and her laptop would be her only lifelines to Jason. Maybe he'd call one more time on his way to North Carolina. Not likely, but possible, and if he did, she'd be ready for him with words of encouragement and support. Rebecca promised herself that no matter how she was feeling, she'd smile and sound happy when talking to him.

All Rebecca knew was that right now she just couldn't face that empty house. Not yet. She'd go back in an hour or two when Joe and the workmen were there. At least then she wouldn't be entirely alone. For now, she'd go down to the beach. Maybe being by the water would make her feel better — soothe her aching soul and tired heart. God, how she wished Whit were with her now. She could sure use a hug and a joke or two. Hopefully, Whitney was having a better time on her adventure than she was.

As she started the Jeep, the engine groaned and sputtered but wouldn't fire up. "Oh, great," Rebecca mumbled aloud. "This is the last straw."

The sun was out now and she leaned over, rummaging through the glove box for her sunglasses. Too much sun always gave her a headache, and that was the last thing she needed today of all days. Not being able to find her glasses, she leaned forward, laid her head on top of her hands on the steering wheel and sat quietly with only thoughts of Jason to keep her company.

Finally, it seemed she had no more tears to cry. Rebecca sat up, found some tissues and decided to give the truck another try. This time it started, and she headed out of the parking lot. A mile down the road, she pulled into an unfamiliar lot next to the beach. It looked as good a place as any for a walk. The best part was that it was completely deserted. She didn't have to talk to anyone.

Even though the sun was out, a slight nip in the air warned of an approaching storm. Rebecca tucked her hands into her oversized sweatshirt sleeves and began walking. It was one of Jason's old shirts. His Burberry cologne still clung to the soft material. Burrowing her nose deeper into the scent, she walked quickly, just needing to move. She had no eyes for her surroundings — just the image of Jason the last time he had kissed her.

They'd been so happy, and she so hopeful when they were together. It had seemed as if their lives stretched out before them like the pearly white beach where she walked. In that space of time no longer than a breath, she'd gone from the highest point of her entire life to one of the lowest—setting all the incidents with her mother aside. Not in a million years had she thought this could have happened to her again. At least seven years ago when Jason left, she hadn't had to fear for his life. Now he could be injured or killed.

It was just too awful to think about. No, she chided herself silently. Just like she'd said to Jason, she wouldn't even let that possibility into her consciousness. She concentrated on the breaking waves crashing down around her bare feet. The tidal waters were cool and foamy. The sand felt rough and wonderful against her skin. There was a slight fishy smell to the air. The fishing boats were out in the dozens.

The sun cast an orange-red reflection on top of the water. Jason had told her that was how the town got its name, Cinnamon Bay. The water looked like cinnamon sprinkling the white shoreline. For the first time that morning, she truly took in the beauty around her. She would draw strength from that, she promised herself. From the power of the ocean, the beauty of the sun on the water. If there was ever a day she needed strength, today was the day.

Taking a deep breath, she turned around to retrace her steps. It was time to head home.

By the time Rebecca returned, Joe and his crew were hard at work. The minute Joe saw her, he put down his clipboard, came over, and put his arm around her.

"How are you feeling?"

Rebecca shrugged her shoulders. "Probably about as good as I look. I feel like one of your machines chewed me up and spit me out."

"C'mon, let's get you a cup of coffee." Joe held open the screen door.

They went inside and Joe made her sit at the kitchen table while he made coffee. She watched him, amazed at how well he did with only one arm.

"Drink up, kiddo." He went to work cleaning up the mess he'd made on the counter.

She took a couple of sips, but the coffee made her stomach jumpy again, and she set it down.

Joe grinned as he walked over to Rebecca. "He'll be okay. He knows what he's doing, and so do the other guys." He patted her on the back.

"Thanks, Joe." Rebecca rubbed her temple where a headache was beginning to build. Joe was a constant reminder to her of what could happen. Whoever was in charge that night didn't do a very good job of taking care of him.

"Rebecca, are you feeling all right?" He looked at her with concern.

"Migraine, my friend."

Joe went to the cupboard, retrieving some medicine. "Hey, would you like us to take off today? You look like you could use some rest, and we'll just be pounding and banging all day."

"Would you?" She felt a wave of relief. The onset of this headache had changed her mind about having company. "I'd really appreciate that."

He smiled, appearing to be happy he'd helped out. "Consider it done. Will you be okay by yourself? I can have my wife come by a little later if you'd like some company."

"I'll be okay." She mustered the best smile she could. "I just need to get some rest."

Within an hour, everyone was gone and the only sounds she could hear were waves crashing and birds off in the distance.

What a day. It had all the makings of a sad country song. Maybe she ought to sit herself down and get some more songwriting done. It would help her get all the turmoil she was feeling out of her system. Besides, it seemed she always did her best work when her life was at its lowest points. And today was certainly low.

Rebecca remembered how the crowd had reacted to the song she had written for Jason, and the memory made her feel warm inside. There hadn't been many songs written since Jason came back into her life. She sometimes wrote in the afternoons and of course late at night, but that limited time was going to change. Now she should concentrate on her writing full-time. It would be great to channel all these emotions into lyrics.

Maybe it was time to heed Jason's advice and take her songwriting to an entirely different level. And what better time to write than now? She'd surprise him with some new lyrics when he returned, and that would be her homecoming gift to him. Yes, J.R. Neels becoming a huge success would make for a great present. Gathering up pen and paper, she went out onto the screened porch where she could see the ocean and began a new chapter in her life.


Rebecca awoke to the sound of Joe's team banging and hammering. She'd stayed up until the wee hours of the morning, putting pen to paper. She was surprised that, given her fragile emotional state, she'd actually written some decent poetry for lyrics.

The construction crew had begun tearing into the walls at the back of the house. Guys were stapling up plastic and hammering plywood into place so the elements and critters wouldn't get in. She peered out the window and noticed all the tools and equipment littering the front yard. The house looked like a demolition zone. Even though she'd seen the plans and the renderings, it was hard to believe that something beautiful would emerge from the ruins.

Deciding it was time to get up, Rebecca thought it would be nice to make Joe and the guys coffee or something cold to drink.

Last night, as she was searching for more paper, she'd noticed all kinds of treasures Jason had packed away—awards he'd won, copies of his videos, family pictures and knickknacks. She'd start going through all the boxes soon, putting things into their proper places. Since the house would remain largely intact as part of the new one, she'd have a lot of cleaning to do. So she went from room to room, investigating their contents and evaluating what work needed to be done.

The previous owners had left the furniture they'd used in their summer home. Most of the stuff just needed a good dusting, while other pieces could be stained, refinished, or painted. She could do that herself, she thought as she pulled out a piecrust table that had seen better days. It would be fun, dragging the old stuff out into the yard and refinishing it the way she wanted. And since she loved to cook for Jason, she'd have to meet with Joe some morning before he got too busy and see what was in store for the kitchen remodeling.

Soon her lonely days turned into busy weeks. Joe and the crew made progress on the house, but the place was still a wreck. There were construction materials, dirt and sheetrock dust everywhere. She tried to keep up with the constant cleaning and laundry that ensued, but she felt tired, as if she'd been fighting a flu bug. It seemed that she never got nearly as much done as she wanted because she seemed to end up taking a nap almost every afternoon.

She called her uncle frequently, and talking to him was often the highlight of her day.

After fixing the construction men coffee, Rebecca headed for the phone. "Are you still liking it at the resort, Uncle Burt?"

"It's nice, but I'm not used to all these people taking care of me. I'm just a country boy, Rebecca. It's almost too much." He sighed.

"So you don't like it," she teased him.

His voice dipped down a bit. "No, it's not that."

"Why don't you just admit that it's a treat to be taken care of like that? Neither one of us have ever had that kind of treatment before Jason."

"Okay, Becca. You win." He laughed. "I love it. I love everything except the curried chicken on the room service menu. It's meat and potatoes for me."

"See, that wasn't so hard now, was it? Just stay away from the chicken." She laughed and jumped in place as if she'd won some type of small victory.

Burt paused for a moment, "I'm worried about something, though."

"What is it?" Rebecca tensed up.

"We left in such a hurry that I forgot to take my metal strongbox with me. It's got my military medals in it, you know, and there are a couple of your songs in there, too. I worry about it going missing."

Rebecca bit her lip. She'd forgotten about it as well. She wouldn't put it past JoAnne to throw it out if she ever found it. "I wouldn't worry about it, Uncle Burt. It's way in the back under your bed. No way JoAnne is going to find it there. It's not like she is going to be doing any cleaning in there."

He sighed deeply again. "Well, if you say so," Uncle Burt grumbled.

Rebecca's stomach was starting to feel queasy. She walked over to the counter to boil some water for tea. "I'll come visit as soon as I get over this bug and we'll go get it together. Next week maybe."

"Don't worry about traveling if you're not feeling well, honey. Take care of yourself, you hear?"

"I will, Uncle Burt."

She hung up and made a note to make arrangements for a trip back to Texas.

# Chapter Twelve

ഇ

"I'm never gonna get through this mess by noon. I wish my supervisor would fall off the face of the Earth," Whitney grumbled under her breath as she looked at her cluttered desk in disgust. "This is definitely one of those good, stiff margarita days."

Originally, she'd liked her job after the promotion had come through, but now the warehouse job was becoming repetitive and boring. Not knowing what new requisition form to fill out first, she leaned forward, tapping a pencil against her keyboard. She stared at the screen, unable to concentrate as her thoughts drifted off to the argument she'd had with Rick the night before. Women were always hitting on him, and he'd been a ladies' man for years. What made her think he could or would change overnight and love only her?

That must be why he wasn't taking her home to meet his family. Committing to her completely was apparently more than he was willing to do, and her heart ached as she thought of it. Still, she knew she'd miss him terribly while he was away. Any part of him was better than nothing at all and ten days was a long time to be apart.

She jumped as the sound of the phone suddenly sliced through the silence, startling her back to reality.

"Ms. Whitney."

"Yes, Gloria." She frowned.

"The boss wants to see you. Says it's urgent. He's waiting in the conference room."

"Okay. Be right there." She leaned forward and rested her head in her hands.

Damn, she thought, her boss must have found out about the screw-up with the Cincinnati shipment. Like nobody ever over-ordered an extra five thousand parts before. She'd been in a big hurry to see Rick that day. The job might be boring, but it paid well and she needed it. But there was no time to think about that now, or dream up explanations. Apparently her feeble attempt at a cover-up hadn't worked. It was time to tuck tail and take what was coming. She grabbed a legal pad and a pen and headed down the hallway toward occupational demise.

As Whitney entered the reception area, she gave Gloria a puzzled glance. The pleasantly plump, gray-haired spinster was looking at her over her horn-rimmed glasses with an odd expression on her face. Whitney knew that Gloria had never been any good at hiding her emotions. So why did she have this flustered, excited look in her eyes?

The receptionist turned to look at the conference area, situated directly behind her desk. The door was shut and drapes drawn.

"Ah…is the boss man still in there, Gloria?" Whitney said with a lilt of hope in her voice. Maybe he'd left.

"Yep," Gloria said as she pointed a pen toward the closed door.

Whitney's mind quickly went to work on a plan to avoid termination. "Think I should show cleavage or leg?"

Gloria shook her head. "Don't think either will help in this situation," she said in a subdued tone.

"That's what I love about you Gloria." Whitney made a face at the receptionist as she moved past her. "You're always the optimist."

Taking a deep breath, Whitney turned the heavy brass doorknob, pushed the door open, and froze. Where was her irate boss? Her pink slip? Had she taken a wrong turn and entered a romance-filled wonderland? All that was missing was the prince.

Vases filled with dozens of long-stemmed red roses were carefully placed all around the conference room and the beige carpet was strewn with red rose petals. In the middle of the table, a bottle of Dom Perignon was chilling in a sterling silver bucket, which was flanked by crystal champagne flutes. Another vase with roses stood at the head of the long conference table and there was a narrow red velvet box with a dark blue ribbon sitting next to the flowers.

Amazed, Whitney took a few steps backward and bumped into Gloria.

"Is this a joke?"

"Nope." The older woman smiled. "Boss said to call you."

"Well, this certainly isn't from J.P. Who the hell did all this?"

Gloria smirked, shrugged and threw her arms up in the air.

A deep voice echoed from around the corner. "I did."

Whitney felt her knees turn to jelly as she turned toward the familiar voice. There was her Rick dressed in a dark blue blazer, white dress shirt and worn blue jeans. A Texas-sized smile illuminated his face. He looked so fabulous that if she weren't crazy in love with him already, she would have fallen for him on the spot.

"Rick," she gasped. "I thought you were gone."

"Now, how can I leave town with my best girl upset with me?" He tucked his thumbs into his jeans pockets. "I think we need to talk."

"I think I just want to be mad for awhile—you know, like the Terry Clark song?"

"I know Terry Clark quite well—and she wouldn't stay mad at me for very long either." Rick grinned and sauntered toward Whitney. Stopping in front of her, he placed his hands around her waist and lifted her up for his kiss.

"We'll be busy, Gloria." He winked at her. "See that we aren't disturbed."

"You got it, boss." Gloria grinned back at Rick.

Shutting the door with his foot, he carried Whitney over to the table, placing her down gently.

"What's all this, Rick?" Whitney said, bewildered.

"It's a peace offering."

"You mean it's a substitute because you can't or won't give me what I really want. Right?" She put her hands on her hips.

"Look, Whit, I really care for you." He held out his arms.

"You care for me?" She gave an offended sniff. "That's what I'd say about my cat—if I had one."

"Whitney, stop it." Rick put his hands on her shoulders and gave her a little shake. "I've never felt this way before, and I need to clarify some things," he said as he gazed into her eyes.

"Yes," she said seriously. "I think you do."

"The reason why I haven't asked you to come and meet my family is that—"

"I know," she interrupted him. "Just say it. It's me."

"Will you stop that?" He paced away a couple of steps. "My dad has a lot of issues with me, and one of them is dating outside my race." Rick stared straight through her. "He's prejudiced, and I'm sorry for that."

"You're a grown man. It shouldn't matter what he thinks." Whitney slipped off the table and went to where Rick stood. "You're no teenager and you can make your own decisions."

Rick's face twisted as if she'd slapped him. "Look, I respect my father. He's a good man, and he wants what's best for me. But I call my own shots. And that's why we don't get along."

"Was it always like that between the two of you?" Whitney asked and touched him lightly on the back, as if to encourage him to keep talking. He'd never opened up about his family and she didn't want him to stop now.

"My dad is very strong and very proud of our heritage. He had big plans for his youngest son." A rueful smile touched his mouth. "My father wanted me to go to college, teach school on the reservation and marry a local girl." He paused.

"And?"

"I disappointed him." He shrugged. "My first love was music. College wasn't my thing. The girl wasn't my type and now—" He looked deeply into her eyes. "Now here I am with you."

With a crackle in her voice she said, "So what are you trying to tell me?" She began tightening her fists in frustration.

"I care for you more than you'll ever know, but I was hesitant to take you home. Dad can be tough. I love him, but sometimes even I can't stand to be around him."

"So I don't get to meet them?"

"I don't want this to tear us apart." The look in Rick's eyes told Whitney that he was serious. "Let's have some champagne and make up." He reached past her, opened the bottle and poured each of them a glass. Looking into each other's eyes, they clinked glasses.

"Why don't you do me a favor and open that box, little lady." Rick gestured toward the rectangular velvet box with his champagne flute. "I've been waiting all morning for you to do that."

Her heart fluttering nervously, Whitney pulled the dark blue satin ribbon from the box, looked inside and saw two round trip plane tickets to Phoenix.

"Does this mean—?"

"I love you, Whit. I was attracted to you the moment I saw you. You're different, fiery, and you've captured my spirit. It's time we kick this relationship up a notch, and I want my family to know how great you really are."

Whitney's mouth dropped open and she remained silent. All sorts of emotions were racing through her. She wasn't one to cry or carry on. "I don't know what to say."

"Now that's a first. My girlfriend has nothing to say." Rick laughed as he reached for her.

"Oh, that's so outta line, but I'm so happy I'll let that comment slide." She jumped up, stood on her tiptoes and kissed Rick madly, running her fingers down his neck to the opening of his shirt. "Girlfriend, huh?"

"Girlfriend," he said with a smile.

Whitney smiled. "That has a nice ring to it. I'm almost speechless again."

Rick kissed her cheek. "So what do you say…will you meet my crazy family? Come to Verde Valley with me."

"But my boss—" Whitney looked as if she were about to panic. "I sort of need this job."

"J.P.'s all taken care of and so is that Cincinnati thing." Rick sent her a wicked grin. "It's amazing what a pair of free front row Toby Keith tickets will do for a person's career."

Whitney felt free as a bird rocking to the beat of Darryl Worley's "Tennessee River Run" while the wind whipped through her hair. Rick had rented a ragtop Jeep so she could enjoy the majestic Arizona scenery. Feeling renewed, she leaned against Rick while her bare feet rested on the dashboard.

Rick really loved her. For the first time in her life, she felt content. No more searching for Mr. Wonderful in all the wrong places. She had the perfect guy, and he was in just the right place—beside her.

She couldn't take her eyes off the landscape as the Jeep climbed higher. Arizona wasn't at all what she'd anticipated. She'd pictured it hotter than hell, with nothing but desert sand, rocks and snakes.

Instead, the landscape with its sagebrush and saguaro cactus and the occasional spiky Joshua tree had a stark beauty. And once they'd reached the top of their hilly climb, the view took her breath away. The land suddenly evened out into a high desert plain with enormous violet-shaded mountains in the background, and above them the huge expanse of blue sky.

"Wow," Whitney breathed. "No wonder people move here in droves."

Whitney glanced at Rick, but he was oblivious to her gaze. His thick black hair was whipping around in the breeze as he drove. By the look on his face, she could tell he was concentrating on thoughts of his family and on the land around him.

What had he been like as a child? Life on the reservation must have been simple. She envisioned a young, lanky boy hunting, fishing, doing chores and taking part in sacred ceremonies with his brothers and sisters. She leaned back against the headrest and put her hand on Rick's leg.

This was so beautiful. She couldn't imagine him ever wanting to leave. And he had family here. He must have left to escape his father's iron rule. She began to feel a little queasy as she thought that in a matter of hours, she'd be face-to-face with a man who didn't understand her, nor would want to. These thoughts made it tough for her to breathe and she reached for the door handle.

"Can you stop for a minute, Rick? I want to get out." She unbuckled her seatbelt and started to open the door as the vehicle came to a stop.

With a questioning look, Rick complied and pulled over to a scenic overlook. Whitney put her hands in her pockets and walked to the guardrail. All she could see for miles and miles was the high desert with its cacti and outcroppings of rock.

Rick waited for a few moments to see if she'd come back to the Jeep and then headed off after her. "What's the matter?" he asked, slipping an arm around her shoulders.

Whitney couldn't take her eyes off the panoramic view, nor its incredible purplish-blue sky. It was the most beautiful scenery she'd ever seen in her life, but she couldn't have felt any worse. There was no way that she wanted to become a source of turmoil in his family.

"This is such beautiful country. I can't imagine why you ever left." Whitney began walking around the guardrails of the rest area.

Rick leaned against the railing as he looked out at the valley. "It is beautiful, no doubt about it. But have you ever lived in a place where all you wanted was to get out?"

"I've always wanted out of Galveston. Figured I'd be the one to leave first, but Rebecca beat me, and I'm happy for her. If anyone deserves happiness, it's Becca." She looked up at him. "Why did you fight so hard to leave here?" She picked up a rock, skipping it across the road.

He shook his head. "Lots of reasons. In the evenings, I'd look down the road and wonder what was on the other side of the mountains. I knew the world held something for me — more than I'd find on the reservation. It was depressing only seeing it through books. There was this overwhelming need to experience it all for myself."

"And you're not sorry?"

"No." He shook his head. "When you were in school, didn't you want to travel after seeing pictures of places like New York City?"

"New York?" Her eyes got as big around as pie plates. Excitement stirred within her. She'd always wanted to go there.

"The first time we played a gig in New York, I was walking around Midtown just mesmerized by all the buildings and the overpowering energy. I stopped and bought a hot dog from one of those vending carts and sat down on the steps of the Public Library. All types of people were walking by, folks from every race. I could hear all these different languages being spoken, but everyone was minding their own business. No one in the city cared who I was." He looked out into the horizon, apparently reliving his New York moments.

"I kept staring up at those mile-high, marble towers in amazement and thinking that everything in the world happens here and how lucky I was to see it firsthand." He brushed past Whitney, taking a seat on a bench. "It was better than anything I'd ever seen in one of those textbooks."

"But how can a city, concrete and buildings ever compare to this?" asked Whitney.

As he so often did, Rick began trying to state his case with hand gestures. "It's not so much the city, it's the fact that I got out of here. I did something different with my life. There's a lot of drumming at ceremonies, but not the kind of drumming I do."

Whitney took his hand. "But there's more to it, isn't there?"

"There was plenty of pressure from my father. He's very traditional and always wanted me to be the same." Rick looked down at the ground as if the memories were too painful. "Believe me, I've never forgotten my roots but I enjoy looking out at the future and the highways ahead of me."

Whitney moved away from Rick, her hands tightly linked.

Rick followed her. "What's on your mind, Whit? Would you mind clueing me in?"

With a troubled look on her face, Whitney turned to Rick, burying her face in his chest.

He caught her under the chin with his finger and tipped her face up toward his. "Will you tell me what's wrong?"

"I'm afraid your family is going to hate me," she burst out. "I've got auburn hair and pale skin. I don't think they'll appreciate my Irish heritage."

He took her hand in his. "Mom will love you and my sisters have been asking about you for weeks."

Whitney was feeling nervous again. "Surprisingly enough it's not them I'm worried about. Normally women don't like me much because I'm straightforward. I relate better to men. It's your father who has me worried, though." She bit her bottom lip.

"Oh, don't worry, darling. He'll come around. Besides, I'll be there with you. He can't break us both." Rick gave her a squeeze.

"That's comforting," Whitney said, punching his arm. She managed to crack a smile. "Do you have any suggestions? Is there anything I can do to make this visit a success?"

"Just be yourself, honey. Remember, I'm the disappointment. He may take things out on you, but it's me he wants a piece of."

Rick pulled Whitney toward him, hugging her tightly while running his fingers through her hair. They both turned simultaneously toward the beautiful scenery God had laid out before them. Rick took in a deep breath of air and sighed. "I guess I do miss this place after all."

"How could you not?" Whitney chimed in while giving Rick's waist a little squeeze. "Think we could stand here a few more minutes?"

"I don't see why not. We aren't on any schedules." He smiled.

Lost in scenery and each other, Whitney's "few minutes more" turned into much longer until thirst interrupted their solitude. "Come on babe. Let's go back to the truck. There's a convenience store up the road. We can get something to drink and finish up the drive."

Within an hour or so, they pulled off the highway toward Camp Verde, where a shop advertising turquoise jewelry caught Whitney's eye. "We'll have to come back here. I'd like to get a gift for Rebecca."

"Sure. Or I can take you to Sedona to do your shopping. Besides, the red rocks are not to be missed." Rick grinned. "Maybe I can get you into some hiking boots and we can go up Bell Rock. It's a sacred place for us."

"Hiking boots?" Whitney looked doubtful. "What about snakes?"

Rick threw her one of those wicked grins he was famous for. "If you're careful where you step, and don't look under rocks, you shouldn't get bitten."

"I don't know…"

"See that red-tail hawk circling up there?" Rick asked.

Whitney shaded her eyes and looked up.

"I always see a hawk right here when I come back to the reservation. It's my welcome home." He murmured something in a language Whitney didn't understand. "It's a greeting for Sister Hawk," Rick explained.

Just as Whitney's favorite Big & Rich song had finished, the Jeep came to a stop in a dead-end street in front of a small house with bluish siding that the sun had mostly faded to gray. The house was so tiny it was hard to believe that Rick's parents had raised six children there.

There were some clay pots with flowers in front of the house and a small vegetable garden to the side.

"My mom loves to garden," Rick said. "She makes the best homemade salsa. I never could figure out when she found time to do it between us kids. Now that we're all grown, she says she's bored and volunteers at the school." He shook his head. "She's an amazing lady."

"Well, where is everyone?" Whitney asked. "Didn't you tell them we were coming?" The butterflies in her stomach were dancing the rumba. As she got out of the Jeep, she locked her knees to keep them from shaking.

"I wanted to surprise my parents, but I told my sister. Let's go around back and see if we can dig anyone up."

Rick gently took Whitney's hand and led her around the back of the house. They walked down a sandy driveway toward an auto repair shop. The shop area was much different than that of the house. It was cluttered with cars and rusty auto parts. A lizard scurried past her shoe, causing her to squeal and jump to the side.

A loud sound came from inside. Rick stopped at the opening of the building and yelled, "Hey, Dad."

The drilling stopped, but there was no reply. Whitney pressed her hand against her stomach, hoping to relieve the jumpy nerves.

"Where are you at Dad?" Rick continued walking in an effort to spot someone.

There was still no answer, but the office door swung open and a petite, gray-haired woman emerged. Her face lit up as she dropped the stack of papers she was holding. Opening her arms, she ran toward Rick.

"Mama."

She reached up as far as she could, throwing her arms around Rick. "It's my little baby boy."

Whitney chuckled. This would be something to hold over Rick's head. He had to bend way down to give his mother a hug. It was hard to believe that a woman tinier than herself had given birth to such a big man.

"Richard, it's so good to see you. I can't believe you're home — and that you didn't call to let us know you were coming."

Rick's father still hadn't appeared. Whitney wouldn't feel better until she met the man for herself. Then she would be able to gauge the situation.

He broke free from his mother's grip. "It's good to be home, Mama. There is someone I'd like you to meet." He stepped aside and took Whitney's hand. "Mom, this is Whitney Harmon, a very special friend of mine."

She was a damn sight more than a friend, Whitney thought. Mrs. Youngblood would sure blush if she knew just how "friendly" they were in their alone time. But she pushed away her initial reaction, realizing that Rick was just trying to break the opening blow.

Whitney extended her hand. "It's so nice to finally meet you, Mrs. Youngblood. Rick has told me so much about you."

"Well, Whitney, it is nice to meet you too. Since Rick left, he's never brought anyone home to meet us before," she said, extending her hand in a welcoming gesture.

Looking up at him, Whitney could have sworn that Rick was blushing.

"Is this your first time in Arizona?" Rick's mother asked.

A smile was on Whitney's face. Things were going better than she'd expected, especially with the mother. "Yes. We stopped at one of the scenic overlooks on Interstate 17. The view was amazing. I'm really enjoying myself."

"We'll have to take you into town. You'll find some nice jewelry at the trading post, and you can do some souvenir shopping before you head back home." Rick's mother turned toward the desk, handing Whitney a brochure on tourist shopping in the area. "Keep it. The Chamber of Commerce sends those to us by the truckload. We give 'em out to tourists."

Whitney reached out to take the pamphlet. "I'd love that." She was sure that shopping would be more fun than facing down Rick's father.

A stern voice broke through their idle chitchat. "Hello, Richard."

Rick jumped and turned in the direction of the voice. Whitney had never seen him look so happy. "Hey, Dad. It's been a while."

Whitney was shocked. Rick's father didn't look a thing like what she'd imagined. He was tall and very thin, dressed in a dark blue mechanic's uniform. Years of hard work providing for his family had obviously taken their toll. His craggy face was deeply creased and wrinkled. All in all, she didn't think he looked mean and was not frightening at all.

"Look what the spirit winds blew in. What brings you back to our humble home?" Mr. Youngblood fully emerged from the oil pit. "Did the lights of the big city get to be too much for you?" he said with a twisted look on his face.

Rick gave his father a sarcastic grin and waved. "It's good to see you, too, Dad." After that last comment, she could tell that he was uncomfortable. He was looking down at the ground, something he only did when nervous. Rick was doing his best to control his temper.

But the older man wouldn't let things go, getting in one jab after another. "Is that your car?" His father said continuing to sport that scowl Whitney had become familiar with in the brief time she'd known him.

"Nope. Actually it's a rental. I thought Whitney might enjoy the sights better with the top down."

His father squinted, as if even that wasn't good enough. "Couldn't drive your own car out here and spend some real time with your family? Always the jet-setter taking a plane and wasting good money."

"Hey Dad, it was simply a travel choice. Let's leave it at that, okay?" Rick's tone seemed to be getting desperate.

Mr. Youngblood wouldn't hear of letting things go. He also continued to light up one cigarette after another. "Did that dead-end band job of yours come to an end?"

"No, Dad. I'm still playing in Jason's band and working in Nashville." He reached into his shirt pocket and pulled out a CD. "I brought a copy of our latest release for you to play here in the shop."

Mr. Youngblood was obviously unimpressed and while he took the CD, he immediately handed it to his wife. "Are you still living in Nashville, as well?"

"Yep, still there. I also have a time-share in Florida and a condo in Texas. I've been spending a lot of time in the Lone Star State lately." He took a step toward Whitney. "Speaking of Texas, Dad, I'd like you to meet a good friend of mine. This is Whitney Harmon."

Despite the heat, Whitney could feel goose bumps rise on her arms as Rick's father looked in her direction but didn't look *at* her. Swallowing past the huge lump in her throat, she extended her hand. "Nice to meet you."

Rick's father returned the gesture but barely touched her hand or acknowledged her. Whitney wanted desperately to say something, but she held her tongue.

The conversation stalled. She looked down at the ground and kicked a small rock between her sneakers. Finally, it was the mother who broke the uncomfortable silence.

"Well, it seems like the men have lost their manners. My name is Mary. This is my husband, Charles."

Mr. Youngblood continued to ignore Whitney, seeming to look over her shoulder or concentrate on other things. Because she loved Rick, she fought back her emotions and refused to make any off-the-cuff remarks that would anger anyone. Perhaps she shouldn't have pushed Rick to bring her.

Mary took a step toward the door. "Come on. Let's leave the men to talk. I've got supper in the oven. I hope you like roast?"

"I do very much, thank you," Whitney lied. She hated roast.

Mary looked delighted. "It's elk roast. Charles went hunting up in the high country of Montana last fall. This was my last one. I hope there's enough."

Whitney felt nauseous just at the thought of eating elk. She'd never eaten any wild animal. If it didn't come from the meat department at Food World, forget it.

"You and I can get acquainted while we finish supper and set the table. I want to hear all about you and life in Texas. I've never been there, but I hear it's nice." Mary took her by the arm, leading her toward the house.

Whitney glanced back at Rick. He gave her a wink and a nod. She didn't feel good about leaving him there.


The women disappeared around the corner of the house as the men stood in silence in the auto shop.

They stood there for a moment trying to figure out what to say. Rick wanted to state his case to his father, but it would be the hundredth time and it did no good. Why bother, he thought to himself. Instead he decided to try and defuse the situation and get along. Making small talk seemed like the harmless choice. Rick thought for a moment, looking for a safe topic of conversation.

Walking over to the vending machine, Rick removed a diet soda. "How's business these days?"

Taking another drag from his cigarette and exhaling, Charles looked calmly at his son. "It's not bad this time of year— those tourists are always breaking down. Your brother Chet should be back any moment. He helps me run things now because he lost his job over at the casino." Rick thought his father looked a bit embarrassed to admit that one of his children couldn't keep a job.

"So he lost another one, huh?" Rick shook his head and laughed without humor.

"It's not funny, Richard," his father said. "They accused him of stealing."

Rick had never seen eye to eye with Chet's way of thinking. They had fought often as children. It was his brother's senior year in high school when Rick caught him robbing his father's tools and selling them for gas and party money.

Before Rick could stop himself, he said the first thing that came to mind. "Well, was he?"

Mr. Youngblood became enraged, throwing down his cigarette butt. "You shouldn't say things like that about your brother. He is family."

"Being family doesn't make him right." Rick, tired and agitated, began scouting the room for a chair.

"Leaving your roots doesn't make you right either. You have no cause to judge anyone else in this family." Rick's father pounded his fist into his hand trying to get his point across.

Rick threw his father a sarcastic smile. "I know what this is about. It's not Chet. You're mad about my girlfriend, right? Is that what you're trying to say?" Getting madder by the minute, he sat his soda down on the workbench and walked over to the door for some air.

"You know my feelings," Mr. Youngblood stated impassively as he reached into a carton for another pack of cigarettes.

He could feel himself getting angrier by the minute. More than anything, he loved Whitney. There was no way he'd put up with his father's stern principles—not this time. "You could have been a little nicer to her. She's a good person." He jammed his hands into his pockets. "I need someone like her in my life. She makes me walk a straight line."

His father chuckled. "That's something I never could do."

Quickly removing his hands from his jeans Rick threw his arms up above his head and began shouting. "I really don't understand what you are talking about. I did well in school, never got into any trouble—unlike my brother—and went on to do something with my life." He turned and pointed at his father. "I'm in a successful band, I make good money and I travel to some of the best places on Earth."

"There is no place better than where you came from— where your family is," Charles declared. "Your roots are what keep you grounded."

Rick could feel his face harden with anger. "I'm still grounded—grounded outside the valley."

Mr. Youngblood continued to stand stoically near a welder. "You know my feelings. There is no place other than the land."

"Yes, there is, Dad. There's a whole world out there, and I want a piece of it. Whitney understands this. I love her." Rick shook his head. "This is hopeless."

Rick's father walked over, repeatedly sticking a bony finger into his chest. "I will not accept her into our family."

"When are you finally going to recognize that I'm a grown man?" Rick demanded. "I do what I please and I love whom I please."

His father did not respond. Instead, he walked over to the soda machine and grabbed a soda.

"We've been over this a thousand times. I've got my own life. Why can't you understand that?" Rick followed his dad, trying to place his hand on his father's shoulder.

Pulling away from his son, he turned back toward the welder. "We are a proud people, Richard. Why do you continue to undermine our way of life?"

Rick dropped his arm by his side. "Undermine? By finding myself? By being the person I want to be?"

"Have you forgotten our struggles? Did history not teach you anything? You were the first of our family to have the chance to go to college. You could have come back and taught our children." Rick's dad pointed out the door of the shop into the valley. "I don't understand this way of life you've chosen. I wanted more for you, my son."

For a moment Rick thought he was breaking through his father's steel attitude. "I'm happier than I've ever been in my life. I'm content with the man I've become, and I have also found someone who makes me happy."

Charles once again started to scowl. "I will never accept that woman as part of this family." With that, he turned his back and started to walk away.

"You don't even know her," Rick said with an angry plea in his voice.

He continued acting cool toward his son. "I know enough. You should marry Delia. Delia still loves you."

"That relationship was over before it began. You chose her for me," he scoffed. "I won't leave Whitney."

His father shook his head in disbelief. "You've forgotten the struggle of your grandfathers. I will not accept an Anglo woman as part of my family. For the sake of our ancestors, I can't. I won't."

Rick shoved his hands back into his jean pockets. "Whitney is not responsible for our past, but she can play a key role in this family's future if you'd just let her."

"It's her people who still judge and stereotype us." He slammed his right hand down on the top of an oil drum.

"You and your shop make a good chunk of money off 'those people' — or have you forgotten that?" Rick paced back and forth in the entryway as if he were a caged animal.

"That's different." He coolly lit another cigarette.

Rick waved his hand in the air trying to get what his father was saying straight in his mind. "So it's okay to use people that we aren't supposed to like to make money, but I can't go out into the world, make a living and love the people who support me?"

"I had such high hopes for you. If you had gone to college, you could have helped our people," his father stated sharply.

"Dad, you should be happy that I found a solid career and someone to love. Teaching history wouldn't have made me happy. Don't you love me enough to want me to be happy?" Rick fought back the urge to punch the door.

"I've put up with your wild lifestyle and halfway accepted the fact that you don't want to live here. If you intend on marrying that woman, this family will turn its back on you." His father turned and walked away.

This was the last time he would do so. Rick had had enough. He loved his father and knew that, in his own way, his father loved him, too, but he couldn't take any more. For years he had taken the torment and negativity due to his nonconformance to traditions. It was time to put his foot down. Unless there was a drastic change in attitudes, he would never be back.

In a very calm voice, Rick answered, "That's how you want it?"

Without hesitation, Mr. Youngblood stood in defiance to his son's desires. "That's how it will be. I will not discuss this any further." His father began moving car parts back and forth on the table next to the drum of oil.

For several minutes, Rick looked at his father's back, hoping that he would relent. Hoping that he would offer him an olive branch. Hell, he'd take half an olive branch. But his father did not turn around.

Rick continued standing there. His body was flushed with anger. He quickly turned and walked toward the house. After a few seconds, his father noticed him gone and began running after him.

The sound of the men's angry voices had drifted down to the house. Whitney peered out the kitchen window in time to see Rick walking toward the backyard with his father following close behind. His mother turned toward Whitney with a worried look as she dried her hands with a dishtowel. The screen door swung back so sharply that it hit the wall, startling the two women.

Rick held out his hand. "Come on, Whitney. Grab your things. We're getting out of here."

Whitney looked shocked and worried. "Rick, what happened?" she blurted out.

"You and your father had another disagreement, didn't you?" Mrs. Youngblood demanded. "I just don't understand why the two of you can't get along. Don't you know how this breaks my heart?"

Rick's head shook and he wrung his hands together. "I don't want to talk about it, Mom. You know I love you and Dad, but I can't take this rigid viewpoint. I gotta go, before I say something I'll regret. I doubt you'll see me again for awhile." He put one hand on the door, the other tightly wrapped around Whitney's hand.

Mrs. Youngblood's eyes welled with tears. "You don't mean it, Richard." The older woman swiped at her tears with the back of her hand and then turned angrily on her husband. "What the hell have you done, Charles? What did you say?"

With little expression and absolutely no regret on his face, he boldly answered, "I told him the truth."

Rick stood in the living room glaring at his father. All Whitney could do was hold his hand while her stomached twisted into knots. She loved Rick, but she didn't want to be the cause of a family split. Why can't things just be easy for a change, she thought. Life didn't have to have so many obstacles.

Mary walked over to her husband, shaking his arm. "What truth would that be, Charles?" She dropped his arm and got into his face. "You are much too stubborn and hard on him."

"Last I checked, I'm still the man of this house." He drew himself up to his full height. "I don't condone this relationship."

"Then it's your loss," Rick said. "Come on, Whitney, we're getting out of here. Some things never change."

# Chapter Thirteen

**ఈ**

Sitting in her overstuffed recliner, Rebecca looked out the window. The water in the bay was calm — by far calmer than the rumblings in her stomach. Every time she stood to do anything, she felt weak and nauseous. Rebecca decided that she'd been spending entirely too much time indoors. It was probably just the construction materials and fumes making her feel so lousy. Maybe it was nothing that a little gardening, yard work and fresh air wouldn't fix.

Rebecca got up, slowly walking to the storeroom for gardening tools. Reaching for a pair of hedge clippers, she stopped. Feeling dizzy, she clung to the edge of a lawn table. Bracing herself, she prayed that whatever was making her so ill would soon go away.

Suddenly, she heard a boisterous female voice coming from the porch. "Hey, what the hell is going on around here?" She could see the shadow of a tiny-framed figure step into the kitchen.

Startled, Rebecca jumped and headed toward the voice and shadow.

Realizing who it was, Rebecca went running toward her friend. "Oh, my God, it can't be! Whit, is that you?" She felt like a teenager who hadn't seen her best friend all summer long.

"You're damn right it's me. Who'd you think it was, Shania Twain?" Whitney wiggled her hips like Shania had done in the "Party For Two" video.

Rolling her eyes, Rebecca laughed. "Not a chance. Not even Shania makes an entrance quite the way you do," Rebecca said, hugging her friend in delight.

Whitney cocked her head with a satisfied look. "Okay, admit it."

"Admit what?" Rebecca questioned.

"That I scared you." Whitney smiled, obviously pleased at herself. "Rick's been teaching me how to walk real quiet-like— like the Apache do." She laughed. "I've been using my newfound talent to sneak up on people, especially him—in the bedroom."

"Oh, Whit, even with that twisted sense of humor of yours, it's so good to see you." She hugged her friend again. "I've been so lonely. But what the heck are you doing here?"

"Since when did I need a reason to see my best friend? I don't remember ever needing an invitation before." Whitney propped a hand against her hip. "Have you gotten so rich and famous that your friends have to make appointments to see you?"

"You know me better than that." Rebecca playfully punched Whitney's arm. "I just didn't think you could take time off work right now, with that new promotion you got and all. Tell me all about your new job."

"It's more work than I bargained for," Whitney said with a frown. "And not as interesting as I thought it would be." She tapped her fingernails against the table. "I've actually been checking out the job situation in Nashville."

"Really? Oh, my gosh, that's terrific." Rebecca began to feel envious of her friend. "I sometimes feel so useless without a job," Rebecca admitted. "Whoa! Never thought I'd hear myself say that one."

Whitney laughed along with her friend and leaned back in her chair, her shirt rising to show her belly as she stretched. "This life of leisure by the sea isn't making you happy? It'd sure do the trick for me."

Rebecca shook her head. "I am happy. It's just that Jason isn't here with me."

"How is our boy doing?" Whitney reached for Rebecca's arm and squeezed it.

"Okay, I guess." Rebecca rolled her eyes. "Not that he'd tell me otherwise. We don't get to talk too often, but he e-mails me when he can." She put her hand atop her friend's. "Oh, Whitney, I miss him something fierce."

"I know, baby." Whitney flung her arms around Rebecca.

Rebecca returned the hug and then pushed herself away from the table. "I'm not about to throw a pity party for myself right now. Besides, I want to enjoy this moment. Would you like a glass of water, soda or something?" She got up, making her way over to the cabinet.

"Um—not right now, thank you."

"During the day, there's plenty going on. But in the evenings, the house gets pretty empty. I concentrate on my writing when Joe and the crew leave. I've cranked out some really great lyrics these past few weeks." She removed some ice cubes from the freezer and poured herself some tea.

"You can write with all these men around? I saw the hunky construction workers when I drove up. What a hardship to look at all those muscles every day." Whitney sent her a mischievous grin. "Looks like I timed my visit just right."

Rebecca plopped her butt back down on the chair, slapping her hand on the table. "Be serious. And besides, you're an attached woman. You're not supposed to be looking at hunky construction workers." She shook her head in disbelief.

"Who says I can't look?" Whitney laughed her husky, sexy laugh. "I may be attached, but I'm not dead."

Sensing Whitney was being polite earlier, Rebecca got back up and fixed her friend a Diet Pepsi, her favorite. Once again sitting, she leaned forward in her chair, raising an eyebrow. "So just how are you and Rick doing these days? Do you get to see much of him?"

Picking up her glass, Whitney nodded a thank you. "I see *all* of him—every chance I get!" She giggled. "We're doing incredible." Then the giggle turned to a frown. "Most of the time."

"What about the rest of the time?"

Whitney shrugged. "You know how a new relationship is…but enough of that. What's up with you, girl?" she demanded. "You're looking a little ill."

Rubbing a hand over her stomach, Rebecca wrinkled her nose. "I've been fighting some kind of bug for a while. I'm so tired and dizzy. It's either the flu or all this construction dust, I figure."

Concerned expressions crept over Whitney's face. "What do you mean flu bug? How long have you been feeling bad, hon?"

"I was sick the night before Jason left, then it stopped. Now, it's back again. I can't seem to shake it this time." Rebecca began crinkling a napkin that was lying on the table.

"I'm worried about you, Becca. You never get sick." Whitney leaned forward, taking another sip from her glass. "Have you been running a fever? Do you have a sore throat or runny nose?"

Rebecca squinted her eyes, thinking. "I did take my temperature yesterday, but it was normal. My throat isn't sore — no runny nose." She rubbed her stomach again. "My tummy is so queasy, I'm sure it's the flu. I haven't been taking that good a care of myself since I moved. Jason and I got caught up in a couple of storms and got rained on. Then I tend to the garden early in the morning, even when it's a bit chilly. Combine that with breathing in all this dust and fumes — my immune system is probably just weak."

"I'm sorry Becca, but that doesn't sound like a normal bug. You'd at least run a fever." Whitney slowly put down her drink and leaned back in her chair, crossing her arms.

Rebecca stopped crinkling the napkin and pushed it aside. "You worry too much. I'm fine, really."

"I know, but my receptionist's sister has Lupus. She feels dizzy, tired and sick all the time. I think you need to see a doctor. Gloria and I talk about this often. Think, Rebecca—do you have any other symptoms?"

"Nope. Nothing other than some really bad PMS." She put her hands underneath her breasts. "These things have been hurting and my nipples are really sensitive to the touch. When I was in the shower this morning, I could've sworn that my boobs looked bigger. What do you think?" She cringed when her hand accidentally hit her left breast.

Whitney looked confused. "I'm not into that sort of thing. Now that you mention it, they do look a little bigger, but that can be from water gain. Mine do the same thing from time to time."

Rebecca waved her hand. "Don't even talk about water gain. I'm afraid to weigh myself. Before this sickness episode, I thought maybe I'd been snacking too much—maybe subconsciously comforting myself with food since Jason left. I swear my clothes are tighter around my stomach and butt. What makes me furious is I'm too sick to eat—no reason for the weight gain. I should get a good diuretic when we go to the store tomorrow."

With a questioning look, Whitney pushed her empty glass to the middle of the table. "Have you actually thrown up?"

"I threw up a couple of mornings, feel like heaving every other morning and then got sick once the other night. Really, I don't think anything is terminally wrong."

"Look, I was there in the hospital with you and I know this isn't probable, but your symptoms sound a lot like what my cousin just went through." Whitney opened her eyes wide. "Misty had a boy." She paused as if it was almost shocking hearing those words coming from her own mouth. "Rebecca I know this question is way off-base. In fact, I can't believe I'm even bringing it up, but when was your last period?"

"What kind of question is that?" Rebecca was surprised that her friend would even imply such a thing. "You of all people know I can't get pregnant."

Stunned by Whitney's preposterous notion, Rebecca was at a loss for words. Memories of that awful night flooded back—the argument with her mother, falling down the stairs only to be repeatedly kicked in the stomach and privates. There was so much blood and pain. The doctors had said it wasn't possible. Therefore she was not going to entertain the idea. That time in her life was too painful. She'd almost lost the will to keep fighting. Tears began to burn her eyes. She quickly began talking to Whitney to avoid the heartache.

"I appreciate you worrying, but I've always had irregular periods. Being late is nothing out of the norm for me." She stood up and walked into the kitchen. "Besides, you heard the doctors. My uterus was too damaged. All the specialists agreed that the scar tissue was too expansive inside for me to ever conceive a child." Going back on what she'd just promised herself, she placed her head in her hands and began to sob.

Whitney got up, walked over to Rebecca and hugged her. "Okay—I can't believe this either, and am in shock myself, but you have to remember what the doctors said exactly. Is your uterus too damaged to conceive or to carry the baby to full term? There is a big difference between the two and I think that you should take a pregnancy test anyway. Whatever the result, I'll take you in to the doctor before I leave."

She awaited some type of response from her friend. When there was none, she made her final plea. "Please do this. Take the test. It would make me feel better."

The following morning Rebecca lay in bed thinking about the bright purple and white box sitting on her bathroom sink. She told herself that all she had to do was pee into a cup. Then she could quiet her friend's nagging once and for all. It sounded so simple and yet so complicated. She couldn't quite bring herself to get up and do it. Whitney's suspicions couldn't be right, could they?

Rebecca rolled over and looked at her sleeping friend. She had shared her bed the night before to keep her company. Good ol' Whitney lay on her stomach with her head cocked to one side, snoring. "What a great piece of video to share with Rick," Rebecca laughed. She'd often teased her about snoring at their many sleepovers, asking how that worked for her in romantic situations. Whitney had just laughed, saying she'd been told she had the sexiest snore on the planet.

Should she wake her? Last night, Whitney was insistent upon being up for the big event. Well, why not? The whole thing was her crazy idea in the first place.

Sitting up, Rebecca lightly shook her friend's arm. "Wake your lazy butt up, Whit," she said. "We've got a test to take."

She barely moved and continued snoring. Rebecca noticed a wet spot on the pillow next to her head. Apparently she was too asleep to realize she'd been drooling. "Note to self, Bec — wash Whit's pillowcase later."

When Ms. Sound Sleeper didn't wake, Rebecca realized she'd have to resort to drastic tactics. Leaning down, she whispered into Whitney's ear in her deepest, most masculine pretend voice. "You'd better get your lazy behind out of this bed — my wife just pulled into the driveway."

Whitney snorted and jumped out from underneath the covers, her hair looking like a fright wig, her eyes barely open and the sheets going every which way. "Ah, she's home...? My underwear...? I'm too pretty to die." Whitney madly ranted while searching for her imaginary clothing. Rebecca couldn't contain her laughter. Looking up and finally coming fully awake, she shot Rebecca a disgusted look. "You're a regular damn comedian, Becca."

"C'mon, girl. This was your brilliant idea. I have that pregnancy test to take, and if I don't pee into that cup soon, I won't be responsible for the consequences."

Rebecca crawled out of bed and stumbled toward the bathroom. "Besides, I want to get it over with and get on with my day."

A few minutes later their eyes were fixed on the white testing strip. Would it turn bright purple or light gray? If it was purple, then a baby was on the way, which was clearly impossible. If it was gray, no baby. Whitney hopped up and down with all the anticipation of a child on Christmas morning.

"How darn long does this thing take anyway?" Rebecca grumbled, "I don't have all day. Are you sure these things work?"

Whitney stopped bouncing and slapped her friend's shoulder. "It takes as long as it takes. If it's any consolation, I wish it would hurry up too. And it'll work. I've used it a hundred ti—"

"Just how many close calls have you had, you hussy?" Rebecca demanded with mock indignation.

With a bright red face, Whitney said, "Never you mind. It's your close call we're talking about here. And I think this thing takes about three minutes—if I remember right."

"Hasn't it been three minutes yet?" Rebecca sat impatiently on the toilet as her stomach twisted inside.

"You've asked that every five seconds." A hint of agitation was in her voice as she leaned her butt against the sink.

Rebecca buried her head in her hands and sighed.

Whitney turned to look back at the tester and gasped. "Look… It's purple." Her voice rose to a squeal. "Oh my God. It's a miracle! Rebecca, I'm so excited about this pregnancy. I get to be the baby's adopted aunt." Whitney began jumping up and down.

Also in shock, Rebecca raised her head, placing her hands over her mouth. "I can't believe I'm pregnant." Her heart stopped. This was all like a dream. She grabbed her friend and began jumping with her, then collapsed back down on the toilet, breathing heavily. So many thoughts were racing through her head. It was almost too much to take in.

"Yup." Whitney grinned. "We're having a baby."

"We?" Rebecca echoed, eyes still wide in disbelief.

"We're best friends, aren't we?" Whitney threw her arms around Rebecca.

"The first thing you have to do is see a doctor, pronto. I hear you have to get on those prenatal vitamins right away," Whitney said, eating the scrambled eggs with cheese, toast and plum jelly that Rebecca had made for her. "You never did answer me last night. How late is your period?"

Rebecca placed the skillet in the dishwasher, dried her hands and grabbed the calendar off the wall. She began carefully counting the days. "Well, I was sick before Jason left, but that was most likely a flu bug the neighbor boys had. Jason loves playing football with those two. When Mrs. Baxter told me her boys were down sick, I knew I'd caught a touch of it."

Whitney twisted her face. "That's great Einstein, but that doesn't answer my question. When was your last period?"

Rebecca continued counting. "It was around the time Jason left."

"Then I bet you're about six weeks along." Whitney looked over Rebecca's shoulder as she counted the days again.

Pushing the calendar aside, Rebecca picked up her coffee cup. "How come you know so much about it?"

"I've done my own research—and had a few close calls." She grinned. "Can you call Jason?"

Rebecca shook her head. "I don't think so. Maybe if it were a family emergency, but then, I'm not even family." She rubbed her hands over her face. "Maybe I should have listened to Jason."

"About what?"

Tears flowed down her face. She tried to force the words out, but couldn't. Finally, after wiping the tears away with a napkin, she took in a deep breath and sighed. "He wanted to get married before he left."

"And you said no?" Whitney's mouth dropped open. "You need your head examined."

Whitney wasn't there when she'd made her decision. Who was she to judge someone else? Rebecca's blood began to boil. Sometimes her friend could be too pushy and overbearing. This time, Rebecca felt like slapping her friend upside the head. Whitey knew her better than anyone. How could she even question her like that?

"It was because—oh, forget it." Rebecca made a tired gesture. She didn't feel like explaining why she'd felt so strongly about not getting married before Jason left. It was none of her business anyway.

"Becca, look—I'm sorry for that last comment. It was out of line. I probably crossed a line here, but I'm just worried about you." She walked over to her friend's chair and rubbed her back to soothe her. "So are you going to write to him? Or wait until the next time he calls?"

"Oh, Whit, I'm not sure I ought to tell him now. He's got enough on his mind over there in that hellhole without worrying about me having a baby." She got up and paced around the kitchen. "I want him to concentrate on getting home safely."

"He should know, Bec," Whitney said, her face uncharacteristically serious. "Maybe he'll be even more careful if he knows he's coming home to a baby as well as you."

"And maybe he'll think…" She sat down and buried her face in her hands.

Whitney shifted her chair over and put her arm around Rebecca. "Think what, hon?"

"His father blamed the fact that Mrs. Engles got pregnant for his singing career not going anywhere. Because it was too hard to tour with a wife and babies." She looked up at Whitney. "You know how bitter he got. I don't want Jason to think this will jeopardize his career."

"C'mon, Becca, that doesn't make sense. His career's already flying high."

"He'll have catching up to do when he gets back. Oh, Whit—" She laid her head on Whitney's shoulder. "There's part of me that wants to sing and shout because I thought I'd never be able to have a baby. But why couldn't it happen after Jason got back?" Tears of joy began to flow once again.

"Well, it did happen. And we'll deal with it. I've been with you through tougher things than this," Whitney assured her. "You just figure out when and how to tell Jason."

The arrival of Joe and the crew put an end to the baby talk.

"So, are you going to give me the nickel tour?" Whitney demanded once the hammering had started.

Pushing her chair under the table, Rebecca slipped on her shoes and headed for the door. "C'mon."

Rebecca showed off her first gardening attempts and then took Whitney down to the beautiful private white sand beaches. They rolled their pants up and waded for a while, gabbing about everything and nothing and picking up shells while looking at the scenery and cargo ships heading for port off in the distance.

"How come you haven't talked about Rick yet?" Rebecca asked as they made their way back to the house. "You're always dying to spill all the details." She sent her friend a sideways glance.

"This is different, Becca. I've never felt like this. I'm really gone on this guy." She twirled around. "I'm in love."

"Love? You?" scoffed Rebecca. "Oh, that's rich."

"Don't laugh. I'm totally serious."

Rebecca looked at her friend. She really did look serious.

"We have so much fun when we're together, it's criminal." She halfheartedly smiled. "I'm just not convinced he is as 'in love' with me as he says." Whitney stuck her hands in her pockets. "Besides, he's always been the ladies' man of the group. You should see the women swoon over him everywhere we go."

What? Was she hearing this kind of uncertain talk from her best friend? The most emotionally stable person she knew? She must be in love this time, Rebecca thought. Usually it was Rebecca having problems in the love department, not Whitney.

"I've never heard you talk this way. Usually you're the one making all the other women jealous."

"I can't help it, Becca. I really care about him." Whitney bent down to pick a rose from one of Rebecca's bushes. She plucked the petals from the flower in a "he loves me-loves me not".

"Why do I hear a 'but' in there somewhere?" Rebecca asked, also picking a flower.

Removing a ponytail holder from her pocket, Whitney pulled her hair back. "Last week he surprised me in my office with dozens of roses, champagne and tickets to Arizona to visit his family."

Rebecca smiled. "That's fabulous, Whit."

"Well, let's just say it was a short visit." Whitney frowned.

"What happened?" This time, Rebecca felt the need to console her friend by grabbing for her hand.

Whitney looked at her friend with hurt in her eyes. "Rick's father told him right there in front of me that he would never accept our relationship."

"And Rick? What did he say?"

"He was spitting mad, and we left barely an hour after we got there. Rick told me that he didn't care whether his father approved or not. That he was done with trying to get his approval."

"So things are okay between you." Rebecca walked over to the water spigot, pooling water in her hands to wash some sand from her leg.

"It seems like it, but I can't help but wonder whether it won't drive a wedge between us." She hunched up her shoulders. "Even though he doesn't get along with his dad, he loves him. He loves his whole family. I just keep wondering if he'll hate me someday for coming between them."

Rebecca held the spigot handle so that her friend could also wash her legs and feet. "It'll work out. His father won't stay mad forever."

"You didn't see him." Her face withered with worry. "He practically looked through me like I wasn't even there."

"Have you talked to Rick about this?" Rebecca questioned as she sat down on a bench, again feeling a bit nauseous.

Whitney shook her head. "Every time I mention anything, he just cuts off the conversation. That's what bugs me. Because I can feel it's bothering him, but he won't talk about it." She took a seat next to her friend.

Rebecca wrapped an arm around her friend. "I'm sorry, Whit."

"Hopefully, Jason will be coming home soon," Whitney said. "Maybe he can talk to Rick then."

The musical ringing of Rebecca's cell phone interrupted their chatter.

"Hold that thought." She fumbled in her hurry to get the phone out of her pocket. "This might be Jason calling."

"Is this Rebecca Roberts?" asked a male voice on the other end of the phone.

Rebecca's heart began to sink. Oh God, this couldn't be the military calling about Jason. It just couldn't. With a nervous, questioning tone she answered, "Yes. Who is this?"

"This is Detective Rowley of the Galveston Police Department. Are you the daughter of JoAnne Roberts?"

It wasn't about Jason, but her heart starting pounding just the same. What had her mother gone and done now? Had her mother gotten into a fight with someone—hurt them? A million wild thoughts ran through her mind. "Yes, I am. But what is this about?" Her hand fluttered up to her throat. "Is my mother in some kind of trouble?"

"I'm afraid there's been a fire at her home." The detective paused for what seemed like hours. "I think you should get here as quickly as you can."

"Oh, my God, is she all right?" JoAnne was constantly passing out with a cigarette in her fingers and all the furniture and carpets had the burn marks to prove it. Had she finally burned down the house?

"We can't tell you much over the phone. How quickly can you get here?"

Rebecca's hands started to shake and she almost dropped the phone. She could barely think straight. Should she call Uncle Burt? Thank God he was safe and sound at the resort.

"I'll take the next flight out. I can probably get there late this afternoon."

"Call the police station once you arrive in Galveston. Ask for me and I'll meet you at the house, Miss Roberts. We'll talk then."

She clicked the off button, numb with shock.

"What is it, Becca?" Whitney questioned. "What's wrong?"

Rebecca was shaking and could hardly stand. She sorrowfully looked up at her friend. "It's my mother. There was a fire. She might not have made it out alive."

# Chapter Fourteen

**ഇ**

"Please, driver, the highway is backed up. Can't you find an alternate route into Galveston?" Rebecca said desperately as she clung to Whitney's hand. "It's an emergency."

She'd been in shock from the time of the late morning phone call until their landing at the airport outside Houston. Despite everything her mother had done, Rebecca had never wished her ill. Rebecca had always hoped that one day JoAnne could stop drinking and straighten her life out. When she was a little girl, she'd pray for that every night—and that her mother would love her.

"The police officer's voice sounded so urgent." She turned to her friend. "If only she's not dead," she said to Whitney. "Maybe there's some way we can work things out between us."

Whitney placed her arm around Rebecca and pulled her close. "Let's cross that bridge when we come to it."

"JoAnne was furious when I got back together with Jason and moved away," Rebecca whispered. "Maybe moving Uncle Burt out of the house pushed her completely over the edge. She was left with nobody. I should have demanded that she go to a rehab center or gotten some kind of help."

Whitney raised her voice. "Look, that statement really angers me. You need to think sensibly here. JoAnne wouldn't have gone for any kind of treatment. You're fooling yourself if you think otherwise. She didn't think she had a problem. There is no helping someone who won't help themselves."

Rebecca leaned her head back against the seat, holding a tissue. "You know what the last thing was she said to me?"

Whitney shook her head. "No."

The words were hard to say and they plunged pains deep into Rebecca's heart. She turned to look out the window. "'The sight of you disgusts me—you never shoulda been born.'"

"Becca…" She put her arm around the back of her friend's shoulders. "You know how your mother is. JoAnne always says evil things like that all the time—and not to just you, to everyone. All we know is that there has been an accident. Nobody's said that she's gone."

Those words did nothing to comfort Rebecca. "If she's dead, those are the last words I heard her say."

Rebecca started to feel dizzy with jumbled-up emotions. She'd lived with JoAnne for years and yet her mother was a complete mystery. There were so many unanswered questions. The biggest was what happened to make her the way she was? What had she ever done to deserve that type of treatment? The beatings? Emotional cruelty?

Whitney again tried to console her friend, but there were no words or comforting gestures that would ease her pain. "I'm sorry."

Rebecca nodded. "So am I."

Fields of tall, swaying sawgrass, ranches and cattle stopped rushing past the window just outside Galveston. The flat countryside turned into palm tree-lined streets with outlet malls, car lots, restaurants and grocery stores. The traffic slowed to a crawl as the parade of vehicles heading toward the ocean for the weekend became an almost solid mass.

Breaking the icy silence in the car, Rebecca spoke up. "I just keep remembering how I'd always follow JoAnne around, putting out the ashes from her cigarettes." She stared out the window, seeing their shabby living room instead of the city-lined streets. "You know how often she fell asleep with a lit cigarette in her fingers? I was always afraid that she'd set the house on fire."

"It's not your fault, Becca. Nobody could expect you to take care of her forever. You are your own person. I admire your strength in getting out and away." Whitney squeezed her friend's hand.

"I know." Rebecca began tearing up. "But it still doesn't make me feel any better. At least Uncle Burt is safe and sound at the resort."

Whitney looked out the window and spotted a medical supply store. "That place makes me think of your uncle. It's a good thing you and Jason got him out of the house. It would have been horrible, had he stayed."

"I was planning a visit to Galveston to see him, but not like this." Rebecca put her hand up to her mouth. "Instead of waiting until the house is finished, I'll just bring him back to Cinnamon Bay with me. I'd thought about calling him before we left home, but there's no sense in upsetting him until I know exactly what's happened."

"Once you speak to the police, we can go have a nice dinner with your uncle at the resort. I just know he's going to be fine."

Seeing a small clearing in the traffic, Rebecca impatiently leaned forward, tapping on the seat. "Driver, can't you go any faster?" Rebecca burst out.

"Lady, just who do you think I am…Superman? You see the traffic. I don't want a ticket. What's your hurry, anyhow?" He threw her an annoyed glare over his shoulder.

"You jerk!" Whitney bristled. "Apparently you haven't heard any of our conversation. There's been a terrible accident involving her mother. We need to get to her as fast as possible."

"Oh, ma'am, I'm sorry." He looked back apologetically. "It's been one of those days and quite frankly I've just been up here paying attention to the road. I had no idea…I'll do my best." He stepped on the gas pedal and began maneuvering aggressively through the congested lanes.

"We'll get there, Becca," Whitney said. "Everything will be fine."

"I hope you're right." Rebecca felt a sudden chill and rubbed her hands up and down her arms. "But I've got a really bad feeling about this."

As the car approached the neighborhood of old, rundown houses where her childhood home was, Rebecca saw that the road was blocked. Her heart sank and she grabbed once again for Whitney's hand. There were fire trucks and police cars all along the street, and an ambulance was parked on the corner. Yellow crime scene tape was being strung on both sides of the road. Why were all the police, firefighters and equipment still here, she wondered.

The cab driver edged the car as close as he could to the family home. Once the vehicle had slowed, Rebecca began to panic. She couldn't see around several large pieces of fire equipment, but she could smell the raw stench of charred wood filtering in through the vents. When the car had come to a complete stop, she opened the door and bolted, running down the middle of the street.

A policeman stepped in front of her, raising his arm. "Miss, I'm sorry, but you can't go any farther. This is a crime scene."

"But that's my mother's house!" Rebecca couldn't control her tears as she glimpsed a heavy cloud of ash and a mound of smoking rubble over the officer's shoulder.

"Are you JoAnne Roberts?" questioned the officer, placing his hand on her arm, holding her back.

"No. I'm her daughter, Rebecca Roberts." She tried to twist out of the policeman's grasp, but he was holding her too tightly. "What happened? Is my mother in there?"

In the most serious of tones, the police officer began interrogating Rebecca. "When was the last time you were home, Ms. Roberts?"

Rebecca became angry. Her mother could be seriously hurt or even dead and this man was asking her questions about her whereabouts like she was a criminal. "The last time I was home was several weeks ago. I live in Florida now. My plane landed about an hour ago."

The officer seemed satisfied with her answer and stopped questioning Rebecca. "Ma'am, before I let you talk to the investigator, I do need to see some identification. It's precautionary. You understand?"

Whitney chimed in. "It's right here officer." She continued to dig through her friend's purse until she found Rebecca's driver's license. "Here it is, sir."

The police officer quickly glanced at her identification and then handed it back. "Come with me Ms. Roberts."

Between heartbreaking sobs, Rebecca asked, "Sir. Can my friend, Whitney, come with me?"

The burly officer looked emotionlessly down at her. "I don't see why not. Miss, please stay with Ms. Roberts at all times." Whitney nodded. "Ma'am this is Detective Joe McDaniels. I believe you talked to another officer initially, but because of the type of case this is, Officer McDaniels is now lead investigator."

Rebecca extended her hand outward, shaking the detective's hand. "Sir, where is my mother?"

The Detective removed a handkerchief from his suit pocket, offering it to Rebecca. "I'm sorry to have to tell you this Ms. Roberts. These things are never easy to explain to family members, but we just don't know." McDaniels put down his notepad and put an arm around Rebecca. "We're just now able to start our investigation. It was an inferno in there."

Rebecca turned away from everyone and began examining the spot that used to be her home. "You didn't find anyone?" She began to feel nauseous again and leaned against the detective.

"No, Miss. We have not been able to locate your mother. Ah—I was just about to interview a gentleman when you pulled up. That guy says he has some information pertaining to the case."

Rebecca touched the detective's arm. "Can I go over there with you?" She could barely talk. The smoke was choking her. "Please!"

"It's not normal procedure to take family members to interview potential witnesses, but given the circumstances." He looked down at Rebecca, putting his arm around her back. "I'll escort you to him."

"Who is he, officer?" Rebecca wondered if this was perhaps one of her mother's boyfriends or a new neighbor.

Detective McDaniels stopped scribbling in his note pad long enough to answer. "He's a local cab driver here on the island."

"A cab driver?" Rebecca repeated. Why would a cab driver have information on her mother?

Brushing passed the detective, Rebecca ran over to the man. "The officer said you knew something about what happened here. This was my family's home." She put both hands over her heart. "Please what do you know?"

The man shook his head. "I drove an elderly gentleman here earlier today, Miss. He asked me to come pick him up in about an hour." The man removed the hat from his head. "When I got here, I saw flames and smoke and I called the fire department. But the place went up like a tinderbox, and I couldn't get inside." His voice began to crackle as his face tensed. "Such a nice man."

Rebecca's head began to spin with thoughts that this man could be her beloved uncle, but she quickly dismissed them. It had to be one of her mother's many suitors. "Did you get the man's name, sir?"

There was a long pause as the driver looked down at the ground. "Burt. He said his name was Burt." The driver put his head in his hands and bent down crying.

Her body began to tremble with the awful news. Rebecca let out a bloodcurdling scream that came bellowing from deep within her heart. "No, that can't be." She pressed her hand tightly against her mouth, refusing to believe what was just said. "No way was my uncle in there! He's staying at a hotel."

The man stood, clutching his hat tightly. "I'm real sorry, Miss, but I saw him go in. He said he used to live here and was coming back to get his strongbox." The man pointed to the house. "Said he wanted to give his Purple Heart to a young wounded vet whose medal hadn't come through yet." He put a gentle hand on her shoulder. "Maybe someone else drove him back to the hotel."

Rebecca's shrill screams filled the air. With tears streaming down her face, she turned toward Detective McDaniels. "Not my uncle. He was my best friend. You all are liars—every one of you."

She continued her rantings until the tall, lanky, dark-headed homicide detective pulled her into an embrace, trying to calm her. Not wanting anyone to touch her, she tried to break free, but even pounding on his chest with her fists didn't deter him from trying to help.

"Ms. Roberts, it's okay. You just get it out of your system, all right?" He patted her back, holding her tightly. "We're going to get to the bottom of this. You have my word on it."

Whitney tried to pry Rebecca away from the officer but couldn't. "You stay away from me, Whit." As the detective lessoned his grip, Rebecca began screaming, "These people don't know anything!" This time she was successful in breaking the officer's hold and began to run toward the fire. She stopped at the sidewalk, shaking. If Whitney hadn't put her arm around Rebecca's waist to support her, she would have collapsed.

"Becca, listen to me. I'll call the resort, and maybe we'll find out if your uncle's there." Whitney looked around for her friend's purse. "Becca, where's your handbag?" She received no answer. Searching the ground, Whitney spotted it next to the cab driver, apparently dropped during the scuffle. Leaving Rebecca's side for a brief moment, she returned with the cell phone in hand.

"The number's already coded into the phone. Look under the hotel." Rebecca was shaking too hard to look for the number herself.

"Officer, is there a blanket in that ambulance you can wrap around her? She's pregnant, and I think she may be going into shock."

As the officer led Rebecca to the ambulance, he waved the medic over to open the back. The paramedic pulled out a blanket and advised her to take a seat for treatment. Whitney walked a little ways away from the ambulance and dialed the phone.

Rebecca sat in the rear of the ambulance and looked at the remains of her former home, tears running down her face. A heavy gray cloud of smoke still hung eerily above the ruins. For the most part, the fire had burned out, and water from the fire hoses was still flowing down the street, pooling in the potholes and ditches.

A heavy, choking stench still engulfed the air. It was hard for Rebecca to breathe. The chemicals also burned in the fire were pungent enough to make everyone's eyes ache and burn. Noticing that Rebecca was having trouble breathing, the paramedics demanded she take a few breaths of oxygen.

One of the firemen came over to speak to her. "The fire marshal will begin his investigation as soon as it's cool enough to go in. We will know more then." He placed his hand on Rebecca's head. "I'll keep you and Detective McDaniels updated."

Rebecca managed to nod, but all she wanted to do was curl up in a ball and continue to cry.

"Becca?" Whitney climbed into the ambulance and gently put her hand on her shoulder. "I'm so sorry. It was the nurse's day off. They said your uncle left the hotel in a cab earlier this morning. He told the desk clerk he'd be back in an hour or two. But he never returned."

Rebecca started to sob harder. Memories of all the good times with her uncle flooded her mind—all his wise sayings, touches, laughter and the way he smelled. Her uncle had a scent all his own.

Whitney hugged her tight. "I'm so, so sorry." There was no response.

Rebecca and Whitney stayed at the fire scene for an hour longer, hoping for new information, but the firemen were cautious about moving too quickly for fear of collapsing what was left of the structure.

"You should check into a hotel or something, Miss," one of the policemen finally said. "We'll call you when we learn anything. I can have one of my officers drop you off." He leaned down to her with a kindly expression. "Maybe your uncle took another cab and decided not to go back to his hotel right away."

Rebecca allowed a little bit of hope to glimmer inside her. Perhaps he was down at the VFW hall or visiting with friends. He could even be down at the jetty fishing with some buddies. Although she didn't know where the spot was, he'd often talked about an abandoned concrete parking lot next to the bay where they'd go and fish.

"Come on, Becca. Let's go to the resort," Whitney seconded the policeman's suggestion. "You should get away from all the smoke and chemicals around here. Think of the baby."

The ride to the resort was fast, an occasional blare of the siren moving them through the crowded streets lining the beach. Here were all these people having a good time swimming, eating and partying. They had no clue that someone's life hung in the balance. Rebecca felt totally numb and couldn't bring herself to talk, and Whitney simply held her close and let her cry.

At the resort, Whitney spoke with the director. The entire staff was sympathetic and let them into Uncle Burt's suite of rooms.

Whitney pulled out the sleeper couch in the living room, which was made up for guests, and went to find an extra pillow and blanket.

One of Burt's shirts was draped across the back of a chair, and Rebecca buried her face in the worn flannel. Her uncle's familiar scent both comforted her and made her sad. She lay down on the bed, wrapped herself up in the old shirt and cried herself to sleep.

Rebecca woke to the sound of Whitney talking on the telephone. The sun shone brightly through the balcony doors, and Rebecca groggily realized it looked like morning. Had she slept the entire night? Part of her wanted to stay asleep forever as the memories of yesterday came flooding back when Whitney walked into the room.

"Whitney," she said weakly, "is my uncle...gone?"

"He didn't come back last night, honey. I'm so sorry."

Her heart felt broken. She'd thought about asking God for strength to get through this, but didn't know if even He could help her. "I just can't believe it." Rebecca buried her head in her hands. "Both of them are gone. My uncle was my best friend—in an instant, he was erased from my life."

"I know, sweetie. It's just too much to take in." Whitney perched on the edge of the bed. "I've been on the phone all morning. The fire marshal wants us to go out to the house as soon as you're up to it."

Rebecca lifted her head, pulling the hair away from her face. "Did he say why?"

"I asked." Whitney shook her head. "But he wouldn't tell me anything over the phone."

Rebecca sat up and rubbed her hands together. "I should try and get a message to Jason. Let him know where I am."

"I've already taken care of that too. I called Jason's base in North Carolina. They're trying to get word to him, but it might take awhile. His base camp is on the move. They should be at their final destination in a couple of days."

Rebecca started to get off the bed. "Thanks, Whit." Feeling too exhausted to move, she fell back into bed. "I think I'll stay here for just a bit longer."

"Can I get you some water or something to drink, eat?" Rebecca waved off her friend. She didn't want anything. "I also called Joe McCoy to let him know where to reach you if he needs anything and told him to keep an eye on the place."

Sitting up again, Rebecca asked, "Is everything okay at home?"

"It's fine." Whitney reassured her. "He said he'd call Opie and Gladys so they'll know where you are. Joe seemed really concerned." Whitney looked down at her friend. "I wished there was more I could do."

"You're a good friend for taking care of all that for me, Whit." Rebecca reached out and took Whitney's hand. "Do you have any headache medicine? My head hurts awful bad."

Digging through her makeup bag, she retrieved two capsules and poured her friend a glass of water. "I bring them along in case cramps should hit me." Rebecca looked up at her friend. "Do you want me to order some breakfast while you shower?" Whitney quickly handed Rebecca the medication.

"No." Rebecca guzzled down the water and tablets. "I can't even think about eating anything." She forced herself to climb out of bed. "I'll be ready soon."

Scraggly, burned palms that stood in the thick pools of mud were all that remained of the lawn, and Rebecca could hardly bear to look at the ruins of the house. The fire marshal was waiting at what used to be the front steps. Rebecca made as if to go inside, but the marshal stopped her.

Removing his gloves, he said, "I can't let you go up there, Miss Roberts. What's left of the structure and foundation is about to crumble."

"Did you find my…" Rebecca's breath hitched, and she clenched her fists until her knuckles turned white.

He placed his hand on Rebecca's shoulder, walking her away from the house. In a soft voice he updated her on the morning's findings. "We located two bodies. Both were very badly burned and couldn't be identified right away. They've been taken to the medical examiner's office for an autopsy. We will also be turning our findings over to Detective McDaniels."

"Autopsy?" Rebecca asked.

"Is there a question of how they died?" Whitney asked sharply. "Other than by smoke inhalation or from the fire itself?"

"I'm afraid there is, ma'am." He stopped and removed a notepad from his jacket. "According to the preliminary findings, eyewitness accounts and a timeline put together by the investigators, we think that foul play may have been involved."

Puzzled, Rebecca asked, "Foul play?"

"We've determined that there was one male and one female body in the house at the time of the fire." He stopped once again to find something in his notes. "The medical examiner's initial finding was that the male victim might have died as a result of a skull fracture—or, in other words, blunt force trauma to the head. The victim was found just inside the front door."

Rebecca leaned against Whitney for strength. Her legs were weak and shaky. "Do you think he suffered?" she tearfully asked.

"I don't think so, ma'am. My theory is that the blow to his head probably knocked him out instantly." He ducked his head. "If it didn't instantly kill him. A heavy brass lamp fixture was found next to his body."

"What…What about my mother?" Her voice quivered.

"Well, Miss Roberts, you'd have to talk to the detective about that. I've probably said too much already. Again, I'm sorry for your loss." He solemnly smiled at Rebecca, turned and began walking back to the crime scene.

Whitney stepped forward. "Can't you tell us anything else?"

He walked back to them. In a hushed voice, he began speaking. "The female body was found near the back door. Likely she passed out from smoke inhalation before the fire reached her. Again, Detective McDaniels will know more in the next few days."

"The back door always did stick," Rebecca said miserably.

"Will there be any criminal proceedings?" Whitney asked the marshal.

"It requires a full-scale investigation. It'll probably take weeks to determine exactly what happened."

"When do you think I can plan their funerals?" Rebecca was eager to lay her family to rest. Maybe now her mother would be at peace. JoAnne was in death as she was in life—always calling the shots.

Thinking, the marshall paused for a moment. "The bodies should be released for burial right after the autopsy. It should take about two or three days." Pulling Rebecca aside, he began speaking again. "There's something for you in my car." They walked down the street to his white, unmarked car. "I checked with Detective McDaniels this morning. He said it was okay to release this to you." He reached inside his vehicle and took out a familiar metal box.

The strongbox was covered with soot and wrapped in a clear plastic medical bag. Rebecca took the box and hugged it to her body, knowing that this was what her uncle had given his life to save. "Thank you, sir, for everything you've done."

The creaking of the master suite's door caught Rebecca's attention as she sat on the bed, alone with her thoughts.

"Becca, it's almost time to go to the funeral home."

Rebecca thought Whitney looked nice. She was dressed in a simple black tea-length dress with pearl earrings, her hair elegantly pulled back and of course, those signature designer shoes she was famous for. Rebecca couldn't have been happier to have her there. "Whit—you look nice."

Whitney gave herself the once-over. "Thanks, Becca. Are you about ready?"

"I'll be there in a bit." Rebecca stood and walked into the bathroom. Looking in the mirror, she hardly recognized the person staring back at her. She looked like a ghost, withered and drawn with worry. Her skin was pale and there were dark circles under her eyes. "Whit, I look like hell. I wanted to look presentable for my uncle's farewell."

Whitney slid her hand around the door casing and then leaned against it. "You look good. A little tired, but good." She paused. "You've had a rough week. Not everyone could deal with a tragedy like this, especially in your delicate condition." Whitney walked further into the room. "Do you want me to get your outfit out of the dress bag?"

The sudden knock at the door interrupted their conversation. "I'll be right back." Whitney disappeared around the corner, leaving Rebecca alone to finish getting ready.

Once again popping her head into the doorway a minute later, Whitney said, "Rick just got here and is ready to drive us over. He hasn't heard from Jason either. They haven't been able to track him down yet."

"Thanks, Whit." She walked back into the bedroom, facing her friend. "I don't know what I would have done without you here with me."

"C'mon, hon." Whitney reached over and rubbed Rebecca's back. "It'll be over in a couple of hours, and then you can rest."

Rebecca nodded, but she knew just how hard rest was to come by these days. The minute she turned off the light, heartache, regrets and old ghosts plagued her.

She scouted the room for her black dress. "Whitney, after visiting hours, we have to go to the VFW hall. There are some people there I need to see."

Whitney began to argue. "You need to rest, Becca. Think about the baby."

Finally finding the dress behind the bathroom door, she turned to Whitney. "I have to go. They're planning a ceremony for my uncle, and the area vets are setting up a memorial fund in his name." She gave Whitney a wan smile. "I'll rest later. Promise." Whitney looked skeptical. Rebecca had always pushed herself. "I'm going to finish up here. I'll meet you in the living room when I'm done."

When she joined them, Rick greeted Rebecca with a strong hug. She almost broke down again, but refrained from doing so. While everyone was making his or her way out the door, Rebecca remembered that she needed to go back for her uncle's funeral policy. The undertaker had mentioned something about a hard copy last night. Rebecca hadn't had the courage to open the box before now.

She walked to the dresser, opening it. Removing the grungy metal box from the drawer, she placed it on the bed. On top of his important documents were old family photographs— pictures of her mother and uncle as children. One picture in particular caught her attention. It was of a smiling teenaged girl standing with her arm around her little brother. How odd, she thought. This was the first time she had ever seen her mother look pleasant.

Continuing to thumb through the pictures, Rebecca saw later family photos showing her uncle during basic training, in his uniform, his tour of duty in Vietnam and finally, JoAnne holding her as a baby and again smiling and looking content. It was nice to see that at one time her family had been happy.

Rebecca wanted to keep looking at the photos, but she forced herself to put them aside and search for Uncle Burt's funeral policy. Then something else caught her attention. It looked like a bank passbook with a piece of paper wrapped around it. Rebecca carefully unwrapped the paper to discover that it was a letter for her.

*Dearest Rebecca,*

*It has been my special pleasure to watch you grow into a beautiful young woman. I'm sorry your life hasn't always been wonderful, but the world is a much brighter place because you are in it. There is so much goodness in your heart. I'm only sorry that your own mother blinded herself to it.*

*Our mother, your grandmother, didn't treat JoAnne very well, often beating and cursing her. I was more fortunate because Mother favored me for some reason. I'm not making excuses for my sister, but I can only guess that this damaged her. And when your father left after he found out that JoAnne was pregnant, that hardened your mother something awful.*

*I know that deep down inside somewhere she loved you, but, unfortunately, she took out all her anger and disappointment on you. Over the years I tried to get her to go to AA, but she always refused. I even encouraged her to contact your father after you were born, in case he'd grown up some and was able to help out, but she refused that suggestion, too.*

*I regret that I couldn't do better by you, Becca, because you surely deserved better. I know it isn't much, but I want you to have what I've managed to save over the years. It's meager repayment for all the years you took care of your mother and me but I want you to have it, my darling. I love you as if you were my own daughter, and don't you ever forget it.*

*All my love,*
*Uncle Burt*

Holding the note and passbook tightly against her chest, Rebecca wept. Even in death her uncle had been looking out for her. In his savings account was a little over $60,000. Although she didn't need it now, she would always cherish the gesture. She quietly placed the box and its contents back on the dresser. Only the military papers, insurance policies and medals would go with her today.

When they arrived at the funeral home, Rebecca was grateful that Rick and Whitney were at her side. Even though Uncle Burt and her mother had to have closed caskets, it would take every bit of strength she had to get through this. Her body was trembling as tears ran down both cheeks. Even Whitney was silently weeping, and Rick kept his arms around both women.

It was hard having the caskets closed. She felt cheated, since she couldn't even properly say any goodbyes. What words would suffice? All she could do was touch these heavy wooden lids that enclosed their remains. She still couldn't comprehend how her mother could have been so sick, so damaged, so drunk that she had actually murdered her own brother. She could only hope that both of them had found some kind of peace, as they had once done during the photographs of long ago, and that her uncle was looking down at her from heaven.

Approaching the front of the funeral home, she lovingly touched her fingers to the slick walnut finish. The wood was hard, cold and lifeless, so unlike the brave man she'd loved so much. He'd been her father figure and her confidant, and he'd always had a smile or hug for her, making her feel loved.

Rebecca dropped to her knees, touching the wooden box where the man she adored even more than Jason lay. "Oh, Uncle Burt," she whispered as she knelt by his coffin, leaning her forehead against it. "I love you so much. Thank you for the beautiful letter. Please watch out for Jason over there, and send me your courage and strength. I'm sorry you won't have a chance to meet our baby, but if it's a boy, we'll name him li'l Burt. Thank you for saving all my songs. Every one will be dedicated to you. Rest well dear uncle. I love you."

She rose and moved to pray over her mother's coffin. "Mama, today I saw a picture of a sweet young girl with a happy face holding a baby. I don't know where that emotionally whole woman went to, but I pray that you will find some peace in the afterlife, rediscovering that happy young woman once again. I forgive you for what you did to me but I will never forgive you for taking my uncle away from me."

As she returned to where Whitney and Rick sat, she heard the faint ring of her cell phone at the bottom of her purse. She moved quickly to the back of the room so as to not disturb anyone's prayers. Her hands shook as she answered it. The funeral home director opened the door to his office and motioned for her to take her call in there at his desk.

"Hello?"

Rebecca's heart stopped. She was so relived to hear his voice.

A deep voice shouted from the other end. "Becca!"

"Jason, can you hear me?"

His voice sounded sad, but rushed. "The chaplain had to pull some strings to get me this phone call, and I only have a couple of minutes. I want to tell you that I love you and that I'm so sorry about Uncle Burt and your mom. I wish I could be there for you, sweetheart."

She tightly hugged her sides, wishing it were Jason holding her. "I wish you were here, too. Jason, when can you come home? Can you get any special leave?"

"I wish. But I'll be home soon. They're moving my unit to a different part of Iraq, but don't worry. Things aren't nearly as bad as they seem on the news."

"There's so much to tell you. I have some news that—"

"Baby, I'm sorry." There was a pause and Rebecca could hear different people talking over the line. "They're telling me I gotta go. I love you so much." She could barely make out what he was saying, there was so much static. "You take care of yourself, and I'll be missing you every day that I'm gone."

"I love you, too." The line crackled. "Jason? Jason, are you there?" She sat frozen in the chair, staring at her phone for several minutes after it went dead, as if willing it to ring again. A knock on the door told her it was time for the ceremony to begin.

Finishing her call, she walked out and took a seat in the front row. The chapel was now packed with people, and every pew was filled. Many of her uncle's VFW friends and their families attended, along with local business owners and other

Galveston residents who knew the family. Some of Jason's band members had come to play the music for the service. Rebecca was overwhelmed with emotion as dozens of eulogies came from her uncle's many friends.

Later, at the graveside services, the band sang "God Bless America" and "Amazing Grace". Then, at the end, an honor guard fired three rifle volleys.

At the conclusion of the services, Rick placed his arm around Rebecca and began whispering. "I'm going to walk Whit to the car—I'll be back for you in a moment. I thought you might need a few minutes."

Rebecca gazed up at Rick, then hugged him. "Thank you."

There were no words for this occasion. Rebecca had said her goodbyes back at the mortuary. Walking over to the place where her mother would be laid to rest, Rebecca whispered, "Goodbye, Mama. Sleep in peace." She then plucked a single red rose from a flower arrangement, throwing it onto her casket.

Next, she proceeded over to her uncle's coffin. Kneeling down, Rebecca began to sprinkle dirt into the hole, rubbing each tiny piece between her fingers. Uncle Burt had always said, *"There's nothing on this Earth worth fighting for more than the land"*. Good ol' U.S. soil, he'd call it. Rebecca buried her head in her hands. After a few moments of silence, she stood.

"This may be goodbye for now, my sweet uncle, but someday we will see each other again. Until then, please continue to watch over me. I love you so." Rebecca turned to a large floral arrangement that a veteran's group had sent. She carefully removed twelve roses and threw them on top of the casket.

"Are you ready Rebecca? The jet is fueling up." Rick placed his hand on her shoulder.

Rebecca nodded. "Yes, I'm ready."

Within a couple of hours, they were packed and the jet ready for takeoff. Although Rick and Whitney accompanied her, the plane ride back to Florida was somber. Rebecca barely talked or even looked up. She sat there quietly, still numb and from time to time absently rubbing her slightly bulging stomach, seeking some type of contact with her unborn child. Now that her childhood home and her uncle were lost forever, Cinnamon Bay was truly her only home.

# Chapter Fifteen

**ɾɔ**

The weeks following the funeral were long and emotionally difficult, but Rebecca had plenty of moral support. Rick and Whitney stayed for awhile after the trip from Galveston and then visited the island as often as they could. Opie and Gladys arrived weekly with groceries and gossip. Jason's mother, Sarah, kept in constant contact through e-mails and phone calls.

Although there was plenty of support, Rebecca still ached to have Jason home, not just because of the loneliness, but because there wasn't a moment in the day when she wasn't worried for him. His phone calls were sporadic and brief. He would never say too much when she asked what he was doing or going through. Rebecca was sure that he was only trying to protect her by explaining to her as little as possible. Oh, she knew that she'd probably worry even more if he did talk about the dangers he faced on a daily basis, but she still wished he wasn't so closemouthed.

When Jason had called her at the funeral home, she'd wanted to blurt out the news that she was pregnant, and if he hadn't had to cut the phone call short, she probably would have. But since then, she hadn't felt right about telling him about her pregnancy. Rebecca was afraid the news might distract him. Wouldn't that be an additional danger for him, she asked herself again and again.

But the biggest question now was when would Jason come home? It had already been six months. She was trying to worry as little as possible and instead concentrate on the good parts of her life. Each day that passed, the stress of losing her family subsided and so did the tears. Instead, the crying was replaced with fond memories of happier times.

Rebecca was tired of problems. It was time she made some good things happen for herself. Every morning after breakfast, she'd settle into a nice routine. First, she'd pick up the house and start a load of laundry. After tending her garden, it was off to take a shower. Joe had finally finished the bathroom remodeling. Rebecca was delighted to find that he'd installed a huge ceramic tile shower with a seat. Letting the hot water hit her tired back was exhilarating. Rebecca's ever-increasing stomach was making her lower back hurt something awful. After the shower, it was time to get to work writing, which she found therapeutic.

Next to the windows overlooking the bay, Rebecca covered the hardwood floor with goose down sleeping bags and dozens of throw pillows. If the morning air was cool, she'd open the window and let the crisp ocean breeze blow in, filling the house with fresh tropical air. Sitting on top of the blankets, she'd surround herself with overstuffed pillows and grab her laptop. Then she'd type away. Not even the constant banging of hammers and high-pitched whine of saw blades cutting through wood distracted her. She was on a mission.

First Rebecca started out writing poetry. She'd worry about converting the words to lyrics after the material was completed. It was the right time to begin composing because lately her life had been one catastrophe after another. Rebecca didn't need to look much farther for inspiration. Skillfully she wrote word after word, sentence upon sentence, until she'd composed a beautiful poem suitable for song. Then she masterfully put those poetic words into verses and choruses. After most of the songs were complete, she loaded the printer. But the ink cartridge was low and the printer stalled.

"Jeez. I don't believe this. Now I've got to go to the mainland to buy a cartridge when I'd rather look over my songs." Rebecca despised reviewing her work from a computer screen. She always felt like she'd miss mistakes and redundancies that way. Getting up from the floor, she went into the storage room, looking for office supplies. "Jason probably has some extra print cartridges in here."

As Rebecca searched through the mounds of storage boxes, her feet became tangled up in the rug and she fell into a mangled pile of lost treasures. Stunned, she rose to her knees and checked her stomach carefully for marks or bruises. The tumble she'd taken hadn't hurt her or the baby. Slowly, Rebecca began picking up the mess she'd made when she discovered old videotapes and music cassettes. Upon further investigation, she realized that the tapes were used to teach people how to play the guitar.

It was as if a light bulb went off in Rebecca's head. Finding these was no coincidence—it was time for her to learn how to play. Quickly, she gathered the tapes and cassettes, putting them in the living room with the rest of her supplies. Then she grabbed her purse, slipped on her shoes and headed outside for the mainland. Only it wasn't just a printer cartridge she wanted this time—she was in search of a guitar. Jason's was back in Nashville. But then it dawned on her. She didn't have to look too far to find the perfect one.

As she opened the door to the bar, a thick cloud of smoke poured out, hitting her in the face. She coughed and shook her head. It was five o'clock, or *beer thirty* as Rick liked to call it, so what could she expect? People were eating, drinking and having fun after being cooped up at work all day.

Rebecca grabbed a familiar friend. "Donna! Have you seen Opie or Gladys?"

Donna, the head waitress shook her head, her ponytail going in every direction. "They're in the back, arguing as usual." She laughed and went about her work. "Rebecca, you can go ahead and go back there if you want to," the waitress yelled back at Rebecca as she began pouring drinks.

Making her way back to the kitchen, Rebecca turned the corner just in time to hear a burly man barking orders. The voice startled her for a second. Realizing who it was, she stopped. "Hey Opie—I heard you and Gladys were back here arguing?"

Opie laughed. "Nope, Gladys left a few minutes ago. I was yelling at Cletus. He dropped the chicken on the floor again.

That man is worse than my sister's kids. Besides, when I fight with the Mrs. it's called love sparring." He reached around, giving her a big bear hug and then went back to cooking on the grill. "What brings you here? Want a burger?" He plopped an enormous beef patty on a plate in front of her.

After hearing what Cletus had done with the chicken, she shook her head. "No thanks. But you do have something I want." Rebecca smiled a wicked little grin.

"You shouldn't talk that way missy—I'm a happily married man." He pointed to his wedding ring.

Rebecca slapped his arm with her hand. "I don't want that."

"Quit it, doll. You're breaking my heart." Opie placed his greasy fingers over his apron-covered chest. "I thought for once this old man wouldn't be...well, quite so old." He gave her a wink.

She could feel the warmth in her cheeks as Opie made her blush. "No, really—I'd like to borrow Jason's father's guitar."

Opie looked surprised. "What do you want with that old thing?" He scraped the grill with his spatula.

Rebecca hesitated for a moment. She knew what that guitar meant to Opie and Gladys and that they might not want to part with it. "It's a surprise for Jason. I...I never really learned to play."

The older man looked puzzled. "You're going to learn to play guitar for our boy?"

Rebecca nodded. "I write songs. Not too many people know that. I've had some success, but I thought if I could learn to play the guitar, it would take my writing to an entirely different level. It seemed like a nice surprise for Jason, too." Rebecca paused. "What do you think?"

"Give me a minute." Opie took off his apron and headed toward the back of the building. Gladys was nowhere in sight. Rebecca figured she was probably making a quick run to the grocery store for a must-have item or two. After a few moments, he emerged from the backroom carrying a dusty case. "You take care of this. There's a lot of good memories tied to that old piece of parched wood."

Rebecca smiled, taking the case from Opie. "I'll take good care of it, don't you worry." She rose to the top of her toes to give him a kiss on the cheek.

Opie grinned. "See? I knew you wanted me."

"Looks like you busted me, Op. My secret is out—I want you." Rebecca turned around, blowing him a kiss with her hand and winked. "See ya soon."

As the days passed, Rebecca was thankful for the life growing inside her. With Jason gone, it was as if a piece of him stayed behind and was with her always. Each day, the tiny being gave her a new sensation of joy and hope for the future while she noticed other new and fascinating changes taking place in her body.

The morning sickness and accompanying dizziness had gotten worse in the first few weeks following the death of her family and she'd had a hard time keeping anything down. Even certain food smells, especially bacon, roasted beef and fried chicken made her sick to her stomach. Smells made her so nauseous that for a period, she had to eat strictly vegetarian. The doctor recommended dry crackers, and she lost a little weight but managed to muddle through. Thank goodness the symptoms eventually subsided.

After her hips began to spread, a plumper stomach lined with bright reddish-purple stretch marks emerged. Rebecca couldn't even look at her belly button. It seemed more like a mining pit than part of her body. Then there were the ever-changing breasts. They grew fuller and heavier with each passing day. Rebecca had always loved to sleep on her stomach, but with her new boobs, that was a thing of the past. She wondered what Jason would think of them and of her new, less lean figure.

Most exciting was what Rebecca called "the flutters". This is what she nicknamed the feelings she got whenever she thought she could feel the baby move or kick. She never was quite sure that's what it was. Her doctor had told her it was too early and that what she'd been feeling was her uterus stretching to make room for her growing child. In private moments she began holding her stomach and singing to the baby. She'd also tell her unborn child how wonderful his daddy was and how much he or she would be loved.

Joe, his crew, and Rebecca worked hard to get the new house ready before Jason returned, which meant keeping the cottage livable even as the workers tore apart both bedrooms to accommodate the huge kitchen, hearth and family area Jason had envisioned. Rebecca moved her bed into the living room next to the French doors leading to the patio, and in the evenings she would often sit outside and write lyrics. She'd gotten used to the weather and these days, when a Gulf storm blew in, she no longer found it frightening but found instead that it refreshed her creative soul. This was never more apparent than during her best friend's last visit.

Back in July, the girls sat huddled in the living area. A huge storm had blown in and the electricity went out. The two friends talked and chatted to ease one another's nerves as the storm continued to rage. Rebecca was more on edge and Whitney did her best to get her mind off it.

"What about those songs in Uncle Burt's strongbox?" Whitney asked once the power came back on.

"What about them?" Rebecca looked up from her first attempt at trying to play the guitar without the tapes.

Whitney stomped into the room with one hand on her hip, the other waving some music sheets. "What are you going to do with them?"

Rebecca shrugged. "I imagine I'll get around to reworking them someday."

"Why don't you give them to me? Rick knows some people who are looking for new material." Whitney took a seat next to her friend.

Rebecca shook her head. "Nope, Whit. I've got plans for those. But I'm not ready to tell even you what those plans are."

"Come on, Becca. I'm your best friend. If you can't tell me, then who can you tell?" Whitney urged her. "And why are you fiddling with that old guitar anyway?"

She looked up at her friend and laughed. "This has to do with my songwriting."

Whitney twisted her face in confusion. "You've sold lyrics before. You're good."

"It's not like the lyrics I sold as J.R. Neels got a major Nashville contract," Rebecca protested. "I'm no John Rich yet. But this new stuff I'm working on will get me noticed. I feel it right here." She pointed to her gut. "And I'm not going to ask for help from Jason, Rick or anyone else. This is something I have to do myself."

"So what if you have help from inside Nashville? Sometimes it's not about the work, but who you know." Whitney pointed out the window with her perfectly manicured finger. "There are a lot of talented musicians out there in the world who haven't made a Music City connection yet. You've got the greatest opportunity – use it."

Rebecca looked up at her friend and shook her head. "Nope. This is not up for discussion, Whit. I went to Waldenbooks and loaded up with books on the business. I've been doing research for days. Now, I don't want to talk about this anymore. Leave my old music alone. I have special plans for it."

The sound of hammering and sawing filled the air. Joe and his crew were putting in overtime to get the frame of Jason's recording studio completed before the storm hit. The weatherman had forecasted that it was supposed to be a big storm front like the one in July, but so far they hadn't seen much—just a little wind and some light rain, which had subsided for the moment. When the sounds of the workmen suddenly subsided, Rebecca walked out onto the porch to see what was going on. Whitney should have arrived for her visit an hour ago.

"Whit!" Rebecca's mouth dropped open at the sight of her friend shamelessly flirting with the workers. She was a little angry. Rick was a terrific guy. Her friend shouldn't be acting so free. Whitney was finally in a great relationship. The last thing Rebecca wanted was for her to blow it.

"Hey, pergola!" Whitney called from the bottom of the path, waving to her friend. "You think you can get any bigger? I'm surprised you can tie your shoes."

"Be nice, Whitney." Rebecca braced her hands at the small of her back. "I already know I'm the size of a small house."

As Whitney sashayed up the path, the workmen put down their tools and followed her progress, some whistling their appreciation. Rebecca could see that Whitney reveled in the masculine attention. Even though she was with Rick now, the woman sure loved to flirt. Rebecca watched as her friend made a production of putting down her bag and bending down to look into it, giving the guys an eyeful of her derriere. This egged the guys on, and they whooped and hollered like animals in the wild looking for a prospective mate.

"Back to work, you losers!" Rebecca yelled to them good-naturedly.

They laughed and got about their business.

"Don't spoil all my fun, girl," Whitney complained.

"You deserve to have your brand of 'fun' spoiled." Rebecca sent her a mock frown.

"That's not fair, and you shouldn't be mean to me." Whitney shook her finger at Rebecca. "Because I've got something for you and if you want it, you'll be nice."

When Whitney got into the kitchen, she set down her bags and turned to Rebecca with a large brown envelope in her hand. "I stopped by the post office and got your mail on my way here. Thought I'd save you a trip, given your most delicate condition."

"What's this?" Rebecca scratched her head and looked puzzled.

"Turn it over, read the return address and then you tell me." Whitney beamed. "I already looked, so I know."

Rebecca turned the envelope over. Her mouth dropped open. The envelope was from Mercury Records in Nashville, and it was addressed to J.R. Neels.

"It couldn't be good news hearing from them this soon. They probably hated my songs," she said somberly, trying to rearrange her pregnant body so she could comfortably sit down on a nearby chair.

"Does this have to do with those lyrics you told me you were working on — the ones you were learning how to play the guitar for?"

"Yeah…" Rebecca looked depressed.

"Well, why do you think it's bad news from Mercury?" Now Whitney looked puzzled.

Rebecca shook her head. "What makes you think just hearing from Mercury is good news? I sent in my submissions less than three weeks ago."

Rebecca could see that Whitney was practically ready to burst with excitement.

"Okay. Let me read what's in the envelope." Rebecca opened the letter, read, folded the paper and put her hand up to her mouth. Then she repeated the ritual as if she wasn't sure what she just had read.

Whitney jumped up from her chair. "Are you going to tell me or what?"

She turned toward her friend, shaking. "They loved my lyrics, Whit, and the record label bought a batch of them, even some of my old songs Uncle Burt had—the ones I reworked. My contract will be coming within a few days."

The two girls started screaming. Rebecca couldn't, but Whitney was jumping up and down enough for the two of them.

With all the excitement, Rebecca had to sit back down. "They're offering me a $15,000 advance, payable as soon as I sign."

"You're kidding, right?" Whitney threw her arms around her friend. "It's about time you got some good news."

"Look at it," Rebecca urged, holding the letter out for her friend. "Plus, I'll get royalties once the songs get recorded and released."

Rebecca took the papers out of the envelope and gave them to her friend to review. She could barely believe her eyes. For the first time, her songs would be making her some real money.

After the shock and excitement died down, Whitney looked up at the clock. "Becca, I'm going back down to the dock to wait for Rick. He stayed on the mainland to pick up Jason's mother."

"Jason's mother?" Rebecca looked up in alarm. "You didn't say she was coming with you."

With a little crooked look on her face, she said, "I thought I'd surprise you."

"I love Sarah, but she doesn't know I'm pregnant you idiot." Rebecca felt a sick pit sitting in her stomach.

"I know. But don't you think it's about time somebody in that family knew?" Whitney said. "You're not mad, are you?"

"No, I guess not." She smiled. "I know that Sarah's dying for some grandkids to spoil. You're right—it's about time she knew."

"Good girl. I'm so proud of you for this." Whitney patted the papers on Rebecca's lap. "Things have been rough for you, and no one deserves success more."

Whitney gave her friend a hug and scooted out the door. Rebecca turned to read the contract again.

As Rebecca sat at the kitchen table, a huge smile broke over her face. So J.R. Neels was going to be a success, she thought. Maybe a major songwriter. It hardly seemed possible. She smiled when she thought of how proud Uncle Burt would be. Bless him for saving all her old poetry and lyrics. She was still sitting there looking at the contract as if it would disappear if she looked away when she heard voices outside.

The screen door opened and lots of rattling could be heard. "Look who's here, Becca," Whitney called from the porch.

Rebecca looked up as the door opened and Mrs. Engles came in, her arms spread wide.

"Rebecca darling." She reached out to give her a hug.

She rose from the chair and returned the gesture, hugging her future mother-in-law tightly. "Sarah! I've missed you." She pulled away, remembering Sarah didn't know she was pregnant.

"Becca?" she gasped. "What's this? You're pregnant?" Sarah paused in a moment of shock. "When? How come you never told me? How come Jason didn't tell me?"

Rebecca bit her bottom lip. "Jason doesn't know yet, Sarah." She stopped, waiting for her reaction.

Sarah's brow wrinkled. "What? Becca, he's the father! My boy needs to know that he has a child on the way. I'm disappointed that you would keep something like this from him."

"Please don't be disappointed in me Sarah." Rebecca tried grabbing for her hand. "I want him to concentrate on getting home safely. I don't want him worrying about the baby and me." She led Sarah toward the couch.

As they sat down, Rick and Whitney made themselves scarce. Rebecca looked down at a throw pillow, fiddling with the fringe, before she looked up to face her mother-in-law.

"Everything happened so fast, Sarah. We were here on vacation and then suddenly he got called up and sent to Iraq. Then my mother and uncle died, and Jason was so upset that he couldn't be here with me. He worries a lot about me, especially since he knows I'm here alone in a new place." She spoke quickly, hoping to make the disapproving look on Sarah's face disappear.

"I don't want to spring this pregnancy on him when there's nothing he can do about it. I want him to keep his head on straight and focus on staying safe." She wrapped both her hands around Sarah's. "Can you please keep this a secret for now? I'll tell him when the time's right. Please?"

"You know, my son might never forgive me if he finds out I knew about this and didn't tell him," Mrs. Engles said. "Are you sure this is the right thing to do?"

Rebecca was aware of how over-protective Sarah was of Jason—and always had been. When he didn't consult her about important things, it annoyed her. He'd probably feel the same and be angry, she thought uneasily. She often wished he'd talk things over with her. But surely she was right about this decision, wasn't she? His very life might be in danger if he were distracted.

Trying to stand her ground, she said, "I do think it's the right way to go, Sarah."

Putting her arm around Rebecca's back, she said, "I'll make a deal with you, then. You allow me to move in here with you and I'll keep your secret. After all, I'm going to finally be a grandmother."

"I can't let you give up your life to help me out," Rebecca protested weakly. It was too much to hope for, that Jason's mother would want to help her through her pregnancy.

"Oh yes you can. What am I going to miss, my bingo games? I can go back to Nashville and check on things once a month." Sarah laughed. "Staying here will make me feel closer to Jason. I miss him, too, you know. Is it a deal?"

"Deal." Rebecca reached out and hugged Sarah tightly. This would be wonderful. Maybe now she'd have the mother she'd always wanted.

Sarah walked into the kitchen and then over to the windows facing the bay. "So, show me around, Becca. I can't wait to see what you've done here. I've only been here once when Jason first bought the place."

The two women hooked arms as Rebecca gave Sarah the grand tour of the garden and the finished rooms.

"Can I help with supper tonight?" Mrs. Engles asked when they returned to the kitchen.

"Not tonight, but I'll remind you tomorrow. I miss your chicken and dumplings." She smiled. "And I want your recipe so that I can make them for Jason." Rebecca knew she'd never be able to fix chicken and dumpling as good as Sarah's. "Since the storm they were predicting blew past us, tonight we're having a picnic and barbecue on the beach, and everything's all prepared. I want you to enjoy our beautiful Cinnamon Bay sunset."

"Sounds wonderful. I can't wait to get out of my traveling clothes and take a shower." She peered toward the hallway, as if prompting Rebecca to show her to the room where she'd be staying.

Rebecca showed her to the guest quarters. The walls of the sunny room were papered in blue and white toile, and a blue-and-white-striped chaise lounge and reading lamp stood in a cozy nook across from the four-poster bed with its lace canopy.

"I love it here already." Mrs. Engles ran her fingers over the thick white enameled wood casings. "The house is beautiful, and this room is perfect." She hugged Rebecca. "Thank you for letting me be part of your life. I was pretty lonely by myself in Nashville."

The ringing and vibration coming from Rebecca's pocket jolted both women. It was her cell phone. She'd forgotten she had taken it off the counter, slipping it into the front pocket of her sweatshirt earlier.

"Becca, do you miss me?" came Jason's impossibly sexy voice.

She quickly turned to her mother-in-law. Rebecca couldn't contain her excitement as she began to shout into the phone. "Jase! Of course I miss you! How are you? Where are you?"

"I'm doing fine, baby girl." He paused for a moment. "Don't worry about me. Tell me everything."

Still shouting into the phone, as if Jason couldn't hear because of all the miles that separated them, Rebecca responded, "I'm so glad you're all right." She took a deep breath. "The news sounds as if things have been heating up over there again."

"Well, not everyone over here is happy we're helping this country become a democracy and have free elections, you know?" Rebecca could hear the popping of static through the receiver. "The insurgents like to bully and threaten us every chance they get to try to get us the hell out of here—as if they have a chance." He let out a deep sigh. "But not to worry. I should be out of here in no time."

Rebecca couldn't contain her excitement and screamed, "You're coming home?"

"They're letting me go in six weeks. My CO told me this morning. With the military, nothing's ever set in stone, but that's what the commander thinks. I can serve out the rest of my tour stateside."

"That's wonderful news!" Rebecca felt like dancing. "Your mother just got here for a visit. Do you have time to say hello to her?"

"I've only got two minutes left. Tell her I'll give her a call at home next week."

"Well, she's not going home right away. She's decided to stay here for awhile. We miss you so much, and she thought we could keep each other company." Rebecca gave her mother-in-law a "please don't tell" look.

"Wow, both my favorite girls in the same place. That's great. I'm glad you'll have the company. Becca, I gotta go. Tell Mama I love her and I'll try to call back in a couple of days."

She hugged her sides tightly, as if she were hugging Jason. "I love you, Jase. I miss you every minute you're gone."

"Me, too. I love you, Becca." The static began popping once again. "Keep the home fires burning, and I'll see you soon."

"I'll be counting the days," she said as she fiddled with the string on the mini-blinds, clicking the phone off.

Rebecca was elated as she grabbed hangers from the closet for Sarah's dresses. "Jason's coming home soon."

"Yes. I couldn't help overhearing. That's wonderful news, darling." Sarah continued removing clothes from her suitcase, placing them on hangers. "I'll breathe easier when he's out of harm's way."

"Me too." Rebecca plopped on the bed and began removing the clothes from Sarah's suitcase.

Sarah looked over her shoulder while hanging a blouse in the closet. "Maybe he'll be able to get a wedding ring on your finger before that baby arrives."

Their chatter was interrupted by a deep voice. They turned toward the sound of the voice. "Come on, ladies," Rick called out from the porch. "I've got the campfire going."

Rebecca and Sarah walked into the kitchen just as Rick trotted in, trailing sand behind him.

"Have you been rolling around down on the seashore with that girlfriend of yours?" Rebecca pointed to the beach of sand that had accumulated on her newly waxed kitchen floor.

Rick grinned while reaching for a spatula. "Ah, you know me too well, Becca."

Rebecca quickly handed Rick a plate draped with tinfoil. "No. I know *her* too well," she joked.

The screen slapped against the back patio door. "Are you two talking about me again?" Whitney inquired as she came inside.

Rick and Rebecca just looked at one another and laughed in unison.

Mrs. Engles also was laughing. "Okay, kids, what's for dinner? I'm starved and ready for that beautiful sunset I've been hearing about."

Whitney took Mrs. Engles by the arm as they all trooped out the door.

"I'm happy to report that we're having grilled steak and shrimp, corn on the cob, campfire-fried potatoes and s'mores for dessert." Whitney raised her eyebrows after saying s'mores. That was her favorite desert.

"I'm glad I'm eating for two." Rebecca laughed, feeling more lighthearted than she had been in months. "You want to grab that old guitar for me, Rick? I think we should celebrate Jason coming home soon with some singing."

"Great idea. I can impress you with my own talent." Rick looped an arm around Rebecca and chuckled. "When your boy gets back, he'll be upstaging me again."

"Not in my book he won't." Whitney peered back and sent him a flirty look over her shoulder.

They were all laughing as they took the pathway down to the beach.


Rebecca had been awake and working on the house for hours without waking Sarah. She had heard about the "nesting" instinct and she guessed that might account for her recent overwhelming urge to get everything done at once. Even though Mrs. Engles had been a big help during the past month, doing some of the gardening and chores as well as her share of the cooking, Becca couldn't stop getting ready.

Suddenly feeling pain, Rebecca began massaging her lower calves and ankles. They were swollen, red and blotchy. She sat on the couch with a glass of orange juice Whitney had poured her earlier, and the abrupt ringing of the cell phone startled her so much that she spilled her drink over her shirt.

She hurried to get up in case the call was from Jason. Maybe he was calling with the date of his homecoming. Perhaps this would be a good time to tell him about the baby and give him something happy to think about once he was safe on the long flight home.

"Hello?" Rebecca was out of breath when she reached the phone.

"Baby. What's the matter? You sound strange."

"I'm fine — just running for the phone. How are you? When are you coming home? We have most of the house ready, and —"

"Becca, honey, I've got bad news." As usual, static ended up troubling the line with loud pops and cracks. "We have to move out, and fast."

Grabbing her stomach, she leaned forward sporting a huge frown on her face. "What?" Rebecca gasped.

As if he couldn't hear very well, Jason spoke up, shouting into the phone. "I'm so sorry, baby. I have to stay."

"How long?" Rebecca bit her bottom lip, fighting back the tears. She couldn't bear having him over there any longer than he'd already been.

There was a long pause, as if he was scared to answer. "Likely at least another six weeks. Who knows?" A loud static pop nearly made her drop the phone.

She couldn't bear this bad news. Not now. Trying to get an intelligible sentence out, she could only mumble the words, "Oh, no."

For the first time since he'd been gone, the tone in his voice conveyed worry about his current situation. "The insurgents are on our tails."

Here came that sick feeling in the pit of her stomach again. "Oh, God, no," Rebecca said, close to tears.

Having trouble hearing her, Jason paused, "Becca, is something wrong?"

"Jase, it's just that...well...I miss you. I worry about you." She looked out the window, holding her tears inside.

"I miss you, too, but I gotta go, darling. Talk to you when we get to the new camp."

The call was interrupted by a rat-a-tat-tat sound. Rebecca knew it wasn't just normal static that she was accustomed to hearing. Then came a deafening sound of an explosion. She could hear men shouting, screaming, but couldn't make out anything they were saying. The connection became worse and Jason voice was garbled and unintelligible.

"Jason, was that gunfire in the background?" she asked anxiously. But there was nothing on the other end of the line but silence. "Jason? Jason!" No answer. Rebecca slowly closed the phone and sat down on the couch.

"Becca, dear. What's the matter?" Sarah came out from the other room, tying her robe. "What's all the commotion about? What has you so upset?"

Placing her head in her hands, Rebecca started shaking. She lifted her head briefly to speak to Sarah. "That was...that was Jason. He's going to have to stay in that hellhole for at least another six weeks." She felt as if she was in a hellhole herself.

"He'll be all right." Sarah patted her on the shoulder, but she couldn't contain the worried expression plastered on her face. "That boy knows what he's doing."

Rebecca knew Mrs. Engles was just saying that to sound reassuring to both of them. Sarah was every bit as worried as she was.

Starting to shake once again, Rebecca looked Sarah straight in the eyes. "When I was on the phone with him, I thought I heard gunfire. I didn't get to say goodbye."

The two women went directly to the TV and stayed glued to it throughout the day. The news anchors briefly mentioned some renewed fighting with Iraqi insurgents, but that was all. Finally when Rebecca got up to get them some iced tea and a bit of lunch, a sharp, stabbing pain hit her in the abdomen, doubling her over. Rebecca dropped to one knee, holding her stomach. The pain was intense. She felt like she would lose control of her bladder at any second.

"What is it, Rebecca?" Sarah stood up, rushing to Rebecca's side, pulling the hair out of her face in order to hear her.

Leaning on the couch for support, Rebecca lifted her head to answer Sarah. "I don't know. I hurt."

"Is it labor pains, child?" Sarah put her arms around Sarah, gently trying to lift her up on the couch where she would be more comfortable.

"I don't know." She grabbed Sarah's hand. "I'm scared."

Sarah glanced at the couch where Rebecca had been sitting. "There's blood on the cushions—we've got to get you to the hospital!"


The next several hours were a blur. Sarah took over like a general, organizing an emergency medical helicopter for Rebecca and a boat ride to the mainland for herself. Opie and Gladys picked her up and they were in the hospital in record time.

Sarah took a seat in the ER waiting room next to Rebecca's friends. Opie had already called Whitney, who was catching the first flight out to be with her friend. They sat in the waiting room for what seemed like hours.

Finally a tall doctor with gray hair and glasses walked into the room. "I'm Dr. Alcox. Are you the folks here with Rebecca Roberts?"

"Yes," Sarah said. "I brought her in. How is she? How is the baby?" Mrs. Engles began wringing her hands nervously.

"Rebecca is stabilized. But there are some complications." He peeled off his surgical gloves and sighed. "I'm not sure the baby will make it."

# Chapter Sixteen

**⁘**

Feeling groggy, Rebecca slowly opened her eyes. Her eyelids felt like they'd been weighted with lead. After a few minutes passed, the cloudiness began to lift and she began exploring her surroundings. Looking around the unfamiliar room, she noticed an IV machine. Following the tube with her eyes, she saw that it was attached to her wrist. As she watched the clear liquid drip little by little into the tube, she moved. Her vein hurt with sharp, prodding stabs from the needle. Every bone in her entire body ached and she was weak. Realizing this was a hospital, Rebecca felt frightened and alone.

The door of her room was cracked open just enough for her to hear the hustling of a busy hospital ward. As people walked past her room, Rebecca could hear whispers and the echo of shoes shuffling against the hard tile floor. A nurse was shouting out Dr. Johnson's name over the intercom and then in a frantic voice called a "code blue".

Rebecca turned her attention to the other side of the room and noticed that the shades were slightly open, allowing a small amount of light to shine through. The television was on, but there was no sound. Rebecca wanted to turn the volume up, but was scared to move her arm again. The IV was pinching her vein. Unable to find the controller, she eventually gave up and decided to turn her head to get a better view of the screen.

The channel was broadcasting pictures of Geraldo Rivera standing in front of an Apache helicopter taking off in a remote desert somewhere. Then it switched to images of soldiers firing upon what appeared to be Iraqi insurgents and buildings. Rebecca watched for a few minutes as Fox News showed pictures of a young soldier. She guessed that something bad had happened to him, as there were pictures of a teary older couple holding up a photo of him in full military dress for the cameras.

These images upset Rebecca. She needed to touch her stomach for comfort. Bringing her hand up to caress her baby, she discovered that her belly was flatter. Rebecca was stunned. There was no baby, only thick bandages covering her midsection. With her fingers, she cautiously explored the wide gauze and wrappings—her stomach was sore to the touch. She began to panic. What had happened? Where was her child?

Even with the IV drip making her slightly drowsy, she managed to reach behind her head, fumbling for a call button, but whatever she pressed only made the bed move up and down. She needed to find someone—anyone who could explain to her what was going on. Trying to get out of bed, she rolled onto her side in an effort to sit up, but the pains in her stomach immediately forced her back down, keeping her from moving. Annoyed, worried and panicked she began shouting, "Please help. Someone please help me. Is anyone out there?"

Suddenly the door to the restroom swung open. Sarah emerged, wiping her hands with a thick, brown paper towel. "Rebecca, you're awake."

Within a few seconds she was at Rebecca's bedside, taking one of her hands into her own and rubbing it to soothe her. "Becca, how are you feeling, honey? You gave us all quite a scare."

"What...what happened?" she asked weakly. With her good arm, she pulled back the sheet and pointed to her tummy. "Where's my baby? Jason?"

"Jason's still overseas, remember? You talked to him right before you..." Mrs. Engles stroked her hair gently. "He can't come home to us right now."

Visibly distressed, Rebecca once again tried to move the lower half of her body, but the pain was too great. "Where's my baby, Sarah?"

Sarah put her hand on Rebecca's shoulder to quiet her. "Hush now. You had an emergency C-section yesterday and you have a little girl."

Rebecca's heart warmed hearing the words. She mouthed what she'd just heard. "I have a baby girl?" she said in wonderment. Grabbing for the older woman's arm, she started questioning her. "Where is she? I want to see her. Is she all right?"

"Slow down, dear. They're taking good care of the little one in the neonatal unit. You'll see her tomorrow." Sarah reached behind Rebecca, carefully straightening her pillow.

Rebecca resented being unable to move and fought her help. "I need to see my baby. Something's wrong, isn't it? Why else won't you take me to her? You have to tell me."

"My granddaughter was over four weeks early and requires assistance breathing. She's getting excellent care. Now you need to catch some sleep and get your strength back. Your body needs time to recover from the blood loss. We almost lost you."

"I have to see my baby," she pleaded desperately while tears of worry rolled down her cheeks.

Sarah pulled the sheet up around Rebecca's shoulders. "Shh, Becca, please calm down." She grabbed for Rebecca's hand, squeezing it tightly. "Don't cry. Everything is going to be fine. The baby barely weighed five pounds and needs to be exactly where she is. You need to be where you are too, dear. They have the baby in an incubator. The doctor and I spoke earlier. If you're doing better tomorrow, they'll bring a wheelchair to your room and you can go and visit your little bundle of joy."

Rebecca nodded her head in agreement. "I promise to do what you and the doctors tell me to do."

"Good girl. My son would never forgive me if I let something happen to you. You're the best thing that ever happened to my boy." Sarah bent down to kiss her cheek.

"A little girl..." Rebecca smiled, letting her head fall back against the pillow.

"A little girl," Mrs. Engles repeated, patting her hand. "She may be tiny, but she's beautiful. I think she'll look more like her mommy than my Jason."

"My little miracle baby," Rebecca whimpered. "I've had two miracles in my life. First I found my Jason again and now the baby." Her mouth quivered. "I didn't think it would happen this way, when we're not together." She rubbed her abdomen as the stitches began to hurt and throb. "And Jason doesn't even know he's a daddy."

"Well, whatever way you did it, Rebecca, you and Jason have your miracle baby now. With that said, you can rest more comfortably." Sarah lowered the bed. "Have you picked out a name for her?"

"Virginia Anne. I loved your mother's name the moment I heard it." She smiled. "Jason used to talk about her a lot. He had good memories of visiting her during those long summers back at the ranch. 'No one could match her baking', he used to say to me."

"Well, Grandma Ginni would be pleased." Jason's mother smiled and pointed upward. "I'm sure she's in heaven looking down and feeling very blessed at this moment."

"Oh God, Sarah." Rebecca clutched Sarah's hand. "Do you think Jase will be happy?"

Sarah patted her hand. "Of course he will, darling."

Rebecca saw the concerned look in her eyes. "What is it?" she asked anxiously. "What aren't you telling me?"

Sarah gave a forced smile, looked down at the floor and then back at Rebecca. "Just that you need to recover from your surgery and the doctors have to take care of little Virginia. We need to get you both healthy so we can tell Jason all good news if..." she looked away as if in pain. "When we get to talk to him again."

"What are you saying, Sarah?" Rebecca demanded. "Did something happen in Iraq? Is Jason hurt?"

A worried look crept over Sarah's face. Rebecca could tell she was hiding something because tears began welling in her eyes. "We don't know much of anything right now." She turned and started rearranging the flowers and balloons that had been delivered earlier in the day. "Just what I've told you and what Jason said in his last call. Try not to worry, and—"

The nurse bustled into the room and interrupted the conversation. "Hello, Ms. Roberts. I'm Kelly, your night nurse. I need to check your blood pressure and temperature." The nurse went efficiently about her poking and prodding and wrote down Rebecca's vital signs on a chart. Once her examination was done, she hooked it to the bottom of her bed.

"Rebecca gave us all a big scare yesterday. Does everything look okay?" Sarah anxiously questioned the nurse.

"Well, her vitals look good—she's stable. We just need to watch for any signs of infection." Kelly quickly replaced the nearly empty IV bag. She then began to check and then change the dressing around Rebecca's stitches. Before she left, the nurse took a syringe and shot additional medication into the IV line. Turning toward Rebecca, the nurse moved the call button closer to her hand. "That was something to help you sleep more comfortably. Push the buzzer if you need me."

Rebecca looked up at the nurse, weakly thanking her.

The nurse winked. "Later on when you wake up, I'll take you down to see your daughter. If you're up to it."

"Oh—I'll be up to it, you can bet on that." Rebecca eagerly smiled.

Almost instantly she became drowsy, continuing to hold on to Sarah's hand. "I want my baby," she murmured. "I want Jason." She started to slur her words. "Maybe…maybe they'd let him come home."

Sarah stroked Rebecca's hand, caressing her fingers back and forth over the top to ease her. "You rest now. Sleep soundly Becca."

"Will you stay?" Rebecca's eyes started to close.

"Of course I will. I'll be here when you wake up." Sarah smoothed Rebecca's sheet one more time and then made herself comfortable in a reclining chair next to the bed. She kept an eye on Rebecca while working on her cross-stitch.

Rebecca slowly recovered from the surgery and on the third day was wheeled into the neonatal care unit. Her baby lay in a huge, clear plastic dome, attached to all kinds of beeping and blinking machines. The baby's lungs were undeveloped and she needed IVs and a breathing tube. Rebecca peered down at her tiny child. Virginia looked like a sleeping angel with her clenched fists and blond wisps of hair.

Another week passed before Virginia was strong enough to be removed from the incubator and Rebecca could hold her, wrapping the teeny infant in a handmade pink baby blanket that Whitney had sent over with a box of baby clothing. "By the time your daddy comes home," she would whisper to her, "you'll be big and strong."

Virginia was so soft and delicate, and Rebecca held her carefully. Rebecca's heart warmed when she looked at her child. She would explore every inch of her baby from the top of her head to the tips of her toes. Ginni's hands were so small and fragile. She was stunning. Whenever the baby opened her blue eyes and looked up at her, Rebecca would melt. What a miracle to be holding this child that she and Jason and their love had made. God, how she wished Jason were here to share these precious moments. He was missing so much being away.

"Hey, little Ginni, do you know how much your mama loves you?" Rebecca kissed her baby's forehead. "I can't wait to tell your daddy all about you, little girl. He'll be just as proud of you as I am." Rebecca gently rocked her as Virginia slept.

As she held Ginni, Rebecca periodically checked her cell phone, making sure that it was on. She was warned not to use one in the hospital, but if Jason had the opportunity to call, she didn't want to miss it. It would be so hard not to tell him about this precious little one. There had been no calls for nearly three weeks.

Rebecca wondered if she had done the right thing in not telling Jason. She still believed that the news would have distracted him, jeopardizing his safety. What she did regret was that she'd talked Jason out of getting married prior to his leaving. If they were married, she thought, perhaps he would have gotten family leave and Ginni would carry his last name. But she tried not to think of that too often because she knew there was no use regretting something she couldn't change.

The most important thing was to get baby Virginia's lungs healthy and bring her home. The neonatal nurse coming into the room to take the baby back to her medical crib startled her thoughts. Rebecca reluctantly released Ginni and asked anxiously, "Is there any news on her blood work yet?"

She was worried about her baby. The doctors were running daily tests, telling Rebecca that it was just routine and not to worry, but she didn't have a good feeling about any of this.

Once Virginia was safely in her crib, the nurse began hooking up different monitors and then turned toward Rebecca. "The doctor is going to bring in another specialist from Boston tomorrow. Her liver functions still aren't giving us a good reading. She looks great though, doesn't she? Good color and all."

"She looks beautiful," Rebecca whispered.

The nurse gave Rebecca an extra blanket. "Now all we need to do is get mama healthy enough to go home."

"Oh, no. The longer I'm here, the closer I can be to Ginni. I don't want to go home."

"Why don't you take a nap? Virginia's going to," the nurse kindly suggested.

Sadly Rebecca wheeled herself back to her room. To her surprise, when she opened the door, Whitney was sprawled in a chair, brandishing a bottle of contraband booze and a paper cup.

Rebecca quickly closed the door. "What're you doing here, Whit? You can't bring that stuff in here."

"What they don't know won't hurt them. I've never been one for rules — you of all people know that." Whitney wasn't her usual chipper self. "To answer your question, I'm trying to drown my sorrows. Here, have a cup. You look like you could use a shot, too." She extended a glass of spirits to her friend and then abruptly stopped. "You aren't breastfeeding, are you? I read somewhere that mothers who breastfed had to be careful what they ate or drank."

"No Whit. You don't have to worry about that. Ginni's on a special formula right now." Rebecca looked at the cup. "However, I'm still on my pain meds. I hope your booze doesn't whack me out."

"Rebecca, sometimes it's good to be whacked out."

The girls both chuckled as Whitney leaned forward, handing her friend the drink. They both clinked their cups together. "How's the kid?"

Rebecca sat down on the bed across from Whitney and took a drink. Immediately the swash of alcohol made her insides feel warm and tingly. Surprisingly the alcohol made her feel light and numb. "Virginia is holding her own. They're calling in another specialist, though." The idea of one more doctor chilled her as she placed her drink on the table. Deeply troubled, she began rubbing her hands up and down her arms. Whitney looked awful. "What sorrows are you drowning with this illegal booze?"

"Well I guess you could say I'm a bit upset you got your figure back so quickly after having a baby — me, I'd probably swell up like a tick." Whitney pointed at her own body.

"I hardly think that's your problem. Now, really what's the matter with you?" Rebecca was concerned. To sneak booze into a hospital ward was just a little outside of Whitney's antics.

Whitney groaned. "Nothing like what you're going through. I probably shouldn't even be saying anything. My problems are trivial by comparison and I shouldn't burden you. You'll just laugh at me if I tell you anyway."

She scooted into her bed, reached across the nightstand for an extra pillow and laid back on them. "Well, what are best friends for? Besides, I could use a good laugh. Something to take my mind off my own troubles. So fess up."

Getting up from the chair and gripping her hands tightly, Whitney reached for another drink, turning back to face Rebecca. "It's Rick. I love him, and I did something really stupid."

Rebecca gestured for her to continue.

"Our relationship has been off-beat, to say the least. The guy literally has women hanging all over him all the time. To deal with the situation, I try and make things in the romance department lighthearted. I figure that way he never gets bored with just me. So, I play these little practical jokes on him." She shrugged. "You know, pretend I'm someone else and try to trip him up and see if he'll fall for another woman."

A puzzled look came across Rebecca's face. She leaned up on one arm, totally engrossed in everything Whitney had to say. "Keep going."

Whitney continued. "For instance, I'll wait in his pitch-dark trailer after a show. I put on a wig or a hat and dark glasses, dim the lights and pretend I'm a groupie who sneaked into his bed."

"And...?"

"For the first few minutes he plays along, calling me Roxanne or Foxy Lady and putting the moves on me. He finally comes clean that he knew who I was all along before we make love." Her cheeks began to blush.

"Well, what's so embarrassing about any of that? Sounds like you're both in on the joke and play along together. Besides do I have to remind you of the time you played Nurse Naughty with that chiropractor over in Texas City? Didn't you call him Doctor Dirty?"

Whitney crinkled up her face. "Shut it! I'd rather not revisit that one, thank you very much. Now let's get back to my problem with Rick shall we?"

Rebecca held back the laughter, which made her stitches hurt. Grabbing her middle to brace her stomach, she put one hand over her mouth. "Okay. I'm sorry — continue."

"If only I'd stopped my escapades there," Whitney said as she poured herself another shot of blackberry brandy. "I thought I'd surprise Rick with a 'present' yesterday. So I went to this costume shop on the outskirts of Nashville. The place is called 'Get Them While Your Figure's Still Hot Erotic Costume Shop'. I had them make me a risqué guitar costume. It almost looked like a real guitar with makeshift strings on it. He could strum them and everything. I spiked my hair and put on this vixen rocker make-up."

Rebecca coughed, choking on her drink trying not to laugh. "Boy, you know, this stuff's stout." She had to quickly cover up her urge to laugh with something, even if it was feeble. "What's the matter? Didn't he like the costume?"

"Rick's been really busy, so I told him I wanted to spend some time alone with him. He said he had work to do in the studio. You know he helps his friends put mixes together for demos sometimes." Whitney set her cup down and tipped her head back against the wall. "When I got there, the lights were off in the mixing room. Like our normal games — I thought he was trying to surprise me. So I took off my trench coat and stood in the middle of the room in all my naked guitar glory."

Rebecca accidentally giggled. "Oops — sorry about that."

Whitney shot her a cross look, but continued. "Then I heard Rick's voice over the microphone, asking me what Roxanne wanted."

"So what did you say?" Rebecca said with anticipation. She couldn't wait to hear the ending of this story.

Whitney rolled her eyes in embarrassment. "Turn the light on, big boy, and see. Tonight, I want you to play me like you play your guitar."

Rebecca pressed her hand against her mouth.

"The lights came on, and there stood Rick with the entire band and some sound mixers. I felt like an idiot, and I probably looked worse."

"Oh, that's rich." Rebecca couldn't contain herself and burst out laughing, slapping one hand on the bed while hugging her stomach tightly so as not to jar her stitches.

"Are you done yet? If not, I can wait. I'd hate for you to miss a good laugh at my expense." Whitney frowned.

Rebecca stopped. "Oh, I'm sorry Whit. I didn't mean to do that—really. So what did Rick do?"

Whitney glared at her. "He looked as surprised as I did, and the guys in the band were laughing like loons. It was just awful, so I snatched up my coat, ran out of there and caught the first plane here. I think I spent most of the night in the airport. Of course, thoughts of all those men seeing my naked, thong-clad butt during my rushed departure kept me company. There was no way I was going back to my apartment, let alone work today. Rick will probably never speak to me again. Do you know he hasn't even tried to call me?" She slumped in her chair.

Rebecca shook her head. "I can't believe you said, 'play me'. That's too funny."

"Thanks for your understanding, pal. My hair was spiked and everything. I mean it, I looked like a guitar."

"A Fender or a Gibson?"

Whitney made a rude gesture.

"Jason always says, 'Nothin' makes music like a Gibson'. Maybe Rick prefers another brand?"

"You are just too funny for words, Rebecca," Whitney said, her voice heavy with sarcasm.

Rebecca laughed. "Whit, with all the bad going on in my life, I really needed a good laugh." She kicked the side of Whitney's chair. "Now, let's put our heads together and figure out your Rick problem."

"There's nothing to figure out," Whitney mumbled. "I'm sure by now he's figured out that I'm one pathetic loser and has dumped me."

"He's crazy about you. That man wouldn't do that." Rebecca sat up in the bed to argue her point.

"Now I've got two black marks against me." Whitney poured herself another drink. "First I flunk the visit with his family, and now this. Maybe I shouldn't have left my job in Galveston and moved to Nashville. We could have taken things slow and easy. Had one of those long-distance relationships. You know what they say, 'absence makes the heart grow fonder'."

Rebecca raised her eyebrows and looked at her friend. "Right. Like you ever took anything slow and easy in your entire life — and the long-distance thing isn't as easy as it looks."

"Yeah, well…"

"How's the new job working out, anyway?"

Whitney perked up. "It's great. That's the one good thing in my life. I'm going to be in Miami tomorrow setting up some promotional stuff for some new singers the company has signed up. They're a good group. I think once their new single hits the airways, they'll do well."

"So maybe the move to Nashville wasn't a total loss." Rebecca sent her friend a sly smile.

A loud ringing came from Whitney's purse. It was her cell.

Rick.

Finally the day arrived when little Ginni could breathe on her own, but the doctors prescribed a nurse and breathing apparatus in case there was a relapse. She had to be watched over continuously by a health care provider until she was at full strength. While they did a final panel of tests, Rebecca paced up and down.

"Come and sit down, Becca," Sarah said. "You're wearing a rut in the floor."

Rebecca perched on the edge of a chair next to Sarah. "I'm so excited, I can hardly stand it." She squeezed Sarah's hand. "The doctor said we can take her home as soon as they're done. I can't wait to show Ginni Cinnamon Bay. They'll call us with the results."

"I know, dear. The nurse was here while you were in the cafeteria getting us coffee." Sarah continued folding clothes, gathering up toiletry items and packing them in the suitcase for the journey home. "It truly is a wonderful day."

"I just wish—" Rebecca paused.

Sarah patted Rebecca's arm. "I know," she said. "So do I."

Most of the work on the house had been finished, so they didn't have to worry about dust impacting the baby's health. When Rebecca put Ginni to sleep for the night that evening, she sat for hours next to the crib, looking at her perfect miracle baby and singing softly to her.

They had only been home less than a week when the hospital called. Sarah found Rebecca still holding the phone and sobbing.

"What's wrong, honey? Is it J—" Sarah pressed her hands against her heart.

Rebecca shook her head. "It was the hospital. I have to bring Ginni back in." She looked up at Sarah, barely able to see through the tears in her eyes. "They think she has cancer." The phone fell on the floor as she buried her face in her hands and sobbed.

Sarah, too, began to shake, and the two women held each other as they wept.

"She can't die," Rebecca finally said. "I refuse to believe that I would have been given this miracle baby only to have her taken away."

"There are so many treatments these days. The doctors will find something." Sarah picked up the phone, placing it on the table. "Did they say what kind of cancer it was?"

"The doctors need to do more testing before they can conclude what type it is. They said it could be a tumor, or it could be in her bone marrow." She pulled in a breath on a sob. "Or both." She bent down and cradled her head in her arms. "What kind of life is my poor baby going to have now?"

Sarah sat down. "Well, we just have to keep going, the three of us, until the doctors figure it all out."

"Sarah, it just breaks my heart." Rebecca held a tissue to her nose.

No longer able to contain her tears either, Sarah reached for her handkerchief. "I know." She slumped a little. "Are you going to tell Jason now?"

Rebecca abruptly stood up. "God, no! How can I hit him with everything all at once? He'd never be able to concentrate on himself."

"What if Ginni doesn't make it?" Tears rolled down Sarah's cheeks. "Then she'll be gone before Jason even knew she was here."

"No! I won't let her die. Do you hear me? I won't let her die!"

Sarah folded her hands as if she were praying. Then after a while she raised her head and sighed. "Come on, Becca," she said. "Let's pack."

Rebecca sat at the table in Ginni's room and doodled on a piece of paper, fiddling with the verse of a song as she waited for Ginni to be brought back to her from her radiation treatment. That was the only thing really working in her life right now, she thought. After that first sale, J.R. Neel's songs were suddenly in demand by big-name artists.

Donna Jo Hughes, a major singer, had recorded "Lonesome Tonight," a song Rebecca had written shortly after Jason left. People were talking it up even though it hadn't even been officially released yet. The record label said that it was a cinch for a Grammy nomination.

Rebecca had always imagined how fabulous her life would be once her songs started selling, but it was nothing like that. She had a beautiful baby who was dangerously ill and every penny she made as J.R. Neels went to her care.

She had been up all night, unable to sleep long after Ginni had fallen into an exhausted slumber. Now she was running on coffee and a prayer.

There was a knock at the door, and before she could say anything, Opie burst into the room. Rebecca looked up from the song sheet she'd been working on to see Opie looking upset, sweating and out of breath.

"Opie? What the heck are you doing here?"

"Turn on the television set." He was still panting hard. "Gladys and I were watching the news. I didn't want to call and tell you about it over the phone. That's why I made the trip out to the hospital, so you'd have someone here with you."

Rebecca could see that he was almost crying. "What is it?" She stood up.

"Something awful happened over in Iraq. There's been intense fighting near the area Jason was last." Opie threw his big arms around Rebecca's body, almost picking her up.

Rebecca felt her blood turn to ice and she began to tremble.

Keeping his arm around Rebecca, Opie switched on the TV, working the remote until he found one of the cable news channels. Just as he turned the volume up, the news anchor flashed on the screen.

"This is Joel Thomas bringing you breaking news from Iraq. There is word this morning that Muslim extremists have captured several Marines."

Rebecca threw her hands over her mouth.

The reporter continued, "The Pentagon has not yet announced how many Marines have been taken captive. Word is that the terrorists are demanding that the United States Armed Forces pull out of Iraq and are warning that unless the U.S. pulls out, any Americans who are taken hostage will be killed."

The reporter paused, listening to what was coming through his ear microphone and nodded.

"Okay, I'm also getting word that we now know that a convoy carrying Marines from Baghdad to Mosul has been attacked. The Pentagon is releasing figures that at least three Marines have been killed and at least three, maybe four have been taken hostage. I'm being told that we should have a picture feed of the hostages at any second. We will be getting this from Al Jazeera, so I apologize for the delay and quality of the footage."

Rebecca had eyes and ears only for what the reporter was saying, and she didn't even notice that Sarah had come into the room and was standing next to her. When Sarah spoke, she jumped.

"This can't be happening to us, Rebecca." Sarah whispered, visibly trembling. "I don't believe for a second that my son is being held captive. Opie, we don't even know if Jason was in that area anymore."

"I'm sorry Sarah, but I got a letter last week from him—"

Rebecca interrupted their chatter. "If he had been one of the ones killed, we wouldn't even know. You're not at your house. How would they know where to go to notify you if—"

"Oh, for God's sake, Rebecca." Sarah's voice was harsh. "Stop talking like that. If you don't have any more faith in my boy than that, what are you doing with him?"

"Ladies, please." Opie raised his voice to get everyone's attention. "You guys need each other right now. I think all Rebecca was trying to say is that she's worried about Jason like you are. She just wants to make sure that you get word on where he's at if they try to contact you."

All eyes once again focused on the television as the reporter began to speak again. "I'm being told that the Marine convoy was brought to a halt with an explosion and in the aftermath of the explosion, a shootout ensued. That's when the hostages were taken."

Rebecca's heart sank, and she began to bite her fingernails. Sarah was visibly shaken. Opie tried his best to console both of the women as all three waited breathlessly for the reporter's next words.

"The names of the Marines taken hostage have not yet been confirmed by the Pentagon, but our sources on the ground have told us that one of those captured is country singer Jason Engles. Our thoughts and prayers go out to his family this morning."

# Chapter Seventeen

છૐ

A scorpion crawled over the laces of Jason's boot as he sat quietly on the ground, staring at his crude desert prison and the three other Marines who had been captured with him. The heat was unbearable in their tiny cement cell, the air rank and humid. Mosquitoes swarmed around the blood, urine and feces that fouled them and the floor. His best guess was that they'd been locked up for about two days. Their watches and military devices had been taken away. The cell had one high window, close to the ceiling, so it was hard to gauge the passage of time with anything resembling certainty.

Damn that major. If he'd cared a little more about the men instead of moving up in rank by making such a bold move, they wouldn't be in this mess. The road conditions for the small, lightly armored convoy had deteriorated, becoming too dangerous for passage. He'd radioed ahead requesting a change of course. Jason's plan was to maneuver the troops several clicks due west and then plot another path to the north. Major Bettis refused, instead barking out orders insisting they detour onto a less secure road, trekking them east. Jason's gut told him this was a bad move, but he was helpless against the orders.

Several Marines were killed as a huge explosion from a roadside bomb rocked their convoy. There was significant damage done to the first Humvee. The lightly armored vehicle veered off the road, careening into a drainage ditch and then burst into flames. During the aftermath, two other vehicles flipped over, pinning the injured men inside. Before Jason knew what hit him, they were surrounded by Iraqi insurgents and taken prisoner. He was staff sergeant and the highest ranking Marine among the prisoners, but he'd be damned if he knew how to get them out of this jam.

Their captors had told them that if the United States didn't meet their demands to pull out of Iraq completely—and he knew that wasn't going to happen—each day, one of them would be taken from the cell and killed. The terrorists had given the United States a forty-eight hour deadline.

Since Jason held the highest rank, the terrorists said he would watch his fellow Marines die before they would make an example out of him with a particularly gruesome and slow death. As he crouched on the floor, he prepared himself mentally for the torture that was almost sure to happen. It would take all the strength he had, but he swore to himself that he wouldn't crack, no matter how brutal the torture. After all, he was a United States Marine, bred to courage and honor.

His heart ached as he thought of the men he was now responsible for. Chad, a private from a farm in Mississippi, was only nineteen. He'd hardly seen more than his home state. Chad had never traveled or experienced half the things he wanted to. His high school sweetheart had sent him a Dear John letter, and he had taken the breakup hard. As Jason continued to watch Chad, all he could think about was the boy back on the farm plowing fields, hunting quail and playing with his dog Shawnee.

About two hundred U.S. Marines and eighty Iraqi soldiers had moved into Haqlaniyah, one of a cluster of western towns in Anbar province, a stronghold of Iraqi insurgents and foreign fighters. Armed, hooded gunmen with rifles and rocket-propelled grenades had attacked their unit. Chad had never encountered actual hand-to-hand combat before. When the fighting turned deadly, he was unsure of himself. Jason suspected that, despite his rigorous training, killing another human being had made him freeze, thus making him easy prey for the terrorists who had ambushed and attacked them.

At twenty-eight, Dale was the oldest. He was a corporal and one of the finest men Jason had ever met. Dale had a wife and three small children back home in Chicago. His youngest, a daughter, had been born only three months before Dale was deployed. Jason winced. It was difficult enough leaving his mother and Rebecca behind, let alone any children. He wouldn't have been able to deal with that type of anguish. How do you tell a child that their father's been taken prisoner or, even worse, killed? Jason couldn't keep his mind off the personal heartache his friend must have been facing.

Jason watched Dale worriedly. He had taken a bullet in the abdomen. God, he could lie there in agony for days before dying. Their captors apparently got a kick out of beating injured men as well as whole ones. It was likely that if Dale survived the next forty-eight hours, he would be the first to die under the terrorists' ultimatum. He was wounded and would be hard to move if the Iraqi insurgents had to pull up stakes and leave quickly.

The final man of the group was Kyle—a bona fide loner. Jason didn't know much about him other than that he was from California and his father had pushed him to enlist. He had barely spoken since their capture. He sat quietly in a corner, staring downwards, drawing circles in the sand.

Jason's head ached, and he tentatively reached up with his cuffed wrists and ran the back of his hand across the open laceration. A piece of shrapnel had embedded near his eye. Only the handcuffs cutting into his skin matched the painful throbbing in his temple. He hated to even move, but the blood and sweat constantly dripping down into his eyes irritated him. Occasionally, he had to try and wipe his face clean to avoid infection from disease-carrying insects.

To escape this pit of hell, Jason tried to fill his mind with happy moments. He thought back to the weeks he and Rebecca had spent together at the homestead on Cinnamon Bay. The time had been all too short, but now, those memories sustained him.

He remembered what it was like to make love to her. Jason replayed how good she felt in bed over and over in his mind until he could almost feel the touch of her fingers, the silkiness of her hair over his chest, taste the salt on her skin and smell the sweetness of her perfume as she leaned over and kissed his neck.

Then there was that day at the beach. It was hot and butter pecan ice cream was melting down her arm. As she licked the cone, he licked the dripping dessert from her skin. He could taste the salt of the water against the sweetness of the cream against her smooth flesh. She looked at him with such devotion. He fell in love with her all over again that day.

Closing his eyes, he could almost hear her whispering to him. *"Anything less than mad, passionate, extraordinary love is a waste of time. There are too many mediocre things in life, Jason, and love shouldn't be one of them."*

He took his mind back to his high school days in Galveston. Rebecca had been a lanky, long-legged kid, just barely showing the promise of her beauty. Still a tomboy at heart, she liked to tease and usually managed to out-fish him during weekends at the lake, often bragging she'd read his mind and the fishes'.

Most of all, if he never lived another day, he wanted to remember the lazy summer nights grilling their catch on the beach and making music after a radiant Texas sunset, only to make love under the stars later. Together they had dreamed of becoming a sensational singer-songwriting team who'd take Nashville by storm. Were all of those dreams now lost?

He had loved her more than anything in the world. Rebecca always knew the best things to say when he felt down or had had a horrible day. No matter how bad her own life was, she always managed an illuminating smile just for him. She'd always been the best thing that had happened to him, and yet he'd left her and wasted so many years. He'd listened to his father and put his career first.

Jason stared death in the face. He now knew what was important in life—to find a soul mate and never let her go. One special person to share life with forever came only once. God how he wished he could wake up just one more time feeling the curves and texture of Rebecca's sweet body, smell the lightly scented fragrance of her long golden hair and hear the crash of the waves against the shore.

Fulfillment wasn't packing an arena with fans and making tons of money. It was spending your years with the person you couldn't bear to be without and growing old with her. He felt a pang of regret that he and Rebecca hadn't produced children. A house filled with kids that looked like her, who could carry on their legacy would have been wonderful.

Oh, the lost years, the mistakes he'd made. Thinking of Rebecca now and the life he'd missed out on made him want to single-handedly claw his way out of the cell and kill any terrorist who tried to stand in his way. He'd be damned if he'd let terrorists screw up his future and keep him away from the woman he loved. He couldn't let Rebecca down again. He wished he had that picture of her he always carried, but, like his freedom and his gear, his captors had taken that away too.

Five hooded Arabs bursting through the cell door carrying Kalashnikov assault rifles interrupted Jason's reverie. He sat there, refusing to rise to attention. Fearing the consequences of disobedience, Chad scurried to his feet. Kyle, too, remained in his corner, looking up at his captors with a defiant stare. Dale could do nothing but lie on the floor in agonizing pain.

He watched as two of the men began kicking Dale repeatedly. The wounded Marine moaned aloud, but he seemed to be only half-conscious. Before he could think about his actions, Jason leaped up and lunged toward Dale's tormentors, forcing them back. The leader turned, threw him against the wall and began punching him in the back, sides and stomach. Jason clenched his teeth together, refusing to cry out. At least they were leaving Dale alone.

Jason stood, helpless. He was so enraged at his capturers that his heart and his blood began to boil. Here he was Dale's superior, and there was nothing he could do to get him out of there. Dale had talked about his family all the time. Images of Dale's family, especially his children, ran through his mind. He became even more enraged.

"You sons of bitches, leave him alone." He landed a punch on the gunman doing most of the beating. Then everything stopped. Jason, bleeding from the nose and mouth, looked up and saw a bearded man dressed in gray standing in the doorway. Jason had seen this man from afar when they were first brought to the cell. He must have been some kind of Mullah, since the men treated him with deference. The man in gray began to speak to him in English.

"Come with me, Sergeant Engles. As the ranking soldier of these pitiful dregs of humanity, I think you should see firsthand what we have planned for the American audience back home. This is what all Americans can look forward to." He gave Jason an evil grin.

Jason defiantly looked the Arab cleric straight in the eye and shouted, "Semper Fi!"

Pointing a dirty finger at Jason, the Mullah commanded him to step forward. Refusing to move, Jason spat on the gunman when he jabbed him in the back with the butt of his gun.

"You will pay for that little stunt," the bearded man said mildly with a faint smile. "You think you hate me now, but just wait until later, infidel."

The Mullah motioned for his henchmen to bring Jason along as two of the men brutally dragged Dale from the cell. Nausea welled up in Jason's stomach. He knew what was about to happen to his friend and was helpless to stop it. The armed men left Chad and Kyle in the cell, preparing to lock it behind them.

Jason turned his head back to see Chad pressing his face against the bars. His arms and hands were sticking outside the cell. "Sarge, don't leave me here! Don't leave me here to die!"

"Chad, you listen to me," he called back over his shoulder, struggling with the guards. "Just keep your mouth shut and do as they tell you. The longer you do that, the longer you might live. Okay?"

Jason looked ahead, walking as slowly as he dared, taking in his surroundings and watching for any opportunity to commandeer a weapon and attempt to break his men free. He was led into what he guessed was a torture chamber. He saw an array of tools, knives and chains laid neatly on a table. In the middle of the room was a light blue Oriental rug and a simple wooden chair. The captors dumped Dale's limp body into the chair and bound him. Jason, too, was bound tightly into a second chair off to one side, but he was left without a blindfold. He knew what that meant.

"Dale, you're a good man. The finest I've had a chance to serve with," he said to his nearly unconscious friend. "God be with you. Semper Fi!"

"Jason, tell my wife and girls I love them," Dale gasped weakly. "You tell Sommer, that I was thinking of her smile right up until the end."

Jason swallowed hard, ducking his head. "I will, Dale. I promise. God bless you, man."

The Mullah shouted something in Arabic and a gag was tightly placed over Jason's mouth. He began to struggle up from his seat, but the guard's grip was too tight.

"Sergeant Engles, we have created a little entertainment for you this evening. I like to call it 'Theatre of the Living'. You can take comfort in the fact that we will sacrifice you last. However, you will get to watch each time one of your friends is executed."

Once again, Jason fought to get free, moving the chair with his legs. A guard came over and kicked his knee, making it buckle.

The bearded man laughed. "Struggle all you want. Your government did not comply with our demands, but you know this, don't you? Thus, we are filming this little event to show all your friends back in the States that we mean business." He gestured to the video camera one of the hooded thugs was holding. "We want you out of our country. The Iraqi people didn't ask for this war. We didn't ask you to come in and 'free' us. For doing so, I hope you enjoy what you are about to see."

Two of the captors instructed Dale to state his name and rank as the camera began to roll. Jason watched, sick at heart, as the terrorists spoke to the camera in words he didn't understand but whose tone he recognized. Dale was about to pay a soldier's ultimate price and Jason couldn't do one damn thing but hope that Dale's wife and children would never see this tape.

One of the men grabbed Dale's hair, holding him, while another picked up a blade that looked like a short sword and held it to his throat. Jason closed his eyes. Dale wouldn't experience a quick death. Even with the sharp blade, the enemy was sure to torture him first, he thought.

The leader gave Jason a karate chop to his throat, making him choke and gag. A razor sharp pain shot through his neck. "Sergeant Engles, you will keep your eyes open and watch our little presentation unless you want to see one of the other Marines go today, too, instead of tomorrow."

Forced to comply, Jason had to watch and listen as Dale's screams turned to gurgles as the blood filled his throat. All Jason could do was pray desperately that his suffering would be over as soon as possible. He blinked back tears as the eyes in Dale's severed head stared up blankly at him, seeming to silently accuse him of failure.

The men who had murdered Dale raised their guns and swords in the air and shouted triumphantly at the camera, though the only words Jason understood as he held back tears at the carnage before him were, "*Death to the American invaders*".

Finally, mercifully, a blindfold was wrapped over his eyes and he was marched out of the compound over rubble-filled terrain. Jason walked for what felt like hours, alternately grieving and feeling a deadly numbness stealing over him. There were voices all around. Once he heard a strangled cry and thought he recognized Chad's voice, but he wasn't sure.

The fact that they were apparently being moved to another location might mean that American troops were on their tails, searching for the hostages. The last thing he felt was a hard blow to the back of his head, and then all he knew was blessed darkness.

# Chapter Eighteen

ജ

Jason lay unconscious upon a woven matt, covered with blood and grime, his wrists bound. He was dreaming of an elevator covered in a brilliant white, almost blinding light that kept going up. Jason thought he was on his way to heaven and didn't want to wake up, but one of his men was tugging at his shirtsleeve.

"Come on, Sarge," the voice anxiously pleaded. "Please wake up. I don't know what to do."

Stunned, Jason tried to shake his head to clear his brain, his thoughts clouded by fog. He felt hot spikes in his head and heard himself moaning in agony as the voice nagged and aggravated him until his head hurt even worse with intense, throbbing pain.

"It's just us, Sarge. Wake up. Please wake up." The voice paused. "Where's Dale?"

An involuntary groan escaped Jason's parched throat and he slurred some words.

Chad bent down, leaning his ear to Jason's mouth. "What are you saying, Sarge? I can't understand you."

Jason continued to feel the boy jerking him into wakefulness. He tried to move his arms and sit up but he felt waves of coursing pain and wanted to scream. Chad's hands on his shoulder held him down and kept him flat on his back. Finally, Jason opened his eyes.

"Chad?" His voice was raspy.

The young Marine looked relieved and sobbed, "I thought they had killed you."

Jason tried wiggling his fingers and realized his wrists were tied in front of him with thick twine. "How long have I been out?"

Chad wiped the sweat off his cheek. "I dunno. They brought you back this morning. Three of them threw you on the floor. You haven't moved since. I thought you were in a coma or going to die. They left some soup and I forced it down you."

Blinking his eyes open, Jason tried to focus on Chad. Talking was difficult.

"Any idea where they've moved us to? And where's Kyle?" Jason whispered. He saw that the new surroundings were slightly better. It was a cement storeroom of sorts, but it was fairly clean, and metal lockers lined the room. He wondered if they were in a school or hospital.

Chad grimaced in horror. "They took Kyle."

Jason gritted his teeth in pain as he lifted his head. "Bring me some water."

He picked up a cup of water and extracted a fly before putting it up to Jason's split lips.

"Could you understand anything they were saying?" Jason said, raising his head and savoring the moisture, foul as it was. He looked around the room again. "Was there anything done by those thugs that would give us any information about anything?"

The young Marine shook his head again. "I couldn't see because of the blindfold, but I could hear them kicking him. Kyle never cried out, not once. I called out to him, but there was no answer. It wasn't until this morning when they removed the blindfold that I knew for sure he was gone." He poured a little more liquid into Jason's mouth. "Do you think they killed him, sir?"

"I don't know," Jason said, letting his head fall back on the mat. "Your guess is as good as mine at this point." But Jason didn't have to wonder too much. It was likely Kyle died the hard way. Chad was next. He had to focus on getting them out of here.

Chad began shivering uncontrollably. "I heard screams last night…"

Jason closed his eyes, his head pounding like a drum. Chad looked like he was ready to snap. The happenings last night were almost too much for the young soldier. Jason knew he'd better shake this headache fast. He was the only one left with enough military experience to get them out alive.

"What are we gonna do? How're we gonna get out of here?" Chad's voice rose shrilly in torment.

"Keep your damn mouth shut, boy," Jason said hoarsely and struggled to get vertical without passing out. "We've got to keep our cool, not panic, and find a way outta here."

"How are we gonna do that?" A dull, haunted look crept over his face. "There's no way we're gonna get out of here alive, Sarge."

"That kind of thinking's definitely gonna get you and me killed."

The boy looked at Jason in disbelief. "How will anyone know where to begin looking for us?"

"I'm disappointed. Have you forgotten our code?" Jason lashed out at him.

The young Marine swallowed awkwardly and slowly repeated the words. *"We will never leave one of our own behind."*

"You're damn right and they won't leave us behind either," Jason snapped. "Now you gotta pull yourself together—think back on your training. To survive, a soldier must calm his anxieties and keep them in the range where they help, not hurt. You want to get outta here, don't you?"

"Of course I do." Jason could see that he had gotten Chad's attention. His eyes stopped clouding over.

"Now help me get vertical…" Jason managed to remain on his feet with Chad's support. Something was cracked or broken—it felt like all his ribs.

"I think you should know what happened to Dale—know just what we are up against." He walked a few steps to lean his back against a wall for support.

"Sir—"

Jason clinched his jaw. "His head was taken off with some type of sword. They had all kinds of blades and carving tools and in the end chose a short sword. Dale's head landed at my feet. Blood was everywhere. Although he was dead, his eyes looked up at me with an expression I'll never forget. Those bastards aren't going to do the same to us."

Chad was visibly shocked. But he regained his composure and Jason listened to the thread of determination in his tone. "You're damn right they won't."

Jason shifted positions and forced his legs to bear his weight.

"Keep believing that Marines will be looking 'til they find us." Jason gritted his teeth. "I want to get home to my wife-to-be, Becca. There were two great loves in my life. One was my music, the other Rebecca. For far too long that pretty lady waited for me to figure out what she already knew—that our relationship should have taken priority. I'm going back home alive."

Chad looked at Jason with a grim smile and nodded. "Yeah, I want to get home too. I want to spend time with my folks and take Dad hunting."

"Let's start reconnoitering then."

With newfound resolve, Chad helped Jason explore their surroundings, looking for anything they could use as a weapon. They carefully searched the row of lockers and a metal desk. Chad stumbled upon two ballpoint pens in a rusty cabinet.

"Here, Sarge," he said triumphantly.

"Good boy, now push a pen up my sleeve. You hang on to the other. If need be, you can stab it into someone's temple or throat and maybe bring him down."

"O-Okay."

His wrists chafing his skin, Jason struggled to recover the circulation in his legs. "I figure we're in some sort of public building, maybe in the middle of a small town. The way I see it, they're probably going to want to keep us on the move. If our guys are looking for us, that might give us better odds. Just follow my lead. When I strike, you follow—got it?"

Chad nodded his head in agreement. "Whatever you say, Sir."

They were left alone except for when the metal door opened for a few seconds and a masked thug slid a box across the floor. Inside was a mixture of soupy rice, broth and stale Iraqi bread, flat like a pita. Chad tore up the bread and poured soup down Jason's mouth.

An eerie silence surrounded them. The two men took turns sleeping so they would always be aware of any sounds.

Finally Jason heard footsteps coming down the hallway and the rattling of keys.

He elbowed Chad, placing a finger against his lips to warn him not to make a sound. Leaning over, he whispered, "It's showtime. Now, remember the plan. You watch me like a hawk and follow my lead. You can't afford to hesitate this time. Either we take them out, or they'll murder us just like Dale and Kyle."

"Got it, Sir. I won't let you down." Chad's voice was deeper, steadier—almost robotic.

The metal door clanged as it was unlocked and four Arabs without masks, rifles slung over their shoulders, strode into the room. "You are leaving with us," yelled the leader.

"Where are you taking us?" Jason demanded.

The man lifted his gun, pointing it at Jason. "Quiet! You'll find out soon enough."

"Here." One of the men thrust U.S. military water canteens at Jason and Chad. "We want to keep you alive." He grinned evilly at Jason. "For a little while."

A guard walked over and cut the rope around Jason's wrists. Wearily, he took the lid off of a canteen, sniffing it for any odd odors. Jason took a sip to see if it tasted suspicious. When he determined that it was okay, he passed it to the young Marine to drink. Then it was his turn. The water was fresh, a temporary but much needed relief, giving Jason renewed energy.

There were no blindfolds this time. The ragtag gang of Arabs led their two captives down a hallway, out a back door and into an alley. The town was deserted. Jason warily studied his surroundings. At the end of the alley, Jason saw something so vile, disgust washed over him. He hoped Chad didn't see it. Next to the trash heap was Kyle's lifeless, bloody corpse, shot full of bullet holes. Jason said a silent prayer.

They continued to march through more rubble-strewn streets. Jason carefully dropped the pen he had concealed in his sleeve down toward his hand. A burning rage welled up in him. He would be ready to strike at the first opportunity.


As the sun began to set, Jason heard the sound of gunfire and explosions in the distance. That could mean the Marines were out there or some soldiers on convoy were being attacked. His captors didn't seem to know and they were confused about what to do.

This retreat appeared to be unplanned and disorganized. Jason could have sworn they were walking in a circle. Unplanned moves were a breeding ground for mistakes and Jason hoped a mistake might mean the opportunity to escape.

The Marines were prodded north with the rifles and headed away from the town under the cover of darkness. Jason could sense the tension in the air as the Arabs stumbled over unfamiliar, rough terrain. They were soon exhausted from the heat and the insurgents stopped to rest. Another band of gunmen joined them. Jason counted a dozen insurgents slumped on the ground, but two rifles remained pointed at them at all times to insure they wouldn't escape into the brush.

"Foolish American. This is no longer a mere guerilla campaign. It will escalate to a full-scale fight," muttered the Arab who had cut his ropes.

Jason sat silently, head bowed, feigning sleep so he could conserve energy and pounce without warning.

A guard came over and spoke excitedly in Arabic. He frantically pointed out into the dark night. All the gunmen grabbed their rifles and joined a heated discussion.

From out of nowhere came a clap of gunfire louder than a Texas thunderstorm, followed by bursts of light and shots in quick succession. Several insurgents screamed in agony and fell to the ground in pools of blood. The insurgents tried to organize and returned fire. Nothing like night vision scopes and goggles, Jason thought. The insurgents' attention was pulled away from their hostages.

"Chad," Jason hissed and caught the young soldier's eye. "Now. And then run like hell."

Jason stood and plunged his pen into the throat of the Arab guarding him. Thick spurts of blood sprayed the air. As the man gurgled and began to fall, Jason bolted, running deeper into the scrubby brush, hoping Chad was right behind him. As he caught his breath, he looked around and to his dismay did not see the young solider.

"Chad! Where the hell are you?" he called over the gunfire. No answer. He yelled again. Still no answer.

From the light of tracer bullets, Jason could see that more insurgents had joined the fight. He finally saw Chad, stuck in the middle of the firefight, sitting on the ground with an emotionless stare as bodies fell around him. Chad rocked back and forth, holding on to his arm. He appeared to be in shock.

Leaping out from his cover, Jason ran toward the helpless boy. As he did so, a blast of white-hot fire pierced his left side, almost knocking him down to the ground. He kept going and grabbed for Chad. As he dragged the kid toward cover, another bullet caught him in the leg. Adrenaline surging, he ran for his life, taking the young soldier with him.

They found a hiding place under a pile of fallen palm leaves next to a lean-to shed. Jason was more dead than alive, but his will to live was strong even though the humidity beneath the heavy foliage made breathing difficult. He and Chad were dripping with blood, exhausted, hungry and thirsty. Yet no matter how uncomfortable their shelter was, they couldn't risk coming out. He and Chad had run as far as they could before collapsing.

As the gun battle raged on around them, Jason did the best he could to stop the blood loss by ripping up pieces of their jumpsuits.

When dawn broke, he pushed the leaves covering him to the side and looked up at the sky. The streaks of red along the horizon told him that the sun would soon be up. He closed his eyes and listened, but it was only sweet silence.

Was the battle over, or was this just a lull in the fighting? Whatever it was, the quiet soothed his grieving soul.

He glanced at Chad, lying next to him. His arm was broken, his sleeve was soaked in blood and there was a trail of dried blood down the side of his face from the bullet that had creased his skull. The boy appeared disoriented, lying there with his eyes wide open and glassy. His skin was cold to the touch and he was shaking, indicating shock.

Jason lay back down, his breathing quick and shallow. Jason knew he was burning up with fever. Both he and Chad were in desperate need of medical care. He didn't know how they were going to do it, but they had to get out somehow. The question was when should they risk movement? If they didn't soon, the vultures would be picking their bones clean.

He closed his eyes. He'd just rest for a little bit longer. Then they would try to find a way out of here.

A loud explosion, followed by faint chatter awoke the men. Jason slowed his breath to listen. It took him a moment to identify the gibberish, but he realized that there were voices in the distance. Burrowing down further under the leaves, he stifled a moan at the piercing pain that ripped through his side and his leg.

The voices gradually grew louder. Unless he was hallucinating, whoever was approaching was speaking English. Of course they could be Iraqis schooled in the language, but they wouldn't be speaking English among themselves, would they?

Chad moved and then started to sit up, but Jason reached for him and pulled him back down.

"Stay quiet," he whispered, then gestured.

This movement sent another wave of agony through his body. He bit down on his lip to prevent himself from crying out. He had to stay focused.

The voices fell silent. For a moment, everything was quiet. Then he heard the crunch of sand and parched leaves under booted feet next to them. Was this it? He had no weapon, nothing he could use to defend himself and Chad. He slowed his breathing, trying not to make a sound.

Suddenly the palm leaves parted, and Jason threw up a hand against the brilliant sunshine.

"Hey guys," a voice shouted. "We found 'em."

Jason was blinded by the sunlight, but he could swear that no Iraqi talked with a Southern twang like that.

"Well, well, well. If it isn't my good friend, Jason Engles, playing possum. You'll do anything to get out of work, won't you? All those years as a singer have made you soft."

"Charlie?" Jason gasped in disbelief. "Charlie Wallace, is that you?" He tried to sit up but collapsed back onto the ground.

"Well, who the hell did you think I was, superstar?" Charlie laughed. "Some pretty little hoochie-mama?"

"Yeah, right," Jason said, and he began to cough. There was a dry burning in his throat and a dizzy feeling in his brain.

Charlie held Jason's head up and poured water into his mouth from the old silver canteen he carried. It had been his father's in World War II and was a good luck charm for the seasoned Marine.

"Looks like we're square now," he said as he assessed Jason's wounds. "You saved me up near Tikrit and now I've repaid the favor by saving your sorry ass. Ah, hell, that's what the Marines get for training a musician to do a warrior's job anyhow. If you were in a battle of the bands, now maybe you would've stood a chance."

"You're a regular laugh riot, Charlie." Jason smiled despite the immense pain. "I never thought I'd say this to you, but, man, you're a sight for some very sore eyes."

"Ain't that the truth? My mama always said I was a pretty boy," he continued to joke as he applied pressure dressings to Jason's side and leg. "Bet you think you dreamed me up, huh?"

"Nope. You're real," Jason bantered back weakly. "I can smell you."

"You're one hell of a mess, Engles. I wish I had my camera. I could probably retire on big bucks the tabloids would pay for a picture of this."

"Charlie, if it makes you feel good, sell the damn picture to the highest bidder. Now, do me a favor and have your men take care of this kid here. He took a hit in the head and shoulder. He's definitely shocky."

"And you? Don't you need some attention, too?" Charlie patted his friend on the arm. "I'm no medic Jason, but I think you need to stay awake. Just keeping talking to me buddy," Charlie said with a grin as he saw the medics approaching.

"Like you said, I'm a damn mess. I don't know if there's any fixing me or not. How come you're here, anyway? I thought you guys had gone home."

"Well, we would have, but when I heard that the great country crooner had been taken hostage, me and the boys here volunteered for this assignment." He helped the medics open the stretcher. "Hell, Engles," he continued, "you know we couldn't have left this God-awful place knowing you might be about to lose your handsome head. Just wasn't an option. Especially seeing as how you saved my life last time."

"Yeah, but how'd you know where we were?"

"Some cooperative Iraqi local gave us a tip. Me and the Bulls put in for the assignment, and here we are for this joyous reunion. We've been trailing that Mullah and his goon squad for a couple of days—even saw them move you—but we had to stay back." He hunkered down next to Jason. "Course, I figured you'd come up with one of your famous stunts."

Jason weakly smiled a mysterious smile.

"So give it up already," Charlie questioned. "How'd you get away?"

"Wouldn't believe me," Jason said and winced when the Marines lifted him onto the stretcher. His eyes began to close.

"Hey buddy. You need to stay awake. Your face is a little pale. I don't want you going into shock on me." The medic patted Jason's shoulder.

Charlie walked along by his side and tapped his chest, also trying to keep him awake. "Try me," he said, once again grinning smugly at his friend.

Jason's voice was scratchy. "A ballpoint pen."

"A what? I'm not sure I heard you correctly." He signaled to alert the helicopter.

"When firing started, I jammed a pen into the throat of a guard. Chad took out another, I think."

"Well, now I'm really annoyed. Instead of me and the Pit Bulls getting the glory for your rescue, it'll be all over the States that Jason Engles escaped by using a ballpoint pen. You're a regular MacGyver, you know that?"

"Nah. Just a plain old guitar-picker." A trickle of warm blood dripped from the corner of his mouth.

"Come on, boys. Step on it. Move those stretchers and get these Marines back to base camp. They need some TLC. Chopper's on the way."

"And you?" Jason said. His words came slower.

"Don't worry about us. We're on our way home, the next flight after yours."

"Tell Tara and the kids hello for me, Charlie. You're a lucky man. I hope I make it home in one piece so I can tell Becca how much she means to me. I didn't realize how much until I thought I was going to die." The jab of a needle made him quiet and woozy. He remembered Charlie yelling "goodbye" as the copter lifted off the ground.

"Keep your powder dry and your nose to the wind." He gave Jason the "thumbs up" sign.

Jason had enough strength to give the all clear before passing into oblivion, but not before seeing that Chad was hooked to an IV and still breathing.

# Chapter Nineteen

80

It was an excruciatingly long night. Rebecca brushed her hand over her tired face — she hadn't gotten one minute's sleep. Ginni's temperature climbed to 102 and she was easily agitated and fussy. The only thing that calmed her was Rebecca rocking her while lightly patting Ginni's bottom with her hand. At times the soothing rhythm almost put her baby to sleep, but the slightest deviation from those movements immediately woke her. She wouldn't let her grandma hold her either. So Rebecca spent the evening alone, awake and worrying about little Ginni's condition. The night doctor assured Rebecca the temperature was from a bacterial infection treatable with antibiotics.

Rebecca felt weary and ready to collapse from sheer exhaustion. She hadn't had a decent night's rest or much of anything to eat in weeks. Beginning to yawn, she decided it was time for a quick nap while Ginni finally slept in her crib. Rebecca pulled a sheet around her tired body and curled up in the cot next to the crib. She clung to one of Ginni's stuffed bears for comfort. Momentarily lapsing into a light slumber, a subtle tapping of someone's hand on her shoulder startled Rebecca back to consciousness.

"Becca." It was Ginni's favorite nurse, Audrey. "I'm sorry to wake you, but the specialist assigned to Virginia's case has arranged a meeting in Conference Room A down on the first floor. You need to be there in twenty minutes. Okay?"

Slowing sitting up, Rebecca wiped her eyes, yawned and nodded. "I'll be there, but I'd like to find my mother-in-law first."

Audrey nodded her head in agreement. "One of the other nurses saw Sarah go into the chapel earlier. Do you want me to find her for you?"

Rebecca stood and shook her head while straightening her clothing with her hands. "No. Thank you for the offer, but I'll go. Who will be here with Ginni? I don't want her to wake up and be all alone. She might think I abandoned her."

"Don't you worry. I'll be right outside checking in on her frequently. Besides, she got a pretty strong dosage of pain medicine and antibiotics earlier this morning. She should sleep for awhile."

The elevator ride to the chapel was long, stopping on every floor. Rebecca grew impatient and began tapping her foot. There were places she needed to be and she didn't have time to wait. The door opened and she quickly stepped off. Walking down the long, window-lined corridor, she squinted and ducked her head as the light almost blinded her. She hadn't left Ginni's side in days or taken time to look out the window.

Pausing for a moment, she opened the entrance to the chapel and went inside. Sarah was consumed in prayer and didn't notice that anyone had walked in.

Rebecca knelt next to her mother-in-law and whispered, "I hope your prayers work. Do you think God hears them? Our family hasn't had the best of luck lately." She ducked her head, almost ashamed of what she'd just heard herself say.

With a hint of tears in her eyes, Sarah looked up at Rebecca. "I believe in miracles and the power of prayers. I know God hears them." She patted Rebecca's hand. "I believe that God forces us to look deep within ourselves for the answers to our problems." She lifted Rebecca's chin with her fingers. "It's just hard to get over the fact that you never think of anything bad happening to such a young soul. Pain should be reserved for older people. A child should never know pain. That's what's so hard for me to deal with right now—and then there's what my own child is living through."

Rebecca placed her hands on her head, massaging her temples. "It seems like the rug's been pulled out from underneath us lately. Both the people we love the most in the whole world could be dying. My whole life has been nothing but turmoil. To tell you the truth, Sarah, I almost feel like giving up. I'm barely hanging on. If it wasn't for Ginni…I think I would."

Sarah turned, facing the front of the chapel. "I know what you mean, but Rebecca, you need to look deep inside your heart and pray for strength. You are stronger than you've ever given yourself credit for being. It's time you reassessed how you handle things and go on from there. One day you will understand what I'm talking about. My son is missing and my granddaughter has cancer. Things can't get much worse, but there is always hope — there is always courage in the face of danger."

Rebecca nodded but refused to answer. Look deep within herself? Whatever. She'd done that for years. Nothing seemed to work and she was feeling bitter. If only something would numb all this pain, she thought, then maybe she could cope better. In a somber voice she said, "The doctors want to see me about Ginni. I want you with me. They expect us in a few minutes."

Sarah wiped a tear from her eye. "Let's say a quick prayer before we go?"


Greeted by an office administrator, Rebecca and Sarah were led into a large room with a sleek mahogany table, video display equipment, television monitors and human anatomy diagrams. Rebecca and Sarah took seats next to each other and sat in silence. Each passing moment felt like long, agonizing hours. Just when Rebecca was about to jump out of her skin, the door opened and a small, dark-haired gentlemen wearing thin, wireframe glasses and a white coat appeared.

"Hello, Ms. Roberts. I'm Doctor Dennis Markum, Chief of Oncology here at Pensacola Memorial. I wish we were meeting under better circumstances. This all going to be a bit overwhelming for you, so I'm going to try to explain Virginia's condition in general terms. Please stop me at any time with any pertinent questions you may have."

Both women nodded in agreement as the doctor pushed a box of tissues closer to them and opened a file folder.

"As you know, we found cancerous cells in your baby's blood work. After extensive consults with my colleagues, we have determined that Virginia has a condition known as Neuroblastoma."

Sarah glanced over at Rebecca, who sat angrily staring at the doctor. "What exactly is that, doctor?"

Dr. Markam cleared his throat and began gesturing with his hands as he talked. "This is a tumor that has attached itself to Virginia's right kidney. To complicate matters, the mass is pushing on the spinal cord."

Rebecca stood and burst out shouting. "I don't believe you! Who ever heard of an infant having a tumor? I demand a second opinion."

Sarah quickly reached up, grabbed a corner of her shirt and tugged her back down into the chair. Sarah snapped, "Rebecca, get a hold of yourself and calm down. It's not the doctor's fault Ginni's sick. Let him finish." Sarah turned back around and faced the doctor. "Sir, I'm sorry for the outburst. These are trying times for our family. Please continue."

"Ma'am you are definitely entitled to a second opinion, but time is of the essence here. Please listen to everything I have to say and evaluate it before making a final decision." The seasoned doctor pulled the folder closer to him. "If we could say with absolute certainty that the baby is in Stage 3 Neuroblastoma, then your child would have an eighty percent chance of survival."

"So, Ginni will make a full recovery?" Rebecca leaned forward, almost daring to hope.

Dr. Markam shook his head. "No, it's not that simple. My fear is that her condition is hinging on a Stage 4 case. My concern, Ms. Roberts, is that the size and positioning of this tumor and Virginia's blood work all point to a much worse case than we expected. I've talked with other specialists in this field — we all concur that she should be sent to St. Jude Children's Research Hospital in Memphis immediately."

"What will they do for her there that you can't do here?" Rebecca said between hiccups and tears.

"St. Jude is the most aggressive hospital for childhood cancer in the country — in the world. I assure you, her care will be second to none there." The doctor removed his glasses. "Virginia's course of treatment involves a risky procedure called nephrectomy, which will remove the tumor from the kidney. Then she will have between twelve to twenty-four weeks of chemotherapy. After she is released from their immediate care, she will be sent home, most likely with a nurse. St. Jude will care for her until the time she is eighteen. In essence, she will be a patient for life — as long as she needs to be. The cost for treatment is free."

"Is she going to live? Can you guarantee me that if we ship her off only to go through all this testing again that she will live?"

The doctor began gesturing with his hands. "Ms. Roberts, there is no guarantee with this type of situation, but St. Jude is a wonderful facility. The quicker she begins treatment, the better she'll be. Her chances of survival depend on the timeliness of the treatments."

Realizing it was in her child's best interest to get the best treatment possible, Rebecca began to calm. "When do we leave?"

"Once we get the parents' approval, my colleagues and I submit a request. St. Jude will get back with us later today and we will advise you when we are good to go." The doctor moved his chair closer to Rebecca. "I know this is an awful time, but I wouldn't refer your baby there if I didn't think it was the best place for her. It's an amazing hospital with the best scientists and surgeons." He patted Rebecca's hand. "I'm going to get the request form faxed out immediately. I'll be talking with you both very soon." With several quick steps, the doctor disappeared out the door.

Rebecca and Sarah remained silent, neither one knowing what to say to the other. This was just another tragedy in her life that had to be overcome. Rebecca felt as if she were going to explode. Where was her escape from all this heartbreak? Did an outlet even exist?

Without thought, she picked up the tissue box and slammed it against the window. A sharp pain in her arm forced her thoughts back to her surroundings. Looking down, she saw that Sarah had her hands wrapped around her upper limb, squeezing tightly.

"I'm sorry I had to do that, Rebecca, but you need to get a hold of yourself. You need to clear your mind of all negativity and focus your full attention and strength on that baby up there."

Sarah was right. Taking a deep breath and patting the hands that held her, Rebecca nodded and tried to mentally prepare herself for the trip to Tennessee.


Rebecca walked over and looked out her daughter's hospital room window. While pondering the morning events, she watched the raindrops fall out of the sky. Violent thunderstorms with hail and damaging winds rolled through Memphis earlier in the day, but now the weather had quieted down to a tranquil rain. Under normal circumstances, she loved days like this. Rebecca believed it was a time for reflection and prayer. But now there was so much to think about — so much at stake.

Time and time again she had picked up the pieces of her broken life and carried on. Some may have viewed her as weak for staying with her mother and uncle for so long, but that was compassion, nothing more, nothing less. Disaster and despair seemed to be all she ever knew. Whitney had always had a wonderful life and Rebecca's living conditions were unacceptable, but to Rebecca they were the norm. Whitney had often criticized her for not finding someone beside Jason to love. *If she could only put herself in my place for once, she'd see that gaining the love of someone is not easy for me,* Rebecca thought. *Even the slightest rejection is an ugly thing. Why take another chance at it?*

"Oh Uncle Burt, if only you were here." Rebecca touched the cool glass with her hand. She'd give anything to feel his arms around her, trying to comfort her as he'd done many times over the years. Where was his wisdom? Where was his knack for saying the right thing at the right time? God, how she missed all that.

Looking up into the clouds, Rebecca clutched a stuffed animal she was holding even tighter. "Uncle Burt, I know you are up in heaven looking out for us. Please send some help. Send me a sign that my child will be fine. I need something, even if it's small."

The sun began to peek out from behind the clouds as not one, but two brilliant rainbows appeared, seeming almost close enough to touch. One end appeared to start at the hospital and the other stretched way out into the horizon. Holding her daughter's stuffed dolphin to her chest, Rebecca shut her eyes and made a wish. "Thank you Uncle Burt for sending me this wonderful sign. Maybe these rainbows will be a good omen for my baby and Jason lost somewhere in a foreign land."

Turning to her daughter's crib, Rebecca lovingly gazed downward. It wasn't fair. Virginia was a brand-new life. She was innocent of anything. She'd only brought joy into people's lives. A baby shouldn't have to go through something like this.

Now the question was, would the treatment work? Would she live long enough to experience her first day of school? Her first kiss? Would she grow up and get married, have babies? Rebecca had so much love to give this child, and when Jason got back home, he'd love her too. Bursting into tears, Rebecca laid her head on the cold metal railing of her daughter's bed.

Her sobs were interrupted by the abrupt bursting open of the heavy wooden door. Rebecca looked up, expecting to see some intimidating stranger enter her daughter's sanctuary. Almost losing her balance, she ran across the room to meet Nurse Melissa.

Rebecca threw her arms up in a panic. "What is it Melissa? Please don't tell me that there is more bad news about my baby."

"No! You've got to turn the television on! We had the set on out at the nurses' station. An update came across on CNN just a few minutes ago. You have to watch it." The little nurse panted, almost out of breath from running and excitement.

"What?" a bewildered Rebecca questioned. "What's going on?"

"Just watch the television. I'm on my way to find Sarah. She needs to hear this too. Someone saw her near the cafeteria." Melissa turned and left as quickly as she came.

What on Earth is going on with that crazy nurse that could be this important, Rebecca thought. My eyes won't even stay open. I don't have the strength for games. Curiosity getting the best of her, Rebecca turned, searching the nightstand and Ginni's bed for the remote, finally finding it between the covers and the mattress. She'd forgotten she'd dropped it there last night when Ginni was fussy. Eagerly she turned on the television and flipped the channels to the news.

Within moments Sarah came rushing in. "Did you hear, Rebecca? Jason's free, darling! Our boy is alive and free!"

Rebecca's legs weakened. Could this really be? She hadn't expected this kind of news, not today anyway. Her head began spinning and her body trembled. Looking at Sarah, she could hear her words, but she could not fully concentrate. Trying to make it to a nearby chair, Rebecca stepped forward just as the room began to spin. Everything went black, as she collapsed. Rebecca had no recollection of her body hitting the floor.

Although she couldn't speak, she could hear people around her hysterically talking, but they sounded hundreds of miles away.

Motionless, Rebecca could hear everything Sarah was shouting. Poor Sarah, there was so much worry in her voice. "Oh my God, Rebecca! Nurse, I need some smelling salts, something! I need help in here!"

From the distant miles of foggy unconsciousness, Rebecca felt cold and could hear herself screaming, but no one answered her cries. Time and life seemed to be carrying on without her. Jason's image appeared and then faded as quickly as it had come. She reached out into the darkness, screaming at the top of her lungs, "I'm here. Please don't give up on me, I'm on my way back to everyone—I just can't get to you right now."

The noise of a heavy banging door jarred Rebecca. She could feel her eyelids trying to open. Melissa had rushed into the room, applying smelling salts directly under her nose. The pungent odor burned the inside of her nostrils and throat as Rebecca struggled for air.

Nurse Melissa continued shaking her. Then she said, "She's breathing Sarah—Rebecca just passed out. You know she hasn't taken the best care of herself, but I think she's going to be all right."

Rebecca fully opened her eyes and began shaking her head in different directions, trying to wake. The pungent, sulfuric odor, like rotten eggs was still burning the membrane inside her nose. Looking wearily around the room, she felt woozy as Sarah and Melissa combined efforts to sit her up. The women helped Rebecca to her feet and into the nearby cot.

Sarah rubbed Rebecca's arm and shoulder. "Are you all right, dear? You gave us a scare. Two sick people in my life is plenty—I don't need another one."

Melissa went about taking Rebecca's vitals. She quickly slipped a blood pressure cuff around her arm and listened to her heart. Then she took her temperature. "Her blood pressure is a little low. I think she just got overly excited. Could be from low blood sugar. I suggest we get her something to eat, and soon. Rebecca do you feel okay? Does anything hurt from the fall?"

Rebecca wearily answered, "Yeah—just overwhelmed. The room went black and I got dizzy. Funny thing is, I could hear everything you were saying, but it was like everyone was miles away and I couldn't get to you. I wanted to answer you guys but couldn't."

She asked again, "Did you eat today?"

Rebecca shrugged her shoulders, not taking the question seriously.

"You've been running yourself ragged and not eating or sleeping. When was the last time you ate? Last night or yesterday afternoon?"

"I ate today." Rebecca looked up. "I had some animal crackers and a soda out of the vending machine." She suddenly stopped, looking up at the television. Pointing, she said, "Look!" A news anchor was showing pictures of a military plane landing at an airstrip, flashing a news alert at the bottom of the screen while Sarah continued ranting about Rebecca's eating habits.

"Sarah, let's listen to this. I'm all right—just a little shocked at the news." Once again, Rebecca pointed toward the television set.

"To recap, Sergeant Jason Engles, better known as country superstar and lead singer of The Flying Eagles, and Private First Class Chad Morwick of Mississippi have been found. They are alive and well. Two of their fellow Marines are feared dead at the hands of Mullah, Mohamed al Zabarra. Engles and Morwick escaped captivity after Marines tracking them engaged the insurgents in a furious firefight.

"The men reportedly sustained injuries, but we're unclear as to the extent of those wounds or their conditions. However, they are reported to be alive and free and on their way to medical treatment in Germany at this hour. What you are seeing at the bottom of your screen are pictures of the C-17 cargo plane landing on the runway at the U.S. Air Force Base in Germany."

"Did you hear that?" Rebecca turned to Sarah. "Jason's okay."

"Lord, yes, child! He's alive! But call it a mother's intuition, I have a feeling there's more to the story than what the news is allowing out."

Rebecca, still seated on the cot, looked up at Sarah and Melissa. "You know — after today's rain, I looked at these two enormous rainbows. I prayed like I never prayed before. Looks like God heard at least one of my prayers in that Jason's going to be okay and coming home to us very soon." Rebecca nervously brought her hands to her face and continued to listen to the television.

One by one the nursing staff came into Ginni's room to congratulate Rebecca and Sarah. Everyone was careful not to wake baby Ginni, as she needed her rest. The ringing of Rebecca's cell phone broke through the exuberant congratulations from well-wishers. The room fell silent with anticipation that it might be Jason on the other end of the phone.

Rebecca fought her way out of the cot and dashed to answer the phone. "Hello?" Her hands trembled, almost making her drop it. "Hello — hello! Is anyone there?"

A weak and shaky voice began speaking. "Becca, sweetheart."

"Oh, Jason — I can't believe it's you." Thoughts were running through her head a mile a minute. "Thank God you're safe." Her eyes filled with happy tears as she reached for Sarah, who was also crying. "They're showing pictures of a plane landing in Germany. Are you on it?"

Sounding tired and barely able to speak, Jason slowly answered, "They're about to let us off the plane, but I don't remember where we were going."

"Are you okay? Are you hurt badly?" Rebecca was nervous and started to bite what was left of her fingernails.

"I'm okay. It's you that I'm worried about." He sounded like he was under heavy sedation and his attention was easily interrupted.

It had been several seconds without hearing Jason on the other end of the phone. "Jason, are you still there sweetheart?" The line was still silent. "Your mom is standing next to me. She says she loves you."

A raspy voice began to speak again. "I gotta go now, baby. Tell Mama I love her."

Rebecca started to speak, but another voice interrupted her.

"Rebecca?" questioned a burly voice on the other end.

"Yes—Yes! Is he okay?" She couldn't contain the worry in her voice. Sarah was sitting on the edge of her seat, only able to pick up bits and pieces of the conversation.

"This is George. I'm a Marine on board taking a weekend hop. I let him use my phone. He was in and out of consciousness the entire flight, but he kept mumbling your name over and over, so I had to offer to let him call you."

Rebecca tried to speak through her tears. "His whole family is here. Do you know anything about his condition?"

"He's banged up pretty badly. Someone said that his wounds looked infected and that he had a fever. I sure hope he makes it."

"Well, how bad is it for you to say 'make it'? Did you see his injuries? Where are the bandages?" Rebecca tried to keep her panic level under control, so as not to alert the others to the criticalness of his condition.

The soldier hesitated. "Look, I don't know how much information I'm supposed to release, but his face has some abrasions and they were working on one of his legs. It looked pretty bad, but I'm not a doctor and then—" The man paused. "He took a gunshot to the side. That's all I know."

She gasped. "To his side. That sounds serious. Did anyone say anything about his legs? Was he in pain?"

"Look, I gotta go. I'm sure the military will be in touch with you soon." The click on the other end indicated he'd hung up in a hurry. She turned off the phone and hugged it against her chest.

The room's attention was on her. "He sounded disoriented and weak. He told me to tell you that he loved you, Sarah." Rebecca looked as Sarah placed her hands over her mouth. Rebecca's guess was she did it to hold back the screams. "The man also said that his face had cuts, his leg was hurt pretty badly and that he'd taken a bullet to the side."

"If he's on painkillers, then I would guess that he's hurt pretty badly," Sarah said.

"I think you should go to him, Sarah. He needs someone there right now. I can't leave Ginni here by herself. I can handle things. You need to contact the base and go—the sooner the better. Jason needs you."

"You're right, Rebecca. I need to be with my son, but leaving my granddaughter and you, sweet Rebecca—it won't be easy." She stopped herself, crinkling up the tissue she clutched tightly in her hand.

Rebecca walked over and put her hand on Sarah's shoulder. "We both need to be with our children. It's a mother's calling. You just be sure to give Jason a big hug and kiss from me. Tell him that I love him and that I missed him every day that he was away." Sarah hugged Rebecca tightly. "He sounds pretty bad. My guess is you'll be over there for a long time. Will you call me every day and update me?"

Sarah managed a small smile. "Only if you promise to update me on my grandbaby. I hate it that I won't be there for you in Memphis. Can Whitney come and stay with you?"

Rebecca shook her head. "Nope. This is my child, my problem. I will be fine. I'm stronger than people give me credit for being." She turned and walked over to Ginni's crib and stroked her wispy hair.

"Dear God, thank you. Jason's alive!" She bent down toward Ginni, who had slept through all the excitement, and whispered, "Your daddy's alive, my beautiful baby girl."

A few minutes later, Rebecca, Sarah and a few nurses gathered around the small set, watching images of the cargo plane unloading passengers. Rebecca and Sarah anxiously watched as two ambulances backed up to the plane. For the most part, paramedics and doctors hustled around the back of the vehicles. Then one young soldier was removed. Several Marines held on to his stretcher, carefully lifting him into one of the ambulances. There was no movement from the Marine.

Rebecca's heart sank. "He's not moving, Sarah. Oh, God— he's not moving."

"That's not my boy. It can't be. From what I could see, that kid looks too young. A mother knows whether it's her child or not." She held Rebecca's hand with such strength, it was as if she was cracking walnuts.

Rebecca's eyes were glued to the TV, afraid to take them off for one second. She didn't want to miss him. "You're right, Sarah. That wasn't our Jason." A second soldier was pulled from the plane and carried by the same group of Marines. "Oh, God, Sarah. He looks ba—"

Sarah interrupted Rebecca before she could finish the sentence. "Don't say it, Rebecca. Just don't even think it."

Twenty-four hours had passed after watching the images on television before the Marine Corp chaplain contacted Sarah about Jason. The minister sounded vague and noncommittal regarding Jason's physical and mental wellbeing. The chaplin told Sarah that his condition was "serious" and "guarded". Like baby Ginni, Jason had a long way to go. Rebecca ran the same questions through her mind—would they both make it? Would she still have a family when all this was said and done?

Within a week, the necessary arrangements for Mrs. Engles to fly to Germany were made. Sarah stepped into the room, taking both of Rebecca's hands into her own. "Well, I'm packed and ready to leave. My taxi will be here any minute. Before I go, I wanted to come by and kiss my granddaughter one more time. I stopped by the store and bought her a new teddy so she'll remember Grandma loves her." Rebecca took the toy, nodded her head and choked back the tears. "Becca—I want you to take care of yourself. I'm never more than a phone call away if you need to talk."

Rebecca hugged her mother-in-law. "I'll miss you, Sarah. It will be hard not having you here with us, but we'll get through all of this. Don't forget to tell Jason I love him and that I'm waiting here eagerly for him to come home."

A troubled look crept over Sarah's face. "What should I tell him about Ginni? Or should I say nothing? It's your call, Rebecca," Sarah said.

Pacing around the room, wringing her hands, Rebecca hesitated to answer. "I don't think it's a good idea, do you? Jason's going to need time to recover. He probably won't be in any condition for a few weeks anyway. It's just not the right time. We'll cross that bridge when we come to it."

Nodding, she said, "I don't like it, but I agree. He needs to get better so he can come home and be with his family." Sarah looked away. "Jason's always been healthy. He's never had a broken bone. I don't know what to expect when I go over there. I pray I have the strength not to break down in front of him."

No words of encouragement came to mind to give to Sarah. Rebecca was living through her own emotional hell. "You are his mother, Sarah—I know you will find a way to comfort him. Just tell him that you love him and that you care. Hold his hand and stroke his hair when he needs comfort. Please remind him of me."

Sarah bent down and lightly kissed Ginni. "Baby girl," she whispered, "I'm off to see your daddy and bring him home to us. You hang in there and Grandma will be back as soon as I can. You will never be out of my thoughts and prayers—not for a minute. I love you more than you will ever know." With a gentle kiss to her brow, Sarah left, hugging Rebecca on the way out.

Once in the jet, the full effect of Jason's being injured in combat hit Sarah. She became nervous and wanted to cry. Within a matter of hours she would see and hear what horrors had happened to her brave son. It was difficult for a mother to take and she began to second-guess the wisdom she'd given Rebecca days earlier. She couldn't wait to throw her arms around Jason and tell him how much she loved him.

She had spoken to his superiors and although his condition was stable, his injuries were severe. If he pulled through, he would need months of care and physical therapy. Sarah had been cautioned that his emotional state was extremely fragile and unpredictable. She was instructed not to ask her son too many questions about the war—what he saw or how he'd gotten his injuries. The doctors said he should remember things in his own time and talk about the atrocities only when he felt they were appropriate.

After being held hostage and witnessing one of his friends being beheaded, he would certainly have PTSD—Post-Traumatic Stress Disorder. Sarah couldn't imagine living through such a horror. What would she say to comfort him? She wondered if Jason would ever talk to her about it. The chaplin had suggested that she enroll in a course at the hospital to learn more about the affliction. Depending on how long she was going to be over there, and Jason's condition, she was seriously thinking about it.

"Excuse me Ma'am, but one of the crewmen let it slip that you were Jason Engles' mother."

Sarah turned to the passenger seated next to her. "Well yes, son—yes I am," she said proudly.

"My name is Craig. Craig Morgan. It's a pleasure meeting you." The young man extended his hand, meeting Sarah's. "I'm a big fan and from Tennessee too. My girlfriend, Maddie and I heard him play a few clubs there. I'm a singer. Maybe one day

I'll be as big as your son. He's the greatest—a real gift to the country scene. Sure glad he's okay. Guess you are too, huh?"

"More than you'll ever know." She smiled. "I'll be sure to pass along your greetings to him. He loves to hear from fans." The boy apparently had no idea how badly her son was hurt. Sarah kept looking at the young Mr. Morgan, imagining after his weekend, he'd be back in the field in combat maneuvers. She didn't want him to suffer the same fate as Jason, or even worse. But she managed to keep a smile on her face.

"We love to hear about him, that's for sure. I can't believe he escaped those Iraqi insurgents with only an ink pen for a weapon. Saved a buddy, too. He'll be a legend now for sure."

"Excuse me, did you say a ballpoint pen?" she said in a disbelieving tone. Her son was the most resourceful person she'd ever known—had been since he was a kid.

"Yeah." The guy's eyes lit up with excitement. "It's true. A Marine buddy told me about it. You should ask Jason about it sometime."

"Indeed I will."

Sarah thought about what she'd just heard. Her son was a bona fide war hero. For the remainder of the flight, Sarah continued to question herself regarding keeping Rebecca's secret about the baby. How could she look into her son's eyes and keep on deceiving him? Would he ever forgive her? Besides occasionally conversing with Private Morgan, she remained quiet with only her thoughts. Before she knew it, the crew was instructing all the passengers to buckle up for landing.

Later, Sarah carefully opened the door to Jason's room. The nurses instructed her not to make any sudden noises in case he was jumpy. Peering around the door, she saw him lying in the bed. Her heart nearly burst with love and sadness. His torso was bare above the covers and wrapped in bandages with traces of dried blood on them. One leg was suspended in the air in traction. His handsome face looked gaunt, cut and bruised. An IV trailed from one of his arms. Her war hero son looked so vulnerable. She tiptoed to his bedside and gazed down at him. Slowly his eyes opened to meet hers.

"Mama! Is that you?" he asked softly, reaching weakly for her hand.

"Yes, baby, I'm here." Her eyes filled with tears as she held his hand. "I love you so much, Jason. We all do."

"Rebecca? Is she okay?"

Sarah quickly looked away. She'd been there less than a minute and already the tough questions were being asked. "Rebecca's fine."

"How come she didn't come with you?" he asked fraily.

"You two aren't married. The military sent for me." Trying to change the tone of the moment, she used her sense of humor. "What's the matter boy—isn't your ol' mama good enough anymore?"

"You're just fine. It's so good to see you." He managed a weak smile.

Jason looked groggy and his eyes were glazed with pain. Her heart ached for her son. Sarah smiled and brushed his hair back. Bits of dried blood from the bandages came off onto her hand. He was burning up with fever and shaking. This couldn't be good, she thought. Heaven only knew what type of bacteria he came in contact with over there.

Sarah began removing the pillows from behind his head and fluffing them. She tried to busy herself so that Jason wouldn't see she was worried.

His feeble voice broke through the silence. "Mama, do you think Dad would be proud of me?"

"What?" Sarah stopped what she was doing and turned to look at her son.

"I saved a life out there. Do you think Dad would be proud of that?" He tried looking back toward his mother.

Sarah slowly refitted the pillow behind his head. "Why heavens yes, boy—he was always proud of you."

"He never said it." Jason looked away as if trying not to cry.

Sarah took his hand again. "Jason, your father was a hard man. He was career driven. When that dream career didn't happen, he took it out on you kids. It was me he wanted a piece of—me he blamed." She was on the verge of tears herself. "You can bet that he was proud of you. He may never have told you that, but he was. Remember when you learned how to play the guitar all by yourself? You must have been five."

Jason nodded. "Yeah, I remember. One of the band members gave me his used guitar."

Sarah interrupted, "And you practiced day and night for weeks until you could play. Your father peeked in on you one night. He had this look in his eyes I'd never seen before as he stood there watching you play. I only wished I could have put that look on his face a little more often."

"Mama, I have to tell you something." He paused and then began speaking very slowly, carefully. "When I was held captive, I had a lot of time to think. I should've waited to go to Nashville and taken Rebecca with me. Dad had it all wrong. I was trying to obtain approval I never had a prayer of getting. He was too broken inside to give anything of himself. The way he blamed us—you. It's not a career, fans and millions of dollars that makes a man whole—it's the woman he loves. It's starting your own branch of the family tree and maintaining it."

Sarah smiled. "Jason, I'm so glad to hear you say that. I was afraid your father affected you with wounds so deep, no one would be able to heal them."

"Well, it took a war to bring it out of me—and if I learned one thing, it's that time is precious and shouldn't be wasted on glitz. It should be spent wrapped around the one you love on a lazy summer afternoon while lying in a hammock in the backyard watching your children running around and playing. There's so much more to life than what I've been living."

"Oh, my sweet boy, you are so much more of a man than your father ever was. Someday you are going to make a wonderful husband and father."

"Mom, I can't be with Rebecca anymore," he said, turning his head while fighting back the tears.

A confused looked came across Sarah's face. "For heaven's sake, after what you just told me, why not?"

"The doctors talked to me today. Mama, they said there is a good chance I could lose my leg. I'll be a cripple and I'm not going to saddle Rebecca with that. She deserves better."

"She wants you. Don't take her choices away from her, not again. By doing that, it's like you left her for something else all over again." Sarah took a seat beside her son. "You need to take some time and think about this."

"I already have—that's all I've thought about since they broke the news to me. Please tell her I'm in a coma. Tell her something—anything—just don't let her be saddled with me. I don't want her staying out of pity. Dad stayed for all the wrong reasons. I don't want that happening here."

"You mustn't talk like that, Jason. We all love you. You would never be a burden." Sarah could no longer hold back the tears.

Jason closed his eyes and began shaking so uncontrollably that Sarah could hear his teeth chattering. "Jason, baby—talk to Mama." His color was grayish and his eyes closed. She began to shake him, but there was no response. Bolting out into the hallway, she hysterically ran to the nurses' station.

"Please. It's my boy. I think he is going into shock from fever. My son is Jason Engles. He's in Room 219. Hurry—please!" Sarah stood to the side as the nursing staff ran past her toward Jason's room.

Sarah followed frantically after them, only to be ordered to take a seat in the waiting area. Minutes slowly turned into hours, then half a day went by and melted into evening. She sat there completely by herself, watching as doctors and nurses continued to hustle in and out of her son's room. Sarah put her head in her hands and began to pray.

When she could no longer take not knowing, Sarah quietly walked to the nurses' station. Clearing her throat, she spoke up. "Nurse Hawkins, is there any word on my son?"

Hawkins turned from the file cabinet, started to talk and then hesitated. "Uh...why don't you come down to the conference room around the corner? Dr. Taylor, Jason's physician, had planned on talking to you. Why don't you wait there and I'll see if she's available now?"

"Can I go in and see Jason?" She took a step forward.

The nurse held out his hand, gesturing for Sarah to stop. "Not right now. The doctor needs to talk to you first, Mrs. Engles. Particularly about his leg and emotional state. Please come with me. It won't take long."

Sarah followed Hawkins and, halfway down the hall, a tall woman with short, blonde hair and a no-nonsense air about her joined them.

"I'm Dr. Taylor," she said, opening the door to a conference room. "Let's talk in here."

Sarah sat down on the edge of a chair, her hands folded tightly in front of her. "Would you mind telling me what's going on with my son, Dr. Taylor?"

The doctor sat very straight in the chair while removing some notes from a day planner. "There have been some serious complications in your son's condition. His fever has spiked to 104 from an infection that set in from his initial wounds. Now, I'm afraid, the infection has spread into the bloodstream. He is in a coma."

"What does that mean, doctor? Can you treat him?" Sarah said with a crackle in her voice.

The doctor hesitated for a moment. "Well—"

Looking straight at the doctor, Sarah interrupted her. "Dr. Taylor, this isn't easy for me to say, but I'm not an educated woman. Please explain these things to me in terms I can understand."

Dr. Taylor placed her hands on the table, one on top of the other. "Mrs. Engles—the infection in his leg and bloodstream is severe enough that I'm doubtful he will ever regain the use of his leg. In fact, we may have to amputate."

"Amputate? I was praying that wasn't necessary," Sarah gasped. "Isn't there something else you can do?"

"We are doing all that we can." The doctor reached out and patted Sarah's hand. "I understand you were visiting with him earlier this afternoon, when he was still coherent."

Sarah was puzzled. "Still coherent? What are you talking about, Dr. Taylor?"

"Before the fever spiked, even before your arrival here today, I had a chance to talk to Jason about his leg. He's taken it pretty hard. He asked that if amputation was the course of action taken, that we send his family home."

"For God's sake. He's my son. I can't just leave him." Sarah picked up a tissue from a box sitting on the table. "Would you leave your son?"

The doctor shook her head. "Mrs. Engles, what I would do is irrelevant here. Jason is going through some very severe psychological turmoil combined with the physical problems and now this coma. He needs some time to get well. The emotional healing is just as important as the physical. Your son stated quite unequivocally there are to be no visitors. Jason will stay here until we are able to stabilize him and then we will send him on to Walter Reed, stateside."

"I don't understand any of this, doctor. He's my son. I love him!"

The doctor wiped her tired-looking eyes. "Mrs. Engles, I will keep in constant contact with you via the telephone, or you can stay here if you'd like, but Jason is an adult. If he doesn't want visitors, we have to honor that."

"And the coma — what can you tell me about that?" Sarah asked.

"I'm hoping that the coma will be short-term. Only time and his reaction to antibiotics will tell."

Sarah looked up at Dr. Taylor. "I...I don't know what to do."

"I know it's hard, but you have to understand that Jason isn't himself yet. He's been badly injured and his emotional trauma is intense." The doctor's voice was low and soothing. "In addition to his experiences in captivity, he's dealing with the fact that he may never be able to walk without the use of some type of device, whether it be a wheelchair or prosthesis. That's been very hard for him to take, especially being in the public eye as he is. He's having a great deal of trouble coping, which isn't unusual in these cases. Most of my patients come around in good time. I'm confident he will too, with the help of therapy."

All Sarah could do was sob as the doctor kept talking.

"Jason feels completely out of control, and that frightens him on a very deep level. He was held hostage, abused by his captors and made to watch his fellow soldier's beheading — these things are the ultimate in powerlessness, in loss of control. Any one of those events would be extremely traumatic, and he suffered all of them and more. Right now he's physically helpless as well, and for a guy like Jason...well...I'm guessing he needs to feel in charge."

Sarah lifted her head out of her hands. "So what should I do?"

"I can't advise you about that." Dr. Taylor bent down to retrieve her notes. "The best advice I can give you is to go back home. Wait for my calls and updates. When he gets to Walter Reed, we can reevaluate the situation. If he cooperates in his recovery, he'll probably come around in his own time. But it's not going to be an easy road."

Defiantly, Sarah rose from her chair. "He's my son. I don't care how tough the road is. I'll be here for him."

# Chapter Twenty

**∞**

Rebecca lifted her head from the armrest, hoping the sounds that awakened her were the footsteps of Ginni's doctors. Cramped leg muscles and a crick in her neck made sitting up painful, but she struggled to her feet, pulling down her sweater as she straightened up. No hospital personnel clad in green surgical scrubs were coming through the swinging door for her. She'd just imagined it. She fell back down, oblivious to the sympathetic stares from the other people in the waiting room.

What time is it, she wondered. She rubbed her tired eyes with the back of her sleeve. The clock on the wall pointed to four o'clock. Her baby had been in surgery for five long, excruciating hours.

She wasn't alone staring at the swinging metal doors. Other children were under the knife at St. Jude and every person in the room looked gloomy and anxious. But the parents were sitting as couples, they were together, oftentimes with grandparents, talking softly or silently consoling each other, occasionally glancing at her as if to say, *"Where is her husband? She's been alone here for days."*

Rebecca lowered her head into her hands, blocking out everything and everyone. She didn't know if the other children were as seriously ill as Ginni, and she didn't care. She was numb. She wasn't up to small talk or hearing about other people's problems. Her mind was on automatic pilot and she knew it. Acting strong for the sake of Ginni's health was crucial, but inside she was paralyzed with fear, unable to feel the need for normal human contact. Her hair hung limp around her shoulders and she looked disheveled, like she'd slept in her clothes. She was barely hand-washing the two or three outfits she'd frantically stuffed into a bag and hadn't touched an iron for weeks.

She was talking to herself in third person like someone crazed. Always a bad sign. Perhaps it was depression, she cautioned herself. A dying baby, a dying lover, a murdered uncle and an insane, dead mother. The words kept repeating over and over in her brain like a broken record.

Rebecca couldn't imagine unconsciously trying to turn these sad, pathetic words into lyrics. Even for country western music, her life was too dark and tragic to ever inspire a song.

Everyone who loved or could love her was gone. This line was also playing over and over when she tried to sleep. If she wasn't so tired, she might write it all down. It might work. If she ever felt inspired enough to put pencil to paper again.

The word inspire came from the word spirit, someone once told her. That was the problem. Her spirits were waning and she wasn't in a songwriting mood.

If only the waiting room was quiet and soundproof, away from hospital noises and blue alerts. Through the glass partition she imagined she saw wounded soldiers being pushed on stretchers, dirt and blood covering their bodies as they were wheeled off to surgery. But this was St. Jude Children's Hospital. No soldiers here, other than the brave little ones battling for life. She was just hallucinating, imagining all that— imagining Jason was here.

When would the doctors tell her something? She wanted to scream, to pull out her hair, but instead she leaned back on the hard-backed chair and closed her eyes, blocking out horrible pictures of Jason. She had such a responsibility figuring out what was best for Ginni and wondering if she was making the right decisions. It would be so much easier to deal with if she had a partner to lean on.

She looked up and her heart skipped a beat. Finally! Ginni's doctors walked through the swinging doors, removing their masks and motioning for her from the sterile corridor. Rebecca jumped up and rushed into the hall. She could smell the overpowering odor of hand sanitizing soap swirling around them. Before she could speak, they led her away.

"What is it?" she said desperately. "What happened to Ginni?"

One of the doctors gestured for her to follow them. "Ms. Roberts, please come with us."

Ginni's doctor, Rob Crane, showed her into an empty office and asked her to sit down.

"Is my baby all right?" She took a seat and stilled her hands in her lap, balling them into fists.

Dr. Mann remained standing while Dr. Crane took a seat behind the desk. "Ginni is resting comfortably. The removal of the tumor was a complete success, but we won't know how the kidney will function. We'll have to wait."

"She will recover?" Rebecca optimistically questioned.

The doctors glanced at each other, inscrutable expressions on their faces. The surgeon spoke first. "Virginia lost a lot of blood and is weak. Her immune system is compromised. Then there is the problem with the chemotherapy. We need to wait until she is stronger before we begin that phase of treatment."

"This sounds pretty much like what they told me in Florida. But what aren't you telling me?" she eagerly asked.

Dr. Mann took over. "Ms. Roberts, your daughter has Stage 4 Neuroblastoma. She will require extensive chemotherapy, but we need to wait until she is stronger before starting such aggressive treatment. This makes her condition critical." The doctor paused, looking over at his colleague. "We will do all we can."

Those were the last words she would remember from the conversation. In shock, Rebecca uttered them over and over in her mind as she was leaving the room. "*We will do all we can.*"

It wasn't until the following day that Virginia was brought to her in a special crib. Rebecca was waiting impatiently to see her, to touch her soft skin and stroke her hair.

"Oh Virginia—what have they done to your poor little body?" She looked so fragile. Bandages and a draining tube stuck out of her battered and bruised tiny frame. They cut you up and now expect you to get better. How does anyone so small ever recover from something like this, Rebecca thought. "If you only knew how much your mommy loves you. You've got to get through this. We'll do it together," she whispered and then began to silently sob.

Ginni was lying on her stomach, arms sprawled above her head and breathing heavy. Except for the medical equipment, she looked like a sleeping angel. Rebecca's finger lightly crept over her bandages and then trailed down her soft blanket. "You need to fight for me, my brave girl. Fight for your daddy too."

At the mention of Jason's name, Rebecca began to wonder why Sarah hadn't called. Surely she would have heard something from her by now. This was so unlike her—she promised to keep Rebecca updated. Perhaps Sarah had called, but Rebecca wasn't in the room to hear it.

"Excuse me. Can I come in?" said a soft voice from the doorway, startling Rebecca.

Rebecca looked up from the crib. "Of course. Everything's fine here, Patsy. Ginni is sleeping."

"I'm not here to check on her. You have a visitor downstairs." She walked closer to the crib to peek inside.

"Oh, it's okay to send them up. They won't be disturbing us," Rebecca said as she tucked the blanket snugly around the little form.

"Hospital procedure—visitors can't just come up."

She gave the nurse a surprised look. "I don't want to leave her," Rebecca said nervously.

"Ginni is under heavy sedation so the stitches can heal. I assure you she won't wake up, not 'til tomorrow. She's stabilized from the procedure." Patsy looked into the crib and then glanced at Rebecca. "I know this is hard, but you need a break. Go on, honey. Have a nice visit with your friend. I'll stay here and take my breaks and check on her every ten minutes."

Rebecca grabbed for the nurse's hands, thanking her profusely. It was probably Whitney waiting for her. She must have driven down from Nashville. As she rode in the elevator to the visitor's entrance, she wondered if Whitney would go with her to a convenience store. She was out of so many things.

Rounding the corner, Rebecca's mouth dropped open. She couldn't believe who was waiting for her in the lobby. "Sarah?" she said. "What on Earth are you doing here?" Mrs. Engles looked tired and was standing next to a suitcase. Then the thought dawned on her—something had happened to Jason. She froze in her tracks.

Sarah stretched out her arms and walked toward Rebecca. The two women held each other tightly, as if they'd been apart for months. Sarah felt like skin and bones under her loose dress. When had she stopped eating? What was wrong? Her shoulders were shaking. Rebecca pulled back to look closely at her. "Sarah, are you crying? What happened to Jason? Tell me!"

Mrs. Engles pulled out a tissue from her purse to wipe her eyes. "The doctors told me he was getting good care and to come back to the States."

Rebecca held Sarah at arm's length. "You should be with Jason. He shouldn't be alone."

Sarah broke away from Rebecca's grasp and turned toward the window. "He's still alive, but just barely. There is no easy way to tell you this. Jason lapsed into a coma shortly after I arrived. I didn't have much time to talk to him. His wounds caused severe infections, his fever spiked, his immune system crashed and then he fell unconscious."

Anger welled inside Rebecca as she lashed out hysterically. "Sarah, he needs someone there with him. How can you just leave your child? I love Jason more than anybody, but I could never leave Ginni, not even to be with Jason."

"Please don't get upset." Sarah wiped her face once again with the tissue. "The doctors ordered me back. There was nothing I could do." In tears, she sat down on a couch. "I was able to visit with him for about thirty minutes—that was it."

"What did he say?" Rebecca knelt down beside her. Her heart ached and she felt stunned.

"He said he loved us, and when he thought he was dying in Iraq he realized what a fool he'd been to ever leave you. You should have been his main priority. That he was sorry he wasted all those years being apart."

In spite of the tears running down her cheeks, Rebecca smiled. It warmed her heart to hear his words, even though they were secondhand. Finally, someone that loved her no matter what.

"His friend Charlie found him and got him safely to a hospital or he would have died in the desert. Everyone was looking for him. I didn't realize he had so many friends."

Rebecca rubbed her hand over her face nervously. "How long will he stay in a coma? Or do they know?"

"They don't know. He had injuries on every part of his body. All the hospital in Germany can do is get him stabilized until he can be flown to the States for treatment at Walter Reed. The doctors are keeping me posted on his condition. There was no need to be over there, especially if I couldn't hold his hand or see him and tell him I love him."

The older woman broke down. Sarah had been the pillar of strength for Rebecca for months—to see her sobbing was the final straw. Rebecca knew that Jason's condition was more than critical.

"He took some bad hits over there. I had no idea he was..." She stopped before saying what was on her mind. "So terribly wounded."

Rebecca sat silently as images of war-torn, bloody bodies flashed into her brain. Jason, beautiful Jason, in a coma. A man she had shared her heart, body and soul with was fighting for his life, yet she couldn't go to him. Glassy-eyed and robotic, she began to speak. "Ginni had surgery to remove the tumor today. The procedure went well, but she is classified as a Stage 4 case of Neuroblastoma. It's almost unheard of in infants her age. The whole thing is kind of ironic, isn't it?"

Sarah removed her hands from her face and sat on the edge of her chair. "What do you mean, Becca?"

"She lost a lot of blood and her immune system is weak. She's not in a coma, but a deep sleep. It's ironic that her father is lying in a hospital bed half a world away in the same condition."

Even though her heart was breaking, Rebecca managed to fight back the tears. Perhaps they would dry up one day, she told herself. Crying was not helping the people around her. The two people she loved most in the world were borderline hopeless, and she was losing her grasp on reality pretty fast. Her head began to throb and the pain behind her eyes grew more intense.

Rebecca began to stand. "Ginni is under heavy sedation and the nurses are looking after her. I need to find a convenience store. Once I get you checked in, I'll run my errands." Rebecca could feel a hand on her back as she began to walk away.

"Do you want me to keep you company?" Sarah stood, looking very concerned.

"That's nice of you, Sarah, but I think a solitary walk and some fresh air will clear my soul. You must be exhausted from jet lag. Stay in my room and get some rest. It will make me feel better knowing you're sitting with Ginni."

Seeing the sky for the first time in days and feeling a breeze across her skin felt almost normal and refreshing. The stringent hospital smells were replaced with the aroma of seafood, fried chicken and hamburgers. The enticing smells hung heavily in the air from all the area restaurants, yet Rebecca had no appetite. The security guard pointed her into town. She sucked air into her lungs and tried to concentrate on taking deep breaths as she walked aimlessly, attempting to clear her head.

She realized she was out of touch with her emotions, not really knowing or caring who she was. But only two things were on her mind — her baby may not recover and her lover was in a coma. How much more pain could God add to her plate? Looking up at the heavens, Rebecca said aloud, "Okay, God. The gloves are off. Whatever else is going to happen, lay it on me. I can't feel any lower."

A bright blue neon sign led her in the direction of a dollar store. She desperately needed shampoo, tampons, toothpaste, gum, washing detergent and some new tank tops. Off in the distance she spotted brewing storm clouds. She was about to get caught in the rain with no umbrella. Or, worse, she'd be hit be by lightning the way her luck was running.

Guess she really could be worse off, she told herself as she ducked under a canopy. As cool raindrops plopped noisily on her head, she dashed into a doorway for cover. The sultry, sweet sound of jazz was coming from inside.

"Ma'am we close early on Wednesdays." The raspy voice that called out belonged to an elderly black man standing behind the bar. The place was empty of customers. Rebecca prayed he wouldn't send her back out into the storm.

"Sir, it's raining cats and dogs out there. Well, maybe just dogs, but please let me stay here for just awhile. I don't have a car. My child is over at the hospital."

"You've got a child over there at St. Jude? Didn't they tell you about the shuttles?" he said with a surprised look on his face.

Shrugging her shoulders, Rebecca said, "Yes, I was told, but I needed to get away by myself. Thought I'd walk. Looks like I picked one heck of a time. Another wrong turn in my life."

The old man walked over and extended his hand. "My name is Earl. Why don't you sit down at the bar and keep me company while I clean up?"

Rebecca nodded. "I sure appreciate your kindness."

"I figure you got your troubles. Anything I can do to help, just let me know. You want a drink? It's on the house, little lady."

"Thank you kindly, Earl. I'm not much of a drinker. I wouldn't know what to ask for. I usually drink wine."

The older man reached for a glass under the counter. "Guess life's been hard on you lately, Miss? Something stronger might help."

Tears filled Rebecca's eyes and threatened to spill over. "You don't know the half of it, Mr. Earl. My baby has been diagnosed with cancer. The man I love more than anything was wounded in Iraq and lies in a coma in Germany. His mother just told me he probably won't make it. I've lost my beloved uncle at the hands of my insane mother. Not much else can happen to me. So if you have a suggestion to help with what ails me, I'll let you pick the poison." She crashed her fist on the bar for emphasis.

Earl thought for a moment, turned and caressed his chin with his bony fingers. Deep in thought, he reached up onto a high shelf and picked out an interestingly tall, old-fashioned looking bottle containing a light brown liquid.

"That looks intriguing. What's that?"

Earl winked. "This is Southern Comfort. It goes down real smooth. Thought I'd show you a little Southern hospitality. Take a swig of this and see if it warms up the innards and soothes the brain."

Rebecca watched his steady hand fill the shot glass to the rim. He poured one for himself and showed her how to toss it back in a swallow.

Hard liquor had been her mother's crutch. Maybe Rebecca had read her all wrong. Perhaps her mother once felt like she did right now and she drank to…what did Earl say? Soothe the brain?

She caressed the shot glass in her hand, rolling it back and forth between her palms as if warming it. Rebecca was watching Earl sweep the floors and clean off tables while she wrestled in her mind "should she" or "shouldn't she".

Stoking up enough courage, she raised the glass to her nose. The odor of the devil brew was strong, sweet, yet dangerously appealing. Rebecca parted her lips, tilted the glass and tossed it back. The warm liquid slid down her throat. Coughing and wiping her mouth with her hand, she tried to catch her breath. Searching the bar for Earl, she saw him in the corner, chuckling at her expense.

"Hey Earl, I thought you said this stuff was smooth? It's firewater."

Earl looked up from his mop. "It won't be when you're used to it."

The effects of the whiskey almost overpowered her. She hadn't eaten all day and the alcohol brought on a lightheadedness, but in an odd way it soon warmed her insides, making her feel cozy. It quieted her down. For a split second, she'd forgotten her troubles. This stuff wasn't as bad as she thought. "Hey Earl, can I have another?"

Earl nodded as he walked back behind the bar. "Told ya you'd like it Miss, but you've got to promise me that after that you'll get on outta here. This is my place and my wife, Emmie, gets real mad when I'm late—especially if I'm in the company of a pretty young lady."

Rebecca winked at her new friend. "You've got a deal Earl. Pour me another round." Rebecca slid the empty shot glass to where he was standing. "Earl, how long have you been married?"

"Me and Emmie been married for twenty-five years come January," he said with a smile.

As she looked around the bar with its bright beer lights, pool tables and high-backed stools, she wondered about his family. "Any kids?"

Earl put his damp rag down on the bar. "We have four boys. Two are in the Army, one is in college and our baby is in high school. Loves playing football, that boy."

Rebecca closed her eyes. The firewater was surging through her veins and it made her calm. "You're a lucky man Earl. You keep your family safe and don't forget to love them every day. And God bless your boys in the military."

She picked up the glass and tossed it back with more aplomb. This time the alcohol went down smoothly and sent her into a state of mild euphoria. Rebecca hadn't felt this relaxed in such a long time. She'd swear she almost felt a bit happy.

She left money on the bar and headed out the door.

"Is it still raining out there, Miss?" Earl hollered from the back of the bar.

Rebecca quickly opened the door. "Yep, Earl. It's still raining."

"You hang on a minute. I'm gonna call you a cab. Are you going back to the hospital?"

"Actually, I was looking for a discount store when I found you."

"Friend of mine named Fatty owns a taxi cab. I'll call him. There's a convenience store two blocks north of here. That's about all you're gonna find open now. He'll take you back to the hospital from there."

"I appreciate your kindness, Mr. Earl." Rebecca sat back down at the bar while Earl made the call. Playing with a book of matches she noticed the logo, "Smooth Times Lounge". Another irony, Rebecca thought. These weren't smooth times—just the opposite.

Back at Cinnamon Bay, Rebecca dropped the suitcases at the door and slipped out of her shoes. Dolores was behind her, carrying Ginni, who was wrapped in a light pink blanket. "Welcome to my humble home," she said and pointed Dolores in the direction of the nursery.

Stepping off the entry's landing, Rebecca sank her bare feet into the luxuriously plush carpeting, digging her toes in tight. It felt good to be back at Cinnamon Bay, in her own familiar surroundings. She'd had it with hospitals, sickness and death. It had almost worn her down to nothing, trying to take care of everyone. She looked around her comfortable home. It seemed like years, not months since she'd lived here. Rebecca walked from room to room looking at the new additions including the fixtures, furniture and art. The walls were painted in desert fawn brown and looked very nice.

Jason's vision of the kitchen and hearth room was nothing less than spectacular. He'd instructed Joe to install stainless steal appliances on the east wall and to make certain the fireplace separated the rooms. He'd chosen handmade sandstone bricks and tiles from Italy for a Mediterranean effect.

The chiming kitchen clock reminded her that it was time to get everyone to bed and show the nurse her room. Dolores had met them at the ferry, carrying a large duffle bag. They chatted on the trip over from the mainland and Rebecca explained her duties. The middle-aged woman adjusted her glasses, listening to every word closely. She appeared to be experienced and efficient, like the agency said.

It didn't take long for Rebecca to get accustomed to Dolores' gentle ways. She was a good manager and the quiet type. They settled into a routine for Ginni, organizing her medications and nutritional needs hour by hour. Every two weeks, Rebecca took Ginni to the local pediatrician. Once a month she flew her to St. Jude for chemotherapy. All the while, Rebecca's heart continued to get ripped apart.

There was no improvement in Jason's condition. She spoke to his doctor at Walter Reed, who informed her he was still in a coma but reassured her that he was getting excellent care. Ginni, on the other hand, appeared to be slightly stronger but her color was pale, as if her blood was still weak. "Too soon to know the outcome," was Dr. Crane's cryptic answer.

Rebecca would escape for walks on the beach in the evenings before turning in for the night. She awoke earlier than usual one morning to cries coming from the nursery. She walked by Dolores' room and whispered that she'd take care of her daughter herself. Rebecca bent over Virginia and kissed her on the forehead. "Good morning, Mama's precious baby." Ginni reached out and for the first time tried to grab Rebecca's nose. Maybe this was a sign things were on the upturn, she told herself.

She giggled at her and softly rubbed her baby's head. Where once a crown of blonde curls had been growing were ratty patches of grayish hair. Ginni was fitful due to the chemo, but Dolores knew how to keep her calm and free from too much pain. The poor little thing couldn't tell you what was wrong, but Dolores was learning to almost read her mind.

Later, Rebecca decided to take a late afternoon walk for a change. She'd called Sarah after lunch as she had done every day since she'd left to get the latest report on Jason. Nothing had changed except that he was responding a little to the music that the therapists turned on by his bed. Sarah was on a crying jag again and that was depressing.

She had to get out of the house. Rebecca picked out a clean pair of jeans and a sweatshirt, grabbed her purse and headed off to the bathroom. Before turning on the shower, she pulled out a collection of hair products from underneath the cabinet. She surprised herself when she caught sight of an old face in the mirror. The woman she'd become had a strange pallor and looked gaunt and unhealthy. Her collarbones stuck out and her hair was flat and lifeless. Rebecca ran her hands down her face and over her shoulders. Yes, that was her all right, but it wasn't a pretty sight. Where was the golden-haired girl of her youth? Her hair was almost as dull and mousy as Ginni's.

Disgusted with herself, Rebecca grabbed her purse and slid down the wall between the toilet and shower. The tile flooring was cold and made her legs shiver. Removing a silver flask from her purse, she tipped the bottle back and tasted some of that smooth Southern Comfort she'd become so familiar with, letting it tickle down her throat until all the pain evaporated.

Rebecca peeked her head into Dolores' room before leaving. She wasn't there. Walking down the hallway, she peered into Virginia's room. Dolores was sitting in a rocking chair knitting while baby Ginni was sound asleep. After popping a piece of spearmint gum into her mouth to hide the smell of alcohol, Rebecca walked over to the crib and kissed her daughter. "Dolores, I'm going for a walk."

"Okay, Ms. Roberts. I'm going to watch a little television and knit. You enjoy yourself."

As Rebecca opened the door, the fresh breeze hit her in the face. It was so refreshing. After being cooped up in Memphis, she appreciated the Gulf breezes that blew into her home. Rebecca took off her flip-flops and felt the warmth of the silky sand between her toes. Except for the occasional piece of a jagged shell or two, the sand was almost as luxurious as her new carpeting. She was truly home.

Walking half a mile down the beach, listening to the tide roll in, she found a comfortable, familiar shady spot on a log where she could be alone with her thoughts. There was no smog or city haze in the sky—just dreamy clouds floating above the first rays of sunset. She looked back at the ocean and remembered just how special this particular place was to her.

It must have been the second week of her first visit. She and Jason had sat here together. Like foolish kids, they went skinny-dipping, just enjoying each other's company and not caring if anyone else was around. Thinking back, she could almost feel skin against skin and how the cool water lapped at their bodies as they came together. From a simple touch of Jason's hand trailing across her neck...

Rebecca forced her head up off her knees. This had to stop. She had to forget how her body responded to his in the water, the taste of his salty skin and what it was like to love someone with her whole being. She could go mad with yearning for something that would never happen again.

Opening up her bag, Rebecca pulled out a bottle of comfort. She carefully broke off the red and white quality seal and removed the cap. Earl was right. This worked. This was what was getting her through the rough nights. Rebecca didn't drink until after sundown—like a real Southern lady, she told herself. She'd read that once in a novel or *Southern Living* magazine.

Drink was making her life tolerable, making her sleep like a log. She didn't have to face anything when she went to bed. Not the pain of losing Jason or losing her child. Alcohol not only dulled the past, but it blacked out the uncertainty of her future.

Above the roar of the waves, a voice began calling her name. Who was that? Rebecca wasn't expecting company.

"Rebecca Lynn Roberts, don't make me walk all the way down this damn beach to find your sorry butt." A high-pitched wailing came from up the beach and she immediately knew who it was.

"Whitney?" She would surely get a lecture from her. Rebecca began to panic. She quickly spun the lid back on the bottle, placing it in her purse. Finding some gum, she stuck two squares in her mouth and chomped down for a few moments to disguise her breath. Only then did she answer. "Over here, Whit. I'm by the tree." She stood up and waved.

"There you are. What a sight for sore eyes." Whitney slid down the slope and gave her a big bear hug. She wrinkled her nose and broke away from her friend. "Have you been drinking, Rebecca? I swear I smell booze."

For a moment, Rebecca felt guilty. Not wanting to speak, she remained silent so as not to admit to anything. Vying for time, she spouted off the simplest thing she could. "What gave you such a silly idea?"

Whitney shrugged. "I thought I smelled it on your breath when I hugged you."

"No way—just this new green apple gum. It's got a strong scent. You're not the only one who's thought that." Quickly she changed the subject. "What a surprise. How have you been?"

"Worried about you, mostly. I chatted with Dolores about Ginni." Whitney took Rebecca's arm and sat down. "How's Sarah?"

"She's back in Nashville checking on things. Then it's back to Walter Reed. Jason is in the Head Trauma and Neurological Care Center there. Sarah says there are so many young men with terrible head injuries, just like Jason. He's getting 'round the clock care, but his brain waves aren't showing much improvement," she said angrily. "I desperately want to take Ginni and go to see him, but I'm afraid to go too far from her doctors."

"I heard," said Whitney, giving her a squeeze. "Rick keeps in contact with Sarah through e-mails. I know you want to see him, but for now it's probably best that you don't. The most important question is how are you doing?"

"I'm not going to lie. Things have been rough. Today was bad. Sarah gets jags of crying. She said I shouldn't count on Jason coming out of the coma. I can't picture Sarah saying such a thing, but she did. She said she's ready to accept it." Her voice trembled.

"Let's go back to your house, get in the hot tub and talk. It's getting chilly out here," said Whitney, rubbing her arms. "A night of Oreos and girl talk like the old days will do both of us some good. My schedule keeps me hopping and I'd love to relax."

Arm in arm, they made their way from the beach back to the house, laughing and talking. Rebecca slid open the patio door. "Let me show you to your room."

Whitney smiled that bubbly smile of hers. "No need for that, my friend. I already found my room and it is gorgeous."

Rebecca was agitated. "You found your room—which one?"

"The one down the end of the hallway to the right—I think you call that color sage green. Reminds me of the color of money," she quipped.

"You should change rooms," Rebecca said curtly.

Whitney looked puzzled. "Hey. You've never objected to me making myself at home before. What's the deal?"

"No deal. I just think you'd be happier in another room. The rooms on the east side get a better breeze from the ocean."

In a somewhat puzzled voice, Whitney agreed. "Whatever. Let's just get our bathing suits on. Meet you in the hot tub, okay?" Whitney quickly disappeared to change.

Alone in her room, Rebecca took another long swig from a bottle hidden in her dresser drawer. The drink was what she needed to get through a long night of probing questions. Immediately, Rebecca could feel the warm liquid coursing through her veins, numbing her mind. She took another big gulp before replacing the cap and changing into her swimsuit.

The patio was quiet at this time of evening. Rebecca took in a deep breath of fresh ocean air before removing the vinyl cover and turning on the jets. From the house a shadowy silhouette appeared, startling Rebecca. Placing her hand across her chest and panting heavily, Rebecca could see it was only Whitney. Upon closer examination, she saw that Whitney was holding up two empty whiskey bottles and appeared to be angry.

"Rebecca, what are you doing? You've never been one to drink, let alone this."

Rebecca refused to admit anything. "Looks like a couple of empty bottles. Where'd you get them?" She turned back to adjust the hot tub gauges.

"Funny thing—I was going through the linen closet looking for a beach towel when I found a big box of empty bottles and two half full ones, just like these."

Rebecca shrugged her shoulder. "Must be from the construction workers. I'll make a note to get after Joe when I see him."

Whitney set the bottles down on the patio table. "Don't play me for a fool, Rebecca. You never could lie. You know damn well it's you who's been drinking, and drinking quite a lot. How could you? After all you went through with your mother's addiction. This isn't social drinking I see here. This is hardcore stuff — what alcoholics do. What JoAnne did."

Fury welled up inside Rebecca and as she turned around, her anger hissed out like a viper. "Who are you to tell me what to do? You've always had the perfect life. Whitney had the family who cared about her. A new car when she turned sixteen. Great jobs at the drop of a hat. Now you have the man of your dreams and I have nothing. My man is in a coma, my child may not live if that last round of chemo doesn't work and I can't sleep because I'm afraid. The drinking gets me through the night."

Whitney tried to get her friend's attention. "Don't turn away. Look at me. You're delusional and you're going to do something crazy. That child needs you, just like you needed a loving mother. Her life is in your hands. And you're not alone. Our friendship should count for something, right?"

"So I lose the friendship of a whore. I don't need you to tell me how to run my life. *You* lecture *me* on life. That's rich." Rebecca walked to a chair and sat down. Her head was splitting and her hands were shaking. She needed a drink.

The hurt in Whitney's eyes was clear. She looked as if she was going to cry. Everybody around her was reduced to tears these days, Rebecca told herself. But an inner voice also told Rebecca that she'd gone too far.

"That's the coldest thing you've ever said to me, Rebecca. Not so much what you said, but the way you said it. When did you turn into your mother? Have you looked in the mirror lately? You look like her, you smell like her and now you act like her. When will you start slapping Ginni around and making her life a living hell?" Angrily, Whitney stalked off, leaving Rebecca sitting there, tipsy and forlorn.

She felt sorry for what she'd said. Whitney had been there through thick and thin with her. Why was everything around her going up in flames? Rebecca waited a good long while, before heading into the house to find her friend. Whitney always needed time after an argument to calm down. Standing up, she walked back into the house and quietly opened the door. On her way down the hallway, she peeked into a half-lit room. Virginia was sound asleep with Dolores watching TV. Dolores didn't even notice Rebecca looking in on them. As she got closer to Whitney's room, she noticed the room was dark and the door open. Rebecca flipped on the light.

"Whitney. I'm sorry about what I said." Checking the bathroom and closet, Rebecca saw that Whitney had packed up her things, apparently in a hurry, and had left.

Rebecca needed to find her. She removed her bathing suit, threw on a skirt and a tank top, grabbed her purse and headed out the door. In her condition, she didn't dare drive. Besides, Whitney couldn't have gone far and no cab could've come that quickly.

Walking toward town, she spotted a tiny bar on the seaport. Whitney was no angel herself—maybe she'd stopped there to make a phone call or have a drink. Rebecca walked through the door and saw it was a sailor's dive with fishing nets and old pictures of boats, navigation wheels and barometers adorning the walls. The tables and chairs were splintered and worn with age, some seats were broken and there were only a few people— mostly dockworkers—drinking beer.

One for the road and then she'd find Whitney. "Bartender, a double shot of whiskey, please." Rebecca pointed to the bright bottle behind the bar.

"Coming up." The bartender wiped his hands on his apron and reached for a glass.

She watched as the man poured a tall glass nearly to the top. This man wasn't as personable as Earl had been. He did his business and kept his mouth shut.

Rebecca took her drink to a table and sat there, downing another and another until she forgot the world, not caring about her missing friend, what she was doing to herself or her child. Feeling dizzy, she stumbled to the bathroom to get sick. Turning on the light, the reflection in the mirror startled her. She gasped in horror. It was as if JoAnne had come back from the dead. She was looking at her mother's face in the reflection. Messy hair, slovenly appearance and a twisted smile on her face. Stunned, Rebecca placed her fingers on the glass and traced the outline of her face. Needing to erase this terrible memory from her mind, she stumbled back to her table for another round.

After belting down several more shots, Rebecca felt that wonderfully warm, euphoric feeling and soon forgot about her mother and the rest of the world. Standing up was difficult—her legs felt like rubber and her head was empty and woozy. She walked toward the dance floor. Feeling nothing but the whiskey, she began to dance, moving her arms and lower torso provocatively and running her hands down her hips and between her thighs. Feeling the tempo of the music, she twirled herself around and around, the room spinning out of control until a pair of hands caught her waist.

"You all right?" came a deep, whispering voice. She could feel the bristle of tiny whiskers tickling her ear. She cringed, turned around and thought she was dreaming. The man looked like her Jason. Squinting her eyes into focus, she realized that it wasn't him. The guy before her was taller with thick dark hair and a well-trimmed beard.

Brushing the hair from her face, she shook his hands off her and stood by herself. "I'm fine. Just here to party and have a good time. I'm here to forget my problems."

"Mind if I help you with that good time?" He looked at her with a devil-may-care grin. "I bet I can make you forget all of your troubles."

Impaired by the alcohol, she was unaware of his forwardness and began dancing again. "If you're here to dance, then we can party."

She twirled faster and faster and could feel her skirt float up around her. For once, she didn't care if her underwear was showing—she just felt numb. She danced up-tempo until she couldn't stand straight or see. The large pair of hands once again grabbed her. When she collapsed, the dark stranger scooped her up in his arms, carrying her out into the parking lot.

Rebecca laughed. "I think I could use some fresh air."

The mysterious man quite coyly replied, "I know what you need and it's not air."

# Chapter Twenty-One

෨

Rebecca inhaled big breaths of air, hoping to clear her lungs from the cigarettes' choking smoke. It hadn't seemed that bad in the bar. But now the thick smell combined with the whiskey burned the back of her throat as her nerves tingled from an artificial happiness which made her feel like laughing at the least little thing.

Feeling disoriented, Rebecca had trouble focusing on objects. The more she looked around, the dizzier she became. Trying hard to get a good look at her new friend, she squinted, drawing her face closer to his. While wrapping her arms tightly around his bulky neck, she buried her head into his chest, trying to make the spins go away.

The handsome stranger continued carrying her further away from the neon lights of the bar to the outskirts of the parking lot. The night was pitch-black and she could feel droplets of sweat running down her neck from the earlier dancing and the humidity hanging in the air.

Maneuvering her face around his, she flung her head backward, as if to go limp, and kicked her feet. She could feel his hand tightly cradling her butt and upper back as he continued to carry her. Finally she felt a jolt as he plopped her down on the ground. Landing on her feet, her legs felt unstable and rubbery. She reached out and grabbed the side mirror of an old rust bucket of a truck that had definitely seen better days.

When she felt good enough to stand alone, she looked up and asked her new friend, "Do you live here in town? I don't recall seeing you around these parts before. You're not a reporter, are you?" For a fleeting moment, she thought he might be a tabloid reporter sent to spy on her — just waiting for her to mess up in some way.

He rubbed his beard with the palm of his hand and grinned. His lustrous white teeth gleamed as brightly as pearls deep in the ocean against his tanned face. The stranger lightly chuckled. "No. I'm not a reporter, but I guess you could say I'm new in town. Depending on how tonight turns out, I may not be here long." He brazenly reached up and playfully kissed her cheek while trailing his finger down from her neck to the crown of her breasts.

This was a situation she needed to get out of fast, but she was so confused. "You shouldn't do that. I'm engaged. I thought we were just going to have some fun," she said, struggling to stay on her feet.

"Oh, I am in the mood for a little fun, believe me." He reached a hand around her, caressing her buttocks and feeling her panty line. Rebecca could feel his stubby fingers digging deeper into the material of her denim skirt. "If you're engaged, where is Mr. Wonderful tonight? He shouldn't let an exquisite creature like you out alone." He reached out, trying to cop a feel of her breasts — this time managing to dive deep enough to finger a nipple.

Rebecca started to feel uneasy but couldn't move. She steadied herself against the truck, feeling as if she might throw up. "I...I think that I'd better go back inside."

"For what, darling?" He caressed her shoulders with both his hands. "The fun's this way," he said as he pointed to the cab of his truck.

She became angry. "Don't call me darling. Only one man can ever call me that, and it's not going to be you. I don't even know your name and keep your hands off my breasts."

"My name is...um, Don," the handsome stranger said as he opened the door. "Get in. We can have some fun in here."

Stumbling, Rebecca began walking backward. "No. I'm not going in there with you."

Don walked closer to her, once again picking her up, this time under the armpits. "It's not up for discussion, honey bun. You're getting in my truck." With one thrust, he hoisted her up, throwing her against the truck frame.

The metal of the truck and outline of the seat dug into the skin of Rebecca's back. She flung her legs around, trying to kick at his knees or whatever else was in the way, but muscled flesh pinned her down. With another shove, he threw her up into the seat, pushing her past the steering wheel, her skirt rising above her pelvis. She could feel a breeze across her stomach.

The stranger climbed in after her, pulling the door shut. Scrambling to get up, Rebecca could feel Don's hand on her belly, forcefully pinning her to the seat.

"You might as well not fight it. I'm going to have my fun tonight. You wanted to party—you need to look no further than my pants, deary." Rebecca watched him lean closer to her. The cab of the truck was spinning. It was becoming harder to breathe and she felt as though she would vomit.

Out of the corner of her eye, Rebecca could see Don turning as he shifted all his weight on top of her. He began kissing her madly. Wet lips devoured her neck, moving down toward the crown of her breasts until buttons went flying and the material ripped away as he forcefully tugged on it. In the moonlight, she could see the glow of her exposed flesh, which made her fight even harder to get up.

Rebecca could feel the burn from his coarse whiskers roughly moving up and down her neck as his hand continued to work its way further up her skirt. She began to breathe heavily as his finger invaded the elastic band of her panties, ripping the material as his fingers reached her private area. His stale mouth felt as if he were devouring her like a hungry tiger in the wild might consume its prey. With one arm around her, he used the other to rip her tank top open completely.

She began to panic. God. What had she done? This was wrong. It was all wrong! She struggled to get him off her, digging the heel of her shoes deeper into the seat, desperately trying to stretch to reach for the door handle. It was her only chance for escape. She prayed he didn't have electric locks so that she couldn't get out.

Trying desperately to do anything to get him away from her, she reached up, pulling his hair. The softness of his hair filtered through her fingertips. Knocking her arm away from his head, he continued to ravage her body. His knee sunk into the side of her thigh, crushing it. With no other choice, she began screaming and digging her fingernails deep into the flesh of his head, causing him to shout out in pain.

"You crazy bitch! You want it as bad as I do," he yelled, pinning her arms behind her. "Now be a big girl and take your medicine. Fight if you want to — Don likes it rough."

Rebecca continued to fight until she could see knuckles coming toward her. The first blow stung like lightning. The sound of tearing cartilage rung through her ears. Don had cracked her a good one. Blood began gushing down her face, probably coming from her nose, she guessed. She continued fighting as she felt his hands between her legs, trying to rip off what was left of her underwear. Feeling his firmness against her pelvis, she calmed down, making him think he was in complete control. As his body relaxed, she arched her leg, kicking him in the groin. Rebecca could feel his body tense as he rolled off of her, moaning in pain and holding himself.

Scrambling to get out of the truck, Rebecca once again dug the heel of her shoe into the seat for leverage. Frantically, she searched the door frame until she found the latch and forcefully tugged open the door. She could hear her attacker sobbing as she fell from the truck into the weeds. Stumbling to her feet, she managed to cross a ditch and ran into the darkness.

She was still drunk and her head spun like a merry-go-round gone wrong. Every so often she could feel thick blood trickling down the back of her throat. As she ran, Rebecca could feel the tall grass and dense foliage cut into her skin. Finding a slight path, she ran further into the darkness, hoping he wouldn't follow her there. After running for what seemed like an eternity, she collapsed on the beach next to a pile of boulders with the tide crashing against the shoreline loud enough to drown out her gasps.

The world continued to spin out of control as the thought of almost being raped made her lean forward. She threw up until there was nothing left in her system. Thick acid covered her throat and mouth as blood continued to dribble from her nose. God, what had she done? But then, the answer was all too clear. Rebecca had become JoAnne. She had put a bottle of booze to her head and pulled the trigger. It dawned on her that she'd unknowingly put the devil liquid above her career, her lifelong friends, her self-respect and, most importantly, her child.

Crawling on her hands and knees to the water's edge, she removed one of her shoes and a sock. She dipped the material into the water to soak it, her hands and body trembling so violently she almost dropped the soggy material into the tide. Shaky and nauseous, she applied the wet cloth to her bruised and swollen face. The salt water stung as she applied firm pressure to her nose and lip. Curiously, she didn't mind the pain—she figured she deserved worse for what she'd become.

Off in the distance, Rebecca heard the faint noise of a truck clamor down the road. Thinking it was the stranger, she crouched down, lying still next to the rocks so as not to be spotted, but the truck passed and once again she was alone.

Rolling over onto her back, she looked up at the stars, tears streaming down her face as blood trickled from her nose. Rebecca let the cool tidewaters rush over her body as the sand deposits were left behind on her skin. She continued to lie there, muttering the phrase, "I'm not anything like my mother," over and over again. Somewhere deep inside, she had more self-respect, more strength than that. All she had needed to do was find it, and tonight she had. Perhaps the image of JoAnne in the bathroom mirror had been a premonition of what almost happened to her with the stranger—only she hadn't heeded the warning, dismissing it. Perhaps the new tidal waters would wash the sin from her ravaged body.

She had so much to live for. The images of the last year of her life flashed through her mind. The most important answer was so simple, yet the most special of all. Virginia. If she drowned in the bottle, it was no better than pointing a gun at herself. Or worse, it would be condemning her daughter to a life of hell, just like she had lived through. Ginni didn't deserve that kind of treatment and abuse. It was time she learned to love herself for what and who she was. Until she realized that, no one could really love her and none of the insecurities would be dismissed.

Rebecca couldn't bear to have that happen to that sweet, innocent child. The cycle of abuse had to be broken and the line started with her so that Ginni would be spared from this type of life. From now on, she would concentrate on her daughter, put her first above all else in her life. Rebecca knew she had walked over a fine line, that she might not have been able to cross back over if her drinking were to go on much longer. If Jason lived and came back to her, it would be a bonus. If not, she would have the courage to go on with her life, write and attend AA sessions to ensure her sobriety.

She must have dozed off for a little bit, because when she made her decision, the moon had dipped low in the sky and the tide had retreated from the rocks.

Pulling herself to her knees, Rebecca tugged at the pieces of loose blouse, trying to get them to cover just enough of her breasts so she wouldn't have to walk the rest of the way home naked. The salt and sand infiltrated the cuts and scrapes on her legs, causing her to cringe in pain. She had done a lot of soul-searching lying in the wet sand. She remembered what was important to her. It was time to do something about it.

There would be no more tears. She'd cried too much her entire life and spent a lifetime waiting for other people to love her. Her parents evidently hadn't had love to give. Rebecca was coming to terms with that, learning to forgive, making peace with it in her own mind. When Jason had left her in Galveston, that had been an admission that he loved his dreams more than her. He'd apologized for that, but what was done was done. It was time to stop waiting for other people and to put her daughter and herself first.

Finally finding her way home, Rebecca slowly opened the door, praying no one would see her in this condition. Stepping into the living room, she couldn't help but think about how her life had come full circle, almost dying only to become reborn again. Rebecca Lynn Roberts was no longer the abused girl from Texas who once had so little hope. She was now armed with a new, bolder outlook on life. While the deep scratches, cuts and bruises would heal, the memory of this night would never fade. God granted that it would carry her through the next portion of her life.

Tiptoeing into the kitchen, she picked up the phone and dialed 411. "Operator, I'd like the local or hotline number for Alcoholics Anonymous, please."


The beach house was in disarray, strewn with crumpled up lyric sheets, medicines, baby toys, blankets and dirty dishes. With Ginni's chemotherapy over with and her immune system working again, Rebecca had thrown herself into writing and let the house go. There was no time to waste cleaning. Her new sober attitude, stress medication and AA meetings had allowed her creativity to shine—not to mention the "fire in her belly" to succeed in all aspects of her life. She cranked out one song after another, submitting to every record company she could think of.

As she fixed Ginni's lunch, there was a knock at the door.

"Now, who could that be, little girl? Dolores won't be back for another hour. Besides, she would've used her key."

She walked over to Ginni, who was banging one of her Playskool toys against the high chair's tray and picked her up. Balancing her baby on her hip, she walked toward the door.

After the fight with Whitney, she was startled to see who was standing at the door.

"Hey, Rick, what are you doing here?" Rebecca felt a flash of hope that perhaps Whitney had sent him here. She was told by her AA advisor that she was to make things right with the ones she'd hurt during drinking binges. Although she had tried calling Whitney, she never could quite complete the call.

Rick looked a little nervous as she opened the door, inviting him into the house. "I need to talk to you."

Oh no, Rebecca thought. She brushed her hand up to her face. The bruises from the assault were almost gone. She hoped Rick didn't ask any questions about them. Then embarrassment hit her. What if there were witnesses or Opie had heard about the incident? Maybe he was the one who had called Rick.

Playing coy, Rebecca began talking like she knew nothing. "Sounds serious." She managed what she hoped was a credible smile. "Come on in." She led the way into the kitchen. "Sorry the place is such a mess. We were just about to have lunch. Would you like something?"

"I already ate, but I'd take a beer if you have one." Judging by the look on his face, she could tell that Rick knew he messed up. Looking down at the table, he tapped his knuckles against its top. "Becca, I'm sorry about that."

Rebecca reached over, gripping Rick's arm tightly. "There is no need to apologize. I figured Whitney must have told you about my problem. We got into a pretty big argument that night. I'm going to AA. Things are much better now."

Rick nodded in agreement. "That's good, Rebecca. That's real good." His eyes traveled up her face to the bruises. "How'd you get the cuts?"

"I'd rather not talk about it. Now, how would you like a glass of iced sun tea? I made a fresh batch this morning. I even hand-squeezed lemon juice in it," she said, pointing to the pitcher.

He smiled at her. "That would be nice. Do you want me to take Ginni while you fix it?" Rick reached his arms out toward the baby.

"Sure." Rebecca stood, carefully transferring care of Ginni over to Rick. As she fixed the iced tea, she glanced back to look at them. He was playing with Virginia and looking like an old pro while he did it. "You look good with a baby, Rick. Gonna have one of your own someday?"

He grinned back at her and looked away.

Rebecca set the cool drink down. Taking Ginni from Rick, she placed her in her highchair and sat across the table from him. "So, what's on your mind?"

"Especially after the baby comment, I'm just going to come right out and say it." He took a deep breath as Rebecca's eyes got wide as silver dollars. "I'm gonna ask Whitney to marry me."

She almost spit her drink all over the table—that was the last thing she had expected to hear. "That's great, Rick." Rebecca felt a surge of joy for her friend. "I'm so happy for you. Both of you."

"Yeah, well, it just seems right. I miss her when she's not with me. Women throw themselves at us all the time, but I'm hopelessly in love with that short, fiery, red-haired stick of dynamite." He grinned. "But don't tell her I said that. Wouldn't want her to get a swelled head."

"So how are you going to propose?" She leaned forward, raising an eyebrow. "Over a romantic dinner? With a song? On an island?"

"Close. At an SOS benefit concert me and the guys are doing down here on the mainland tonight."

Her heart ached at the memory of The Fighting Eagles' last benefit concert and how it had changed her life. "Wow," she said aloud. "Better be careful. That can be tricky terrain. Look what happened to Jason and me. We haven't had the best of luck."

"I know. I've kept in contact with Sarah. It sure is awful what the two of you have been through." Rick put his big hand over hers.

Rebecca almost teared up, but then remembered AA's steps toward recovery. "You know, I want to cry right now, but my therapy has me taking one day at a time baby steps, as they say in treatment." She looked over to Ginni who was banging on her high chair, impatient for her lunch.

"He saw some pretty bad stuff over there. Do you think he will remember any of that or be the same when he gets out of that coma?" Rick set his glass back down on the table.

Breaking softer parts of her peanut butter sandwich and giving it to Ginni, she sighed. "Maybe. Who's to say? But I haven't heard anything good since I don't know when." She wiped her baby's mouth with a soft cloth.

"Do you still love him?" Rick gave Ginni her bottle.

Rebecca smiled. "I never stopped loving him. I never will." Needing to do something so that she wouldn't get a headache, she slid her chair closer to her daughter and started feeding her again. "But what difference does that make?"

Rick shook his head and reached for her hand again. "Might make all the difference in the world. You have to have a little faith."

"So, getting back to your plans. Tell me about the big night." She wiped the grape jelly off Ginni's face and hands with a cool rag, removing her bib.

Taking another sip of tea, Rick said, "Well, you heard how my dad was throwing a fit that Whitney wasn't Native American, right? We had a pretty big blowup months ago."

"Yeah. She said she'd flunked the visit with your folks. She was really upset, too."

"Well, he and I had a long talk, and let's just say he's seeing things my way now." Rick stood and walked to the trashcan, tossing Ginni's disposal bib away for Rebecca. "He finally understood that no other woman is going to make me happy and that I'm not coming back home to live."

Rebecca picked Virginia up, placing the baby in her lap. "That's great, Rick. I'm sure Whitney'll be relieved about that."

Rick came back to the table. "You know, it's customary for our people to present the bride and her family with a pony. I'm going to bring a war pony out onto the stage tonight and present it to her. Then just when she's wondering what the hell's going on, I'm going to pull her up onstage from the front row—which is where you come in—and ask her to be my wife."

"That's so romantic. She'll love it, but there is no way I will be there tonight." She shook her head and turned toward the window, remembering the cruel things she'd said to her friend.

"I need you there to make sure she's in her seat when the time comes." His piercing dark eyes winked at her. How could she deny him? He looked so in love and happy.

She managed a feeble smile. "I really don't feel much like coming to a concert right now, Rick. I hope you understand. I said some pretty hateful things to my best friend and then seeing The Fighting Eagles perform—I just don't want it to be too much and fall out of recovery."

Rick twisted his face and sharply said, "Come on, Rebecca. Whitney's gonna need her best friend there. She's missing you as much as you miss her right now. You've known her for years. There's no way she's just going to pick up the phone or call here. She acts like a tough cookie, but on the inside she has her vulnerabilities."

Rebecca thought about all the times Whitney had been there for her. "I'll tell you what, Rick. I'll go—because you're right and I need to be there for my best friend. But once I apologize and you propose, I'm outta there. I don't want to mingle with the band members or anything. I don't think I could handle making small talk with Jason's closest friends."

"Deal." Rick stood and threw his arms around Rebecca and Ginni.

Rebecca gave him a quick, one-armed hug. "I'll get Dolores to baby-sit for me."

"I almost forgot." He reached into the back pocket of his jeans. "Someone in Nashville wanted me to give you this. Something about a check for the rights to a song you sold."

"Oh, yeah?" Rebecca was puzzled as to why Rick had it. "What gives, Rick? How did you end up with it?"

Walking toward the back porch, he turned and grinned. "Nashville may be a big town, but it's a tight-knit community. There isn't anything a musician or songwriter can do or say that doesn't get back to someone, especially if they're down on their luck."

"There has to be some mistake." Her mouth dropped open. "Down on Your Luck" was one of the songs she'd started when she was in a drunken stupor and finished right out of her first rehab session. "There's a check in here for $60,000. My standard contracts usually go for $6,000 plus royalties."

Rick shot her a sheepish grin. "Gotta go."

He waved, turned and waltzed out the door.


It took her awhile driving around lost before Rebecca found the modest brick armory building where the SOS benefit concert was to be held. Gauging from the number of cars and pickup trucks in the parking lot and the noise coming from inside, there was already a good-sized crowd.

Even though she knew Jason wasn't going to be here this time, she felt butterflies darting around in her belly. Thoughts buzzed through her brain and her emotions were on edge. She was getting on with her life as best she could, but it still felt as if a big part of her was missing — her heart. Then there was seeing Whitney again. She was never one to hold her tongue. She'd probably let loose on her with a fury.

Rebecca had changed so much from the weeks before. She was gradually beginning to look and feel better, healthier. To bolster her confidence, she had dressed to kill, her sandy hair pinned up with combs in a classy, elegant fashion, her long legs shown off to perfection in a black sequined mini-dress. Dolores had said she looked divine and that when any man saw her, he'd eat his heart out.

She made her way into the venue and showed her ticket to the burly guard at the front entrance. Then she heard a familiar voice behind her.

"Oh, my God, Becca. Is that you?" Whitney rushed to hug her friend. "Killer dress." She pushed Rebecca away and made her turn around so she could get a good look at what she was wearing. "Looking good."

Rebecca turned to hug her friend back. "Whitney, I've wanted to call you a thousand times." Whitney was staring at her with a pleasant smile on her face. "I did once, but hung up before you answered. I am so sorry for what I said — what I did."

Whitney interrupted her. "I forgot all about that stuff the moment you apologized. Oh, and Rick talked to me." She hugged her friend again. "In a way I owe you a thank you for what you did say."

Rebecca was confused. "Why on Earth would you owe me a thank you? I'm the one who was so cruel to you. I drove you away."

"Because you forced me to take a good, long look at the way I act around people — men. You were right about the way I flaunted myself. It wasn't right and if I didn't stop, I could have even put my relationship with Rick in jeopardy." She grabbed for Rebecca's hand. "How is that baby of yours? I mean, we've kept tabs on her through Sarah and Opie, but I've missed her so much and can't wait to see that little girl again."

"Much better now, and getting bigger every day." Rebecca removed some pictures of Ginni from her purse. "She is into everything and starting to crawl. See how big she's getting?"

Whitney shook her head. "She looks just like her mama." She bounced up and down. "Well, I'm glad you made it, Rebecca. It'll be just like old times — us sitting in the front row."

Rebecca raised her eyebrows in surprise. "Yeah, just like old times." She couldn't forget the last time she and Whitney had been to a concert. Her heart skipped thinking about Jason—the way he moved that night, the way he smelled, the look of love on his face when he saw her again for the first time. If only the hands of time could be moved back. She'd give almost anything.

Realizing what she'd just said, Whitney turned red with embarrassment. "Oh, shit. Sorry. Foot in mouth and I meant shoot—I'm trying not to cuss so much lately." She gave Rebecca a hug. "C'mon. Let's go find our seats."

As if time really had stood still, the two friends made their way toward the front row. The crowd was pumped with excitement. Except with Jason not being onstage, it was almost déjà vu. Rebecca couldn't help thinking back to that wonderful, joyful day and remembering how it had felt to see her love after all those years. It seemed almost a lifetime ago, when she had still believed in fairy tales and happy endings. In keeping with her treatment, she tried to think positive. At least she had those good memories to hold onto.

Settling in their seats, she looked up at the stage. Closing her eyes, she could almost feel the electric jolt of being pulled up onto the stage by her one true love as the vibrations of thousands of fans tapping their feet and clapping rocked the floor. Looking over at Whitney, she smiled. Tonight was her best friend's chance to savor that wonderfully warm feeling of love and excitement, and Rebecca couldn't wait.

The band blasted onto the stage and flew into a rousing version of the national anthem. Flags proudly flew as hundreds of fans crossed their right hands over their hearts to take part in the ceremony to honor America's favorite sons and daughters.

It was more than a little strange not seeing Jason performing with his tight Wranglers, devil-may-care attitude and opening act of lofting his Stetson out into the crowd. Rebecca stared at the new lead singer. He wasn't her type with his long, straggly brown hair, pierced ear and black leather pants. He looked more like a biker than a singer, but he did have a nice voice. All in all, he wasn't bad. The audience must have agreed because they were clapping and hollering.

After the opening number, the crowd went wild with applause and then quieted a bit. Rebecca saw Rick looking down at her. He nodded and winked. Rebecca knew Whitney's surprise was about to happen. The new lead singer tossed the microphone to Rick.

Rick began thanking everyone for coming to the Support Our Soldiers concert. When he seemed to have finished his patter, he said, "Ladies and gentlemen, I hope you'll bear with me as I pay tribute to a very special woman out there in the audience. A woman who I hope will be my wife."

Again the crowd went wild with hollers and cheers. Some people lifted their flickering lighters to show their blessings. Whitney turned to Rebecca, her mouth hanging open. "What the hell is this? Do you know anything about this?"

"Shut up, Whit," Rebecca said with a grin, "and listen to what the man has to say."

"In keeping with the tradition of my people, the Apache, it is customary for the groom to give the family of the bride a gift. Whitney, my love, this is my gift to you."

Whitney looked at Rebecca again in disbelief, for once speechless, lifting her hand to her mouth as a white pony ornamented with leather, feathers and beadwork was led out onto the stage.

"Whitney." Looking at her, he held out his hand, bending over the edge of the stage. "Would you please come up here and join me?"

Stunned, her eyes filling with happy tears, Whitney once again turned toward her friend. "Rebecca, you have to come with me! It's all because of you that Rick and I are together. It all started with you and Jason and it wouldn't be right if you weren't up there with me. Please."

Rebecca's heart was breaking, but she couldn't say no to her very best friend. So she smiled bravely as they both stood and walked up the steep stairs. As self-conscious as last time, she hoped no one could look up her dress and see her underwear.

When they arrived on the stage, Rebecca stepped back as a huge, brilliant beam of light shone in a circle where Whitney was to stand. Rebecca was more than happy to relinquish her time in the spotlight to her friend.

"Whitney, I've come to realize that I can't live without you." Rick got down on one knee, taking her tiny hand in his big palm. "Will you marry me?" he said simply, sweetly as he carefully slipped a three-carat diamond ring on her finger.

The crowd erupted in cheers. Rebecca couldn't contain her emotions either. She had watched her friend go from a lovelorn wanderer looking for Mr. Right in all the wrong places to a woman of importance in the recording industry and now she would be a wonderful wife to an amazing man. She couldn't have been happier. Rebecca wiped a tear off her cheek, hoping not to smear her makeup. Being on stage was no time to get a case of raccoon eyes.

Whitney jumped up into his arms, kissing him madly. "Oh Rick, I'll absolutely marry you." She smiled as she cupped both her hands around his face, pulling him forward for another kiss. "But we've got to get this darn horse off the stage before it makes a mess. I don't think the Roadies' Union will allow them to clean this up."

"How about that, folks—engaged less than a minute and she's already starting to nag me." Rick put his arms around Whitney's waist and hoisted her up to kiss her.

The crowd went wild with laughter and excitement as Rick scooped Whitney up into his arms, still passionately kissing her. Finally letting her down gently, as if she were made of glass, he led her to the pony being held by a man in full Native dress.

"I would like to speak to you, Whitney Harmon," a low, deep voice said.

Rebecca watched as the tall man holding the pony's reins, his black hair streaked with gray, his face scored with deep lines, addressed her joyful friend. Her gaze went to Rick, and she realized that the man could only be Rick's father.

The older man began to speak. "I was opposed to your relationship with my son. I saw only a white woman, not a suitable wife for a Youngblood, and my prejudice blinded me to your worth." He stepped closer to her and took both her hands in his. "But my son loves you. This I could see. And he tells me how you take care of him. How you've immersed yourself in our culture. How you work with Native charities every chance you get. I welcome you to our family, my daughter."

Rick beamed as his father and Whitney embraced.

Rebecca knew her time in the spotlight was up. She gracefully backed away from the couple and made her way down the stairwell. Trying to decide whether to take her seat and continue to watch the show or go home, an icy silence fell over the auditorium. Continuing to walk up the long row toward the central aisle, she thought she noticed something new on the stage behind her, but thinking it was the glimmer catching off the sparkles on her dress, she dismissed it.

Carefully, so as not to block anyone's view, Rebecca ducked and dodged people, finally walking faster once she reached the aisle. About midway through the audience, a sudden clapping erupted. Almost in unison, individuals began to rise with stunned expressions. Rebecca turned to see what was happening.

Jason! The jolt of shock she felt was so electrifying that she was taken back in time to that meeting at the benefit concert in Houston. Was this a hallucination? He was in Walter Reed hovering near death in a coma. She once again looked back at the audience as they began talking among themselves. Rebecca was frozen and couldn't move. The image before her stood with the use of a cane and looked thinner, more wrinkled around the eyes, but it was her Jason.

Oh, Lord, she still loved him so. He was the only man who could make her feel happy, safe and electrified. Jason was the one man who made her heart beat slow and fast and weak in the knees all at the same time. Her heart was so confused, it felt like exploding.

With his mother, Sarah, at his side to steady him, Jason made his way to the center of the stage and microphone. Apparently Sarah had been hiding two very big secrets. Rebecca didn't know whether to be mad at him for not letting her know he was okay or overjoyed by his recovery. She was confused and her head started to spin. Her heart was pounding.

She heard Rick announcing Jason's triumphant return to The Fighting Eagles. Obviously, his return was as much of a surprise for the audience as it had been for her, and the crowd immediately began screaming and chanting his name.

Suddenly, an all-too-familiar voice came over the microphone as the music began. The melody was unfamiliar, but she knew the words, she realized. The words she had written.

It dawned on her that he'd bought "Down on Your Luck" for sixty grand. She was unable to move or speak until he finished the song. She stared up at him in amazement and shock. He hadn't lost his touch. Jason was still the smooth country crooner he'd always been. Although he wasn't as energetic, his vulnerability made him all the more mesmerizing.

"Ladies and gentlemen, I guess this is your second unscripted surprise of the evening," he said.

A spotlight fluttered toward her as she stood in the middle of the auditorium.

"Oh, God, no."

"You see, I'm in love with a woman in tonight's audience, as well. That one right down there in the spotlight. I want her to be my wife. You see, I proposed to her many, many months ago before I went off to war. I was injured very badly and living in a military hospital most of the year. I've done a lot of dumb things in my life, but the worst of them was letting that wonderful woman down. Not once, but twice. Big-time. I've done some major soul-searching since I got out of Iraq—"

All eyes were on Jason and what he had to say. When he paused, the crowd started applauding him and chanting, "God bless America!"

"Hold on, hold on." He held up his hands. "I'm no hero. In fact, I've been a complete ass. I screwed up worse than any man ever should, but I think I've healed enough to finally be the man she needs, the man she once loved with all her generous heart. Rebecca, I've prioritized my life. I'm no longer seeking approval from anyone. I'm happy with myself and I want to be happy with you. What do you think, audience? Should she give me another chance? Do I even deserve another chance?"

Rebecca knew he was talking directly to her. The crowd started chanting, "Yes! Yes! Yes!"

In her heart Rebecca wanted nothing more than to return to the beach house at Cinnamon Bay with her beloved to raise their daughter together. But she knew they had a lot of talking—and a lot of healing—to do first, especially if Sarah had maintained their secret about the baby. Could she afford to risk her heart again? Oh, God, could she afford not to? How would this affect her recovery?

"This next song, 'Lay Your Heart Next to Mine', is an appeal to her to let me back into her good graces and marry me." He paused. "Will you do that, Rebecca?"

The crowd cheered as Rebecca reached up, touched and then twirled the ring he'd given her so many months before, around her finger. Despite everything, she'd never taken it off. It must have been by the grace of God that it wasn't lost during her many stays at the hospital, the attempted rape and her passing out at the beach.

"By the way, she wrote the lyrics of the song I just performed, and it'll be released on our new CD. I'm sure you've all heard of J.R. Neels." The crowd broke out into applause. "Apparently it was a big secret from me for a very long time. You see, the person who wrote it wanted to make a name for herself without my help. I guess she figured my helping would cast doubts in her mind about her ability as a writer. I admire her for that, but then again, this lady's always been strong—more courageous than even she would admit to.

"I found out quite by accident from my label that the writer J.R. Neels is someone I've been involved with most of my life. That little lady is standing right there. Oh, I knew her passion was to write songs and that she'd sold a few, but I had no idea she was who she was." Jason pointed at Rebecca.

He sang the song. His body was weak and trembling, but his voice throbbed with emotion and Rebecca knew she had no choice. This was the one man she'd always loved, and nothing would ever change that.

She almost melted like a pat of butter hearing the words to the song. At the words, "*so many times, you danced through my mind*"—how many times had the thought of him danced through her mind while she was waiting for him to come back from Nashville and from the war? "*It will be all right when you hold me tight*"—those were the words that made her envision his arms around her when she needed it most. Tears welled in her eyes and she began crying, only this time they were tears of joy. She wanted nothing more than to run up onto the stage and throw her arms around him.

"So, what do you say, Rebecca?" Jason asked from the stage, his heart in his voice. "Will you lay your heart next to mine every night for the rest of our lives? You're the only woman I'll ever love, and I want us to be a family—forever and always."

All eyes were on Rebecca as Jason extended his hand. Just as time had stood still back in Houston, they were once again frozen in emotion at a concert hall filled with people. The tides of time, the tides of life had come full circle and she was a much better, much stronger person than she ever had been.

Crying, Rebecca decided to bolt toward the stage, not the stairs. She gazed up at him with pure love in her eyes. Aided by Rick and another band member, Jason leaned down, again extending his hand out to Rebecca. She could only imagine part of Jason's dignity was saved pulling her up on stage, reenacting what he'd done so many months before his injuries. To her he was no less a man, but to a man like Jason, one overridden with pride, he would constantly need to prove his self-worth.

Once Rebecca was on stage, Jason pulled her close. He swept the hair back from her face, just like he'd done many times before and bowed his head, lovingly placing his lips over hers. If Rebecca thought she was weak in the knees before, she was so wrong. She began trembling as his lips sweep across hers. Returning the passion, she plunged her fingers deep into his thick hair, pulling her body closer to his. The embrace was stronger than any ocean wave and their love was limitless like the tides.

Jason broke the kiss. Holding his girl with his good arm, he looked out into the audience. "As much as I love my career and all you good fans, I love this little gal more. We were to be married before I left for Iraq. That chance didn't come. So, my dearest, Becca, once again, what do you say? Do you still have enough of that Texas grit left to handle me and one more song?"

Overcome with emotion, Rebecca could only manage a nod.

With that, Jason turned to the other band members. "Hey boys, are you ready for the next song?"

Rebecca leaned into Jason's side. "I have an idea. Why don't we perform an encore of 'Lay Your Heart Next to Mine'? This time let's sing a duet."

"Duet?"

Rebecca threw him a devilish smirk. "You aren't the only one carrying secrets, Mr. Engles. Seems I have one or two up my sleeve as well. Now hand me a guitar, make it a Gibson and we'll do this song up right. Come on boys—hit that tempo and let's get going. These people want to see a real show."

As the band began to play the first chords of the song, Jason smiled and bent down to kiss her once more. Cheers from the audience erupted. "Boy Rebecca—seems you are full of surprises."

Rebecca wickedly grinned back at him. She was the one with the ultimate surprise. "You don't know the half of it, Mr. Engles. Just wait 'til we get home."

# Bonus Gift for *Tides of Time* Readers!

ᴔ

Mercury recording artist Steve Azar, who scored his first No. 1 smash hit in 2004 with "I Don't Have to Be Me 'Til Monday", was so touched by the themes and Azar Family Dedication in *Tides of Time* that he joined forces with Sonya Kate to package his love song "Lay Your Heart Next to Mine" with copies of her romance novel. **Azar endorses *Tides of Time*, calling it "an uplifting, inspirational and heartwarming read for people of all ages".**

To give you a taste of how powerful the song and love story are, Sonya's favorite line is "I can't count the times/You danced through mine/While I'm trying to be who I am/But you got to believe/I'm not really me/'Til I'm back in your arms again...".

For a limited time only, the first 5,000 readers purchasing *Tides of Time* and returning this coupon will receive a special edition CD single from Mercury Recording artist Steve Azar. This song entitled "Lay Your Heart Next to Mine" is from his 2004 release "Waitin on Joe", available in stores everywhere. For new music, tour schedules and more visit SteveAzar.com.

To redeem your special copy of this touching CD single, please photocopy this coupon page and mail it with proof of purchase to Uptown Marketing & Promotions, Attn: Sonya Kate, P.O. Box 870, Springfield, LA 70462. All CDs will be mailed after January 25, 2007.

## *Special Thanks to Steve Azar*

**ନ**

Steve Azar, one of country music's most promising stars and prolific songwriters, began writing songs at a very early age. A Greenville, Mississippi native, Azar was initially influenced by bluesmen like Eugene Powell and Sam Chapman when they would play behind his dad's liquor store. He loved their sound so much that he was immediately hooked and knew that music would be his life's journey. By the time he graduated college with a business management degree, he was playing 200 shows a year and touring with two 28-foot trucks and 10 men on the payroll. He was financially successful, but artistically unfulfilled, so he gave it up to become a better songwriter and moved to Nashville in 1991. Within days after he arrived, Azar was offered three song-publishing deals and later, a major recording contract with Mercury Records.

Azar launched a radio phenomenon with his self-penned hit, "I Don't Have to Be Me ('Til Monday)". The song not only topped the charts, but has since received more than three million spins on the radio. Another one of his big hits was the Top 10 *"Waitin' On Joe"*, that also produced a #1 video featuring Academy Award-winning actor Morgan Freeman.

Lately, Azar has been touring across the United States and writing songs for his upcoming album, *Indianola*, that will be released on his own Dang Records. In addition to writing or co-writing every song on the new CD, including the debut hit single, "You Don't Know A Thing", he produced and engineered the entire collection and also plays slide guitar, mandolin, acoustic and electric guitar on various tracks.

## Your Purchase Helps
## St. Jude Children's Hospital

ϵ⌒

Sonya Kate is a life-long sufferer of Lupus and Anti-Phospholipid Syndrome. However, these illnesses were never diagnosed until 2000 when she suffered a stroke at age thirty-three. Since that time, Sonya has vowed to do good in the amount of time she has left. Therefore, for every book purchased from SonyaKateChilders.Net, a portion of the profits from the sale of each book will be donated to St. Jude Children's Hospital.

Sonya's vision for the future is to raise enough money to help children not only beat cancer, but also contribute funds to St. Jude's Auto-Immune Disease Research Lab. It is the author's dream that someday auto-immune illnesses can be detected in children at an early age, a luxury Sonya herself never had.

# Why an electronic book?

We live in the Information Age—an exciting time in the history of human civilization, in which technology rules supreme and continues to progress in leaps and bounds every minute of every day. For a multitude of reasons, more and more avid literary fans are opting to purchase e-books instead of paper books. The question from those not yet initiated into the world of electronic reading is simply: *Why?*

1. *Price.* An electronic title at Ellora's Cave Publishing and Cerridwen Press runs anywhere from 40% to 75% less than the cover price of the exact same title in paperback format. Why? Basic mathematics and cost. It is less expensive to publish an e-book (no paper and printing, no warehousing and shipping) than it is to publish a paperback, so the savings are passed along to the consumer.

2. *Space.* Running out of room in your house for your books? That is one worry you will never have with electronic books. For a low one-time cost, you can purchase a handheld device specifically designed for e-reading. Many e-readers have large, convenient screens for viewing. Better yet, hundreds of titles can be stored within your new library—on a single microchip. There are a variety of e-readers from different manufacturers. You can also read e-books on your PC or laptop computer. (Please note that Ellora's

Cave does not endorse any specific brands. You can check our websites at www.ellorascave.com or www.cerridwenpress.com for information we make available to new consumers.)

3. *Mobility.* Because your new e-library consists of only a microchip within a small, easily transportable e-reader, your entire cache of books can be taken with you wherever you go.

4. *Personal Viewing Preferences.* Are the words you are currently reading too small? Too large? Too... ANNOYING? Paperback books cannot be modified according to personal preferences, but e-books can.

5. *Instant Gratification.* Is it the middle of the night and all the bookstores near you are closed? Are you tired of waiting days, sometimes weeks, for bookstores to ship the novels you bought? Ellora's Cave Publishing sells instantaneous downloads twenty-four hours a day, seven days a week, every day of the year. Our webstore is never closed. Our e-book delivery system is 100% automated, meaning your order is filled as soon as you pay for it.

Those are a few of the top reasons why electronic books are replacing paperbacks for many avid readers.

As always, Ellora's Cave and Cerridwen Press welcome your questions and comments. We invite you to email us at Comments@ellorascave.com or write to us directly at Ellora's Cave Publishing Inc., 1056 Home Avenue, Akron, OH 44310-3502.